TYING
DOWN
THE LION

JOANNA CAMPBELL

Brick Lane
Publishing

First published 2015 in the UK by

Brick Lane Publishing Limited

London

www.bricklanepublishing.com

1

A CIP catalogue record for this book is available from the British Library.

ISBN: 978-0-9928863-3-2

Illustration: Adam Regester

Design concept: Andrew Macdonald

Graphic design: Renni Johnson

Printed and bound in Great Britain by
Marston Book Services Limited, Oxfordshire

For Adrian, Alexandra, Olivia and Georgia.
For Mum, Dad and Chris.
In memory of Peter Fechter.

Remember, no matter where you go,
there you are.

Confucius

CONTENTS

ACKNOWLEDGEMENTS

I would like to thank

Adrian, for his role as plot consultant and technical wizard, but mostly because I couldn't be a writer without him.

Alexandra, Olivia and Georgia, for endless enthusiasm, encouragement and inspiration, and for never raising a complaint about the cobwebs.

Cornerstones Literary Consultancy, for their invaluable report on the first draft, particularly Rachel Connor, because without her perception and understanding I might never have seen the wood for the trees.

Lara Schonberger, for reading my words and fulfilling my dream.

Tim Challenger, for his valued memories and sensitive insight into the world of divided Berlin.

Richard Carter (journeytoberlin), for his historical knowledge and helpfulness.

Betty Hill, my mother, for reading to me when I was small, then reading my own stories when I grew up, and my wonderful father for soldering my glasses back together every week.

Berlin, 1967. The Palace of Tears

Mothers are never ill, they never give up searching for lost things and they never cry.

At this moment my mother is doing all three. At least she's in the right place. Everyone else here is crying too.

"Jacqueline, I wanted so much to come home," she says. "But it isn't here."

"Mum, it depends what you mean by home."

She keeps shaking her head and clutching my hand. She doesn't know.

This is the Palace of Tears. We have to say goodbye to Ilse here. She can't come with us. And we can't turn back. The visit is over.

"Mum, we have to keep moving."

My mother led me here. But I must lead her back.

Mothers always hum in public, wear old elastic bands round their wrists and speak even when everyone wants them to shut up. But my mother is doing none of these. She isn't behaving like a mother at all. I wish I could say something hopeful, the way she did when I was small and scared. But daughters don't speak in that way. I just steer her into the station.

"I did not say goodbye to my mother, Jacqueline. I looked away," she says, pressing her hand to her side where her inflamed appendix is sending out sparks.

Mothers are supposed to know what to do. And always get it right. Mum can't break down now. Not at the East Berlin border control with our pass about to expire. And looking as if she might expire along with it.

Daughters vow never to utter the corny old chestnuts their mothers trot out, never to fuss about the time and never, ever to wear Gay Geranium lipstick.

"Come on, Mum. Keep your chin up. If we don't join the queue now, we'll end up running for that train. Quickly now. Er...chop, chop?"

All right, I won't say never. Apart from the lipstick.

1

DESPERATION

"Jacqueline, I'll be going to Berlin over my dead body."

"That won't be easy, Grandma," I tell her, trying to coax her bulk out of the front-door. "Here, have a jaw-clamping toffee."

Mum has lived here for twenty years, but she still doesn't call it home. When he finally tore up his L-plate, Dad said the winds of war had wafted the seeds of her to 31 Audette Gardens, but like the dandelions caught in the cracks of the pavement, her roots were trapped in Berlin. Grandma pointed out it wasn't Dad talking. It was the rum and pep.

This is our most important moment since last Friday, when Dad's win from the three-thirty at Haydock finally earned us enough to have the Morris Traveller welded back together. Dad didn't actually win the money himself. It was a filly called Gay Hostess.

Gluing Grandma's mouth with toffee is the only way to watch *Opportunity Knocks* without her shouting, "Take the money, you daft git!" or "Open the box, ugly!" We don't have the heart to tell her she's got the wrong programme. She thinks the clapometer is a temperature gauge for the television set.

But she won't take the bait today.

"I'll not set foot in that car. It's riddled with death-watch beetle," she says, a cigarette clamped between her lips even when she's talking. Which is all the time.

"Grandma, Dad paid fifty pounds for it," my little brother, Victor, says, glancing up from *Commando*. "The seats are real vinyl."

"And in this heat it'll stick to my arse something chronic."

"Grandma said 'arse'," Victor announces before returning to the Battle of Britain.

"Let's go then!" Dad shouts, one hand clapping Grandma on the back and the other clipping Victor round the ear. "Pack up your comic, Victor. Come on, Ma."

"Not bloody likely, Roy." Grandma says, lumbering towards Big Stan's butcher's van and shoehorning herself into the back seat. "I've got the jitters. Anyroad, since it's a Monday, Stan and Elsie will have bought a quarter pound of buttered Brazils and set their cribbage out."

She squeezes in between half a pig and two dozen blocks of dripping. She'd want to visit their pre-fab even if they were offering tinned-pear with top-of-the-milk and a game of Russian roulette. They've only come round to collect her parrot.

"It'll just be temporary, Deborah," Grandma croons to the daft bird. "You shan't be uprooted for long."

"Roots! Do your bloody roots, Elsie!" Deborah squawks. Elsie's hand flies up to her blue rinse.

"I'll tell you what, son!" Grandma screeches above the din. "Why don't you stop at home? Put your savings on a nice accumulator instead. Stan would devil me kidneys for tea."

"Your kidneys can go to the bloody devil, along with the rest of you," Dad mutters, already in despair with Grandma for teaching Deborah to warble "House of the Rising Sun" after changing it to "House of the Striding Hun".

"Nell, I shall crawl to Berlin if I must," Mum calls out, pacing between the car and the van.

"Jesus wept, Bridget," Dad says to Mum. "Calm down. At this rate we'll have World War Three before we've driven to the end of Audette Gardens."

He paces around the car, a cigarette fastened to his mouth. Stan climbs down from the van and clamps his ham-like hands around Dad's. After that they do a lot of back-slapping and make manly noises, Dad's beetle-black hair flopping over his eyes. When Dad spent hours practising double-declutches and kangaroo-hops up and down Audette Gardens, Stan sat beside him in his bloodied apron, which is why the car still stinks of lamb's liver.

On Sundays, Victor, Mum and I all squashed into the back seat to be bumped around the scrubland at the back of the mop-and-brush factory because it was more fun than watching *Ice Cold in Alex* on the television again.

"Talking about your trip, Roy, guess what I've just read in the *Meat Trades Journal*?" Stan says. "Some East German butcher's only gone and strapped on a whole load of gammon slices and sausages, hasn't he? Covered himself in raw meat and threw himself over that Wall. Shot at left, right and centre, he was. Bullets flying all over the shop. But here's the best bit. The meat only went and took all the bullets, didn't it? Can you believe it, mate? A slug in the rump. A pellet in the pork chop. And he's not got a mark on him. What d'you think of that, eh? Want to take some best end of neck with you, eh, Roy mate?"

"Tell you what though, Stan," Dad says, "it must have made an offal mess."

They share a belly laugh, the male sort that goes on and on, and get so excited their hair falls out of its Brylcreem.

"Bloody ugh," Victor says. But I bet he's planning on wrapping a bacon rasher round his Action Man.

Once the laughter ends, Dad starts lighting one cigarette from another. His hands are shaking so much he can hardly strike his matches.

"I'm hot, Dad," Victor shouts, his face shining like basted beef. "Why can't I wear my shorts? I think my legs are suffocating."

"All packed, aren't they, Bridget?" Grandma shouts to Mum from the van. "Only temporary, mind. We won't get further than the end of Audette Gardens. Soon be unpacking it all again." Deborah joins in with the cackling until Elsie throws a cardigan over the cage.

"Nell, please," Mum says, nervous as a spider spinning in the wind.

"Unpacking it all and hanging the whole lot back up," Grandma repeats, tittering.

"Nell, Roy will drive us safely to Berlin."

"I can't travel on an empty stomach, Bridge."

"I gave you a shredded-wheat."

"And it's worked its way into my denture. I'm having to talk through a haystack. Not the same as a fry-up, is it? Even the way you cremate a sausage, Bridge."

But Grandma is already taking out her big blue roller to test if her front curl has set firm, and she only does that when we're going to the Berni steakhouse or for Her Majesty's speech on the television.

"Nell, please come," Mum persists.

"I'm busy."

"No, you are hiding in Stan's van."

"I'm inspecting his pork loins, thank you."

Victor and I climb into the back of the car, and Dad, smelling new and leathery in his car-coat and driving-gloves, takes his place in the front-seat. We all swelter while we wait.

"Grandma would live on Jamaica Ginger cake and tobacco if she stayed here alone," Dad says, gripping his steering-wheel, the horrors of last night already forgotten.

"Why can't she stay at Elsie's?" Victor asks.

"Elsie won't have her anymore. She rubs up a bit close to Stan."

I imagine her heaving her sixteen stone across their card-table, enquiring after his premium sausage-meat.

Dad stubs out his cigarette in the ashtray, lights another and asks, "Can you smell that?"

"Smell what?" Victor asks.

"That funny old whiff."

"Grandma's not in the car yet, Dad. She'll have pumped in the van by now."

"Not that, Victor. Sniff it. Go on."

The car fills with snorting. My friend Gillian's Ford Corsair smells of the French Fern talcum powder that clogs up her mother's cleavage. They used to have a green Mini, but she didn't fit.

After humouring Dad for a minute, Victor and I give up.

"It's the smell of travel," he says, beaming. "You see, Mum shoved that old bag in..."

"No, Dad. Grandma's not..."

"Victor, I'm warning you, son. I mean the pong of that tatty tartan bag in the boot, full of old sand and the stink of those rubbery shoes you wear at the seaside. Nothing in the world smells like travel."

I don't know about that. I reckon holidays are all about blundering through obstacles. In fact, I can't think of anything else they're good for. Rock-pools and funicular railways are all right, but even those will be thin on the ground in Berlin.

I don't mind the new haircuts and the old case packed full of clothes with the tang of last summer. But this time we're driving. Abroad. To Berlin. In the Cold War. Checkpoints. Miles of barbed wire, armed guards with hungry dogs, Dad's weak stomach for food that isn't white or beige. And the Wall.

Uphill all the way. Mind you, downhill would be worse since our brakes don't work properly.

In Audette Gardens, the best grass grows in the worn-out pavement, parents shout with the back-door open and dads sit in their vests to watch the wrestling, but it actually looks pretty with the neighbours' curtains flapping out of their open windows and the sun drying out the damp on the pebbledash. I wouldn't mind being at home all summer, especially now Mum and Dad have recovered from their Saturday row. He lost a whole week's housekeeping on a horse, and she threw an entire brick of ice-cream at the television.

"Your outsider looks more like a constipated mule. And his eyes are crossed," Grandma said before the screen was obliterated. "No wonder he's galloped in a circle and bounced off the railings."

Dad was hunched in his jockey's crouch on the patchwork pouffe, banging his hands on the floor and yelling, "Come on, my son," at the dreadful old nag. I don't mean Grandma. By then she was busy side-stepping puddles of Neapolitan.

Mum couldn't go to the shops without money, so our Sunday dinner was a bashed-up packet of frozen braised-beef-in-gravy Dad bought from the corner shop with the emergency shilling sellotaped to the underside of the sick-basin.

"Tastes like cardboard in a puddle," Victor whispered.

When Elsie and Stan arrived this morning, Grandma hissed, "Say you had prime-rib if anyone asks."

Elsie is shoving Grandma out of the van and saying, "Oh, Nellie, you may never come back, you know. There's soldiers on every corner and you're bound to rub them up the wrong way."

"Chance would be a fine thing," Grandma says, patting her curls before launching herself at Stan for a goodbye kiss that nearly sends Deborah's cage flying and prompts her to shriek, "The Hun's here!"

I have asked to cross through the Berlin Wall with Mum because I'm writing about it for a school project. But this is a project for her as well. I'm on a mission to make her look at me again. At the moment, all I have is a picture of a Berlin factory cut out from a magazine and a lot of blank pages in a Woolworth's notepad. But I'm dying to see how she looks at me when I show it to her.

When Mum arrived in England after the war, she had lost touch with her family. Their house in Berlin had been bombed in an air raid and she had no idea if they were still alive. She wrote nonstop to old friends in the city until she found some who had survived and were able to track her two sisters down. Beate and Ilse lived together at that time, but six years ago, the Wall came between them. Now Beate lives in West Berlin and Ilse is behind the Wall in the East. They can't visit each other, but Mum plans to see them both.

I pick up a few of Grandma's jitters now we are about to leave. I wish Mum could be English, with me still young enough to sit on the kerb and wait for the jangle of the ice-cream van and have Mum reach for my hand while we queue for a Mivvi.

Her face crumples when she touches her sisters' faded faces in an old picture on the sideboard. It leans against the honeymoon photograph of my parents on a tandem in Ruislip, which is black and white with smudges of experimental colour. Dad has apricot cheeks and Mum's blonde curls look like a cluster of egg-yolks. The way they're smiling makes me think about having a husband. I don't know why, when being married is all about buying fridges and paying the coalman and having someone's teeth grinning at you from a glass by the bed.

While Dad tries to start the engine, Victor and I melt into the baking seat and squabble over a barley sugar stuck to the road-atlas. Victor presses his tongue against the window. I have no idea why. Seven-year-old boys do that kind of thing.

Assisted by a final push from Elsie, Mum tugs Grandma away from Big Stan and frogmarches her into the car, promising her the front seat, a U-turn after five minutes if she doesn't like it and custody of the Everton mints.

"Since you like shifting folk from their homes, Bridge, you should do a better job of knocking down the bloody great cobwebs on my front-room ceiling," Grandma says, squeezing into the car, not so much a fish out of water as a whale in a sardine-tin. "Forcing us to God-forsaken places. Packing poor Deborah off to Elsie's. She'll have to watch Z-Cars. And you know how the sirens make her feathers droop."

For weeks, a spider has been weaving a web between Deborah's cage and the standard lamp-shade tassels. It's probably clinging to the bars of the cage now it's been torn away, hanging by a thread and about to find temporary refuge in Elsie's hair before throwing out a new line of silk and beginning to spin all over again.

"Ma, Deborah will be fine with Elsie," Dad tells her.

"She'll scatter millet over the trifle and grind her beak on the bars."

"Elsie should know better at her age."

"Oh, you've got me over a barrel, I suppose."

Not an attractive image.

"Come on, Mum, you know fine well you'll treat Beate's place like a home from home," Dad tells her.

"Home is where the heart is," she says, clapping her hands together on her mountainous chest and rattling her necklaces against her white holiday cardigan.

"More like home is where the fart is," Victor hisses in my ear.

Dad stalls thirteen times and just as we can't hold our breath anymore, we launch out of Audette Gardens with Grandma winding down the window and shouting, "Lock up your children, there's a madman on the streets!"

Sod it. She's sitting on the holiday chocolate. Five-Boy bars cost 7d, so we can't have them all the time like Bluebird toffees, which actually taste of bicycle oil. I didn't even get to see the pictures on the wrapper that show five different chocolate-wanting expressions on the face of a frightening boy in a sailor suit. Desperation, Pacification, Expectation, Acclamation and Realisation are now melted and oozing, sandwiched between the hot vinyl and Grandma's crimplene frock. I sympathise with the first of the five.

I look back to see our neighbour, Mrs Pither, vaulting over the fence with her shears and snipping the heads off our goutweed. Dad thinks it's a proper plant called Snow-in-the-Mountain, but Mrs P says it's a wild flower that smells of cat-piddle. Two sides to everything, I suppose.

Although he's nursing the car along like an old man in a flat cap, Dad is a live wire fizzing with electrical current. Every time we knock the kerb, the stern contours of Grandma's curls quiver like a dozen dead field mice perched on a pink iced bun. Victor makes racing-car sounds and also commentates, holding his fist to his mouth. "Scarfiotti wins at Monza with his amazing braking…"

"Can't I be Jackie Stewart?" Dad asks.

"OK. But we'll have to switch to Monaco."

"Boys are peculiar," I tell them, closing my eyes as a cyclist swerves out of our way in the nick of time.

"Here we go then," Dad says. "Motoring towards our dreams, Bridge."

"You shouldn't follow dreams," Grandma announces.

"Why?" I ask her.

"Because it's a road paved with disappointments, that's why. People should get on with what they've blinking well got at home."

"You can't tell people what their dreams are meant to be."

"I can. But they never listen, do they?" She raises her voice. "Your father should just tinker about with his daft car on a Saturday afternoon like any other bloke. And your mother ought to take on a few hours at the mop-and-brush. Then back across the road to put her apron on before you get home from school. It'll stop her becoming a lard-arse. They run to fat, Germans do."

Mum and Dad ignore her, too busy dreaming.

"What did slick Mick-the-mechanic charge you for fixing the car then, Roy?"

"Don't ask, Ma."

"A bloody monkey would know more than him and only charge you peanuts. I reckon he's stuck it together with sellotape."

"Don't spoil things, Ma."

"I can hear cardboard."

"No one can hear cardboard."

"I can."

"Give over and let me dream."

I'm wearing two twin-sets because the spare won't fit in the case, so this is a bloody hot dream. The seats are like boiling jam. I concentrate on my notepad, but even a Cold War project feels limp and tired in this heat.

Victor says you aren't even allowed to look at the Wall without the East Berlin police leaping across and arresting you at gunpoint. He says even licking those bricks is like asking to be shot at. I don't know why anyone would lick them, but that's how boys think.

Every morning after Dad goes to work, Victor quietly play-fights with himself on the front-room carpet, whispering, "Aargh, not my guts again. Christ, not my guts." After rolling about, he machine-guns the enemy from the trenches behind the settee. If he survives, he teeters on the rope-bridge of the fireplace fender before parachuting into the ironing-pile cornfield where he bleeds almost to death, writhing and moaning, "Got a last fag for me, Ginger?" The Cold War is a lukewarm affair to a seven-year-old who digests blood-and-guts for breakfast. Victor, like Grandma, is unimpressed by Khrushchev.

He is wedged between Mum and me in the back. Victor, that is. Not Khrushchev. After a manic session of bouncing up and down, electrified that we're on the move at last, he realises Dad's driving is less Stirling Moss, and more Stumbling Mouse. The car vibrates if he goes over thirty, so he creeps along in the gutter. Even ancient delivery-men on bicycles have to overtake. We can't open the windows because the draught blows Dad's hair over his glasses. The car fills with smoke and swear words.

Ever since his first lesson, and even after he passed the test at last, Dad has never sat still at home. In his lumpy old maroon armchair, he rests his feet on a small tin of stewing-steak, acting as the accelerator, and a brake in the guise of a Heinz potato-salad can, while we shout out hazards for him to avoid.

"Watch the Panzer!" yells Victor.

"There's an overturned lorry ahead with a load of venomous spiders jumping into cars," I shout.

"Hark, is that woodworm gnawing at your timber frame?" Grandma sniggers, helpful as always.

But now this is the real thing and progress is not much faster. The brake pedal might work better if it actually was a tin of potato salad.

After making Messerschmitt noises in my ear, Victor resorts to walking Trevor-Keith, his ancient Action Man, over my legs and mumbling, "Smithy bought it at Dunkirk. I'm afraid, old boy." His boiled-sweet breath is nauseating. Victor's that is, not T-K's.

"Move over, can't you?"

"Why should I?"

He kicks my ankle and I kick him back, hooking our buckles together. Our conjoined footwear flails against the back of Dad's seat until his hand reaches round and flaps at the air.

"What?" we chorus.

"I'll not have your great clod-hopping feet on my centre console, if you please."

Clod-hopping's the word. I should be wearing white patent boots and a Biba dress. I should be a model called Tuesday. But Mum thinks fourteen is the gateway for geriatric twin-sets, nylon bell-bottoms, square nautical blouses and, worst of all the horrors, navy driving-shoes with rubbery soles that creep up over the toe to prevent scuffing, a hideous decorative buckle and a punched-hole pattern to make them...groovy. Being designed, if that's the right word, especially for women-drivers, we found them piled a mile high in the Freeman-Hardy-Willis bargain tub. Mum dived straight in.

"Mum, no."

"But they are so sensible, dear."

Yes, and she's so German. When Grandma saw my feet in these monstrosities, she said, "Strike-a-bloody-light, Jacqueline, a pair of ruddy shoeboxes would look daintier."

"*Pass auf*, Roy!" Mum yells, relapsing into German. It sounds like pass out, but I think it means pull your finger out and do an emergency stop at the traffic-lights. Fortunately we are travelling at eight miles an hour.

"Lawks," Grandma says, lighting a Senior Service. "You'll have us joining Jayne Mansfield in her grave before we're much older, son."

When the lights turn green, the car stalls time and time again. The back of Dad's neck changes colour beneath the straight edge of yesterday's haircut.

"Pink," whispers Victor.

"Red."

"Maroon."

"Blushing red salmon."

"Boiled bloody beetroot. I win!"

Grandma stuffs in so many mints her cheeks swell into hamster's pouches, but she manages to mumble, "Give it some choke, lad." And, at the ninth try, and with at least nine cars beeping behind us, the engine starts. Dad pats the steering-wheel as if all the attempts and accompanying swear words are normal procedure. On the move again, he rasps his leathery hands together.

"Pass us a sweet, Ma."

"Keep your daft hands on the wheel. You're getting cocky now, son," Grandma says, crumpling the empty bag.

Mum's face is like starched linen. She keeps pressing her hands to her grumbling appendix and moaning like the wounded badger that once crawled into our shed. Dad was pacing in the garden on one of his Bad-Moon nights and heard it. It was also a bad night for the badger because it was dying on our collapsible deckchair. But it turned out well for Dad because, instead of staring into the dark, he could kneel on the shed floor and call us to bring an old towel. Grandma opened a new bottle of milk and poured some into a saucer. Not the cream on the top. She always keeps that for herself, hidden in her denture mug.

Dad spent the night in the shed and buried the badger the next morning. But when he asked me to give it a name, I said no and slammed back indoors. I stormed up to bed and pressed my face into the pillow because we hadn't been able to draw him out of the Bad-Moon girls' horrible clutches when this battered and stinking old creature could. No reference to Grandma intended.

The Bad-Moon girls, Dad calls the slatterns in his head. I imagine washed-up can-can dancers, older than they should be, with crêpey eyes and wizened breasts, high-kicking on a stage with a worn velvet curtain.

They appear on days when Dad doesn't know what he is thinking, or even if he is thinking. Those days can weigh less than air or more than an ocean. He has blank thoughts without feelings, followed by heavy feelings without thoughts. Time means nothing. A minute ticks by in the same rhythm as an entire day.

He can look at one thing for an hour without moving. He can see me or Victor without knowing we are in the room, peering at us as if we're underwater, moving in warped slow motion.

After the nothingness, he wades through a stagnant lake with the moon reflected in it, waiting for daylight to rinse it away. He almost drowns while time ticks on. The sky is filled with black milk. No stars. Two days can pass before he surfaces.

Dad's brain-switch, the focusing thing that the rest of us flick on to make things look better, is a bit buggered. Those are his words, not mine.

The Bad-Moon girls whisper evil in Dad's ear, the sort of women who would set their own mother on fire if there were no other way to light their cigarettes. The trouble is, they can follow. Just as we were setting off to Clacton last autumn, they hunted him down.

***

THE BAD-MOON HOLIDAY

The leaves were turning to cornflakes, and the sun was bulging like a blood orange. A coach smelling of other people's ham sandwiches was waiting at the end of Audette Gardens to take us to the guest-house with brown oil paintings of dogs and fruit and an ancient sticking-plaster over the light-switch.

In the family-room that smells of shrivelled grapes and prehistoric board-games, Mum and Dad never argue. Other people do and it is better than television. One time, we were all waiting in there for breakfast, savouring the prospect of salted porridge and boiled prunes, when the family hogging the better settee, the one with a stain the shape of Sweden on the arm, rowed about their Caroline's bosoms.

"I sewed up the front of that bathing-suit, Caroline. I sewed it double. How come you've unpicked it? They'll look like two spaniels in a sack."

"Why do you always spoil my fun, Mum?"

"Just you sew it back up, lass. I won't have the world and his wife getting an eyeful of what our Caroline ate for breakfast. If we ever get any."

"Oh Dad, I'll look a right sight. Might as well keep my cardigan on. And a muffler. How about an overcoat as well?"

"Fine, lass. As long as there's nothing bobbing."

Grandma stayed at Elsie and Stan's last year because she refused to go near the seaside. "Bloody daft season to be paddling," she said. "They lock up the conveniences at the end of August, you know. And I'm not broiling my ankles in a sea of someone else's widdle."

Victor was planning to fish for crab and be reunited with an old Action Man he'd left in the trouser-press. But we couldn't leave the house.

Mum and Victor went as far as the pavement to tell the coach-driver we weren't going. From the front-room window, I watched the fine drizzle stain Victor's new gabardine coat. Afterwards, the rain never stopped.

Dad was sitting on a chair in the box-room, staring at nothing, his head filled with concrete. The light left his eyes. I stood near him, my hands still full of fruit pastilles for the trip.

"You go. You, Mum and Victor," he said, sounding like a stranger. They were the last words he spoke for three days.

"But the holiday won't feel like a holiday without you," I said, knowing home wouldn't feel like home either.

Mum came in and said the coach had understood. Because I imagined the coach nodding, I let out a stupid laugh, like a hideous, echoing bark.

We couldn't even reassure Dad he would feel better, because there was no knowing how long it would last. When Grandma trod on Victor's Messerschmitt in her new suede Norvics, we didn't promise to glue the shattered pieces together. We distracted him with a box of Pontefract Cakes. With Dad, it would be like trying to mend a burst balloon. We crept out of the room and he didn't notice.

Victor and I found a handful of Rich Highland Shorties and played Battleships way into the night. We shared a flattened Wagon-Wheel Victor found in the lining of his dressing-gown and made shadow-rabbits on the bedroom wall.

"A boy at school's dad sometimes goes away," Victor said, destroying my last submarine. "His mum and dad are always shouting about a barmaid. The dad knows her shoe size. But the mum doesn't think he should."

We never wonder out loud whether our mum or dad might storm off one day, but the colour always drains from Victor's face when they argue.

While I destroyed his patrol-boat, he announced he didn't believe in God anymore.

"I'm going to believe in someone real, like the Beatles," he said. "Even Ringo."

"It won't change anything, Victor."

He looked haunted after that, so I didn't tell him how the wolf spider from Kauai Cave is no longer born with eyes because in the dark caverns where it lives and hunts and dies, it has grown used to eternal night. If Dad ever stays in his darkness and gives up waiting for a light to guide him out, I don't think even George Harrison could help us.

A non-holiday is almost as much hell as a real one. Mum played Newmarket with us once, but it lasted five minutes because Victor hid a halfpenny in his mouth and turned blue. Even *Opportunity Knocks* seemed horrible. I put on my sun-dress, but changed back to slacks. Bare arms and legs felt awkward in the silent front-room with the curtains half-drawn.

Every lunchtime, Victor said, "Rissoles and mash taste like bird-seed and glue." And he knows because he's tried them.

The trouble was, we only had ancient potatoes, a tub of custard powder and three tins of Spam, but we couldn't go shopping because Grandma didn't know we were still at home. It would have upset her to see Dad that bad. Plus, Mum became extra-German and said, "If there vill be no holiday, I vill at least have a rest from Her Ladyship."

In case we bumped into anyone, we had to stay in, creeping about the house and hiding when the doorbell rang. It never looked like anyone interesting, just people in long coats with Bibles or in sports-jackets with encyclopaedias. But crouching at the top of the stairs and seeing their sawn-up shapes through the ridged door-glass, I still felt we were missing something.

***

Today the Bad Moon is not in sight. Soon we'll be flying along the auto-bahns, if the Traveller stays in one piece and if flying is another word for thump-grunt-rattling.

If I speak, just to mention feeling car-sick, Mum says, "No talking, Jacqueline. Dad has to concentrate."

I wish I could sit next to Dad while he's so happy. Gillian is allowed in the front seat of their Corsair, but that's because her mother is so huge that Gillian's dad wouldn't be able to find his gear-stick.

"Is there a problem with the brake?" Mum asks, unwrapping Dad's cigarettes and passing one through to the front for him, stretching to post it into his mouth before Grandma snaffles it.

"No problem at all, Bridge," Dad reassures her, feeling for his matches.

At least they aren't arguing, but the car responds with a thud from underneath, making us all look down, even Dad, which is a bad idea because we drift into the middle of the road just as a bubble-car is trundling past.

"Missed that by a gnat's whisker, son," Grandma says, pulling out her cotton reel and snapping off a thread. She strums it between her teeth like a Jew's harp, continuing her commentary in between twangs. "Christ, lad, you're on a hill, mind. Ooh, watch it. The rag-and-bone-man's horse is thundering up behind."

"Hardly thundering, Grandma," I point out. "Bridgewater Boy is past fifty, dawdles if he spies a privet hedge and has two arthritic knees."

He has to spin a U-turn—Dad, that is, not Bridgewater Boy—because we're driving the wrong way down a one-way street. And off goes Grandma again. "Watch out lad, you're arse-about-face here. Oh Christ alive, now you're face-to-face with the coalman's lorry. Is he cheering you on? Oh I see, that's his fist. Tch, tch, shall I give him a black look?"

In the shadow of the coalman's rage, Dad executes a fifteen-point-turn and the car limps on like a beaten dog.

"Come on, lad," Grandma says. "You're driving like an old woman."

"You've changed your tune, Ma. You were saying I'd kill us all before we set eyes on a white cliff. And here I am, driving as if a dozen eggs were perched on the bonnet, and you're still bloody well moaning."

"Well cover me with breadcrumbs and grill me 'til I'm toasted," Grandma says. "I'm just worried we'll miss the bloody boat. And talking of missing things, I'll not be able to go to Elsie's cheese-and-wine now."

"She's deliberately having it while you're away, Ma," Dad says.

Grandma sniffs. "She said she's got that pricey cheese with ruddy great holes in it, but I expect she'd have handed me an inch of mouse-trap on a bone-dry cracker."

"Grandma," Victor adds, "you can't go to a party without an invitation."

"True," I chip in. "Gillian did that once and Tessa Horlock's mother was too polite to send her away. Gillian won all the games, and by the end every child was in tears because she'd burst all the balloons with a pickled-onion fork."

On the clapometer for holiday-spirits, we'd be hovering around the halfway point if Dad wasn't frowning at the gear-stick.

"I must have a go at changing to third," he says. "But this clutch is a bugger. And now I can't let go of the wheel to stub my fag out."

"Why not, Dad?" Victor asks, perching his tin Sitting-Bull and General Custer on one knee to fight the plastic Dalek pointing his plunger at them from Mum's handbag. In his world, even cowboys and Indians join forces against strangers from outer-space.

"Just can't."

Dad's face is pressed to the windscreen now and his leathery hands are gripping the wheel for dear life.

"Have you forgotten how to drive, Dad?" I ask him. "It's like the Cycling Proficiency. As soon as Gillian passed, she forgot to squeeze her back-brake before her front. She did a full-speed victory circuit around the playground, somersaulted over the handle-bars and catapulted into the long-jump pit."

It was a soft landing, so I didn't feel too bad about enjoying the sight of a friend in trouble. If she'd been me, she'd have felt the same.

"There's always dog's muck in sand," Grandma adds, as if that's the moral of the tale, and it probably is.

Mum says, "Let your father drive without all this destruction, Jacqueline."

"You mean distraction, Frau Schweinhund," I whisper, staring at the road lines to take my mind off the blistering heat, cigaretty car-fragrance and my hopeless mother. I think about being married. I'm cooking prawns, or something equally exotic, for my husband, Peter. I'm wearing a cocktail dress. Not a prawn-cocktail dress. In fact, even more exotic than prawns, I'm actually tipping a Vesta curry onto the best plate. He's wearing flares and lighting candles. My white boots tap on the lino. I can smell the crispy noodles. Or maybe we walk to somewhere romantic like *Le Pomme Frite* restaurant in

Upper Bakewell Street. Just as Peter's beautiful lips are about to kiss my hand, Dad shouts, "Jesus wept!"

The car shudders and swerves. Other drivers honk their horns. "Cor!" Victor shouts, gripping onto my arm with both hands. We finish with a gravel-exploding hand-brake skid into a lay-by with an ice-cream van.

Everyone gasps. Grandma's teeth slip out.

"Can I have a Kinky, Dad?" Victor asks, pointing at the van.

"Only girls have those," I tell him. "And they're ninepence anyway."

"But this is a holiday," he whines. "I've brought eleven wounded Arapaho to glue back together. I've been saving them for this. Holidays are for doing everything you want."

"Look, Mum and Dad had to cash in their Winston Churchill death-crown just to buy petrol," I point out.

"No one's having anything," Dad says, sounding jittery. "I didn't mean to stop here."

"Roy, dear," Mum says, "are you all right?"

The cold breath of a Bad-Moon girl is tickling the back of my neck, unless that's because of Peter kissing me. I'm never sure of the difference between love and fear.

"Look, we're getting on the ferry if it's the last thing I do," Dad says, taking out a cigarette.

"I have no doubt, dear," Mum says, reaching forward to pat his arm.

Thank Lennon for that.

"Mum's foot's on your centre-console, Dad," Victor yells.

They both smile at him. It's revolting how small boys manage to charm grown-ups. But he pushes them too far.

"Can we go to the fair on the way?"

"No, we bloody can't, Victor," Dad says. "This holiday isn't something we're doing for fun."

"Victor, there's more chance of Winston Churchill climbing out of his coffin and giving us a velvet bag full of death-crowns," I tell him.

"Honestly, young man," Grandma says, ramming her teeth home. "Your dad's as white a peeled potato and there you are in a buggering chair-o-plane, if you please."

"Can't get this stubborn-arsed thing going again anyway," Dad mumbles, lighting the cigarette with one hand and pulling out the choke with the other.

We all wait.

In her super-quiet voice, Mum says, *"Ach du liebe Zeit, mein Liebling."* I think it means, "Bloody hell, mate." Just a bit more loving.

Mum changes places with Grandma 'for navigation purposes', but really so she can hold Dad's hand on the gearstick. It won't last. They once made up at the start of *Opportunity Knocks* and fell out again before the clapometer. Just as the applause reached a crescendo she hurled his toad-in-the-hole at the wall. As Hughie Green announces the winner, we watched it slide down and belly-flop on the lino.

Victor and I hunt for our comics to take our mind off Grandma eating Liquorice Allsorts and easing her foot out of her new Shebas to saw off her corn.

When Victor opens *Commando*, she pauses the amputation. "Hey lad, I expect your mum'll want to read that, eh?"

"Why? This is a war comic. Just for boys," Victor tells her, indignant that a female person might turn his hallowed pages.

I give her a glare. "You shouldn't keep on, Grandma."

"Well, my daughter-in-law's a Sausage-Eater. No denying it."

"But she wasn't in the War, was she? She didn't fight England, Grandma. Nor did her family. They were too busy staying alive in Berlin." I pause for breath, uncertain of the details.

Grandma pokes her dentures, releasing the miniature blue bobbles from her Allsort and spitting them into her hand.

"Plus, Mum hates sausages." Victor feels this clinches it.

"It's just words, lad. Like Jerry or Hun. Amounts to the same thing. Foreign." Grandma lights up a Senior Service and coughs like a miner, her massive chest billowing like a pair of blimps.

Thankfully Mum is busy telling Dad that when she says, "go straight on", she means, "take left-fork".

I turn to *Mandy*. I swear fourteen is too old for this comic, but Mum thinks I'm too young for *Petticoat* magazine. It pushes girls on too fast, she says. I think she's holding me back as usual, frightened I'll read it and elope. Or worse, start plucking my eyebrows.

At this rate, I'll never progress from daydreaming. My future husband could be walking past our house this actual moment and I'm stuck in the scorching car, wearing two courtelle twin-sets that make me look like a librarian in *Peg's Paper* or a sad woman in an advert for Beecham's Pills.

After a desperate flick through the car handbook, Dad starts the engine and we lurch into the traffic again.

"Bloody brake," Dad mutters. "I put my foot down and there's nothing there."

"Are you mixing it up with the crutch, Dad?"

"Clutch, Victor. No, of course not. The clutch is under my left foot. Feels like fresh air under my right."

"Dad," Victor says, "how will you drive without a brake? I mean, what if a dog ran into the road because its lead snapped? What if a hippy threw himself off the bridge again? What if a bomb dropped and a crater opened up?"

"The dog and the hippy would fall into the crater before we hit them," Dad says, coasting to a stop outside the turf-accountant and pulling a crumpled newspaper from his car-coat pocket.

"Will we reach the boat in time?" Mum asks, clutching her side.

"Course, Bridge. Don't fret."

The shop door is open, and Dad is busy watching Trixie in her tartan mini climb onto the table to reach the blackboard where she chalks up the racing results. I would sell my brother for a pair of her long shiny boots, but Dad calls them jack-boots, as if wearing them would encourage me to march about annexing something. But I bet the Gestapo didn't wear white patent.

To reach the top of the board, Trixie does a little hop, which flips the skirt right up. Her bosom creates a total eclipse over her clipboard.

"Dad, the lights are green."

Dad just puffs his cigarette, grinning at the perfect view and at his great road adventure ahead. For a moment, his life is pure magic.

"People are hooting, Dad," Victor shouts. "You're sticking out."

"All right, hold the bus," Dad says, crushing out his cigarette. "Sit round properly," he adds, even though we are. He drives backwards and forwards a few times to fit into the parking bay, making the starts and stops with the hand-brake.

"Hold on to your teeth, Nell," Mum says.

"That Trixie buys frozen faggots. I've seen her in Mace's."

"You shouldn't judge her for that, Ma," Dad says, feeling for his wallet.

"I don't judge anyone, Roy. I'm just saying she should get up off her big blonde arse and learn to make her own gravy."

Dad glances at Mum. "Hey, don't judge blondes."

"If it's from a bottle it doesn't count," Grandma says with a sniff of finality. "And Germans are different from everyone else anyway," she adds.

"Ma, give it a rest."

"Ooh, now I'm thinking of Stan's fresh faggots. Heaven. Do you know, last time I was there, Elsie gave me macaroni cheese from a tin? Tried to kid me it was her own, but I heard the can-opener. Slopped it into her fancy Pyrex, sliced a couple of tomatoes on top and flashed it under her grill. If that's home-made, then I'm Mandy Rice-Davies. And talking of rice, I don't like it. Elsie gave me rice from a packet. Blood and sand, it was all colours! It had raisins and toadstools in it."

Dad leaps out, his brown crimplene trousers detaching from the warm vinyl like a tangerine being peeled.

"Shall I get in the driver's seat?" Victor whispers.

"No, you bloody shan't," Dad says, reaching back in for the keys.

"I said we wouldn't be going anywhere," Grandma says, winding down her window to hear the results of the two-thirty at Haydock.

"We bloody will be," Dad calls over his shoulder as he hurries inside, holding his car-coat together and jingling in that strange way men do when they run. "I'll speed up to forty soon."

"That'll be handy when we're dodging bullets," Grandma shouts after him, taking out her knitting and a Chelsea bun.

"What are you making, Grandma?" I ask, not really interested, but the alternative is knocking down Red Indians for General Custer.

"A matinée jacket," she announces, holding up a pattern with a picture of a gargantuan infant squirming inside a dreadful cardigan.

We all sigh and fan ourselves, Grandma's corset creaking under the strain and Mum's appendix preparing to detonate. A frantic fly pummels the windscreen, too demented to escape through an open window.

"Bridge," Grandma says, "I don't mind saying I've got the jitters about letting Roy loose abroad. The roundabouts go the other way, Elsie says. And he only passed the last test because he gave the examiner a dead-cert for the Gold Cup."

"He only failed the fourth time because the examiner was foreign. He misunderstood half the instructions," Mum says.

"He understands you, Bridget."

Grandma snaps off a length of knitting-wool to lever the currants out of her teeth.

"Grandma, Mum isn't a proper German," Victor shouts, vexed. "She can swear in English, and she knows 'God Save the Queen.'"

"Enough," Mum says. "We will all stay in one piece."

"Unlike your Berlin," Grandma says, searching for cigarettes in her enormous navy handbag.

I watch Trixie teetering on the edge of the table, about to jump down. Dad catches her and she wobbles so much when she lands, she nearly takes his eye out.

"Jayne Mansfield was killed in a car crash. Death traps, they are."

"Nell, that was in America. They don't drive Morris Travellers there."

"Her head came off."

"Nell, I'm warning you..."

"I'm just saying. Clean off."

"Nell!"

"What's wrong with the charabanc?"

"They don't bloody exist now. That's what's wrong with them!"

We all gasp. Mum never bloodies. Since car squabbles seem to stew with more violence than quarrels at home, I concentrate on the display of Nudit for female moustaches in Woolworth's window.

"Getting the hang of the lingo at last, Bridge, are you? Ooh, remind us again, what were the only English words you knew when Roy first found you?"

"Angry monkey, peach-stone, Horlicks and May I become the little donkey. I had a terrible start at school. My English teacher believed he could levitate. He was carried from the gymnasium roof on a stretcher. And then came Hitler."

"What, into the school?" Victor asks. "Did you have to do the salute?"

"No, Victor. Thankfully not. I have always avoided him. Oh, I hope Roy is quick. I'm like a boiled spring."

"Coiled, Mum," I tell her. She ignores me. She has shown me her frosty face since last night when Dad had one of the night-terrors, which he's suffered since the war. He pushes Mum away and I help him instead. The next morning, she seems to push me away. As Grandma always says, families aren't all about clean white shirt-fronts, unscratched bannisters and beaming over the cornflakes.

"Nell, we must not spoil Roy's dream," Mum is saying. "All he wants is to drive."

"I know that fine well, Bridge. Been driving me mad for years."

Chortling, Grandma reaches into her bag and pulls out a bacon sandwich.

"He has always wanted to take me home, Nell. Our two dreams are joining together."

I clench my jaw when Mum says Berlin is home.

Grandma's eyes screw themselves back into their sockets as if rummaging for her imagination. "No idea what you're on about, Bridget. Why can't we just take a coach to Clacton like everyone else?"

"Because of Dad wanting to be king of the road, master of all he surveys," I tell her, trying to be helpful.

"*He's* not German." Grandma says, rolling up her bacon rind and cramming it into her mouth. She passes Victor a Tupperware pot of last night's pudding.

"He promised me Berlin," Mum says. "It will kill him if we do not arrive."

"It'd take more than that to kill my Roy. Your lot didn't manage it, did they?"

"But what will happen if the brakes fail, Nell?" Mum dabs at her damp forehead with the hem of her cardigan. "Oh, I do hope Roy can take me home."

"He won't."

"Oh, Nell, can you not let me dream?"

"If hopes and dreams were big ice-creams, the world would be right sticky. Now come on, Bridge. Pull yourself together. Jesus wept, look at the state of you. You're as much use as a knitted knife."

"But if the car breaks down, what will we do?"

"Go on the bloody train, Bridget, like anyone else," Grandma says. "And then walk onto the ship. How's he to get this heap of kindling across the bloomin' sea anyhow?"

"Oh Nell, he will drive onto the ferry."

"You'll be telling me he can walk on water next."

"Can he, Mum?"

"Of course not Victor. Eat your Instant Whip."

"Oh, *Sieg Heil*," mutters Grandma.

"Bum it," Victor whispers. "Bloody Butterscotch."

While we wait, I look out of the window. I'm not a sky-gazer, but being trapped makes a person desperate. According to the calendar, there will be a new moon tonight. I picture the unlit half as a round of damp white cheese sandwiched between the earth and the sun. Carved into it is the evil smirk of a Bad-Moon girl, or maybe Mum's face.

2

NEW MOON

Some Saturdays, I'm still waiting for Dad to emerge from the betting-shop an entire packet of strawberry sherbet later, complete with scarlet tongue and fingertips. But today, he nips in and out in record time.

"Just put a bob each way on an odds-on favourite, love," he tells her. "It's called Midsummer Night's Dream. That's the tune you like, isn't it? Couldn't pass that one by. Trixie'll hang on to my winnings."

"I bet she will," Grandma says, disentangling a cavalry soldier from her necklaces.

Mum reaches out and squeezes Dad's hand. "Thank you," she says, for once not making a complaint about him betting. "Thank you for all this."

"A bob each way won't make your fortune. Not at five to four on," Grandma says. But Mum ignores her and lights Dad a cigarette while he tries to close his window. The handle falls off and he roars with laughter. The holiday clouds are lightening from purple Quink to the grey-white of school mash. Hours from now we'll be on the transit roads that syphon us into East Germany and through border controls bristling with guards.

"They're sons of Nazis who don't want to miss out on being Nazis even though the war's over," Victor tells us.

"We can see your drawers, Jacqueline," Grandma chips in, busy sucking Dolly Mixtures. She unsticks a domed jelly, lime and shining like a bogey, from her bottom denture and drops it in the pull-out ashtray.

"Victor, don't drum your feet on the back of Dad's seat. And Jacqueline, pull your skirt down," Mum says, turning round and talking through a needle between her teeth. She's sewing a trail of white running-stitches around an old navy dress. Her idea of fashion, they look like broken lines dividing a long dark road. "You are not recent," she tells me.

I tug at my skirt. "You're spot-on there, Mum. These twin-sets make me look like someone from the Dark Ages. But, decent or not, minis are meant to be in fashion. I'd show you if I was allowed a proper magazine."

Mum would love to still see me skipping on the pavement, jumping over the rope and singing "I'm a Little Bubble Car". But I should be sitting in a little bubble-car, courting a gorgeous young man in winklepickers and wearing a silk headscarf and a girdle. That's me wearing those, not the gorgeous fellow.

"And guess what?" I say, pushing my luck. "My skirts are this short because I've worn them since I was ten, and my legs do actually grow."

"Mind you, Bridge," Grandma says, her corset creaking as she delves in her bag for *Woman's Weekly* and a quarter of liquorice comfits. "If I had legs the length of our Jacqueline's, I'd wear a skirt as small as a cake-frill. And Victor duck, I can well believe there are still Nazis about. Indeed yes. They get everywhere. Comfit, love?"

"Nell, I'm warning you..."

"I was only referring to Mrs Pither, Bridge. Who did you think I meant, dear? She's putrefied of anyone made different," Grandma says, tapping off her ash. "'Oh, do we have Ten Ton Tessie staying?' she said when I hung out my smalls. Tch, the cheek of it. I'll go back to hanging them out after dark and then up at the crack of dawn to fetch them in."

Grandma scared Victor half to death last winter when he found her wrestling with a rigid, frost-bitten girdle. He launches into a re-enactment, earning a slap from Dad for trespassing on the centre-console. The East Germans couldn't possibly protect their border with greater efficiency than Dad's hand patrols his treasured strip of territory.

"Why won't Mrs Pither say our name properly?" Victor asks Grandma, waggling his hands behind his ears and sticking out his tongue at Dad's back.

"Out of spite, love. She just won't say Bishop. 'Oh, Reginald, Mrs Bitch-op's underpants is blockin' my light', says she, loud-as-you-please, to her stoat of a husband."

"She's made a hide in the hedge," Victor says. "For when her laundry's on the line and I'm in the yard with my catapult."

"Oh, I can imagine her crouching in the lavender, waiting for you to blast her silken bloomers. Nothing's allowed past her boundary."

"Oh, and have you seen how she paints her mouth?" Victor asks. "It goes over the edges?"

I'm sure normal seven-year-old boys shouldn't know about lipstick.

"Oh indeed. And if she stands with her left cheek facing the sun, you can see black hairs sprouting from a mole the shape of a Scottie dog. Yes, a terrible thing, spite."

Mrs Pither's Nazi-spite seems to brighten our cloud even more. Dad bursts our eardrums with occasional bouts of yodelling. Mum unfolds maps, saying such unhelpful things as, "Should you not be on this wavy blue line, Roy?"

"Doubt it, Bridge. That's the Thames."

Eventually, Victor tires of the yodelling and even of the drive. His bare legs are stuck fast to the seat and one of T-K's has pinged off and flown into Grandma's foot-well. I did try to tell him men couldn't do the splits.

"It's like driving to a funeral, Dad," Victor says.

"And we'll be heading straight to yours if you don't pipe down."

"Blood and sand, lad," Grandma adds. "Any slower and we'll be in reverse. I'll be back in Audette Gardens in time for *Crossroads*."

"Is this trip one-hell-of-a-gas, Mum?" Victor says, watching a Lambretta buzz by. "Because Dad told me it would be."

"Can you not drive faster, Roy?"

"Oh, hoity-toity," Grandma says. "Your patience is wearing thinner than a cream cracker, Bridge. Ooh, have you been eating your calves-foot jelly again? I swear I can smell hoof. Beats me why you don't have a British bacon buttie like the rest of us."

Mum ignores her. "How are the brakes, Roy? *Mein Gott*, I think sometimes we will not set a toe in Berlin."

"Ooh, if only Hitler had said that about the Sudetenland."

"Ma, stop it. Bridge, just hold the bus, love. Climb down from your Panzer. The brake's as sweet as a nut. It's your appendix I'm thinking about. Softly, softly, the doctor said last time, didn't he? Not too much excitement. If I go haring off like a rocket it could give you a relapse. You'll never get there then."

"Mum," Victor pipes up, "your appendix is a hand-grenade. If the pin is pulled out you've only got seconds. You don't want to detonate it, do you?"

"Spot on, Victor," says Dad, who has coached him. "Think of it that way, Bridge. A hand-grenade inside your guts. No wonder I'm sticking to twenty miles an hour."

"More like two," Grandma says, pulling her knitting apart to pick up a dropped stitch. "And to think I was terrified. I'd be more scared on a milk float."

Everyone except Grandma is too hungry to be pleasant. When Mum asks Dad if he definitely picked up the Deutschmarks from the hall table where Grandma keeps her battalion of china ladies and he says he asked her to put them in his wallet, the stew really starts to simmer. It's all how-am-I-supposed-to-find-anything-among-that-crinoline-mob? And you-know-I-would-never-touch-your-wallet. Reasonable enough. Then we have why-is-everything-always-left-to-me? Followed by some-of-us-were-busy-unblocking-the-toilet. Inexplicably, this leads to it-wasn't-me-who-forgot-to-defrost-the-turkey (four Christmases ago). But it reaches the point where Grandma has to tie her headscarf around Victor's ears and I hear the German word for arse-hole.

Tears are burning my eyes because my parents actually do love each other. Dad doesn't really think Mum's a know-all who blames him for everything. And Mum honestly doesn't hold Dad responsible for Victor ending up in Casualty last Christmas. It was all the fault of the Space-Saving Easy X-tend table.

We only use it once a year because it's a nightmare to unfold. The flaps must be released at the same precise moment or else they jam. Last year, Dad lost patience with them and instead of getting his toolbox out, he drank a lot of Bristol Cream. While we were eating the turkey at the sloping table, Victor's drumstick glided into his lap. He had just coated it in steaming gravy.

Until nine o'clock that night, almost to the end of *The Black And White Minstrel Show*, we waited in Casualty with his sizzling thigh glistening from the butter Grandma had plastered on. When we came back, our abandoned dinners were shrunken and black in the oven like yesterday's coals. Grandma was asleep in front of the blaring television with a box of jelly-babies under her feet, her slippers in her hand and Deborah shrieking "Mammy."

Victor and I ate Ritz crackers and cheese on our laps with a jar of pickled onions wedged between us and him crying all the way through *The Ken Dodd Show*.

When they row, Mum and Dad always stir the silt at the bottom of the grudge-pool.

"All families do the same, duck," Grandma keeps saying. She holds one of Victor's hands and one of mine while we glance inside the other cars on the road as if hoping to see all their insults flying about.

"At least your mum and dad never throw punches," Grandma adds. And, as if this is a souped-up version of I-Spy, Victor and I look out for black eyes too.

Was it Neville Chamberlain in his "peace for our time" speech who said we should go home and get a nice quiet sleep? Well, I wish he was here now. I don't want to be one of those car-people who fall asleep with their mouth open and their head thunking against the window-pillar.

I'm tired because of Dad's terror last night. Grandma reckons the war shredded his nerves like a cheese-grater. He had to shoot a very young German, not much older than me, who spun round three times before he fell, like a dancer in a terrifying ballet.

***

NIGHT-TERROR

I wake up to the gasping. It explodes through the wall into our room. The luminous hands of my clock, evil in the dark, point to half-past one. Half-past one on a Thursday should mean I'm halfway through my warm school mince and lemon-curd tart, but the night version is a time I shouldn't see, or hear.

Victor and I used to stay in bed and plug our ears with plasticine, but now I'd rather be with Dad.

I get up to help, but the room has no shape. I can't find the door and crash into the dressing-table. My hairbrush and Victor's Action Man clatter to the linoleum. Why do things that fall never land on the rug?

Victor's *Commando* slithers off the nylon sheet. How can a half-ounce of paper actually make a thud? He stops grinding his teeth and mumbles, "Argh!" That's a German soldier. And then "Aieee!" That's a Japanese one. Nothing to do with terror in Victor's case. Just comic war.

I stuff his pillow into his ear, but it springs back again because Mum bought the new foam kind. He wakes up.

"Will Dad say the bit about the soldier having a mother?" he asks, as if comforted by this repeating pattern. That's seven-year-old boys for you.

"Yes, he will."

"Will he take aim?"

"Probably."

"Is it a real gun?"

"No, it's the pole with the hook for hoisting up the Sheila-Maid."

"What about the trigger?"

"Oh use your blasted imagination, Victor, can't you?"

There are only so many questions a sister can take.

Dad's gasps grow louder, more rasping, with a horrific pause between breaths, as if all our good breathable air has been sucked out of the house. Has he died? My heart thumps like a road-drill. Ah, the mattress springs are twanging. He's alive. His feet are out. I can hear his callouses scraping on the floor. And he's off.

He gallops across the landing, almost tumbling down the stairs. The first time I heard him, I thought a horse had come into the house. The landing shakes and the bannisters tremble.

I take a deep breath, wishing I could extract it from my lungs and send it to him. Mum used to follow him down. Once, in his desperation to breathe, he thrashed his arms about just as she reached him and caught her with an uppercut. The next morning, Mrs Pither saw Mum putting out the milk bottles, spotted her black eye and threatened to call the police. Not for putting out the bottles. She thought Grandma had thrown a punch.

A while ago, Dad started being nasty to Mum during the terrors. He kept telling her she scared him, but he never remembered it the next day. We were told not to mention it to Grandma. She would never let Mum forget it. Mum could forgive Dad because his mind was so muddled. It was easier than forgiving him for sloping off to the two-thirty at Kempton on the Saturday she turned forty.

She resents me for being the one person Dad tolerates during these hellish nights. She cried about it at first and I tried to say something helpful, but mothers are supposed to mop daughters' tears, not the other way round. When Gaye Kennedy's grandfather died, her mum kept reaching for her, all blurry-eyed, and Gaye had to keep one eye on the clock because *Crossroads* was about to start, and she wanted to see Andy and Ruth's wedding.

Dad is crashing about in the kitchen, fighting to inhale. When I reach him, I try not to touch him or speak first. Either of those can really rattle him and he goes berserk, so I just stand there. Once he's breathing properly, he starts a conversation with the German soldier he killed, trying to spool back time.

"Oh Christ, don't fire, son."

"Shush, Dad."

"You're still a boy. Not ready, mate."

"Come on, Dad. Shush."

"Don't shoot. I'm begging you. I'm looking at your eyes. Look at mine. Think of my ma waiting for me."

A tear drips onto his pyjamas.

"Please, Dad."

"Mate...it's you or me. I'm so sorry."

"Dad. It's all over now," I tell him.

"Yes," he says. "He's down. That's it. He's gone. But his mum'll be waiting."

"Yes, I know. But we're waiting for you too, Dad. Come back to us."

Eventually, our Dad comes back from the war. After twenty hours that are actually twenty minutes, he trudges back up, just an ordinary, tired man.

Mum's slippers tap across the floor above. Grandma, famous throughout our home-town of Oaking for sleeping through Doodlebugs, is spared the entire trauma.

I fill the kettle and press the plunger on the tea-caddy mounted on the wall. It coughs three times into the pot. The mantelpiece clock chimes two when I take the tea-cups upstairs to them. Sometimes it's later than that if I forget to fire the gas under the kettle.

"Put the light on, Jacqueline," Victor says when I come back into our room. My flung-back sheets look uninviting, and I wish someone could tuck me in.

I pass Victor a hanky from under my pillow and tell him, "It'll be all right now." I find him a weary old peppermint-cream and a flat toffee left over from a Jamboree Bag. I even sling my arm round him.

We listen to the china cups clinking. The tea steam seems to curl under our door. While we fall asleep, the house settles down from the upheaval, although I think Dad wanders on the landing for a minute after his tea, because I hear the floorboards squeak, as well as a gentle murmuring.

The next few hours of sleep are a blessed relief. My arm is still across Victor's bed in the morning, his small hand rounded underneath mine like a contented tortoise.

Nothing is said the next day. Toast is burnt, the wash-basin is stained with toothpaste-spit and milk boils over. Situation normal.

Like the moon rolling through its cycle and round to the beginning again, the recurring terrors are an oddly acceptable feature in our lives, the same as dentist appointments or the dreaded window-shopping. Awful, but always there, like being too tall or having enormous ear lobes. You have to grin and bear it, and even though the grinning part is excruciating, we are still the same people in the same home.

The Bad-Moon girls are different, an evil invasion. Dad's silence makes the house swell. Too much air. Too little sound. His shadow becomes a long ink-stain on the floor.

The Bad-Moon girls slither in unannounced and uninvited. They coil themselves around the furniture and sometimes stay for days, like the worst kind of visiting cousins, the sort who eat the one shiny apple you've been keeping an eye on in the bowl, or the sort like Auntie Freda who leaves her bristles in the wash-basin.

***

Grandma announces every shop-sign and pub-name we pass.

"They've moved all of them since I was last this way," she keeps saying.

"Who's they?" I ask her.

"People," she says. "People who move things. Look, there's The Green Man. He definitely used to be further along."

We stop to eat the remainder of our picnic—Grandma found the cheese-and-HP sandwiches before we left Oaking—on a patch of brown grass next to the car. The sun disappears and we all flop on the prickly ground, too glum to get the rug out of the boot, although Grandma hauls out the tiny milking-stool she always takes on picnics.

Dad would usually whisper, "She looks like a heifer perched on three cocktail sticks," and Mum would wink at him. But the air is still so stiff from the car-squabbles you could slice it.

No one speaks. While we wait for the picnic food to be unwrapped, Grandma crams a pink coconut Allsort into her mouth and lights up a Senior Service. She makes those throat sounds and puffs out those sing-song sighs old people always have to make when the conversation dries up.

But once the wicker basket is emptied out, the plastic picnic-plates distributed and the greaseproof paper unfolded, Grandma launches into attack.

"Ugh, strike a light! Tastes like a clod of German earth," she says, flinging Mum's homemade pumpernickel into the cow-parsley. "And it looks like cackers, Bridge. The constipated kind."

Mum mutters some German words I try to memorise. I don't blame her. She's had to suffer all kinds of disgusting English food. She didn't heave after a basin of winkles. Or even after a dish of Grandma's Gooseberry Surprise. And the surprise is, it's inedible.

"Nell, do you want a piece of my Herman-the-German cake or will it give you stomach-pain in the car?" Mum asks in her strained voice, not even trying to pronounce stomach properly.

"What she means is," Victor tells me, "will it make Grandma erupt like Vesuvius?"

I smile, trying to be sisterly while Mum and Dad are not speaking.

"There is also cold chicken schnitzel, Nell."

"Bridge, when will you get the hang of meat? Ooh, I could just sink my teeth into a bit of cold pork and soggy crackling."

"I still have much to learn about foreign food, Nell."

"We're well aware of that, love. Hold the bus a minute, English food isn't blooming well foreign. But honestly, it's still like war rations at times with all those dried-up kugel buns of yours, whatever they are when they're at home."

Mum searches through the tartan bag, utterly defeated. I nudge Grandma hard. I have to or she can't feel it through the whalebone. She takes the hint.

"If there's a pilchard bap, Bridge, I'll have it. No onions mind. They get me inflating and I've not got my good stays on. Can't trust these Woolworth's poppers."

"Only corned-beef, Ma," Dad says, handing her a sandwich wrapped in a Sunblest wrapper.

"Oh, that'll do. At least I can see the meat in yours. Elsie gets a hundred and ten slices out of a tin and one of them's the white fatty lagging on the end. I don't know. Married to a master-butcher and the scrawny old bird's as tight as a fish's arse."

"Have a potato crisp, Nell." Mum says, offering the bag.

"Thanks, duck. You've not put on a bad spread, I suppose. Better at picnics than you are at the stove. Lawks, those chicken dumplings last night! The pawnshop could hang three of those up on an iron bracket. Good as any stonework."

This is a top-notch compliment—the bit about the picnic anyway.

"She's really creeping," Victor whispers. "She's trying to make Mum happy again."

"This is better than Elsie's kidneys would have been," Grandma says. "She won't open her sherry when I'm there, you know. Doesn't like Stan and me singing 'Blue Moon'. Dry old do, it is. I'm glad I came along with you all. Thank you for having me, son. And you, Bridge."

Mum tries to smile and Grandma beams. Mum and Dad start talking to her, rather than each other, but Grandma eats and talks to everyone, salvaging our crusts for a grey squirrel who keeps inching closer. Eventually he takes a digestive from her, clutching it in his tiny hands. "Must be like nibbling at a ruddy great cart-wheel," Grandma says and everyone laughs. Dad steals a glance at Mum and the thaw begins.

"I hope Elsie doesn't feed Deborah grapes when she's on the perch," Grandma says. "Or else Stan will have to change the wallpaper. And she won't scratch properly if there's more than a dozen stinkies in her gravel."

"Dad, there's only one other cub in my pack whose Dad's got a car," Victor says. "And his has only got three wheels."

Sometimes, even seven-year-olds know how to soften icicles. Even though the clouds are packing together, the thermos is leaking and the salted peanuts have all fallen out of the packet, this picnic has become officially groovy. Last time we had one, Victor fell in a cowpat, and Dad had to fish out T-K and wipe him clean with the last of the lemonade.

And Mum is actually showing an interest in my project. She thinks it's still the one about spiders' webs from last year, but at least she's talking to me. I don't have the chance to explain it properly to her yet because it starts raining hard. We pile inside the car with the leftover food, our damp clothes and sweaty Spam steaming up the windows.

We set off again, Grandma sitting in front with the flattened Five-Boys on her lap.

"Dad, where will we eat on the way to Berlin?" Victor asks. "Will you stop at a German café? Will it have those hot-dog things?"

"Well, there are rest-stops on the autobahn. Hey, Bridge, once we hit that stretch of road in the East, couldn't Ilse just meet us there for a cup of tea?"

"Then you wouldn't get shot at, Mum," Victor says, thrusting T-K at her, his well-chewed hands bent in prayer.

"How about it, Bridge?" Dad says. "It's not as if there'll be much to see on the other side of the Wall. It's all miserable flats in great blocks, isn't it? Shops with nothing on the shelves. Sandwiches with nothing in the middle."

As he slows down even more to avoid smashing into the lorry in front of us, I hear him murmur, "Christ, this pedal feels like melted caramel under my shoe."

Mum sighs. "I wish you could all meet Ilse. She is so enchanting. We all took ballet lessons for a while. Beate and I were like baby-elephants, but Ilse was so light on her feet. She was never still. During air-raids she was like a caged bird."

"Isn't she still like a caged bird?" Victor says.

Sometimes he is less bone-headed than most seven-year-old boys. He even has a girl's train of thought. I make a note of the caged bird idea for the project, wanting to understand the broken pieces of Mum's Berlin, although why I think I can do a better job than Churchill, Roosevelt and Stalin, I haven't the foggiest.

Mum is stroking Victor's head in an absent-minded way, as she often does when she's misty-eyed about the past. I know for a fact she'll find nits. I can see one steeplechasing through his fringe.

"Yes, Ilse is in a kind of cage, Victor," she says. "Beate is confined in a different way. She can travel everywhere she likes except to the other half of her own country, and not even into the other half of her own city. Ilse is so completely trapped that even if she met us at the rest-stop, she would be in danger of arrest."

"But she'd still be in the East, Bridge," Dad says. "It's a sort of motorway funnel, isn't it?"

Mum shakes her head. "Meeting someone from the West in that way is not legal. The border guards know the amount of time needed to reach the exit from the moment of entering the transit route. If Ilse took longer than that, she would be interrogated. We might never see her again."

Dad reaches back and holds Mum's hand, his thumb kneading her finger, pushing her wedding-ring round in circles. It's a bit disgusting to watch, but it means the air has cleared, apart from Grandma's jubilant deflating after an entire packet of Garibaldi.

"Ilse must be careful of the secret police," Mum continues. "The Stasi can take you off the street or out of your home for no reason. They even remove both parents from their children, who are then adopted by strangers. Informers are everywhere. No one can trust anyone, not even close friends or family. If the Stasi believe you are an enemy of the state, they make you disappear."

I imagine husbands spying on wives, sons on mothers, nieces on uncles. Even on Christmas Day, a grandmother could be examining the innards of a cracker for coded escape plans while an auntie stuffs her head in the roast goose to search for blueprints of a secret tunnel.

"Hey, Bridge," Dad says, "don't scare the children with these Stasi thugs. They sound worse than the Cybermen."

Victor's eyes are bulging like poached ostrich-eggs. Oh dear Ringo, he's actually whimpering.

"Christ alive, lad," Grandma says to Dad. "How could you bring up them ghastly Cybermen at a time like this?"

"Well, Bridge brought up the bloody Stasi."

"Yes, but they're only in the East," Mum says. "And when Jacqueline and I cross over, they will leave us in peace. I only want you to realise how careful Ilse has to be."

"I suppose if they think she's planning on escaping with you," Grandma says, "then those Stasi will torture her. Maybe you as well, I shouldn't wonder, Bridge."

Victor howls.

"Mum," I shout above the din, "the Stasi may not be in the West, but the Cybermen aren't in Oaking either. It doesn't mean Victor isn't scared to death of them. Before he goes to bed, he even checks they aren't hiding in his toy-cupboard. Which means his Totopoly falls out and whacks him on the head."

I'm not telling them I still check behind my door for escaped train robbers.

Victor is so distraught he crawls through to the front and perches on Grandma's lap. Dad flails his hand about because of the trespassing and his cigarette scorches Victor's sandal.

"It's made a hole in my sock as well," Victor wails.

"Oh simmer down. Fart-arsing about over socks when I've got less than half-an-hour to get us docking on the Maid-of-Bloody-Kent without any brakes for God's sake. God-all-bloody-mighty, son."

There's a foul smell of melted nylon and a torrent of German swear words, after which Dad and Mum refuse to exchange a word for miles. He mutters the worst word of all, twice. Once when he realises Dover isn't as close as he thought it was and Grandma suggests they might have moved that too. And the second time when the thermos rolls onto the centre console and disgorges the last of the tea.

As Grandma falls asleep, it's up to me to ease the tension in the stuffy, sun-baked car. I ask Mum what school is like in Germany, working on the basis that adults respond well to serious questions. If olden days are thrown in, they are compelled to show a keen interest.

"The first day is the best," she says, casting her mind back before the war. "Every child is given an enormous cone of sweets and small presents. Every family has a photograph of their child with the cone. Mine was taken by the piano. I remember seeing my reflection in the marble floor, and my mother smiling when I said the cone was as tall as I was."

Victor sniffs and sits up straighter. He asks if we'll ever see the picture of Mum with her cone of sweets and she looks sad. "No, Victor. It was lost. In the war, almost everything was destroyed. Years later, in one of her letters to me, Beate remembered how she felt the foundations of the house shifting just before it fell, and as she ran for her life, it seemed to sigh."

"I'd have been furious," I say to cover up Victor's *Commando*-style war-mongering noises.

"They were too tired for fury," Mum says. "Too hungry and thirsty. After the bombs had wrecked the city, the triumphant Soviet soldiers looted the banks for money and jewellery. They demolished shops for fun, throwing the shelves, the counters, out onto the street. The people of Berlin, desperate for food, had to watch these shrieking, laughing men toss out all the bags of flour and rice, spilling it everywhere. No one dared pick it up, not with rifles pointing at them. They had to creep out at night to collect what they could find in the rubble."

I imagine the horrible contrast between plump little girls clutching cones of sweets and hollow-eyed young women wasting away.

"Where were you, Mum?" I ask her.

She is quiet for a moment, the side of her face speckled with leaf patterns from the sunlight flickering through the passing trees. Dad murmurs something to her while the mad spotted shadows prance through the car. I can't hear him. He is concentrating on her, not the road ahead in the blinding sun. I have to scream that the traffic is slowing down for the turn-off to the docks.

Dad grapples with the steering, his feet dancing all over the pedals.

"Christ, lad."

"Oh, *mein Gott*, Roy!"

"Dad, watch out!"

"Fuck me."

Number Three.

He jerks up the handbrake an inch from the car in front. Everyone lets their breath out.

"Wow, Dad, a perfect pit-stop," Victor shouts.

More like a resurgence of everyone's picnic.

"Hey, Dad," Victor goes on, "did you know you said..."

"Yes, son. All right. No harm done."

"Yes there is. Every time you say that word a dormouse dies."

There's the proof. Victor is not like other boys.

Dad lights three cigarettes at once and passes one to Mum and one to Grandma.

Mum has avoided answering my question and I can't ask again because her face is like candle-wax. When she turns to look at Dad, I can see tears swelling. But she doesn't let them fall. She just whispers, "I should have been there with them," as if the subject is a gob-stopper wedged in her throat. And I know that's painful because it happened to me in a hockey lesson. Gillian had to bash me on the back to get it out before Miss Monger saw, and it flew on an impressive trajectory from deep-field straight into the shin-pad box.

When Mum talks about the past, she usually starts with the part about meeting Dad in Berlin after the war and moving in with Grandma in Oaking.

"I felt like an intruder," she always says. "When I first arrived, wearing the perfume your father had found for me, the one unbroken bottle in a ruined shop in Berlin, Grandma sniffed the air and said the toilet must be blocked. When Dad and Grandma went to work, I listened to the noise of his motor-cycle until it disappeared. It took an age. Afterwards, the only sound was the tick of the clock. Grandma taught her first parrot, Winston, to turn his back on me as soon as she left the house."

It seems that Dad and Grandma were forever in the prison. Either A or B-wing, Dad was then. I can't remember which. It was high security anyway because he had to wear the clip-on tie. He's a warder and Grandma became a cleaner there after she was widowed during the war. My grandfather didn't fight. "Too pickled," Dad told me once. "When he had a blood-test, the syringe was filled with pure Three Barrels. He fell in the river one night, and when the police were searching for him, they said the hedges alongside the road to The Slug and Lettuce were bristling with empty bottles."

So Mum left a privileged family with a grand piano and a shiny floor, or at least that was the case before the house and the city were blown to pieces, to live in a pebble-dashed terrace with, shamefully, a shed for a porch.

"An old English dictionary and an even older radio kept me company," Mum often tells us. "I never dared to sit back against the cushions for fear of denting them. After translating the newspaper into German and back again, I folded it exactly as Grandma had left it. I could hardly wait for your dad to come home. I ran into the yard the second he zoomed in through the back-gate, even before he had a chance to lever Grandma out of the side-car."

New English words and half a Lincoln Cream were Mum's only nourishment until dinner, because she was confused by Grandma's cantankerous cooker and terrified of disturbing the contents of the biscuit tin. Words, she says, became her Sustenance and her Salvation. I imagine she worked through the dictionary alphabetically.

I wish she would talk now, but she seems niggled and tense. It seems useless trying to help people troubled by the past, because you can't go back and change anything for them.

The car clatters through the miles until we're on the stifling ferry at Dover. The boat smells of chips and eau-de-cologne. Dad is perspiring after a spectacular hand-brake turn into the parking bay. Stacks of moist people in their brand-new holiday clothes pack the steps to the restaurant deck. Dozens of Belgian teenagers are eating potato-crisps, then blowing into their empty packets and bursting them in people's ears. Grandma, nose in the air, sniffs the salty air in a stiff British way, as if no one foreign understands how to behave.

The boat is shabby and noisy, and looking through the grimy portholes at the grey sea rocking and rolling us along is making me queasy, but being out of the car is a relief. We sit down to eat even though all our stomachs are heaving with chocolate. But there's not much else to do, and we don't know when we'll next have a meal after Ostend.

"Once we're back on the road, there'll be no stopping unless you're dead and I have to tip you out to get rid of the stench," Dad tells us. "And even then I might just bung you out the window."

No one laughs. I feel sorry for Dad, but he is being a bit pathetic.

"That handbrake must be feeling the strain by now, eh, lad?" Grandma says. "And what about those beetles nibbling the wood? I can hear them, you know. The floor's about to fall through. Sounds like Pinky and Perky are trapped underneath."

"I'll set the Cybermen on you," Dad whispers.

There's an end-of-tether note in his voice, so we all fall upon the dog-eared menu for distraction.

"Blood and sand, there's gammon and pineapple-ring," Dad announces, brightening. "I fancy something exotic."

"Now that's just mixing your dinner with your pudding," Grandma says.

"No, it's high class grub, Ma. The pineapple juice cuts through the grease."

"Like Vim then."

"I had it last year after we won the World Cup and I went to that posh restaurant with D-Wing."

"Can they eat with handcuffs on, Dad?" Victor asks, balancing T-K commando-fashion across the cruet set.

Seven-year-olds have brains the size of walnuts, the shrivelled kind.

"If you save the pineapple, I'll wrap it in a serviette," Grandma says. "And when we get home I'll have it with a drop of custard. I'll make it myself, Bridge. Don't want my bowel stopped up for a fortnight again, do I?"

We carry on looking at the strange menu while Grandma trundles off to find the Ladies, casting terrifying glances at anyone remotely foreign, even a tiny French nun on crutches.

The man at the next table is busy spreading out leaflets and maps of France. He looks up and smiles across at Dad. Dad smiles back, rasping his hands together in their driving-gloves. He keeps them on, but he takes off his car-coat, all excited about his glamorous meal. He's wearing his sagging cardigan with the weighty leather buttons like big toffees and for a moment it feels like home.

The waitress explains we have the wrong menu. Cooked dinners are not available for the afternoon crossing. Dad seems to shrink inside his cardigan at the non-appearance of our tropical meal, worried he's let us all down. We all stare at the faded photograph of the pineapple-ring until it looks like a clapped-out life-belt from the Lido. The holiday mood darkens again.

We listen to other people's rustling and crackling, the clink of glasses and the rasp of tongs in the metal bowl of sugar-lumps. No one speaks. Victor doesn't even dare to eat the sugar lumps because Mum is still quiet and Dad is holding her hand. We sit like stuffed dummies, not looking at each other and awfully interested in the scribble patterns on the melamine table. A money-spider is attached to the serviette-holder, springing up and down in a wild dance. It'll be a dance of death if he falls in the milk-jug.

The woman at the next table is wiping her daughter's mouth. She looks too old to be fussed over, but acts as if she's still a baby. Her coarse hair is like a shock of fuse-wire, shorn as short as a school-boy's. She turns towards me, her mouth gaping like a cut plum. Her teeth are as jagged as a row of tilting gravestones.

She stands up and points at me, but the patient mother catches hold of her daughter's cotton frock, bunching it in her patient hands, trying to restrain her.

But the girl breaks free, her large open sandals, brand new Clark's with a rubbery sole like a thick sandwich, clacking on the smooth floor. Even I was allowed to stop wearing those when I was eleven. This girl could be fifteen or more, although it is hard to be sure. She lurches to our table and holds out her dress like a ballerina.

"Bwa, bwa," is all she can say. Her voice is deeper than Dad's.

Black hair smothers her arms and legs, as if she is a wild animal in a frock.

Bwa-Bwa is wearing a white dress with cornflower sprigs, a large version of a child's party-frock, the sort that comes with matching frilled pants. I wish I was still young enough to wear those, although when Peter proposes to me by the Danube, or it might be the Severn, depending where our jet-set life has taken us, my Biba maxi will be fluttering in the breeze. But not enough to show my underwear, matching or otherwise.

"Bwa-bwa-bwa."

Desperate to pull the girl away, the mother scuttles across. It becomes quite a tussle, but she doesn't shout or lash out. The father pretends not to be involved. He folds one leaflet and opens another. Perhaps they take it in turns to be the one who sits with a patient smile while the other dashes and sweats and grabs, hoping to attract less attention that way.

The mother wears a full apron and solid shoes. Her hair is wound into a tight bun. She must stud it with a thousand pins like the Christmas oranges we decorate with cloves. She probably sits in her quiet bedroom for the ritual, taking as long as she can to push in the last pin even though her arms are tired, until she hears "Bwa-bwa" through the keyhole. Then she sighs, but not loud enough for anyone to hear.

A family with sensible matching hair-cuts all stare at the mother trying to lever the girl's fingers off the edge of our table. She's gripping so hard they turn bluish and she barks, "Bwa-bwa!" the whole time. I'm staring too, not at the girl's strangeness, but at her elegant nails, each one filed to a perfect arch and buffed into oval pearls. I feel ashamed that her beautiful fingers and her feminine dress shock me.

The pudding-bowl-headed parents, whose pudding-bowl-headed children sit up straight with their elbows tucked in, begin talking as if this is the Ritz.

"Do you think there's an alternative dining-room, dear?"

"Possibly. I'll call our waitress."

"Which is ours—that one with the bushy eyebrows?"

"I didn't notice her face, dear, but she had rather sturdy legs. I can't see her. Shall we just toddle back in half-an-hour?"

They say nothing about Bwa-Bwa, but that somehow warps their well-spoken sort of politeness into plain rudeness. Bwa-Bwa's parents keep their smiles glued on. They have to. It's a performance and they must keep up the show.

Mum is stroking the girl's hand and inching her chair towards her, marvelling at the exquisite nails, tracing her own finger-tip around them. Bwa-Bwa quietens down, surprised.

"How pretty they are, dear," Mum says. "Look at mine. A mess!"

The girl's eyes never leave Mum's face.

"And mine," I say, picking up Mum's thread in a kind of human weaving. We present our ordinary nails, comparing them with the flawless set clutching the table. The girl burrows her face into her mother's apron. Saliva froths onto it. I'm willing Victor to keep quiet.

"Thank you," whispers the mother. "You've made her happy."

Mothers, I realise, are kinder to strangers' children than their own. When Gillian's mother arranged for me to win pass-the-parcel at her fifth birthday party because I'd only just recovered from measles, Gillian spent the rest of the afternoon on a mission to steal my dot-to-dot book prize. Her mother eventually found it behind the toilet. But it was no good. Gillian had sat in there joining all the bloody dots with permanent felt-tip.

The mother shepherds Bwa-Bwa back to their table, where the father cups her face in his hands and presses a kiss on her nose. "Sit by me and eat this peach," he says. "I'll pare it for you."

She plays with the fuzzy trimmings while he posts peach segments into her mouth. Afterwards he wipes her lips with his blue handkerchief. All this time, the mother eats her own peach in peace. When they walk up the steps to the deck, Bwa-Bwa holds everyone up while she tucks the whole of her dress into her knickers. The smile never leaves the mother's face.

"How come we don't get peaches?" Victor grumbles. At least he doesn't stare. He just thinks about his own stomach. As usual.

"I think that family's got it all sorted down to a fine art, Victor," Dad says, reaching across and holding Mum's hand again. "The parents know the girl likes peaches so they packed their own."

"Does that mean you've brought me a slice of Manor House cake and a cream-soda?" Victor asks.

Anything would be better than wrestling with the hard butter and flabby slices of toast our waitress calls High Tea. The toast is more like face-flannel, the worn grey kind.

"What was wrong with that girl?" Victor asks.

"Nothing," Mum says.

"But she can't talk properly."

"No, but her feelings are the same as anyone else's," Dad says, folding his toast over a spiral of butter and posting it into his mouth. "Maybe she thinks there's something wrong with us."

Victor thinks about this, but seven-year-old boys have heads like coconuts—ungainly, tufty-haired and weighed down inside with ghastly senseless liquid brains. "She's as hairy as..."

"Pipe down, son," Dad says.

"But when we went to the zoo, Dad..."

"Now hold the bus. I'm warning you."

"But they've gone now, so why does it matter?"

"Because other people are listening and they're prejudiced enough," Dad manages to whisper through his toast.

Victor looks blank and tries to stab an icy butter curl with T-K's crampon. The spider panics and falls into the milk just as Mum pours it into her coffee.

"Something shifted in her brain before she was properly created," Dad says. "But she's as human as we are."

"Created? Isn't that what God does?"

"Well, yes, that's right, Victor. God created her the same as he created us." Dad looks pleased with this, certain he's off the hook now. But Victor is still dangling bait.

"She's not the same as us though, is she, Dad? I think her Mum's egg must have gone off."

Dad has no idea how many facts circulate in the junior playground in these enlightened days. He almost chokes on his crust. Not that it's actually crusty. It's as soggy as bread left out in the rain on a bird-table. He lights a cigarette and Victor's face lights up too because he got the last word.

I keep thinking about Mum's kind voice when she held the girl's hand. I wish I could tell her how nice she is. But, apart from in sickening films, no one talks to their parents like that. I can't remember her being as nice as that to me since I was small. So I sip my tea and try to eat the strangely round Dutch toast from a packet. Dad almost breaks his front teeth on it. "Call this food?" he says, staring at the toast. "I could use it as a tension pulley for the fan-belt."

Conversations around us heat up. Cutlery clatters. Without Bwa-Bwa's gruff voice and clacking sandals, people relax. Her world rotates on a different axis from ours, their smug knives and forks say. The two collided for a moment. Now we're spinning properly again. Normal service resumed.

I wonder if Bwa-Bwa can actually feel angry or sad or homesick. Or if she even understands what home is. Is she ever at home anywhere? And how would she cope without her parents and their aprons and peaches? I don't know. I reckon they cope with her because they have to, but I suppose it's mostly because of love.

"What's this flat sausage?" Victor asks, poking at the round of grey stuff on his plate. "It looks worse than school dinner. Are we going to have to eat this stuff in Germany?"

"It'll be better there, son," Dad says, unravelling the plastic rind off Victor's slice of pâté. "When I first met Mum in Berlin I made us a picnic. We ate it on the banks of the Spree. Blood-sausage from a butcher in a dark alley whose shop survived both the war and the Soviets, and hot tea from the NAAFI mobile canteen."

Mum takes his hand and she's talking only to him when she says, "Oh Roy, I thought my stomach was being pulled out of my back."

"And that was nothing to do with the pickled gherkin," Dad says. "What was it, Bridge, you always said? Your insides turned inside-out and became all heart." He kisses her hand.

"Parent-love? Bloody, bloody ugh," Victor whispers.

"Better than arguing," I mutter.

"We danced by the river under the moonlight and he..."

"Please don't tell us any details, Mum," I shriek.

"I only wanted to say he trod on my toe and thought the German word for sorry was *Mistkäfer*. That was the moment I fell in love with him."

"What does it mean then?" Victor asks.

"Dung-beetle," Dad says, mortified. We all have to put up with Mum ruffling his hair and making horrible fluttery cow's eyes at him.

Gillian says words are not needed for love. It's all about looking and trembling and one tongue circling round the other. When we played Do, Dare, Double-Dare, Love, Kiss, Promise in the second year, she had to twirl tongues with Gaye Kennedy and said it tasted of junket gone hard.

"Can I go on the deck?" Victor asks. "That lot over there are eating semolina. It's got rats' droppings in it."

"They're prunes, Victor," Dad says.

"You shouldn't call people prunes, Dad," Victor replies.

Grandma comes back and chuckles to see Mum and Dad clinging to each other and I remember the time in Clacton when she snorted her top teeth into a samovar. I can't stop laughing and the holiday seems more bearable now everyone is slightly bouncier, although that could be down to the choppy sea stopping us putting one foot in front of the other without cannoning off the High Tea trolley.

Up on deck, we lean on the rails and watch the ship cutting through the endless water, which is so different from the seaside. Rinsed of colour, it blends with the sky. Gulls circle and squeal, livelier than their murky surroundings. Eventually, the solid mass of the sea seems to heave us along while the ship becomes static.

The wind whips the side-wing of Dad's black glossy hair out of its Brylcreem and he struggles to smooth it back. He gives up, pulling on his cigarette as if he's about to face a firing-squad. The dream he's living at last seems to be weighing him down. He catches my eye and I see fear. Either that or he's about to throw up the Dutch toast. No. It's fear. This is how he looks during the night-terrors.

Grandma offers him a nip of her brandy. Trouble is, she's not really used to alcohol. She's only brought it to ward off sea-sickness. And for every nip she offers Mum or Dad, she has one for herself. When Victor's hamster was ill she gave it a nip. By the time it revived, she couldn't see straight to put it back in the cage and it disappeared. Dad took the entire settee apart before he found it comatose under the antimacassar.

We try to enjoy the strong cooling wind on the deck, but all the wet wooden seats are occupied and Grandma keeps saying, "Oh bugger, there go my curls."

After the seagulls quieten for a minute, Mum, her face flushed and girlish, says to Grandma, "I'm so excited, Nell. Soon I'll be home at last."

"I wish I bloody-well was, Bridge. All I want is a cup of English tea. Not this foreign gnat's piddle. And I tell you what, I'm worried sick about Berlin." Her face looks white and withered and her mouth is folded in as if her teeth have fallen out. I can see her silver moustache. She's doing her 'frail old lady' impersonation, which doesn't suit a woman built like a Sherman tank.

"Germany is just an ordinary country, Nell," Mum says.

"What, with all that sausage?"

"Oh Nell, listen. My family are people like you and me. They laugh and cry. Their sky is blue. Their rain makes puddles. Some work in prisons. Some keep pigs. They have dreams."

Grandma sniffs. "German pigs have dreams?"

"Oh, Nell."

"Anyway I've seen that sausage sliced up in the delicate-nessan, Bridge. Great white lumps of green in it. I don't trust green."

"Nell, those are peppercorns."

"Pepper's white, Bridge."

The sea-spray and rain are driving people below again. But in her determined we're-English-and-won't be-beaten-by-a-shower way, Grandma unfolds her plastic bonnet, and Mum helps tie it under her chin. The rest of us go back inside. Dad, fortified by the brandy, is trying to pick up the holiday spirit in the way fathers do. While mothers fuss over flasks and wet feet and finding toilets, fathers make it fun. Dad discovers a pack of cards someone has abandoned. They're a bit battered and damp, but have been designed by fashion-gods.

"Fab, Dad, they're Biba."

"I aim to please, Jacqueline," he says, giving my name a French accent. "Is this what they call a gas?"

"This is definitely a gas, Dad."

The backs of the cards are decorated with the Biba black and gold pattern and the fronts are all coloured drawings of impossibly beautiful model-girls in not very many clothes. It's a bit embarrassing to see Dad blinking away at them while we play Newmarket. He holds some of the girls very close. I can actually hear them brush against his glasses. And he looks a bit agitated when he lays down the Queen of Clubs in her frilly white swimsuit, especially when he has to put his threepenny piece on her. But better these girls than the Bad-Moon variety. I hope Mum and Grandma stay on deck for ages. I hope they get swept over... No, maybe not.

Bwa-Bwa and her parents pass by, wild-haired and red-nosed from the deck. Even though she is restrained by a harness and reins, she lunges at us, determined to touch the cards. She pulls free and snatches them, knocking Victor's money to the floor. She barks. She yelps. She wants Trevor-Keith. While Dad picks up the scattered cards and I lob T-K into the tartan bag, we all launch into endless rounds of English-style apology.

"I think she likes the shiny colours, dear," the mother says. "I'm so awfully sorry about this."

"No, no. Not at all. Sorry to spread ourselves all over the shop like this. Er, would you all like to play?" Dad asks. "The stakes are reasonable."

"It's all right, Sir," the father says, looking pleased to be asked, but sad that it could never be possible.

"You'd be welcome," Dad insists through a cloud of smoke, shuffling and smiling like mad.

"She wouldn't understand, I'm afraid," the mother says, trying to prise Bwa-Bwa's hand off the elegant lady-joker wearing one red and one black shoe.

I can see what has to happen. There is a sticky old pack of cards from Clacton in our bag. The ace of spades is missing and the jack of hearts has a bent corner, but isn't that always the way? I give the Biba cards to Bwa-Bwa. I have never done anything as nice as that before. I would never have given them to Gillian.

"You can have them," I tell Bwa-Bwa. "To keep."

And after the no-we-couldn't-possibly and the-pleasure's-all-ours rituals, they accept the beautiful Biba cards. The smiling father looks back at us and his face shows he's thinking, "How nice and ordinary they are. I'll never have that."

Once the ship drones towards the Belgian coast, we return to the deck. The spray leaps up, stiffening our faces and turning our hands wet and cold on the metal railing. Dad holds his cigarette to Mum's lips and she breathes hard, leaving her apricot lipstick on the tip. Her hair is trapped under a blue scarf with an anchor pattern, a few blonde wisps flying free in the briny wind.

"I am so nervous, Roy."

"Have another drag, love."

"Beate resents me for leaving Germany," she says. "Was I wrong?"

I imagine Mum as a dragonfly skimming past a spider's web, while the ordinary insects are caught.

"Hey, hold the bloody bus, love," Dad says, trying to push the escaping hair under her scarf. "I found you hanging on by a thread. I took you away to start again. That's not scarpering."

"But I left them," she says, her smoke snatched by a sea-breeze. "They had always tried to make me safe, but I made no difference at all. I was always just a... ach, what is that odd sea-creature that stands on its head and eats with its toes?"

"I can roly-poly underwater with a beach-ball between my knees," Victor suggests.

"A barnacle, love, do you mean?" Dad asks her.

She nods. "Yes, something that always must depend on someone else." And she frowns at the bleary crayon-line of the horizon, unwilling to leave the no-man's land of the boat yet.

The thrilling discovery of land excites everyone else on the ship. We all turn into Vasco da Gama. Children are held up to see it and put down again, disappointed with the dun-coloured streak in the distance.

"When I first saw England," Mum says, "I wanted the ship to turn round and take me back."

"I feel like that now, Bridge," Grandma says.

The sight of land doesn't mean stepping off the ship. It takes ages to actually reach it, longer than it took to cross the everlasting sea. Dad takes Grandma and Victor to look at the shop while Mum and I squash into seats scattered with pastry crumbs at yet another scribble-patterned table in a smoky bar, surrounded by crowds of clammy, yawning people.

"So, Jacqueline, I'm going home at last," she says, sounding more German than ever.

I grit my teeth, but this business about going home is the gist of the project, so I'll have to grin and bear it, if it is possible to grin through gritted teeth. It must be, because that politician, Edward Heath—the one who wants to sail round the world and Dad says he blooming well should and take as long as he likes about it—manages it.

"Mum, for this project, we used pictures for inspiration. And I found one of a factory in Berlin."

I want to say how I saw the little building, what's left of it, and thought of Mum. "I thought of you." Do daughters say that to mothers?

"I...thought...it would be good," is what burbles up instead. Pathetic. But she is looking at me as if no one could have told her anything better. She even holds my hand for the first time in ages. Sort of awful in public, but all right too.

"It's about how things are. And how things were. Miss Whipp says we have to show contrasts," I explain. "Something with a shadow. She wanted me to do Sandie Shaw."

"Well, Berlin is built on sand."

Heaven help me. Mind you, shifting sand sounds about right for Berlin. Or quicksand. The entire city might sink without trace before we get there.

Mum is staring into the distance now, disconnected from our stumbling conversation. She often detaches herself and wanders to the front-room window to watch the women streaming off the bus for the early shift at the mop-and-brush when she's meant to be giving Victor and me our breakfast. She unhooks the enamel let-down in the kitchen, but I have to set it with bowls and spoons, cut the grapefruit and find Victor's tie. Once I found her cutting our shredded-wheat in half thinking it was toast. And she's always watching the women climb onto the bus again when we come in from school, even when she's meant to be minding one of her beery slab-cakes in the oven.

"You are still so young for knowing the sad things about Berlin," she says at last.

"Fourteen isn't young anymore. Maybe in your day it was."

"It was," she agrees. "I was happy to still wear dirndls and white socks."

Blimey, this won't be a good moment to ask her for a Berlei Gay Slant. Especially at thirty-two and six.

I must find a way into the project, even if everything I ask sounds unkind. "How does it feel, Mum, to be treated as foreign?"

"Not easy, Jacqueline. 'Oh, I've always wanted to meet a German,' a mother said to me last week at Victor's school, peering at me as if I have a disease that has left interesting scars, but thankfully not something she would catch."

"And do you actually still feel as foreign now as you did the first day you came to England?"

"I have always felt foreign, Jacqueline."

She is staring at nothing again. She isn't on the Maid-of-Bloody-Kent at all. She is lost somewhere else. I may be listening and writing beside her, but she is absent.

"Can you tell me about running away, Mum?"

With my notepad soaking up coffee spills from the table and passengers jogging my arm, I keep writing Mum's story, leaving out her grammar mistakes.

At long last we return to the car and merge with the swarm raring to roll down the ramp. We rattle out into the cold dusk of Ostend, which smells, according to Grandma, of rotting fish, with Dad's feet balanced on the clutch and accelerator as if he's on a tight-rope fifty thousand feet above the Grand Canyon. While he side-steps the brake, I copy up the heart of Mum's story, a stranger's tale, and if I didn't feel her sadness between the words, I would be made of stone.

***

CONTRASTS PROJECT

Bridget (My Mum) in Berlin, November 1938
Part One - Disorientation

Friends used to stream into our house every day. Always, always, music would echo through the rooms, following everyone up the central sweep of stairs, even outside into the gardens and further down to the fountain and orchard. My father was a gifted composer and taught me to play the piano when I was still small enough to need three cushions on the stool. My mother was always setting out dishes of silvered almonds and rows of crystal glasses sparkling with champagne.

In 1932, when I had just turned twelve years old, I was invited to join the waltz for the first time. My rustling gown was the bronze of autumn leaves. Over the next six years, my parents gave me dresses in spring green, poppy red and silver white. I wore out a dozen glittering pairs of dancing shoes.

But the parties gradually became less frequent as friends with wealth or connections slipped away from Berlin. Overnight, yet another house would fall silent, yet another group of guests would be missing from our gatherings. My home grew darker, as if endless rain was falling.

Whenever I passed Father's study, he was sitting, not at his piano but in the tall wing-chair, a tiny, defeated man who no longer beckoned me inside to play duets. Once his room fell silent, our home became a strange, uneasy place, not only because of the unsettling hush, but because I knew my father was afraid.

One day, he hurried into the ballroom where I was playing a Mendelssohn sonata.

"Stop," he shouted, trying to grasp my music from the piano. His hands were shaking and the sonata skated across the polished floor.

From someone so quiet and modest, almost afraid to shine, this sudden forcefulness was a shock.

"Forgive me," he said, packing the offensive sonata into a sack along with all the other sheets of music from the pile on top of the piano. Afterwards he closed his eyes for a moment, as if order might be restored while he was not looking.

"No one can risk keeping this music in the house, let alone playing it."

"But why?"

"Apparently Mendelssohn's music is degenerate. It has to be rewritten."

He sounded weary, unable to find any logic in pretending the composer had never existed. But this was life in the Third Reich. People either obeyed or fled.

We took the sack into the freezing night. The wind was hurling leaves into the air. After many attempts, Father struck a match that lit up the fear in his eyes and Mendelssohn's work soared into flames. I had tried so hard to master Piano Concerto Number One and knew every crease in the paper that blazed to nothing in seconds.

Father stood so close to the fire the charred fragments flew into his face, but he remained still, watching until not a single note remained. He flashed his torch at the embers, searching for stray crochets. At last, we left the ashes and walked inside, back to the piano.

My mother came in, elegant as always, her clouds of perfume drifting through the room and the lace edge of her handkerchief foaming beneath her silk cuff. Whether trying on picture-hats, arranging flowers or dancing in the ballroom, she radiated joy. But that day, her smile was a thin, tense line.

"Please play Beethoven for us, dear," Father said to me.

"Beethoven?"

Father cupped my face in his cold hands as if to press the point and restrain me from defying him. "Please understand."

"All right. I promise to fill this house with the heroic German spirit," I said, not understanding at all.

After lighting the candles on top of the piano, I thumped out the music we were told was the essence of the Germanic soul, while my parents sat close together in the shadows. When my mother cried, Father held her tight and told me to play louder.

In the autumn of 1938, the three of us celebrated my eighteenth birthday with an elegant meal in the dining room. I had always imagined an enormous party, a gold ball gown and a small orchestra, but the miserable tap of forks on fine china was the only sound. After the cake was cut, a suitcase appeared in the hall.

"You are going to visit your aunt and uncle and the two girls. Just until this madness is all over. You can be their third daughter," Father said, as if it were customary to send daughters out on loan.

"Just until it's over," my mother repeated, twisting the sudden separation into a mere inconvenience, like a burst pipe or a lost glove.

Father tried to hold me, but his thin arms felt like old string. I pulled away, frightened of his hoarse voice. Fathers shouldn't cry.

I was to become someone else's third daughter, not my parents' only child anymore. I ran from them, trying to hide, but they caught me in the orchard, marched me to the front of the house like an intruder and bundled me into the cold back seat of a waiting car.

The driver's face seemed carved from pumice stone, his voice like gravel. "Your poor mother is crying, look," he kept growling. "Come on, you. How about sending her a smile through the window, eh?"

They were standing on the steps in a downpour. Hail pelted the car roof, lashing at the windows. Crisp leaves that had skimmed across the ground in the wind the day before lay sodden and still. My birthday present, a tiny dog, cowered on my lap. I pulled off the red ribbon round his neck and ground it under my shoe.

"Give them a wave," the driver said. "Who knows when you'll see them again?"

I refused to look up. "No," I said. "This makes no sense."

"Nothing makes sense now," he said.

The car reeked of damp cloaks and tobacco, reminding me of our vanished party guests, and my own coat had absorbed my mother's perfume, the scent of mauve roses after rain. As I was driven away, I heard my father playing Debussy's banned "Clair de Lune", the defiant notes following me through the open door, down the steps and into the car.

My legs shook, battering against the cold leather seat, making the dog whine throughout the journey into the heart of Berlin.

The city was too quiet, the shops shuttered and the streets empty, apart from small groups on corners. The pavements shone from the rain and the sky was still swollen with clouds like enormous, tender bruises.

"You get out here," the driver said, stopping at the corner of Unter den Linden. "Someone is waiting for you under the trees."

I stood alone after the driver had gone, my case between my feet and my dog in my arms, listening to the unsettled, metallic rustle of the leaves until my uncle, glancing around, stepped out from the shadows.

After we had walked along a side-street for a few minutes, we heard windows smashing. As we came around the corner, youths armed with bricks and sticks surrounded a beautiful shop that sold fine leather goods, screaming, "*Juden raus!*"

Jews out.

One stubborn spike of glass stuck fast in the frame. On it, I could see part of a white-painted letter J for Jew. By this time, there were many of these on the shop-windows of Berlin, a sign for German people not to buy goods there. I watched the young men destroy the shop and take as much as they could carry. No one would be able to buy from it now.

Six policemen stood nearby, closer than us, just watching. One of them was grinning.

"Quickly," my uncle said, grasping my arm.

The thump of heavy boots echoed in the alleys as the Hitler Youth joined the rampage. A huge explosion from a building behind us made the dog squeal in terror, struggle out of my arms and scurry into the night.

"Let it go," my uncle said, steering me away from the flames. "Someone might take him in. We can't get caught up in this. These streets will flow with blood tonight."

The dog had no name to call. I never saw him again.

We tore through the streets, my uncle pulling me along. I thought my feet would leave the ground.

"What the hell is happening here?" I asked, gasping for breath. I knew it was wrong to speak that way, but he was not angry. We stopped running for a moment. His face was in shadow, but I heard him weep. All good men were breaking down, their spirits exhausted after such a long time of assuring wives and children that reason would win through.

He took a shaky breath, holding my arm with great tenderness. "Hitler has fascinated us for an age," he whispered. "We've all watched him like a bird watches a snake, knowing he will strike without knowing when. But I think we know now."

"So what is happening tonight?" I asked again.

He swallowed hard before he said, "This night is the end of hope."

We ran faster through the smoke, followed by the stench of burning and the splintering of glass. While we paused to catch our breath in a quieter street, a linnet began singing.

"Do you think he's trying to explain?" I asked in a small attempt at cheering my uncle.

"No, my dear girl, it's just song," he replied. "Not an answer."

But we listened anyway, while the moon that had crossed the sky behind the sun, sank with it, and left the raging fires to light the sky.

We listened while Nazi stormtroopers attacked Jewish homes, stores and schools. Not even hospitals were spared. A hundred synagogues were burned to the ground. Thousands of Jewish men were rounded up and sent away. Afterwards, those brutal hours were called Kristallnacht, the Night of Broken Glass.

3

PACIFICATION

Cars slide out of the boat like the release of a slow zipper, one tooth at a time, nose-to-tail in the hope of rolling faster off the gangplank, or whatever it's called. Our car protests at first but coughs into life at last. Most of us inside it are flagging too, but Dad, fully car-coated and driving-gloved, is plugged in and switched on. During the long wait to go back to the car, he fell into conversation with the bushy-browed waitress, who had changed into a mini-skirt.

"Very nice girl," he says. "She's studying car mechanics."

"I bet she is," Grandma says, opening her box of Newberry Fruits.

"Very substantial legs," Mum says, pursing her lips.

While the queue comes to a standstill, Dad insists on moving Victor into the front seat, muttering, "Bloody women."

The waitress was wearing Sunflower stockings. "Captured from the Riviera. The in-shade, the fun-shade, the sun-shade." And all for three pounds eleven. I might not stand a chance of walking about with Sunflower legs, but there's no point watching commercials about gravy or baby-food that slot you into the kitchen. Television should take you at least as far as the Riviera, wherever that is.

I might become a ship's waitress, travelling the seas, then peeling off a silk stocking to repair Paul McCartney's fan-belt before purring to a Belgian restaurant in my tangerine Beetle.

"Do you think the waitress lives by the sea when she's not on the boat?" I ask Dad. "I wouldn't mind waking up to the crash of waves on the sand."

"She's got digs over the fish-gutting sheds in Macclesfield," Dad says.

"Ah."

Ring-roads scoop us around darkening towns and villages. Narrow slip-roads draw us off onto motorways. Occasional jams and delays overheat the car to boiling-point as we ooze into the heart of Belgium. The landscape thickens into navy-blue fields merging with enormous sky. We try to admire it, but it looks a lot like England. The rain has a foreign smell that none of us can explain. It becomes one of those rare, family-uniting holiday moments.

We pull off the main road for Dad to shine his torch on the map and piddle out the car door.

"Roy, please be discreet," Mum pleads, her hands over my eyes.

While we're listening to the hearty stream of wee hitting the grass, Mum shares out the last of her lettuce and piccalilli sandwiches. Like us, they're limp and soggy, but we can't rely on a food-stop later.

"Will Roy park somewhere for my ten o'clock cup of tea?" Grandma asks. I feel almost sorry for her because she sounds small and lost, uprooted from Audette Gardens, parted from her parrot and her rituals.

"I bet he won't," Victor says, lording it from the front. "And guess what, we all have to sleep in the car tonight. Except Dad."

Excellent. Maybe I can take the night off from filing Grandma's verruca.

"Belgium smells funny," Grandma says, spitting out a Parma Violet and going back to her fruit-jellies.

"Try sleeping, Nell," Mum suggests.

"I have to lie flat, Bridge. It's only those ruddy great carthorses that drop off upright, duck."

"You could try."

"And they keep their eyes open. Mind you, I had to do that when my Bill was alive. Otherwise he'd be ferreting for ale-money faster than a rat up a drainpipe. In the end, I tied bells on my handbag."

Sleeping in a Morris Traveller sounded like an adventure when we were at home, but it really isn't. You convince yourself your head is comfortable jammed up against the window, but however tightly you close your eyes, you never actually sleep. There are no owls hooting. No velvet darkness. Nothing out there except the slim, sinister crescent of invisible moon we are towing. And inside the car, just the smell of well-sucked, synthetic orange sweet flavouring mixed with clouds of smoke, the sound of matches being struck and a strange creaking that could be the car's death-rattle, but turns out to be Grandma's stays staging a protest.

Mum tries to keep awake to read the maps, but she's hopeless, partly because Grandma keeps snatching the torch to avoid the tongue-puckering green Newberry Fruits, but mostly because her navigation skills are even worse than Dad's. His rule is Never Go Back. No matter how lost he is, he presses onwards, even if that is the wrong direction.

"How you and Bridge found your way back to England after the war is a mystery to me," Grandma says.

"We used the Tardis," he says.

"Did you?" Victor shrieks.

"Oh yes. Bumped into William Hartnell in the console room and rematerialized in Oaking High Street."

Victor sighs, wanting to believe it. Grandma sniffs, licks her finger and gathers up all the fallen sugar scattered in her jellies box.

My eyelids droop against the irritation of sugar-crusted seats, the grumbling engine and the deadliness of being bound to people I have looked at too long and smelt too much. Even their rumpled clothes are too familiar. I discover that an air-deprived car-family is connected purely by stench.

I open the window for something to do and close it because of the roar in my ears. Mum snaps because I'm fidgeting. Dad reaches back to cuff my leg when actually both are folded under me on the seat.

"Where the hell are your legs?" he shouts in a panic.

"Thought you didn't want shoes on your console. Now I'm in the wrong for not having them there."

Being a back-seat passenger is so dismal I even miss school and find myself thinking back to Miss Whipp's lesson the other day, when she told the class to choose topics for our projects. It became Day One of my mission.

***

THE PROJECT

Piles of magazines and newspapers thump onto our desks. Miss Whipp has raided her home, her elderly mother's magazine rack and the launderette on the Parade. We were all supposed to contribute, but she put an embargo on the *Daily Mirror* and I'm not admitting to *Mandy* in public.

The *Grocer*, *Angler's Mail* and the *TV Times* are our inspiration. I wanted to carry on with my spider-webs project, but Miss Whipp is the type to shudder if she spots the tiniest *frontinella communis*. I've explained how they hang from an upside-down dome woven above a lacy flat sheet for minuscule insects to fall onto, instant picnic food spread out on a rug. But she sees no beauty in that.

After the Head took her to task for not encouraging us to make mature distinctions, Miss Whipp was forced to give this year's project the theme of Contrasts. Light and Shade. New and Old. Pretty and Not So Pretty—Miss Whipp won't say ugly. If she had her way, we'd be studying the rise of the Genoa cake or the rebellion of the Bourbon biscuit.

"Did Miss actually steal these?" Gillian asks, leafing through a *National Geographic* with someone's biro sketch of a bitten sandwich over the headline "Pakistan: problems of a two-part land".

"She can't have," Lynette Margolis replies, snipping out a picture of fungi clustered on a silver birch. "They're for anyone to take, aren't they?"

"Of course she didn't and of course they're not," Gaye Kennedy scoffs, huffing on her Form Captain's badge and giving it a polish with her cuff. "Pamela and Derek asked our dentist for all the dog-eared mags he would have thrown out of the waiting-room and put a donation in his Blind Dogs box."

"Your dentist's dog's blind?" Gillian says.

"It's Guide Dogs," Lynette chips in.

"Same difference," Gaye says. No one argues. She knows everything because she has progressive parents. They told her the labels 'Mother' and 'Father' were costing them their identities, so now she has to call them Pamela and Derek.

"It's a good job those are their names then," I said.

She didn't get it. People who know everything never get it when someone else comes out with a gem.

Gillian spots an article about Jean Harlow's new husband being found dead. "It says here he killed himself because of im-po-tence. Fancy them spelling that wrong. But why would someone die from that? I mean, Jesus might have been too important for this world, but I shouldn't think Jean Harlow's husband was."

We all agree.

Gillian peers at me through her fringe, her eyes like two sequins in a magpie's nest. She's burning to find about my project. That makes two of us.

"What's yours about then, Jacqueline?"

"What's yours?"

"Promise you won't copy?"

"Cross my heart."

She sits up straight. "I'm doing Naomi Sims."

Who the hell's that?

"I've already got a fab picture of her. Naomi won't be in this lot of rubbish," she says, poking her ruler at the motley magazines. "My picture's from the *New York Times*. My father got it from his members-only club. It's so secret the street isn't even on the map and the blinds are made of black rubber."

"I told my dad I had to write about 'something nice, but with darker shading', as Miss Whipp puts it, and he thought I should do Nobby Stiles," I tell her. "Dad said there was nothing more bafflingly beautiful than Nobby dancing on the pitch with the World Cup and his teeth out."

"He's not Naomi though," Gillian says. And I have to agree with that.

Projects are the worst invention ever. Teachers make us do them when they run out of proper lessons or want a bit of peace to get on with their shopping lists. My project on the gruesome pig-and-poultry farm we visited in the first year earned me third prize and a book token worth two-and-six. Gillian scooped the booby prize, a Quality Street chocolate, but she didn't deserve the Montelimar. Her project wasn't even worth the solid toffee that pulls your fillings out. It was only half a page and most of that was a sketch of a pork chop.

But after the pig-and-poultry assignment, she turned into a gladiator and kept coming top. I had to congratulate her over and over again. It's so much easier to sympathise with a friend's defeat than applaud their success. A prickle of excitement crawls up my spine. This time, I want to beat her.

I imagine going home with the news that I'm top. Mum would sit up and take notice if I struggled through the front door with the big prizes—a two-layer box of Contrast chocolates and an inscribed copy of *Selected Poems of Inspiration*, co-edited by Miss Whipp herself.

Gillian's mother has cut out the hallowed Naomi Sims with pinking-shears and curled her up in a Toni Home Perm box for protection. I imagine her tucking it, along with a Bandit and a red apple, into Gillian's briefcase.

Once I stopped feeling quite so much like a child, Mum seemed disappointed I was changing, although I keep willing her to understand. I can't help wanting a girdle, preferably a Berlei Gay Slant, and every girl reaches the point when *Twinkle* comic is just for catching clippings when you nail-scissor yourself a Marianne Faithfull fringe.

When I first showed an interest in clothes, Mum used to sit on my bed when she came up to say goodnight and ask me what colour I'd like for my winter coat. But the next morning, when the coat still mattered to me, she had already forgotten about it. Sometimes, when we have to ask Stan if he can spare a few chops or Victor has to scrabble among Grandma's toe-nail trimmings under the sofa cushions for a sixpence to pay for school dinners, I suppose Mum has to forget about things that cost money.

But I would like her to notice that growing up scares me. I have changed quietly, like wallpaper peeling. Without a sound, the pinkish plaster underneath becomes exposed. I have somehow shed a layer of skin and I miss it.

The trouble is, Mum's past has risen to the surface the way her hefty bagels float up to the top of the pan. "I prefer me bread without a ruddy great hole in it, thank you," Grandma always says, reaching for the Sunblest.

Grandma thinks Mum should have a job to "shake herself out of the mess of Berlin." A few mothers work part-time on the parade or do earlies at the mop-and-brush. Pamela works all day at BOAC. Gaye thinks she's still an air-stewardess, but Grandma says, "Pamela Kennedy? Tch, she's past being a dolly-bird now. She just minces down the aisle after the plane lands and fishes the false teeth out of the sick-bags."

Derek spends hours helping drug addicts when they're shaking all over and their insides are falling out, but he won't help Gaye with her French, even though he used to pick figs in Fains-la-Folie.

Pamela and Derek swan in at all hours with frozen tubs of mousse, which is all Gaye ever gets for her pudding. She wears a house-key on a length of shirring-elastic round her neck. "It has to have some give," she explained. "Pamela and Derek thought someone might try to strangle me if we used string."

"Bagsy first go," I muttered, watching her suck on the key like a dummy.

My mum watches me drop my bag in the hall when I come home. She has the tea brewing   and she lets down the let-down, ready for us to eat her gritty cake with plums that taste of penicillin. But then she disappears to wash the stairs or clear the grate. It's Grandma who remembers I've had a geography test or notices my hem unravelling. She sits down and looks at me when I talk, even though she interrupts all the time with essential matters in hand, such as, does Deborah need a bigger mirror so she'll think she has a beefy companion, or do I think the Queen eats dates.

The other day she said, "Project? Can't they just teach you how to turn a cuff and make a fatless sponge?" But she bought me a pad of yellowish ruled paper and a soft rubber from Woolworth's when she went into Oaking for her surgical stockings.

Mum's brain disintegrates into fluff when I ask for help with Venn diagrams or the point of ox-bow lakes. She lays down the handkerchief she is embroidering for Beate, stares into space and mumbles about life thirty or forty years ago. Ancient times anyway. Nothing makes sense. Once, she remembered being sent to the back of the class even though she had mastered her Latin pluperfect. Her mind is muddled, the memories drifting about like dandelion seeds in the wind.

Grandma says to her, "Pull yourself together, Bridge, and make the dinner. Berlin's got bugger-all to do with Bisto. You need to think more English or you'll always be a foreigner, duck. You know, there's a gap between what we dream of and what life gives us. So, come on. You invited yourself here. And you'd settle down better if you learnt how to make a decent hot-pot."

Grandma is right. Mum shouldn't still feel like a visitor. Audette Gardens isn't just her mother-in-law's house. It's meant to be her home. We want her to sit in the front-room at Christmas and smile at us all over the roast turkey, instead of staring into the steam.

"Look, here's Naomi," Gillian says, nudging me and opening out her picture of a beautiful coloured woman.

"She's a role model," Gillian says, although she has no idea what that means.

"Finger or bridge? White or Hovis?" Gaye Kennedy asks.

Gillian doesn't know, but she writes her sentence on the first page of her project book.

Naomi Sims is a roll model.

"What's your Contrast, Gillian?" Gaye demands to know.

"She's the only black model."

"Oh."

Miss Whipp hands out scissors and demands silence. She watches us work for a minute, then sighs as she pulls a stack of marking towards her. It's just a barricade. I know the sound of a Wagon Wheel being unwrapped when I hear it.

I am beginning to sweat. Our notepads will be inspected at the end of the lesson. Above the blackboard the clock keeps clucking. Pages rustle. Scissors snip. Stiff old brushes scrape. And I am more stuck than the ton of blotting-paper confetti a million fourth-years before me have crammed into the inkwell.

"Now remember, everyone, cheerful projects please! No dead people. And no toads that squirt poison please, Timothy Forrest. Oh, and Jacqueline Bishop, no more spiders, dear. Let's have something nice."

Nice is Miss Whipp's favourite word. Our other English teacher has labelled it lightweight, antiquated and unfashionable, which sums up Miss Whipp pretty well.

I sneak another look at Gillian's project.

Naomi was a foster child. She was bullied at school for being so tall. Today she is a beatiful model on the cover of the New York Times, *Fashion Suplimint.*

I pick up a Sunday newspaper that falls open at the women's pages. Everything there reminds me of mothers. A sketch of stewing steak beside an article on how to brown it. A picture of a new-born baby with a tube in its nose. An advertisement on how to clean a staircase with Ajax. An interview with Enid Blyton about Noddy. Apparently his name is Purzelknirps in Germany. I'm not sure he'll catch on.

Flicking through a withered supplement, I spot an article about the Cold War. Turning the limp pages, mildly interested, I read a short article:

September 1962, Klein-Glienicke, a Berlin village on the border.

The priest led the funeral party as far as the barbed wire. At last the family were united, but only in the bleakest sense.

The priest raised his voice to ensure both sides could hear the service. He stood at a distance to make it easier for the family in the West to see their relatives and the coffin in the East.

The family had fled to the West in the fifties, but their grandmother stayed behind. Too old, she said, to escape; too old to begin her life again.

They were not allowed to cross back, even for her funeral. They were not considered to be mourners. They were defectors. They would have been arrested and might never have seen daylight again. All they could do was look through the gaps in the wire.

Two policemen in the West watched the armed guards on the other side and stayed close to the mourners, just in case. Both sides stood as near to the divide as they dared. Separated by barbed wire, guns and dogs, yet united by the same grief, they could not even comfort each other with a touch, or a kiss.

I am barely aware of the others snipping and murmuring. Someone asks me to pass a ruler. When I hold it out, my arm doesn't feel like my arm, and is still hanging in mid-air after the ruler has been taken. I am with the mourners on the desk.

An ordinary family is forbidden to hug at a funeral. Guards watch their tears and restrain their panting dogs. Daughters clutch the wire fence as they stare at their mother's coffin sinking into the ground. A little boy passes a handkerchief to his father and struggles to remember his grandmother's face. This is the last time they will all be together, looking through wire, this ordinary family.

I turn the page and find a photograph of a tiny German factory in an old terraced street that used to be lined with tall, dark tenements. The factory made felt shoes and slippers. It reminds me of the "Elves and the Shoemaker" story. Dad used to read it to me from the Grimm's book of fairy-tales he has kept since he was a boy. Mum would never read them, even though the Grimms were German. She begged Dad to get rid of the book in the end. It really upset her. And Victor never liked the thought of the ugly little men marching through the house in the middle of the night and taking over. But Grandma said it was a very German thing to do.

The felt-shoe factory's ground-floor windows are walled in. On the first-floor they are boarded up. The heavy doors are sealed. The stone walls are crumbling. Crazy wildflowers are growing out of the ledges like hippy hair. The shop front lettering is still clear, painted in bold black. My patchy knowledge of the German language doesn't extend to footwear. I only know it says felt shoes and slippers because there is a paragraph about the factory.

The street, Bernauer Strasse, is in East Berlin, but its front doors and windows once opened into the western sector. The residents woke one morning to the noise of hammering and discovered their front doors had been nailed shut. Some leapt to freedom from upstairs, leaving everything behind and falling into blankets held out by friends and relatives.

At first, the residents in the higher apartments could lean out of their windows and talk to friends who looked up from the cobbled western pavement. But the East German police led all the families out the back way and sent demolition crews to tear these tall, gracious border homes down to their ground-floor façades. They are now a core section of the Wall and no one can cross this street.

I reread the last sentence and, like a flickering segment of cine-film, I see Mum tearing to the parade at closing-time when we run out of salt or shoe-polish or denture-glue while, plank by plank, I watch the light disappear from the frosted glass panel Dad fitted into the front door at the cost of half a thumb.

The owner of the deserted factory had to pack up his nails and pieces of felt while other, stouter nails were hammered into place, gradually leaving him in absolute darkness.

I wonder if he cuts out the felt somewhere else. The other side is probably not a soft-shoe sort of place. Communists probably wear one hideous, approved style, similar to my driving-shoes.

I look hard at the picture. It's a desolate place, the kind you see in England. The pre-fabs where Stan and Elsie live are on a bomb-site. A year before the war ended, one Doodlebug took out a whole street. A few years later six pre-formed sections, six men and one day were all it took to make each new home. They built rows and rows of them and made a sort of village, but they are still surrounded by wasteland.

"Right from the start people said the pre-fabs made it all look bleaker," Big Stan always says. "Because they're temporary, you see. That's what we keep being told. Not built to last. They remind folk of the bombing. Hurry up and turn the whole lot into a nice estate with proper foundations, they say. But from day one we settled right in, me and Else. Lovely fitted kitchen. Walls already painted a lovely cream. Mongolia, I think they call it. Our neighbours are our friends. All from day one. Never been temporary to us."

When Bernauer Strasse survived the bombs, the families and the felt-shoe man must have thought their homes and businesses were safe, but a different, more chilling desolation has set in; a silent war without an end.

The east side of Bernauer Strasse has electric wire, anti-tank barriers, a tar-mac strip for the guards to patrol, gigantic lamps and watchtowers. The sandy death strip is well-raked to reveal footprints and is sprayed with anti-plant chemicals. The west side is deserted, convenient for people washing their cars, or just for somewhere to park.

I keep looking at the blind windows of the little factory facing the cobble-stones congested with weeds. I imagine Mum's face if I made this project about the contrasting halves of her city, one free and one captive.

The page flutters in my hands while Gillian's pen skates over her pad.

"Jacqueline, what are you doing?" she hisses. "It's nearly ten to."

"It's all right," I whisper back, pulling my notepad towards me, not even looking up. "I've got it now."

"About time. Oh no, my cartridge is empty. Have you got any?"

I scrabble about in my pencil-case. "It's Platignum, mind."

"Oh bugger, I need Osmiroid."

Miss Whipp glances at us and we set to work, Gillian switching to pencil.

"I hate having to go over it in ink afterwards. It never looks the same."

"Don't forget to leave the rubbing out until the ink's dry."

"I'm not a twerp, Jacqueline."

She sulks for a while, but soon I hear the furious whisper of her pencil across the page.

Naomi is a pieneer for black women. Her mother gave her away. Doors was slamed in her face. She felt...

"Jacqueline, how do you spell aliernated?"

I tell her, but she doesn't believe me.

I speed up. Not just because the bell is about to ring, but because my project is writing itself. It took me an entire geography lesson to finish one sentence about ziggurats, but Berlin stirs me more than Mesopotamia. The words are being sucked from my pen, each with its own shadow because my nib is split.

"Remember you can't do spider-webs again," Gillian says with the vague sneer that close friends somehow get away with.

"Actually that one was really about homes."

"Cobwebs aren't homes."

"They are to spiders."

"They're death-traps to flies."

"Well some things have two uses."

"Oh."

I don't want to show her the factory. I can't explain this project to her and probably can't explain it to old Walnut Whipp either. All I know is the Bernauer Strasse picture is printed onto my brain, and I'm still thinking about homes as if the spider project was never finished.

"Aren't you cutting anything out?" Gillian asks, frowning at me.

"Might do."

"We've got to. It has to be illustrated."

"I'm not bothering with...illustriations yet."

"Be like that then."

Gillian makes a show of gluing Naomi Sims onto the cover of her book. I do snip my picture out, but I'm not sure yet if it will explain anyone's story. To Miss Whipp it might just look like a derelict building and there are plenty of those here. No one knows how Oaking Potted Meats is still standing.

The bell rings.

"Take your projects home, but hold them up as you pass me," Miss Whipp calls above the racket of scraping chairs.

"Now you'll have to say what you're doing," Gillian says.

But what I've written makes no sense yet. It's just questions about the boarded and bricked-up street. Not whys or how-could-theys, but questions about where people go when they say they're going home, and how they might feel when they can't say that anymore.

While the stone crumbles, wild plants thrive, weaving in and out of the fragments of Bernauer Strasse's stolen homes. Nature is taking over, a quiet and final conclusion.

Home is where your mother waits for you. All roads ought to lead there. And when they arrive, people are meant to have a front-door they can open and close behind them.

Mothers should never have to take frightened children out of their homes, and children should never need to wrench their weeping mothers' fingers from the edge of the let-down and lead them out of the back door.

Gillian and I join the queue filing past Miss Whipp.

Naomi Sims wants to lift the spirrit of the africkan-american woman.

"You must sympiate with that," Gillian says, watching me look at her work and trying to see mine.

"I'm not African-American. How come I should sympathise...er, sympiate with Naomi Sims?"

"Well, feeling foreign and that. You're half-something, aren't you? Not from one place or the other."

"No, it's only my mum who's foreign. I know exactly where I come from."

"How come?"

"I've just never felt out of place."

When my turn comes to show my work, Miss Whipp, a chocolate sliver garnishing her front teeth, holds my book out, peering at it without her reading-glasses, which are buried under a mountain of foil wrappers.

"Well done, Jacqueline. Lots of nice writing here. Jolly good. Keep it up while you're off on your hols, won't you?"

"Yes. Thank you. I will," I say, relieved to scuttle past without being questioned.

But the relief is short-lived.

"Mine's on Naomi Sims," Gillian is saying.

"Right, dear, I'll make a note of that. Is she a pop-star? Oh, Jacqueline, hold on. I haven't entered your subject on my list yet."

I look back. Her pen is poised. Gillian is grinning with the satisfaction of a girl whose best friend is in a hole.

I am a spy about to deliver a dead-drop at dawn. Old Walnut will discover the whereabouts of the hidden gen from a discreet chalk-mark on a wall. All she can do is wait for my next move. I am in absolute command of my mission.

"It's all under control. I'll let you know," I say, suddenly hot and prickling because no one ever says that to a teacher. It's probably what people in offices say when, for an entire fortnight, their out-tray has contained nothing but a fold-up windcheater and three broken staplers. "I'm just finding out, you see. I'm... er... sort of writing my way in. Actually, I need to go to Berlin to suss it all out."

"Please don't say that dreadful word, Jacqueline."

She refuses to leave a blank space on her list. Her fingers claw at my arm. I can hear her chins chafing her frilly collar. "You should do that nice Sandie Shaw, dear. For the contrast aspect of the project, her dismal side is obvious. Absolutely dreadful pair, aren't they?"

The *Daily Mirror* said Sandie was being named "the other woman" in someone's divorce. Does Miss Whipp mean that? Ah, I see. She's referring to Sandie's penchant for bare feet.

"Have you seen them, dear? Why she insists on baring those callouses, I'll never understand. But there's such a nice picture of her in the *TV Times*, her bare feet thankfully cut off."

"Oh good idea, Miss. Thank you."

Satisfied, she writes S Shaw in the box beside my name.

Bugger Sandie Shaw. My project is all in my head. And if Miss Whipp unearthed her glasses and squinted at her *TV Times*, she would see, clearly visible through Sandie bloody Shaw's crocheted blouse, there is a nipple. And I'm not sticking that in my notepad.

4

YOUNG MOON

"The car's running on a teaspoon of petrol, Bridge. There's nowhere open at this time of night. I can't go on much longer."

"And I can't manage another minute with this bladder," Grandma says.

"Me too," I add in sympathy, even though I can. It's just that I actually feel sorry for Grandma. Normally I would have said, "With whose bladder could you wait then?"

"Oh, Jacqueline, you should have gone at the last stop," Mum says. "You are a pest."

"And you're Attila the Hun," I mutter into my hand.

At last Dad finds a petrol station that is not only open, but has a primitive Ladies. Grandma and I take our time. Well, she does.

"Jacqueline, this is no more than a hole in the sodding ground. And it's not easy in whale-bone," she wails while I wait outside the door.

"You should wear a Berlei Gay Slant, Grandma. It's a step-in garment in floral frosted-satin."

"A girdle needs good bone and elastic. Not arty-farty frills and fancies."

And all I need is a shape. Grandma's corsets, incredible rubber-and-bone contraptions, are just for sucking in her heaving hummocks, which are not unlike the geography department's polystyrene relief map of the Pyrenees. Every Sunday afternoon, a cigarette trembling on her lower lip, she plunges them (not the Pyrenees) into the sink and scrubs them with Lux flakes. Mum hangs them on the Sheila-Maid and winches up the pulley. They sweat away in the steam from Sunday night's tea-towels that stew in the enamel pan we use for boiling loganberries.

"Are you calling me burly, Jacqueline?" Grandma shouts from the toilet.

"No, Berlei. It's a girdle for girls."

"A girdle?"

"For girls."

"A girdle for girls?"

"Not a girdle for grans."

"Girls' girdles?"

"Gay Slants."

"Good God."

Mum and I have already spun in this same circle.

"It's step-in."

"Step in?"

55

"With a secret panel."

"Secret? How do you know it is there?"

"Don't be so German."

"Jacqueline, please."

"Sorry. But please, everyone's got one."

"Gillian?"

"No."

"Lynette?"

"No."

"How much do they cost?"

"Thirty-two and..."

"No."

I'll never be allowed to grow up. Mum still buys me *Rupert* annual every Christmas, and the most annoying thing is, I still read it.

Grandma eventually emerges, saying, "While your dad's fart-arsing around with the map, sit down with your old grandma a minute, love, just while I have a quick snifter."

With the evening wind billowing car-fumes into our hair, we sit at a battered metal table and Grandma takes out her brandy, cigarettes and Newberry Fruits.

"Ah, nice to get away from Bridge, snapping and snarling like an Alsatian."

"I thought you'd be the uptight one, Grandma. You were terrified of the car."

"Not the car so much, duck. Although I'd say it's held together by no more than a couple of sticking-plasters and an overstretched rubber-band. No, it was the thought of your dad's driving after Lord knows how many tries at his test. Nerves, you see. Behind that wheel, he looks like a rabbit answering the door to a fox. And do you know what Elsie said? She said...she said they'll lock my Roy up."

"Grandma, the war's over now."

"I know that, duck. Can you open my tin for me? Thanks, love." She taps her ash into the ancient Elastoplast tin she carries everywhere. "No, I don't mean the war, dear. Elsie said they'd take him away if he had one of his turns. They don't allow turns over here."

"Grandma, the Nazis have gone."

"They're on the other side, though, aren't they? Those red communists are the same species. That time your dad glazed over in the fishmonger's and I had to lead him out looking the dead spit of the goggle-eyed prawns, I could see what people were thinking. They were thinking strait-jacket. And that's England for you. Christ knows what this lot would be like."

The wind buffets the ash out of her tin, but she keeps tapping away, unable to speak for a moment.

"Elsie's middle name should be Wooden Spoon. But why did you come, Grandma? You could have stayed at home."

"Jesus wept, no." She snorts at the idea, her cigarette nearly dropping out of her mouth. "I couldn't leave your dad and you two mites in her clutches, could I?"

"Grandma, come on. I'm not a mite, Victor's indestructible and you know Mum's not that bad," I tell her with great hypocrisy.

"Blood and sand," she says, stubbing out the cigarette. "Do I have to spell it out? All right then. I came along because I didn't fancy sitting on my Jack Jones for a week. But don't tell Attila."

"Oh Grandma, that means you quite like us all really."

"No it bloody doesn't. You know the old saying, don't you? Why keep a dog to bark yourself?"

"What?"

"I'll put it another way then. Why pickle your own pig-trotters when you've got a daughter-in-law to souse 'em for you? Not that she's stuffed a decent bit of pork-belly in her life. But she's supposed to be looking after me in my dotage, so I had to come along, didn't I? I'm not rubbing me own bunions. And she's not the only one who can tell you something for your project, love."

"But it's about Berlin, Grandma. About the division."

"Well, all these walls and whatnots boil down to one and the same thing, Jacqueline."

"What's that?"

"Blockage."

"Oh."

"And you know what causes blockage, don't you?"

"Er..."

"Not enough meat. That's the problem. They say Hitler was a vegetablarian. So, there you go. Too much swede. His bowels were the root cause of all this. As I always say, never make a decision when you're stopped-up."

"I'll remember that, Grandma."

"Anyroad, one day back in thirty-eight, while your grandfather was still staggering back from the Slug and Lettuce, I had a visit from Big Stan. He had brought me an ox-heart, bless him. Always a pleasure to see his meat-tray, it was."

I have to wait while she extinguishes a small inferno. Same old story, trying to blow her nose without taking the cigarette out of her mouth. My childhood memories will be forever clouded with the stench of smouldering hanky.

"All right, Grandma?"

"Yes, duck. Now where was I? Oh yes, Stan had just come back from Liverpool Street station, where he and his friends had met a train full of homeless little Jewish kiddies.

"'They've just had the floor shift from under them, Nellie,' he said. 'The Nazis set fire to their orphanage in Berlin.'

"'Oh,' I said. 'Berlin, eh?'

"'That's right, Nellie. In Germany.'

"'I'm aware of where Berlin is, Stanley,' I told him. 'I know my geology.'

"It turned out the orphanage went up in flames the night they set all those Jewish shops and senna-pods on fire. I didn't know much about it. I often turned the wireless off in those days, Jacqueline. Load of poppycock about whether a war was coming or not. There are some that say the bit of paper Neville Chamberlain was waving about when he came back from his chinwag with Hitler, the one that said we'd have 'peace for our time', was just his blooming laundry list. And I say, never trust a man with a moustache. But anyroad, Stan knew a lot of Quakers at the potted-meat plant, you know, and they set this mission up to shift thousands of Jewish children out of danger. Stan said not a single one was safe. Tch, children not safe. Jesus wept."

Grandma rummages in her bag for an unburnt hanky, her face crinkled like old tissue-paper. I pass her mine and she keeps nodding her thanks, the way old people do when they can't speak.

"Hey, Grandma, you usually talk the moon out of the sky."

"That's exactly what Stan said, love," she says, sniffing, her voice three octaves higher. "I was choked up that day same as I am now. Stan never had kiddies of his own, you see. Elsie said she couldn't cope with jammy fingermarks on the furniture or the whiff of nappies stewing in a bucket. But he longed for them, he did. It upset him to see all those little ones clutching their suitcases. He wanted to take an orphan home with him, but the thought of Elsie screwing up her mouth as small as a press-stud and ordering him to take it back soon forced him to turn away. And I never said this to him of course, but she wouldn't have had a clue how to feed a child, especially later when rationing started. I already had two chickens in the back yard and a part-share of a wilful goat in Shakespeare Avenue. Smashing omelettes, Jacqueline."

"You made omelettes from a goat?"

"Tch, get away with you. What in God's fine garden do they teach you at that school? This project malarkey just goes to show, doesn't it? They can't be buggered to teach you themselves. They have to get your grandmas to do it for them. Now, where was I? Oh yes, poor Stan. I left his ox-heart to soak in salt water and made him a cup of tea. There was no more I could do to bring him comfort. Poor Stan was too shaken up even to dunk his ginger-nut. Great bear of a man he might be, Jacqueline, but he fetched hold of my hand like a baby grips its mother's finger.

"'You know, Nellie,' he said. 'None of the children were allowed to cry at the station in Berlin. Gestapo's orders. The ones with mums and dads could say goodbye, but not with tears.'

"He could hardly speak, my Stan, after that. Fancy. And him a master-butcher with a full set of precision boning-knives."

I push Grandma's cigarettes closer and she stares at the packet as if she isn't sure what it is.

"Stan wondered which misery was worse, saying goodbye without breaking down or not having a soul to say it to."

She holds my hand for a moment before she says, "Who could turn a child out of its home, even a foreign one?"

Dad calls us and we're on the move again. I fall asleep at last, thinking about home. Yesterday is a million years ago: Victor lining up his Red Indians in the evening square of sunlight that always appears on the kitchen lino, gunning them down with his pea-shooter; German words containing lots of 'sch' erupting from the kitchen when the handle fell off the potato-masher; onions sweltering in lard; eating liver on the wobbly let-down, discovering a tube-thing in my piece, and Victor saying, "Ugh, is that a pig's willy?"

I dream about endless fields where harvest has begun and colossal wheat-drums throw long shadows. The drums become gigantic sculptures standing guard over us, their shadows thrown over our mock-Tudor car that makes other drivers hoot and point as they pass.

The shadows are alive. The car screams to a stop in the middle of the road. The wheat-drums advance, towering over us, crushing our car. Gillian is whispering that she's hidden my smuggled copy of *Petticoat* inside our telephone because she has invented a way to make things so small they can disappear. I want to ask if she can bring them back too, but my tongue is paralysed. She says she can cut me in half and make me two people.

Now Grandma is shaking a packet of Trill over me. "Ziss vill make you talk," she says.

Victor is driving. Mum is screaming. A guard aims a gun at Dad's head and orders him to throw his cigarette away, but it falls inside the car because the window won't open and flames spring up everywhere. Mum is suddenly young and beautiful, playing a piano that turns into ninety miles of bricks. The car becomes a boutique filled with crocheted dresses and Gillian is walking towards me, slim and ravishing in a mini, half-black, half-white, with a golden chain-belt, whispering how sorry she is for being evil. My tongue starts working and I yell at her to leave me alone.

"Stop shouting, Jacqueline! You've been dreaming since Cologne."

I've missed miles and miles of pitch-black Belgium and woken to the glaring early sun of West Germany. We judder to a stop for Dad to stretch his legs. My mouth feels as gritty as the floor of Deborah's cage. Victor climbs into the back again, horribly bright and fresh.

"T-K saw Cologne Cathedral," he says.

"Christ, I can't believe this, Bridge. I can't bloody well believe this," Dad is saying, overcome with pride that he's brought us so far. "Last week I was in a cell with a new prisoner, all cocky-like, saying how this ain't a bad hotel for the money. You know, all talk. And then he just sank on the bed and broke down. Weeping into his hands like a woman. Ten years he's got. He couldn't trust his brother to stay away from his girl and he didn't think his Mum would live through the shame. He'd been planning on learning to drive. His girl was keen on having a go too, he said. He even thought she might be quite good at it. Just hang on to the dream, I told him, or else your nights will be too bloody long."

"Vee are now in the Auto Corridor. It is linking Vest Germany with Vest Berlin," Mum says, seeming vastly German now and ignoring Dad because she is glued to the window.

"Is Berlin a country?" Victor asks, aiming T-K's rifle at a French car that looks like an upside-down pram.

"No, Victor, it's a city, a kind of island bobbing about in a communist sea," Dad says, watching the French car trundle past. "It's actually in East Germany, but the west half of it belongs to the Allies. Some of Hitler's old autobahns have become transit routes. We get on at one end and off at the other. No stopping."

A bobbing island sounds quite friendly. Victor and I settle back.

"That old pig Khrushchev called Berlin a tumour," Grandma says. "One of the nasty sort that goes bad. That's how wars start, you know. When thugs like him spread talk like that, they get people worked up and wanting trouble. I wouldn't trust him with a jelly-baby."

"He did not wish to start another war, Nell," Mum says. "He was trying to keep the peace."

"Old Eisenhower was solid as rock though," Dad says, thumping the dashboard to smother an ominous rattle. "Refused to take the troops out of West Berlin, didn't he? Wouldn't let Stalin hand access rights over to the East Germans."

"But that's why the Wall's there, son," Grandma says. "A bloody great barrier keeping people in. Keeping families apart. The tumour needed surgery, Khrushchev said, but look how the old sod did it. More butcher than surgeon if you ask me. And that's no disrespect to my good friend, Stan."

Not so much a bobbing island then. More a floating crocodile. Bugger.

"Yes, but at least no war has happened, Nell," Mum says, pressing a hand to her appendix-grenade. "There is peace, no?"

"Anyone would think you quite welcomed this Wall that's cut your sisters off from each other, Bridge. This Wall where they shoot people who just want to bob across to see their family or go to the job they used to have before it stopped them in their tracks."

Blimey. Grandma actually pays attention to the news on the wireless. I knew she loathed Khrushchev, but I thought she only ever listened to *The Clitheroe Kid*.

And I am listening, too, sensing my project about to grow as I make the decision to include Peter Fechter, partly because I wish I could fall in love with him and partly because he made my mum cry.

Peter Fechter was eighteen when the East Berlin police shot him. He might have just started loving a girl. That's when it begins, at eighteen.

When the news of his death appeared in the paper, I was about nine, rolling a small Victor round the room on the pouffe, but aware of Mum sitting still for ages with the newspaper on her lap. I could see a picture of Peter's kind, ordinary face.

Eventually, she cut out the article about him, stood up like an old woman and went to cook tea. It was Deutsche mince that evening and for once I didn't worm out all the slippery strips of tinned pimento because she was still so quiet. I helped Victor shovel up his peas and gave him half my Heinz pudding. I used to be quite nice.

I asked Dad why Mum kept the article and he said Peter was a symbol for freedom.

When I told Gillian about him, she said, "He's just a person breaking the law of the land. Not a war hero."

War isn't all about bombs dropping, I would have said, but when Gillian's uncle's house was flattened by a Doodlebug, he shoved her grandfather down the coal cellar in the nick of time, so she knows different.

Peter's newspaper face haunts me at night, not in the scary train-robber way, but because I wish I could marry him. I did have my eye on Kevin Hatherley in 5B until I realised that after Games he smelt like boiled beef.

I try not to think about Peter's small sad body on the ground, just his lovely face. I didn't ask to see the cutting in case it made Mum cry again, but before we came to Berlin, when she was busy snapping at Dad for making her burn the fish fingers when all he did was wrap his arms around her waist, I took it out of her ottoman.

On August 17th, 1962, Peter Fechter, a bricklayer, was helping to rebuild his country. He had an ordinary life in East Berlin, as part of the workforce restoring a palace destroyed in the war. There was an abundance of labour for young men like him.

His older sister lived on the west side. Before the Wall was built, he and his family used to be able to visit her. A few days after the first anniversary of the Wall, he and a friend decided to climb it and cross over, a youthful snap decision, perhaps made in a fit of high spirits.

They hid in an old workshop by the border, peering at the West through a small window not yet boarded up, the prospect of failure generating fear, but the need to escape repelling it.

They removed their shoes, opened the window and leapt out.

Peter's friend scaled the Wall. "Hurry!" he called. But Peter hesitated. Perhaps he had changed his mind. The East German border guards, however, did not arrest him. They started shooting.

Even though Peter had given up running, the storm of bullets rooted him to the spot. They left him lying in the death strip, alone and crying with pain, watched by horrified people from both sides.

A West Berlin policeman climbed a ladder, threw bandages over the Wall and asked Peter his name. No more could be done. West feared retaliation from East. Afterwards, the East German border guards said they could not have answered his frantic calls for help because the West Berlin police were pointing guns at them.

For the East, Peter's fate serves as a warning to anyone else considering escape. For the Western world, however, he will become a symbol of the border regime's cold-blooded brutality.

Peter lay dying for almost an hour before the East German troops sent up a cloud of manmade mist. Behind this shroud they carried him away at last, but it was too late. People will remember Peter Fechter as the young man who was almost free.

"Here it comes," Dad warns. "Checkpoint Alpha's up ahead. This one takes us into East Germany. The one after this, Checkpoint Bravo, will take us into West Berlin."

Armed look-out towers loom from forests stripped to make a free-fire zone in a world of concrete and steel gates, where people are stopped, their papers examined, their faces scrutinised. Forms are stamped, orders are barked. Razor-wire scores the sides of the corridor like a long tunnel-web. In the Auto Corridor, the gaps between watch towers become shorter. Instead of looking out for the next one, we watch them flash by. I swear I can see lights bouncing off field-glasses. Kilometre by kilometre, a world of tyranny is hurtling towards us.

When we queue for the Allied checkpoint in Helmstedt, the atmosphere shifts from oddly foreign into a mood of non-welcome. Ordinary families like ours are being watched and checked. Normal life has skidded to a stop.

But we are the Bishops. We have a pebble-dashed house with keys in the fruit-bowl and bird-seed on the lino. We peel potatoes and watch Hughie Green. Victor keeps soldiers in a biscuit tin, and I suck the ends of my hair when Mum isn't looking. Grandma flirts with the fishmonger. Dad looks after men in prison, and Mum makes blancmange that could re-grout the bathroom tiles. But now we are all foreigners.

The military police look over our car, open the boot and kick the wheels. "They need to know we have a spare tyre and enough petrol, and that we could cope with an emergency," Mum explains.

"Christ, the back-door's dodgy, Bridge," Dad whispers, panicky hands running through his hair, then sliding greasily off the steering-wheel.

A guard walks by with a long-handled mirror on wheels for searching under lorries. Dad is staring, transfixed, like the badger in the shed. I pass Victor my last Opal Mint, but he's too terrified to move, so I make T-K open the wrapper.

While Dad leans forward like a jockey waiting for the off, the guard bangs the flank of the car. We all flinch, Dad almost cracking his forehead on the steering-wheel.

"We can go," Mum says. "Come on, Roy. Before they bang again."

The car stalls. The guard bangs. Victor whimpers.

"Roy, please. We have to move."

"Come on, come on," Dad growls as if he's watching the last furlong of the Grand National.

"Come on, come on," Victor squeaks, clutching my hand.

I want to say shove off, but I might actually need him.

"Lawks what a fuss foreigners make," Grandma says, sucking at the liquorice-pipe from her Sherbet Fountain. "Just give it some choke, lad. And a bit more rev, I'd say."

The guard is rapping on Dad's window. Victor squeals. Grandma almost swallows her pipe.

"Fuck-me-sideways-said-the-queen," Dad says, revving hard. It may sound like the worst word, but it doesn't count because he runs it together with the others to make one long new word. The Germans do the same. Think of *Schwarzwälderkirschkuchen* or whatever it is. Mum banned f-m-s-s-t-q from the house, but on a freezing night when Dad's scuttle comes out empty, I have heard it emerge from the depths of the coal bunker.

The engine starts.

"Thank Christ!" Dad cries, giving the guard a thumbs-up.

We roll forward to the next barrier. More of a jerk than a roll actually, since Dad is using the handbrake for every stop.

"I know we've nothing to hide, but I'm dreading them making window-winding gestures at you," I tell Dad.

"I'll have a job, Jacqueline. My window-handle's buggered," he says, sweating like a man who has a great deal to hide.

"Just be natural," Grandma says, patting on face-powder and touching up her lipstick.

"Anyway, you can't be all la-di-da here, Jacqueline," Dad says, excessively bucked with himself for crossing the first hurdle. "When in Rome, you know."

"They are sure to be very polite," Mum says, giving Dad a belated glare for the bad word earlier.

"They can probably remain polite while ripping out a person's toe-nails," I tell her, receiving a glare myself.

"You're going a bit fast, son," Grandma says as we gather speed.

"I'm allowed to go fifty, Ma, and we haven't got long to reach Checkpoint Bravo. If it takes more than four hours, they come and search for us."

"Who's they?" I ask. "Do the West Germans come tearing along the autobahn to help us? Or do you mean the East Germans march us to a cell for questioning?"

"I mean this lot," Dad says. "The East. We're in their country now, Jacqueline. It's their rules."

Mum looks suddenly wretched.

"This is worse than Daleks," Victor whines in absolute misery, peeling his Opal Mint from T-K's hair. "Why can't Mum be English like everyone else's mums? Then we'd be in Clacton."

"Dear old Clacton," Grandma murmurs, tipping the tube of sherbet down her throat.

Dad swipes his hand around, but our feet are carefully tucked back. "That's enough cheek, young man," he says. But his hair is falling out of its Brylcreem, and he keeps tapping his pockets to check for passports and matches.

I miss the ordinary summer, even the reek of Dad's sweet-William in the back yard, even the lavender polish and stewed-pear smell of the Clacton guest-house. But at least there is one advantage over Clacton. While Dad is busy being as nervous as a racehorse on the starting-blocks, or wherever they start from, the Bad-Moon girls can sleep off their hangovers.

The car lurches towards the police barrier at Marienborn, almost stalling on the approach, but Dad reins it in with an expert kick on the clutch.

"Shall I choke you?" Mum asks.

"No, Bridge. It's under control. Don't worry," Dad says, yanking on the hand-brake and talking at supersonic speed.

A soldier orders us out, demanding to see our papers. We stand in a line as close to the car as we can, toasting against the sun-baked metal. If we end up in a windowless hole, I will never forgive Mum.

One guard watches us while another shuffles through our passports and takes them away.

"God, they're slower than a millpond in June," Dad mutters.

"Sh," Mum says.

"I can't stand long," Grandma says. "I'm a slave to my veins, don't they realise?" She raises her voice. "I've got blood-pressure, you know."

"Haven't we all, Grandma? Thankfully," I whisper.

"Get a move on," she tells the nearest guard. "Best hurry before the car falls apart."

"Sh," Mum hisses.

"It'll not stand much prodding," Grandma continues. "A wing, a prayer and a rubber-band are all that holds it in one piece."

To illustrate, she does a flapping bird impression, then presses her hands together and finally clutches Mum's wrist and twangs the rubber-band round it.

"Ow," Mum shrieks, scowling.

I swear the guard's lips are twitching.

"Not a bad lad really, is he?" Grandma says. "Just not a terribly talkable fella."

We are surrounded by other armed guards, so alert they're almost quiver-ing. I glance at Victor. Although this is T-K's world of guns, uniforms and fear in living, breathing Technicolor, Victor has smuggled him away in the glove compartment and looks lost without him. A rush of sisterly love surges, the first since he was about nine months old and learnt to clap, which made him seem so much more human.

I am shaking. The vital thing is that no one must see. Fear is one of the Emotions we have learnt about in biology. "So-called Finer Feelings," Miss Lobb said, curling her upper lip as if Feelings carried a bad smell. No chalk was wasted on them. Before hurrying back to the safer topic of ovaries, she ticked the most delicate Emotions off on her fingers. "Love, Fear, Sympathy, Excitement. Now, if you feel any one of those, keep it to yourself. Show too much and you weaken." That was it. Feelings covered in five seconds.

I am an older sister, a sensible daughter, an almost-adult. In 1971, I shall rechristen myself Tuesday and wear glorious Sunflower stocking-tights. I already have a powder-compact. I'm just not allowed the powder yet. I must pull myself together and be mature for Victor's sake. I am not the smallest bit afraid. I am a dignified woman. Oh Christ alive, is that a Kalashnikov?

My Emotion is hard to hide now. Grandma tries to hold my hand and I want her to very much, but as I'm not six I shake it off.

The nearest guard is staring at us.

"Shall we tell him a joke?" Grandma asks.

"No, for George Harrison's sake, Grandma," Victor whispers.

"What do you call a cross German, eh?"

Sod it, she's already tittering.

"Grandma, stop it."

"Sour kraut!"

"Grandma!"

"He doesn't understand, Victor love. Look, his face is blank."

"But one false move and it'll be ready-aim-fire."

Victor's right. If I look at the ground, the guard will assume I have something to hide. If I look him square in the eye, I'll seem brazen. I can glare well enough to wither a geography teacher, but they're quite a scrawny species.

"All out!" he barks, pointing at our car. "Become everyzing in zee auto out. Now, please."

He takes a step towards us.

"He means get everything out of the car," Mum says.

I've already worked this out. Their word for 'get' is *bekommen*, which used to confuse Mum too.

"Please all out now!" he shouts.

"Yes, yes, we do understand you awfully well, my good man," Mum says in her primmest English.

Blimey. In a minute she'll be holding out her handbag and saying, "Oh my dear fellow, please would you care to consider the contents of my reticule? Thanks awfully."

If I spoke up like that, it would be called backchat.

The guard, at the end of his tether, keeps jabbing his finger in the direction of the car. The handcuffs tied to his belt jangle and his gun glints in the sunshine. Sweat is collecting in the creases at the back of my knees.

"Hold the bus," Dad says as the guard opens the passenger door and Mum's reel of crochet cotton unspools over the rough ground. "We've shown you all we've got."

"He wants all that is in the car, Roy. Every little thing."

"Fu..."

"Roy."

In deathly silence we all help to unload, although it's difficult with damp shaky hands and an over-inflated bladder. It seems to take hours. My face is scorching. We have to place everything on a slab of concrete like a small railway platform, and they want it stacked, not just in a heap.

"You'll not have my diamonds, you swine," Grandma mutters, all jokes forgotten as she fastens her cardigan up to the neck over her bead necklace.

"They won't pinch the iced-gems will they?" Victor whispers, watching a guard take our tartan shopping bag and pick out the remains of our slimy sandwiches and orange peel.

"How do I know?" I tell him, dumping cardigans and comics onto the sacrificial altar.

A guard picks up *Mandy* and *Commando*, flicks through the pages and tosses them into a bin. He confiscates all Victor's Red Indians, even Sitting Bull. Happily, the Comanche tribe and their horses stayed at home.

Victor bursts into tears and I have to deal with it. Mum and Dad's hands are full explaining the thick coil of rope we packed in the boot in case we need a tow, a distinct possibility.

"Apparently rope strong enough for a hot-air balloon is not allowed here," Mum says. "People have escaped that way."

"They've banned it?" Dad says, the disbelief in his voice painful.

"There's a bandit?" Victor squeaks.

"Victor, we'll get you another *Commando* and some Apaches when we're back in England," Dad promises. I can tell how badly he wishes we were on a quiet English back-road to Clacton.

"King of the road indeed," Grandma says, her voice quavering. "The open road's only open when you're allowed to use it on your own terms, son."

In this hostile place, a stomach-turning trail of homesickness is winding through me, probably through us all, except Mum.

"Why have they thrown my Navajo away?" Victor persists.

"Because they're not allowed to see all our nice things," I explain, hardly understanding it myself.

"The Navajo aren't always nice."

"Well, all your toys seem especially nice here."

"They aren't toys."

"Sorry. I mean, your tribes would make everyone here want nice things too."

"I don't mind them having a read of *Commando*."

"I know. It just isn't allowed, Victor, and that's that."

From our stack, the guard pulls out a Dusty Springfield LP Dad thought Beate would like. We own three of them because Dad's great-aunt has sent the same Christmas present since 1964. But the LP is thrown away. Dad's cigarette is just about balancing on his lip, while, lost for words, he stares at Dusty in the bin.

After we are allowed to rescue our belongings, minus the ones too exciting for communists—and that includes Grandma's liver salts—we are allowed back inside the car. It felt like a tortuous sweatbox before, but is now a haven.

By a miracle, T-K survived the search by camouflaging himself inside the bundle of windscreen rags.

"Lucky he was on night manoeuvres," Victor says. We all laugh in a moment of total family harmony. And when the car starts first time we laugh again in total relief. Grandma pats the beads under her cardigan then rubs her glasses on it to unclog the mist on the lenses.

After a short drive, we have to stop again and get out. Guards guide us into a crummy little building with Lenin staring at us from a huge portrait. A tiny hatch opens. A hand reaches out. Mum explains in German, using their harsh tone of voice, that the other guards still have our documents.

"You could get yourself a job here, Bridge," Grandma says. "You'd be well suited to it, duck."

Yet again we wait. Some holiday. The only sound is my own heart clanging. Lenin is trying to read my mind, but there's nothing else for me to look at. Victor is sobbing, but I've exhausted my entire range of sisterly patience. Mum searches for a tissue but gives up and, with a furtive glance round, uses the hem of Victor's shirt to wipe his nose. Bloody ugh.

"They arrest people for being a cry-baby," I whisper in his ear. This country has turned me evil. Where did the serene Tuesday go? I can only hear the retreating echo of her clicky white boots.

We wait ages for the papers to be returned, like greyhounds watching for the release of the hare, and have to pay a toll of ten Deutschmarks for the privilege of using the transit road. I hope Dad can find the money, but I also hope he can't, so we could turn round and go home.

It takes him an age to uncurl the note. The back of his neck flares up like a beacon. The waiting guard sits motionless, trapped in his little booth, staring, appearing not to breathe. He seems mechanical, not in a robot way, but like a person whose fellow-feeling has been sucked out. He still has a rounded baby-face, so I can imagine him wearing a bonnet and sitting on his mother's lap while doctors in long black boots inject him, and in among the usual jabs is an extra one that dilutes Emotions.

An indifferent nod dismisses us outside into the sunshine that seems drab here, and channels us into a long queue. The funnel tightens. No space to turn round, to retreat.

Another show of papers and a tedious wait before we are rubber-stamped and furnished with a pass. The next barrier is raised.

"Free at last," Dad mutters.

To me, it feels like being sucked deeper inside.

"Light me a cigarette, Bridge," he says. "Bloody hell, it's more of a struggle to get you back into Germany than it ever was to get you out."

"Yes," Mum says. "I feel like a criminal when they stare unwinking at my passport, as if I am being snuggled in."

"Er, smuggled, Bridge, I think."

"Ah yes. But you know, Roy, snuggled or not, I have nothing to hide. I am an ordinary citizen for the first time."

Call this ordinary? At least her grenade doesn't seem to be sparking and she's actually almost bearable.

"Right we're off again, folks. Berlin, here we bloody well come. Study the map, Bridge, mate," Dad says, blowing out plumes of smoke like steam from a thoroughbred's nostrils. "There are three turn-offs to West Berlin. If I don't get it right first time we might fall off the transit route and be floundering around in East Germany. And keep that map safe because I think we have to give it back again."

"It's like that daft Monopoly," Grandma says. "Do Not Pass Go."

"I don't think Get Out of Jail Free would work here though," I tell her.

Every vehicle travels at the same speed in a long procession, the slow-motion world of a dream. Dad has to concentrate harder than ever. No one passes, although we should be used to that in this car.

Dad pauses for a wee at one of the approved places and, after the usual stalling session, we set off again and the road mutates into a steep track into the woods.

"This isn't bloody well right, Bridge."

"Please do not speak as if it is my fault, Roy."

"Well it's not T-K holding the map, is it? Mind you, he'd have more road-sense."

If it is possible for a map to make aggressive noises, this map does. The tension stretches tighter than Grandma's whalebone. Victor hides under my cardigan.

A huge shadow wraps around the car and aircraft noise hovers overhead. Mum opens her window and strains to look up.

"It is something big," she says.

"Very helpful, Bridge."

Victor cranes his neck and announces, "I spy a helicopter gunship."

"Christ Al-bloody-mighty."

"Roy, you must not panic."

"What else can I ruddy well do, Bridge?"

The car is spluttering as if it's being throttled.

"Dad, the helicopter's right overhead. T-K can see guns."

"Bugger T-K, Victor," Grandma says. "Just let your dad drive."

"But Roy, this is not the right way."

"I'm not turning back, Bridge. They might start firing."

This is too much for Victor. His arms bristle with goose-pimples.

"Now you know why they call it the Cold War, duckie," Grandma says, offering him a nip of her brandy. I drape my cardigan over his knees, its waft of home-smell conjuring the relative peace of Audette Gardens.

"I want to go home," Victor whispers. "Mum and Dad don't know what they're doing. And Dad said bugger. He said it about T-K."

Since he's whimpering all over my twinset, I have to take a stand.

"Dad, for once, just turn round and go back. All you did was veer off the road after your wee-stop. So just turn round and veer back on it again. Just this once, Dad, please veer."

"Veer? What is veer?" Mum asks. It actually seems like an invented word now I've said it so many times, but, thank the Beatles, all four of them, Dad gets the message.

"All right. I'll show you how to spin a youey," he says.

The Traveller objects to U-turns.

"Sod it, I'm going nowhere."

"Dad, it's bound to be hard because this track is all rutted and narrow. Just keep going."

"That's what I'm trying to do."

"I mean just keep doing what you're doing. Backwards and forwards."

"I should just put my hands up and surrender."

"Well, for God's sake don't. You need both on the wheel."

The manoeuvre becomes a twenty-eight-point-turn, but, as Dad keeps telling us, considering it was executed with dodgy brakes on a sloping path with a camber, whatever that is, and in the shadow of a gunship, it is a triumph.

On the move again and with no more turning back now, I grow tired of looking at Mum's car-crazed hair and the damp back of Dad's neck. I draw a cobweb on my notepad cover and try not to think about home, which I suppose is what Mum has done for years. I scribble a cluster of petrified flies and a forked twig caught up in the delicate threads. Spiders discard unwanted foreign objects that drift into the web by cutting off that section and letting it fall, which reminds me of Peter.

I draw a black-widow, the star of last year's project. She weaves a tangled structure, a coarse and criss-crossed funnel-shape with a prey-trapping tunnel at the core, wide and open at the top, easy to topple into and impossible to leave. She might as well be the star of this project too.

Victor is still uneasy, but I have used a year's worth of patience on him.

"Get lost," I growl, trying to draw another fine line of cobweb while he burrows his head into my arm.

"What's cobweb made of?" he asks, snuffling.

With a chance to show off, I unearth a stockpile of patience.

"Well, it's made of spider-silk, which is five times stronger than steel of the same diameter. If you have enough, it could tether a lion. The faster and tighter the spider draws the strand, the tougher the silk becomes. When the strand is under massive pressure, it breaks off to spare the rest of the web. If it tried to cope with the strain, all the other crisscrossed strands would be weakened too. One snapped connection, one sacrifice, means the whole structure is safe."

This is straight from last year's project. I don't know how Gillian managed to beat me with Famous Dogs. But her star page featured Pickles the mongrel sniffing out the stolen World Cup trophy in someone's back garden, and with Miss Whipp being a Dandie Dinmont breeder, she was bound to mark it high.

"But doesn't the spider need every single strand to make the pattern?"

"No, one thread isn't missed. He can lose the odd bit. It's still his lair and still a death-chamber for flies."

I let Victor rub out two or three lines to show the web still holding fast, but this has to stop when he wears a hole in my paper.

"So they've twitched the Iron Curtain aside to let you back in, Bridge," Grandma is saying. "First the war drives you out and now you've slipped through again. Blooming game, isn't it? You land on the wrong square, you miss a turn and now you get another go. Maybe you could stay on when we all leave, eh?"

"Hey, Ma, just hold the bus," Dad says. "Bridge is here for a visit. That's all there is to it."

"But Batty's a widow coping alone with a little lad, isn't she? High time you gave her a hand, Bridge."

"It's Beate, Nell. Bay-arter is how you pronounce it."

"Well, why don't we drop you off with Bee-tear, leave you to it and bugger off to Clacton?"

"Nell, put that brandy away or I vill confiscate it."

"Ooh, you and whose army?"

"Ma, stop now or I'll get T-K to take his hatchet to your teeth and chuck them out the window."

"Son, that's no way to talk to your mother."

"And that was no way to talk to my wife."

Grandma stuffs in three pink marshmallows and starts a chorus of sniffing until Dad apologises and Mum promises to buy her an ashtray in the shape of a flugelhorn.

T-K is battling a tube of Refreshers. "Blam, blam, take it on the nose, you pig-dog."

I concentrate on my project until Checkpoint Bravo. Grandma falls asleep, her curls fluttering in the rackety breeze that cuts through Dad's maximum half-inch allowance of window-air.

"We are near the canal in the south of Berlin," Mum says. "But it is part of the border now. And instead of a hedge or a fence, some of the houses near here have the Wall twisting around their gardens, even when it separates an entire village."

I look at the picture of Bernauer Strasse tucked inside my notepad and want to tell her that some houses have actually become the Wall, but the reflection of her face pressed to the window looks sad, as if she is lost inside her old German self.

After a long silence, she rummages in her bag and takes out a creased photograph, one edge looking a bit singed. She passes it to me.

"Careful with it," she says, keeping her voice low to avoid waking Grandma.

I am holding a portrait of a little girl in a puffy party frock, clutching a china doll. Her parents smile from behind, their hands clasping her shoulders. The girl has long black hair and dark eyes. I only know she's my mother because she's so close to being me.

"Is that Jacqueline?" Victor asks. "What an ugly face."

"Thanks," Mum and I both say.

"I meant the doll," he says.

"Anyway, it is me, Victor," Mum says. "I loved the doll. It had blue glass eyes and real hair."

"Your hair's funny."

"Yes, I was not blonde then."

Other children in their best clothes can be seen in the background.

"Who are they?"

"My friends. Lena, Julius, Shoshanna..."

"Funny names."

"Yes. Very funny names."

I turn the photograph over to see if anything is written on the back. It says Eleora, 1935, in italic script.

"Eleora? Is that your name in German?" Victor and I ask together.

"In a way. It was my name when I was born. Then I just used Birgit instead, an easier name, which turned into Bridget in England."

I would have hung onto Eleora. Elegant Eleora. Exquisite Eleora. Peter and Eleora, the perfect couple.

"Why didn't you pass it on to me, Mum?"

"Well, it might have confused people. Very unusual in England, a name like that."

"Doesn't really fit in with all the Susans and Debbies, I suppose, but better than having the same name as everyone else. There are four Jacquelines in my class and seven in the whole year."

Mum sighs, already aware of this, and that I loathe Idit, my German middle name. At school the boys love adding an 'o' to it. The whole Idiot problem could have been avoided with the sumptuous Eleora. I feel short-changed.

Dad lights a cigarette from the stub he's just smoked. "Come on, Bridge," he says in a testy tone of voice. "Concentrate on looking out the window. You're missing it all."

The next checkpoint is coming into view. The tension in the car is wound so high I can hear a crank turning, although that might be the engine, which grumbles on even the gentlest slopes. The strain makes Victor fidget. I have to do something before that ribbon of snot trails out of his nostrils again.

"Where's T-K going on manoeuvres then, Victor?"

"Berlin. Where else?"

"I wouldn't count on it. He may not be allowed in. The East Germans may say he represents the fascist enemy, especially in that rainbow jersey Grandma knitted him."

I honestly don't mean to inflame the situation, just distract him from the guard about to flag us down.

"Shut up, you girl," he says, lunging behind Grandma to whisper it in my ear. "Shut your cake-hole."

"Pig-dog," I hiss in his eardrum.

He gives me a dead leg, I give him a Chinese burn and Dad slaps at the air between us, with Mum shouting at him for taking his hand off the wheel.

We arrive at Dreilinden, where two guards give the car an inspection like a medical exam, running their hands everywhere, screwing up their eyes and stepping back a pace to frown at the timber frame.

They march around the car, keeping us waiting, but, to be honest, we are all quite cocky now. Having survived Checkpoint Alpha, we're old hands at this business. Grandma is snoring. Dad is blowing a smoke-ring, which he only does when life pleases him. Mum is cleaning his glasses and he smiles at her. No Row. No Bad-Moon girls. Bliss at Bravo.

The guards ask Dad to drive a little further so they can watch the car moving. He adjusts his gloves as if he's Jackie Stewart about to race at Monaco. I look at Mum. She looks at me. We both cross our fingers. That, at least, is a common language.

The car stalls. Grandma's head lolls onto her chest. Flustered, Dad tries again, blasting the horn by accident, and somehow setting off the trafficator arm as if we're turning right. We do roll forward but, just as the guards look as if they might wave us on, we hear an almighty creak and one of the back doors falls off.

The guards watch over it as if it's an unexploded bomb. Dad leaps out, rubbing his gloved hands together.

"Sorry about that, gentlemen. Quite all right. Happens now and then. Only when the car's stationary though. Wouldn't happen on the move. Not at all. The aerodynamics keep the doors sucked on."

Victor has to help Dad. It involves a lot of grunting and pushing, but somehow they sit the door back on its hinges. Grandma lets out a mammoth snore that rocks the car. There's a terrible, lengthy whine, which could be either Grandma or the hinge, but thankfully the door stays put.

"Ziss wood is bad, no?"

"Seasoned English ash it is, Sir," Dad says. Victor nods and hides behind him.

They want to know if the wood is part of the structure, which it is. Without it, we would have no doors.

"No, no, not at all. Just a bit of rust on the hinge," Dad keeps saying.

One guard keeps prowling all the way round the Traveller, eventually blundering straight into the trafficator, which snaps off.

"Ach," he says, blushing and holding the stump of it in his hand. "Ach."

The two guards disappear and we dare not breathe, but they come back with a chunk of wood and some glue to patch the split piece on our broken door. They help Dad fix it on, but the poor trafficator is a lost cause. Dad will need to use arm-signals, they explain with gestures. At least I think that's what they're suggesting.

Dad gestures back until they are all windmilling away like *Playschool* presenters. He offers his cigarettes, which they accept, and we are allowed to move on at last with the pointless advice, "Wood good. Car good. Wood and car togezzer, not so good."

"You could be right there, mate," Dad says. "I'll bear it in mind."

A barge rumbles from the canal, guards shout instructions, cars rev their engines and we all move on again. Unable to stop, more because of the dubious brakes than the law, we join the queue for the road to West Berlin with a chorus of thankful sighs.

The autobahn continues through East Germany for another two kilometres, during which we pass crowds of hitch-hikers, their assorted children and dogs and baggage heaped up at their feet.

"With no stopping or turning allowed, at least when they want a lift back the other way, they're guaranteed a two hundred kilometre ride," Dad points out, ready to stop and offer someone a lift, but swiftly outvoted by the rest of us.

Grandma wakes up, refreshed and excited.

"So what's this Bat-Ear like then, Bridge?" she says, reaching for my aniseed-balls.

"It is Be-a-te, Nell."

"Oh I've no time for how foreigners announce perfectly good names. I shall call her Beattie."

"The war has broken her spirit, Nell. I can tell from her letters. She feels a terrible guilt about those years, as many of us do. She was never an easy person, but now she is a shadow of herself."

"Can she cook?"

"No, she was always a terrible cook, I'm afraid."

"So that's where you get it from."

Grandma pops in three aniseed-balls and pauses until they've reduced in size enough to be crunched. The noise is deafening.

"So," she says, "Beattie's a bit prickly, can't cook for toffee and she was widowed after she had what's-his-name, the boy."

"Sebastian, he is called, Nell."

"Oh, fancy. Seb-arstian indeed. What's wrong with Bob or Ken?"

"Well, they are not very German names, Nell."

"You'd think they wouldn't want German names, wouldn't you? You talk about their guilt. Well, what better way to show it than to use nice plain English names?"

"Come on, Ma," Dad says. "It's not as if anyone's likely to be called Adolf, is it?"

"Bridge has an English name now."

"If I did not," Mum says, clipped and frosty, "I would always be putting up with bigots."

Grandma takes her teeth out and folds her lips in. She pretends not to be listening and refuses to speak apart from whispering to Victor to pass the sherbet-pips.

"Beate misses the past," Mum says.

I think she's speaking directly to me now and I reach for my pad and pen. "Carry on, Mum."

"Beate and Ilse both used to live in a flat in a tall, old corner house in East Berlin, where Ilse still lives now. Beate misses it."

"But how can you miss somewhere that spies on people and traps them behind a wall?"

"Because, whatever it is now, it was once her home, Jacqueline. Poor Beate. She was this big, brisk girl who liked to obey. She took her Hitler Youth group meetings so seriously."

"Weren't they for boys?"

"For girls also. They taught her how to become a good German housewife. She wanted to finger the line."

"Toe it, Bridge," Grandma says, shoving her teeth in.

"Thank you, Nell."

Grandma pulls them out again and folds her arms.

"Were you in Hitler Youth, Mum?" Victor asks.

"Yes, Victor, it was compulsory."

His level of interest sky-rockets. "Did you have a machine-gun?"

"No, it was nothing to do with war. The girls were shown how to stay healthy and become excellent housekeepers. There was also a cookery course."

Grandma's teeth resurface. "Did you miss that bit, Bridge?"

"In a way," Dad chips in quickly, "Ilse was on the right side the night the Wall went up. She was at home in the flat she and Beate had lived in since the war."

"I imagine Ilse sewing a frock that night in August, sitting by the open window," Mum says. "A brown frock. A brown window frame. Everything is brown in the East. Even the coal is brown. And I wonder if she heard the bricks scraping together at midnight."

"I think they started off with barbed wire actually, Bridge," Dad says. "The bricks came later. But the message was the same. No entry. No exit."

"It reminds me of Victor's kaleidoscope," Mum says, sounding timid, as if she expects a rude remark from Grandma. "One turn and the pieces spill into a different shape. I imagine Ilse waking up that Sunday to see the sun lighting up the dreadful barrier, as if some trick of the night had split her city down the middle and cut her apart from her sister."

"So where was Beate?" I ask.

"She had a kidney complaint and had been admitted to a hospital, but it happened to be in West Berlin."

"Fate set her free," Dad says, almost drifting into the left-hand lane.

"You see, immediately after the war," Mum goes on, "people could cross the border, back and forth, without a problem. East Berliners swarmed to the West for the cinema and concerts, buying tickets with their East German money. They bought a million things missing from the shelves of the shops under Soviet control in the east. The exchange rate in the West was five to one."

"I bet the East German money's made of chocolate. Leave it in the sun and it melts," Grandma says.

"And West Berliners travelled east," Mum continues, ignoring her, "for the wonderful opera and theatres. They used East German money to eat fine food in the grand restaurants for a fraction of the price it cost in their own sector."

"What did they leave as a tip, a Smartie?" Grandma asks, causing a silence broken only by striking matches.

"Before the Wall," Mum says at last, "Beate and Ilse's home was in the East, but they had jobs and friends in the West. Ilse's fiancé, a pastry-chef, had a bakery in the West, but she only ever saw him there. Like so many from the

East German countryside, he had travelled to East Berlin with his belongings on his back and the visit turned into a subway trip to the West, from which he never returned. Terrified of being detained, he never took the risk of going back to the East, not even for a day. So, after the Wall came, he could never see Ilse again."

"I bet she missed his plum strudel."

"The night the Wall went up was the only time Beate and Ilse were in different sectors. Beate feels such terrible guilt. I can understand it. I also feel ashamed that I am free to go anywhere I like."

"Except down Widgery Lane where that tramp with more beard than face tries to show you his carbuncle."

"Yes, Nell, that is true, but poor Ilse is completely trapped. The guards watch and listen, waiting for ordinary people like her to dare take one wrong step."

"So even though Beate feels guilty, isn't she thanking her lucky kidney that she wasn't trapped too?" I ask.

"Perhaps, Jacqueline," Mum says. "But do not forget that overnight the Wall made her homeless and alone, trapped in a different way from Ilse. The hospital let her stay because she had nowhere else to go. She met a man in there, a soldier recovering from yet another operation on his terrible wounds from the war. She married him a month later, and they lived in his flat in Schillerpark. Their son was born after a year."

"Lawks, she didn't waste much time," Grandma points out.

"Well, her husband was weakening and she had waited a long time for marriage and children, you see. Poor Ilse had to peer from the window of a friend's top-floor flat near the Wall to catch a glimpse of Beate in her wedding dress."

Even Grandma falls silent and Mum stares out of the window at the city cut in half just as its people were trying to put it back together.

City driving with Dad is hair-raising. Or in his case, hair-flopping. We keep shrieking at him for forgetting to stay on the right side of the road. In the end I rip out a page of the notepad, find my felt-tips and draw a right-pointing arrow on it, thick and bright-red, rather like Dad himself. Mum props it on the dashboard to remind him.

New, shining towers of flats and glassy office-blocks flash by. Mum detaches the tinted clip-on lenses from her glasses and lets Victor hold them over his eyes. He pretends he's a spy for about five minutes, but apparently it can't be done without an invisible-ink pen, a fedora and a cheroot.

Mum identifies a few buildings, dark and damaged beside the sharp new skyscrapers. We pass some tall, puffed-up houses from a grander era, like gentlemen fallen on hard times. She thinks she might know them, but I can tell she isn't sure. Too much has changed.

"These will be torn down for more sky-shakers, I'm sure," she says, a catch in her voice. "I know this street. My school is nearby, but it is on the other side now."

"Were you called Eleora at school?" I ask her.

She looks at Dad, biting her lip. She holds out her hand for the clip-on lenses that are now T-K's laser-beam shield and, all fumbling fingers and thumbs, finally attaches them to her glasses, determined to hide her eyes.

"You don't have to talk about it, Bridge. Forget it for God's sake, love," Dad says.

"Talk about what, Mum?"

I wait for her to speak while we drive into Wedding. Nothing to with brides and confetti. This is an area stacked with monumental houses and factories. An old brick pumping-station with a long chimney is crumbling behind a mass of overgrown trees. The remaining walls are a pale rose colour and the damaged brick is shot through with monstrous weeds. Children are playing King of the Castle on the rubble.

"West Berlin is holding on then, Bridge," Dad says, finally mastering the art of lighting his cigarette without taking his hands off the wheel. "Tons of new buildings springing up all over the shop. Look at all these neon lights and tower blocks. And the old places are being cheered up with these painted mural things. Not easily shaken this place."

Mum looks doubtful.

In the hippy, Turkish area of Kreuzberg, yet another division in a city already divided, we trundle through side-streets dotted with tiny artists' galleries, their windows glassless. The sun slides old rain off the bright awnings. A thin black dog flops beside a tin bowl of rainwater. Children stare at our car, half-amused and half-afraid, tearing at little black loaves of bread. A tiny old woman, her face like a wasp-attacked apple, sweeps the gutter in the shadow of the Alhambra, an enormous cinema that looks as if it should be grand inside with a deep orchestra pit and golden candelabra, but is probably gutted, damp and harbouring spiders. Maybe this new community can make it beautiful again.

"All refugees here," Dad says. "Their roots torn up by war and scattered every which way. Blown here on the wind to start afresh in this fantastic city."

He glances at Mum, but she has nothing to say.

I think of the felt-shoe factory owner being forced out of his back door, leaving his things behind: workbench, tools and materials, a photograph on a mantelpiece, a set of dentures soaking in a mug, perhaps a morning cup of tea with the imprint of lips on the rim.

We see the rebuilt hospital in Augustenburger Square where, six years ago, Beate fell asleep, knowing her kidneys were recovering, but not realising her heart would be taken out.

"It was once beautiful enough to take your breath away," Mum says, looking at the new building. "Like a small palace. Ah, the chestnut trees are still here, all around the square. Thankfully not even war has disturbed them."

We pull over because the back door is swinging open and other cars are hooting. Dad tells us to climb out and stretch our legs while he and Victor fix it.

"I'll stay put," Grandma says. "I don't need stretching."

"What were you going to tell me?" I ask Mum.

"Don't, Bridge," Dad says.

"Roy, it's time. She will understand. She is making a project about my city. And this is about me."

We sit on a bench a few yards from the car, where, in this city of ruins from the past and new monuments from the future, inside the history of the Weimar Republic and the legacy of the Third Reich, I learn I have a different story, a new one that eclipses the old.

"Just listen and I will explain," she says, looking at the defiant and altered face of Berlin while I watch hers and wait. She takes a gasp from her cigarette before she speaks.

"Eleora is a Hebrew name. I am Jewish."

My first thought is Lynette Margolis sitting out school assembly and lighting her Saturday candles. My second is that for fourteen years my mother has hidden this enormous secret like a caged bear in a locked room.

"I had a happy family," she goes on. "Our home was a grand house in a square with so many steps leading up to the front doors. When I was a child I learnt my numbers from climbing those steps, losing count and running down to start again. You know how people say the sun was always shining in their childhood. Mine was so."

Mine was so. Such a German type of expression. Mine was so. So, she is Jewish. And that means so am I. Half-German. Half-English. And half-Jewish. Maths is not my strong point.

***

CONTRASTS PROJECT

Eleora or Birgit, or whatever her name is, Berlin, 1938
Part Two - Provocation

During my final year of school, all of us Jewish children were made to stand up in biology class. The teacher chalked Jewish heads on the blackboard, insisting they had a different shape.

"Nature has made you second-class people," he said.

I nodded when he glared at me for some sign of agreement, but said nothing at home because my parents were already frightened. I cried alone in my room.

No one would mark my work and I was banned from lessons on German history. My teacher, now wearing the Nazi brown shirt, moved me to the back of the classroom. When he refused to acknowledge I was there at all, I felt a lid closing.

I turned eighteen, too old to be included in the trains transporting Jewish children to Britain. Time had almost run out. Our world was being reduced to nothing. It was in a desperate attempt to keep me alive that my parents sent me to my aunt and uncle just before the vicious hours of madness erupted on the Night of Broken Glass.

"The country's boiling over," my aunt said as soon as I arrived with my uncle, meeting us at the enormous front-door with its stone lion guard.

"Mother, be calm," Beate said. "We have nothing to fear. At least, we didn't until she arrived."

Her eyes narrowing, she stared at me. She was straight from the pages of a Nazi catalogue. Broad-shouldered and buxom, with long fair hair plaited around her head, she wore flat, functional shoes and a printed frock that matched her mother's. Both fitted the template for the Hitler-approved, non-smoking, un-permed, non-trouser-wearing, beefy German housewife captured in the familiar rhyme:

Take hold of the frying pan, dustpan and broom
And you shall marry a German man.
Shop and office leave alone.
Your true life's work, it lies at home.

No lipstick. No preening. No thoughts of going out to work. Before she turned twenty, Beate planned to marry a thoroughly blonde man and bear dozens of babies, Several would play at her feet while another fed at her breast, the next already growing inside her. The Nazi party arranged a generous loan for young couples. Once they had produced four children, the money need never be repaid. Upon production of her eighth baby, Beate would receive a medal. At eighteen, she was already excited about it.

The inferno lit the dismal drawing-room where we all waited for that night to end. I could smell beeswax and boiled potatoes. My stomach growled with hunger, but dinner was already over.

Beate hurled old curtains across the huge bookcases and covered the glass-fronted cabinets and grand piano with sheets, a pitiful attempt to protect their treasured possessions should the rioters reach us. She glared in my direction, letting me know none of this would be necessary if I had not intruded.

I asked to look out of the window, but was told to sit still. Ilse, a slender, gentler version of her sister, gave me a kind, fleeting smile. They had dressed her in the same stiff frock and wound her braids around her head, but she loosened her white collar and pulled out her hair-pins, letting her long coppery hair trail free.

Beate poured coffee and sliced a tough-looking strudel that only she and her mother ate. I listened to them chewing in the silent room while Jewish homes and shops shattered and burned through the night.

At dawn, the sky was streaked with a strange tawny light charred with black and the air smelt scorched, but the neighbourhood, a fair distance from synagogues or Jewish shops, was almost untouched.

"Which direction is home?" I asked, hobbling to the window, my legs stiff and aching from the long night in the chair.

"This is your home now," my uncle said.

"But are Mother and Father safe?"

"Let us hope," my uncle said.

But I already knew he had none left.

I banged on the glass, hammering with my fists and screaming, "Take me home, Mother. I hate you."

I wish I could forget saying that.

"Be quiet," Beate shouted in my ear. "Would you rather burn?"

"Stop it, please," Ilse said. She was hunched on the floor, her thin arms wrapped around her knees. I saw their childish scabs, but in her face I saw adult fear. She knew the world would soon be on fire.

Although a young adult, I had always been pampered and I missed it. I needed Beate and her mother's maternal bossiness, the rustle of their identical starched dresses and the clumping of their stout shoes. I had grown out of warm milk, but I accepted some, sipping it with my hands wrapped around the steaming beaker, while our leaders cleansed the country.

Beate took me to a pretty bedroom with a pink satin quilt that felt cool and soft, inviting me to close my eyes to the long terrible night.

"You should thank your parents," she said, throwing the covers over me. "Our home is a safe place. You must respect it."

She closed the door and I fell asleep to the distant sound of her humming as she took down the blankets she had pinned to the windows. In a terrible nightmare, I wound my hair around my head over and over again, until it snapped off. I held onto it, this black rope, until a Nazi snatched it from my hands and began tying it into a noose. I woke in a panic and almost fell down the elaborate, curving staircase in my rush to find my new family.

My uncle was also a gifted composer, but unlike my father, he was not Jewish. They had met during easier times, before the Nazis erased the line between music and politics, and had even been working on a sonata together until all Jewish musicians were forced to withdraw from public view. By then, my uncle had fallen in love with my aunt, Father's half-sister. She was a crossbreed, or *Mischling*, as the Nazis termed it. She, Beate and Ilse were fortunate that the Nazis favoured my uncle's work and presented his family with a German Blood Certificate proclaiming them honorary Aryans. After that, Beate and Ilse knew better than to mention the trace of rogue blood in their veins.

"Time to dye," Beate said when she saw me in the kitchen doorway. She held up a bottle of bleach, a grin displaying her uneven teeth. I hoped the grin was friendly, but it was hard to tell with her.

We all crowded round the sink. While Beate uncorked the bottle, Ilse gave me a hug to pretend this was nothing to do with living in danger. Beate peroxided my hair the way people rubbed vinegar into putrid meat to disguise the rot. Her father checked through my roots for remnants of black, his musician's hands careful and precise, as if plucking the strings of a harp.

"You know, monkeys do this. They pick at their babies' fur to find fleas and such horrors," Beate said. I could not see her face because my head was in the basin, but I heard her mocking tone.

"By the way," she said, "we're telling the neighbours your parents have died in an accident. And we, for our sins, are your distant relatives."

"No," I said, my voice booming from the depths of the sink.

"Beate means you are a part of our family now," Ilse added.

"No, I don't," Beate said. "And you have to change your name as well. Your real one marks you out."

"Eleora means 'God is my light'," I said.

"Well it means it in Hebrew, so forget it."

I tried to nod under the weight of the towel she was wrapping around my head. Only I would remember who I was. That would have to be enough.

We sat at the table with Beate's seed-cake to honour my birthday. My head stung from the bleach. Orange-yellow wisps of hair poked out beneath the towel. When I didn't respond to my new name of Birgit, Beate's eyes turned to flint. Every part of her was slow-moving, apart from those hard, glinting eyes. They never stopped watching, disapproving, judging.

"Give me time," I said. "I'm not used to being someone else."

"Better get used to it fast."

"I'd rather just disappear. Why don't you turn me out onto the streets?"

"You would survive for less than one day," she said, stuffing in a mouthful of dense cake and spitting the caraway seeds into the empty grate.

Harsh words, but their tone a touch softer.

"You are one of the lucky ones, Birgit," my aunt said.

"We're taking risks for you," Beate added. "Without us, you could be rounded up and herded somewhere God-forsaken."

"Beate, you promised to be nice," Ilse whispered, her eyes enormous. "You are very safe here," she said, turning to me and ladling whipped cream onto my cake.

I felt far from safe. One wrong move and Beate might relish turning me over to the enemy.

"Will you miss your synagogue?" she asked.

"We hardly ever went there anymore."

"God is always with you, dear girl," my uncle said in his soft, insistent voice. "He is in our hearts no matter what else is lost. He still guides us all. Look for His light in honour of your old name."

I nodded, pushing the cake and cream into my mouth, trying to believe him. I knew he expected obedience. At the dinner-table, I mouthed the words of their unfamiliar evening Grace until the day my uncle told me to recite it alone. When I had done so, he asked me to repeat it again and again until my voice was croaking and Beate's diabolical dumplings had congealed in their gravy.

"We mean well, Birgit. If you do not comply, it will single you out. The woman next door is almost certainly anti-Jewish," my aunt said.

"Are you asking me to throw my identity away?" I shouted, so homesick I no longer cared how ungrateful I sounded.

"Yes," she said, as if it meant nothing. "Don't you want to live?"

I looked away, not answering.

"Then you have no future," Beate chimed in as always. "You will never marry or bear a child. You will be taken away to die."

Ilse was looking at me, willing me to obey. Without her, I might have walked out of that forbidding front-door, crashed it shut behind me and run home through the shattered city. I had no idea that, hours after I was driven away on the Night of the Broken Glass, my home, among thousands of others, had been ransacked and burnt to ashes. It was already too late to forgive my parents. I would have found nothing, and no one, at home.

5

EXPECTATION

"I can't take this in," I tell Mum, although now I know who provided the role-model for my Hitler Youth-inspired shoes.

Dad is hitting the car-door with a hammer, Victor is burping the alphabet beside him and, even though the metal bench is hotter than Mars, I feel as if Mum has pegged my insides out on the line in a howling gale.

This explains the matzos at Easter. I thought they were just a German thing, but maybe I've been innocently celebrating Passover. Grandma always gives hers to Deborah, whispering, "Here's your burnt wafers, duck, with extra water to wash them down."

I know very little about being Jewish, except odd things Lynette Margolis says about fish and bread and candles. I suppose if I don't tell anyone, I won't have to sit out assembly, although it might be handy to skip the embarrassment of Harvest Festival with all those garden-reared marrows and home-made jams beside my small tin of marrowfat peas and an elderly onion.

I am not unwilling to face the unexpected and can cope with the day, or night, or even an entire holiday, being turned upside down by matters beyond my control, but I do have something against my mother lying to me.

In biology, Miss Lobb talked to us about becoming adolescent and how new 'personal discoveries' might seem peculiar, but are actually normal and happy. None of the girls felt happy or normal. We all blushed beetroot and stared at our shoes while the boys sniggered. But the lesson really centred on The Identity Crisis, and how we might all be in the middle of one. It sounded like an epidemic or a horrific crime: The Great Identity Crisis.

Although she curled her lip with distaste because this was not a lesson on osmosis or alimentary canals, Miss Lobb explained that we might have begun to question who we were. If so, adolescence had begun. Reading tonelessly from a textbook while she speared her plastic pancreas on its spike, she said we were at the start of a quest to find our true self.

Most of the boys thought they were Bobby Moore.

"Perhaps I'm really a Pekinese dog," Gaye Kennedy whispered. "I must try to find myself. Let me know if you find me first."

And slower-witted Gillian said, "Perhaps I'm from Sheffield."

Asking about new things and understanding simple explanations is the way of a child. Being older means that not only is the way ahead awkwardly hard to fathom and you feel too embarrassed to ask for directions, but every sign pointing towards a recognisable place has somehow warped. Growing up is like studying an old map that has been folded so many hundreds of times the markings and symbols along the fragile fold-lines have disappeared. But the road you need to find on that double-bed-sheet-sized piece of useless, bendy, crackling paper is always on a crease.

The felt-shoe factory made me want to find the mum I used to have before she decided I shouldn't grow up, and I wanted to stop her mind wandering back home to Berlin. I thought I could bring back how it was—holding her hand when we had to run to the greengrocer's before it closed and suffering a stitch from laughing so much, cracking monkey-nuts and playing rummy after Victor went to bed, explaining the plot of *Peyton Place* to her while she pretended to understand.

I thought my project would answer some questions, but now I don't know what the questions are. I just know she has told me a lie and I cannot forgive it.

"If there's something about you that makes me who I am, then I should have grown up with it," I tell her, watching her bite her lip. "It's a gigantic part of Lynette's life. She's known all about it since she was born."

Lynette's special lamp for Sabbath has movable parts that block or expose the light, so she can't break their Saturday law that says they mustn't operate switches. It's nothing like Grandma's standard lamp with the long dusty tassels Victor wipes his nose on.

I envy the Margolis family's calm rituals that gather them all together. Lynette understands her roots and how she fits in. I would have liked the same chance, but here I am, not knowing if I'll be singing "We Plough the Fields and Scatter" this autumn.

Does Grandma know? No, she can't possibly. She'd bring it up every two minutes. She was upset about Stan's Jewish orphans because she loves all children, however foreign they are. She says a toothless new-born talks more sense than her toothless husband ever did, even when he did remember to stick his dentures in his cakehole.

Despite Miss Whipp being terribly nervous about the subject-matter, Lynette's project is about a gruesome German picture-book from the nineteen-thirties. The book is called *The Poisonous Mushroom* and it warns children to beware of Jews. At first, Miss Whipp thought Lynette was studying *The Observer's Book of Common Fungi*, but when she discovered the real spore producing the mushroom project, she tried to make Lynette adapt it. Death-cap, pig's ear, green-spored chanterelle, any common-or-garden mushroom would do, she said. But Lynette stood firm.

The Poisonous Mushroom shows a mother and son in the forest. The mother explains about gathering good mushrooms and avoiding dangerous ones as a way of advising her child to be on his guard against poisonous, or evil, people. She asks if little Franz knows who the bad people are, and he proudly tells her they are the Jews.

The mother praises him and then describes the different kinds: the Jewish trader, cattle-dealer, butcher and doctor, reminding him that all these different types, like the poisonous mushrooms, are capable of misery and killing. All

German children must learn to recognise the many guises a Jew might take on to hide the fact he is the Devil, and they must alert others too.

This book was warning people about Mum. And about me. I feel sicker than if I've eaten a bagful of toadstools. Not because of being Jewish, but because of the sudden weight of history I have gained.

"How could you do that?" I spit out the resentful words, tasting my own sour breath. "How could you keep that to yourself?"

Dad comes across to the bench and holds Mum's hand. She grips onto it. Her face is white, her voice low. "Jacqueline, I lived in Berlin when Nazis and informers patrolled the streets. Being Jewish became my secret. When I came to England, I kept it that way. It seemed safer, although I hope it will never matter again."

"Not matter? Maybe not to you. But it matters to me. It changes who I am, doesn't it?"

"Of course it doesn't, Jacqueline," Dad says. "Nothing's changed, has it?"

"Of course it bloody has."

"I beg your pardon?"

"Oh, you'll never understand. It hasn't happened to you, has it?"

"Did you just bloody, young lady?"

"No."

"Well, back in the car, Miss, before the bloody door falls off again."

Misery reigns in the car. Mum is dissolving. Dad slaps wildly at the centre console, hoping for a direct hit, and catches Victor's ankle. All hell breaks loose. Victor howls in outrage and confusion. Grandma knits at a furious pace, maybe hoping to stitch us all back together.

"Jacqueline, please understand," Mum says, sounding desperate.

"How can I?"

"Can I help?" Grandma asks.

"No, you can't," I snarl, immediately regretting it because she was actually being inoffensive for once.

Dad stops the car and tells me to get out. "Go on. If you can't be civil, you can bloody well walk."

"Oh Roy," Mum pleads, "how can she? Please let's zimmer down."

"It's simmer," I say in a pathetic gulping way.

"Oh Christ, now I've gone and dropped a stitch," Grandma says, her wool unravelling all over the car.

We all sit there, not knowing how to behave with each other. Mum seems horribly strange and foreign, not because of what she has told me, but because she looks so utterly defeated.

"You're as bad as the bloody Nazis," Dad growls at me, getting out of the car. "I'm going for a wee."

I boil with the injustice. How did they expect me to behave? 'Oh, smooth, Mum. Great. I dig suddenly being someone else. Far-out, man.' I'm not actually a hippy, but I might as well become one of those as well.

Dad is standing in a mist of wee-steam in front of some stupid German tree and I wind down the window and shout, "I'm not the Nazi round here. I distinctly saw you goose-stepping across that grass."

He can do nothing from over there, right in the middle of it. He can't even turn round. But Mum gives me a look of absolute disappointment that matches the one I give her back.

"What's wrong, Jacqueline?" Victor gasps, wiping his nose with the back of his hand.

"I don't know. I don't know anything. You may as well ask T-K, because no one's thought of explaining it to me," I tell him, practically savouring my own bitterness and pretending not to notice Mum whipping round in her seat again as if I'm firing poisoned arrows into her head.

While Victor interrogates T-K Gestapo-style, Dad climbs back in to carry on with the trip that's pretending to be a holiday. Mum has to advise him that Victor saying, "Vee haff vays of making you tock," is not intended to add fuel to the fire.

Dad freezes me out of every conversation and gives Victor the last three Everton mints from the glove-box. I feel more like a stranger with every mile.

"I must shove my bottom in properly before meeting Beattie," Grandma says.

So we make a corset-adjustment stop, which prompts me to leave the car and follow Dad while he stretches his legs and studies the map Mum is in no fit state to read. I touch his sleeve and give him a quick sorry hug that he says I should be giving to Mum.

"It's these halves. They're getting in the way, Dad. I don't want labels that say I'm half-German or half-Jewish."

"More like half-bloody-witted if you ask me."

I ignore that. "Didn't pigeonholing people start the war in the first place?"

"But that's what people do, Jacqueline." Dad attempts to fold the map, his eyes unbearably sad. "It's human nature. Not what Hitler did, I don't mean. More like inhuman nature, that was. But people want to cram everyone who's different into a box and when it gets out of hand, they want to shut the lid. It's because of fear."

I think about the Great Identity Crisis. No wonder people suffer from it. It doesn't come from inside. It's an infection of fear that spreads from people who cure themselves by passing it on, making you feel lost inside your own skin.

"Dad, does Grandma know Mum's Jewish?"

"God, no. Mind you, it's war that scares her most, and foreigners mean war to her. It's understandable. My bit of trouble at night and my Girls, all that comes from the war. And Mum came from the country that turned me into this raving loony."

"But Dad, you aren't afraid of Mum, even though you fought a war with Germany, and you aren't afraid of me either."

"Want a bloody bet?"

"But you aren't, are you?"

He lights a cigarette. As he blows out the smoke, he says, "Well that all boils down to love, doesn't it?"

Back in the car with Mum still tearful, Dad's gloves lying slack on top of the steering-wheel and Grandma wheezing from her tight stays, I struggle with the facts. The gap between Mum and me has opened out like one of Stan's spatchcocked chickens. The project was meant to unfold her story and break down a barrier, but she has built yet another one. Mothers are not supposed to build walls that daughters can't take apart.

She is someone else. I am someone else, someone who has caught The Great Plague of Identity Crisis and its worst symptom is feeling alone, without warning.

I flick through the pages of my notepad and draw spiders in the margin, using the pre-punched holes as the bodies, fanning out whiskery legs around them. Although there are so many different kinds, their story is always the same; they send out a dragline of silk, spin and wait. When the web is blown away, beaten down or trodden underfoot, they begin again. And again. Always the same.

I turn to the wrinkled page where, clumsy with the Gloy, I pasted in the felt-shoe factory. The building looks ready to crumble away, but its sign is intact, hoping for history to swerve off-course again and bring everyone back to their street.

Dad glances at a police-car driving past. It slows down and the policeman looks hard at us, but he doesn't stop. Dad lets out an enormous sigh and switches on the engine at last.

Back on the road, Grandma teaches Victor cat's-cradle with a loop of her wool, but they both fall asleep, their fingers tangled together.

Mum turns to me, her eyes dark and watery, and does what all mothers do when it might be better to keep quiet and let things stew. She starts talking.

***

CONTRASTS PROJECT

Birgit, 1943
Part Three - Exclusion

Ilse became my one bright spot in those wretched years. She used to take my hand and make me fly through the garden with her. My feet barely touched the paths that zig-zagged the vegetable beds and wound past ancient trees. Their leaves sounded like tambourines in the wind. When we reached the pond, alive with trout, we threw in bread saved from breakfast and watched the water simmer as the fish gathered and rose. While they gulped the food, the entire pond seemed to boil.

Ilse talked to me about music and asked about my father's compositions, creating a link to my past. The future could never happen while we lay on the grass, listening to the water. A row of chestnut trees screened us from the house, concealing us from Beate and her endless cookery lessons. We never did learn how to keep air in a cake or make meat fall from the bone.

Ilse once asked, "Are we all going to die, Birgit?"

"Of course not," I said.

She smiled, unwound her plaits and jumped into the water fully clothed. She shook her long mermaid's hair out of her eyes and beckoned me in.

"If you mean that, you'll jump," she shouted.

I was lying, but I pulled off my shoes.

"Thank you," she said while I gasped and floundered beside her.

With her trust invested in me, I had to conform. I prayed to God for her sake. I went to the youth meetings. Even now, when I make the beds, I imagine Hitler inspecting my hospital corners.

In the summer of 1943, Beate summoned me into the vegetable garden and told me I would never see my parents again.

"Forget them, Birgit. And forget who you were," she said, stabbing the hoe at the soil in the potato patch. "That person no longer exists. It's getting worse for people like you. And if you're weeded out, they'll take us all away. They're watching this house."

She held out a trowel, but I slipped upstairs and lay down on the pink bedspread that now felt cold and slippery. The sun never reached that room. I lit the candle by the bedside, remembering how my mother used to read to me in the evening light and trying to remember her voice. But I could not even recall her scent.

I dug out my old coat, the one I had worn when I left, and when I held it to my face, there, deep in the weave, was her damp-rose perfume, bringing back my father's dignified final performance of "Clair de Lune".

I was from nowhere, a nothing-person. By contrast, Beate was growing rosier and rounder, as if she were ripening. She could recite all the rules of child-rearing. She could darn socks and turn cuffs. She had even made her own wedding-dress. No one had asked for her hand in marriage, but she would not be unprepared when the great day came.

That summer, Beate fell in love with Rainer. The mention of his name melted her like butter on a warm window-sill. His fate had been sealed years before, when she seized his hand on the first day of kindergarten. Once he started working for the railway, he became her captive. She often caught the late train and sat in the front car, her eyes drilling into the back of his head all the way to the terminus and back.

She invited him for coffee and cake every day. His mother often sent feather-light pastries with him, but Beate insisted on feeding him herself.

Ilse and I stifled our giggles in cushions when she served her traditional German tree cake, its layers resembling the growth-rings of a tree. When Rainer dropped it on his plate, the crash was like a falling oak. We were tempted to shout, "Timber!"

If he called when she was sewing, she would kick the wedding-gown under the sofa. "Don't look. It's bad luck," she squealed, coyly allowing a trail of lace to show. But he made no attempt to catch a glimpse of it, nor did he ever propose.

While Beate sliced the cake, she looked on with affection at Rainer playing whist with Ilse and me. She beamed if he let Ilse win, but screwed her mouth into a knot if he paid attention to me.

Because I had to be distrustful of everyone, I interpreted the kindly light in his eyes as pretence. For all I knew, he could be a Jew-catcher.

After coffee and concrete cake, Rainer struck up a lively waltz on the piano and watched with amusement as an exasperated Beate tried to teach me the steps. And when it was my turn to play, I thumped out Beethoven with my foot pressing hard on the sustain-pedal in order to prove how German I could be. Beate would shout at me to quiet down, but I played on, aware Rainer was watching, his sandy eyebrows raised and his wide mouth stretched into a huge smile, until Beate lumbered across the drawing-room and slammed the lid.

One afternoon when I was alone, my fingers slid to the positions for Mendelssohn's "A Midsummer Night's Dream". After a long hesitation, I touched the keys just enough to make a discreet sound, the echo faint, but enough to stir memories of home. I played the entire piece, sweating from nerves. Someone might be opening the letter-box or crouching in the shrubbery to listen.

"Can you play it louder?" a voice behind me asked as I lingered over the final chord. Ilse, so light on her feet, had crept in through the garden door. Unfamiliar with Mendelssohn's work, she knew only that the music had moved her.

"I love it, Birgit, but you play like a mouse."

For the first time in years, I cried for the end of simple pleasures. Ilse took my hand from the piano keys and held it between hers. There were no words she could say. She gave her wise smile instead, and it felt like a gift. After I had dried my eyes, I saw one of the long curtains billow and knew Rainer stood behind it, listening.

The Nazis cast their net wider. Beate began urging Rainer to buy her a ring, always afraid of her few drops of degenerate blood, hoping marriage to a non-Jew would provide her with the same shelter her father had given his family.

One afternoon in the drawing-room, Rainer offered to play the piano so us girls could dance. Beate sat in her chair, measuring her sausage-like ring finger, while Ilse and I rolled up the rugs and Rainer pushed back the furniture, causing no end of squealing when the wedding-gown flopped out from its hiding-place, exposing the huge bell-sleeves sewn from the lace curtains in Beate's bedroom.

"Go and find something else to do, you two," Beate told Ilse and me, bundling the dress back into its hiding place.

"Oh, Beate, let us just enjoy ourselves," Rainer said. "While we still can."

I think he meant the war, but she took it as a hint that marriage was a dreadful bind. Determined not to give up, she dragged him outside and down the garden-path to discuss wedding-flowers, thrusting roses under his nose. But this time, Rainer hurried back to the house as if stung by a bee. With a regretful glance at our makeshift dance floor, he picked up his jacket and, recalling a sudden errand, dodged the proposal as well as the strudel Beate tried posting into his pocket as he fled.

At his next visit, he explained that during his free afternoons, he would be taking up fishing. It was in the national interest. Hitler, he told Beate, encouraged it.

"But only for men. You women must sit at home and sew."

When he passed the house with his fishing-pole, he speared little notes for Ilse and me on the hook and cast them up to the bedroom window.

Beate started eating too much of her own marzipan, sitting about with plates on her lap while she fretted over rumours of more round-ups of Jews. Ilse and I tried to keep them at bay, but she took out her anxiety on me.

"Stop loving them for God's sake," she said, catching me with a photograph my parents had slipped inside a poetry book. My aunt had told me to burn them, but I refused to give up the only keepsakes I had left.

Beate more or less frog-marched me downstairs, fetched her mother from the kitchen, where she was hauling a chocolate log from the oven, and made her agree I must throw both the picture and the book in the fire.

"Better perhaps to throw in that chocolate log," I muttered as they held my arm towards the flames. But at the last second, when I let the book fall, I slid the picture inside my cuff. It was a small victory, not over my aunt and Beate, whose fear I understood, but over the Nazis who thought they could destroy everything we valued.

I trained myself not to care whenever I was reminded of my status as the third daughter, the one who did not fit and made them all so vulnerable. They were not cruel people, but I was the stray mongrel they could never shoo away, and worse, one day I might bite.

When occasional treats were bought for Beate and Ilse, I was banished to the kitchen. It was unfair to expect them to divide everything three ways. Sweet-wrappers and new hats were always tidied away before I was allowed into the drawing-room again, but, despite the well-hidden evidence, it was hard to ignore what I was missing and pretend I did not care.

However, as I grew up, the exclusion gave me a comfortable sense of apartness, a kind of pride. Standing in the kitchen, warm from the steam of cabbage-soup and noodles while they ate violet-creams in the chilly best room, I was on the edge of their life. But at least I was reunited with myself.

Slipping off a shoe, I slid my toes over the seams between the mosaic floor tiles until I knew every bump, every rough edge, every inch of the pattern, until I was more familiar with that mosaic than with my own name. I felt a strange pleasure that I knew it better than they did.

But as the danger increased, the fact that I was different became too heavy a burden to shrug off. Spot-checks were being carried out in the streets. Papers must be produced.

My uncle bought me a passport on the black market. He sat at the kitchen table with his white cuffs folded back, prised off the photograph, carefully laying it aside out of respect for the dead owner, and replaced it with mine. My aunt hard-boiled an egg and he peeled off the hot shell, blowing on his scalded fingers. He rolled the egg over the official stamp inked on the dead woman's photograph. The warm, moist egg absorbed the purple ink so that when he rolled it over my picture, there I was, a valid person.

But false papers could not guarantee protection. While Jews produced their new identities, informers were handing lists of real names to the Gestapo. In the mission to rinse Berlin clean, these lists displaced all other paperwork.

My proud sense of being 'other' turned into a disfigurement. People were staring. Neighbours no longer said hello in the park. On sunny days we spotted the flash of binoculars from our neighbour's window. Ilse's schoolteacher began asking her questions about me, demanding answers until Ilse darted out of her lesson and raced home, crying with fear.

"She's panicking," Beate told my aunt, clutching Ilse and turning away from me. "She'll say something. We can't take the chance."

"I won't tell," Ilse said, mouthing me a heartfelt sorry. I gave her a smile. 'Not your fault', I hoped it said.

My aunt ushered me up to the top floor staircase, and we crawled into the attic. "I feel unsafe with you near windows and doors," she said. "Tell me, why could you not bring home the fish I asked you to collect this morning?"

I had hoped I would not have to explain. "The shopkeeper wouldn't give it to me. It was wrapped up with your name on the paper. But he said he had changed his mind."

My aunt cupped my face in her hands, the way my father once did. I saw compassion in her eyes, but I also saw horror, reading her expression as clearly as I had read the family name on that wretched fish.

"Birgit," she said, "the price for harbouring Jews is severe. The whispers about you are now deafening. Soon, we must decide, either to save your skin or our own."

A whisper is a terrifying sound.

I had to stay in the attic, where at least there was peace and the homely smell of warm blankets. I was told not to go near the gap in the wooden struts, but I gazed all day, drawn to the stripe of light, wondering what I would do if I saw the Gestapo marching through the iron gates.

At first it felt like a game, a temporary relocation. Maybe Rainer could pass food up to me on the end of his fishing-line or my dog would be found and allowed in with me if he didn't cock his leg on the linens. But soon it became a sweltering cell.

"Please let me out," I begged my aunt one day. "I can't breathe."

"Don't you dare risk it," she said. "Even some Jews have become catchers, turning their own kind over to the Gestapo. And God knows what they would do to us Jew-helpers."

"Could I please come down for a minute and play a little quiet Beethoven?"

"No such thing," Beate said, looming into the tiny space, never able to let her mother out of sight for long. "For God's sake, let us save you, Birgit. We're trying to think of a way. Just keep quiet until we do. Another huge round-up of Jews is being planned. Thousands, they say. You have to be absolutely concealed."

But sometimes I slipped out at night, just to feel air on my face. The dark streets of Berlin seemed neutral to me, almost benign. I stood under trees in the park and listened to the leaves, watching for torches. If I saw a beam, I hunched deeper into the shadows. The world had become so disturbed that instead of being a guide, a simple stream of light was now a shaft of warning.

One night when I came home, inching the heavy front door closed, I knocked over the hat-stand. It woke Beate. She clumped downstairs to see me struggling out of my uncle's big dark coat that I used for camouflage. She wrenched the stand upright, quite a feat since it was mahogany, and flung all the hats and coats at me until I begged her to stop.

"When will you learn?" she shouted. "There is no disguise for you."

My time with the family was over.

None of us slept that night. Ilse and I listened to September rain pelting on the kitchen windows while my aunt and uncle murmured into the telephone and Beate threaded needles.

"I'm sorry, Beate," I said. "I was no good at this wretched hiding game."

"Who could be?" she said. "No rules, are there?"

I nodded. It was the closest we came to an understanding. I wished I could hug her. She had become my sister in her own way. I had evaded most of her lessons, yet she managed to teach me how to embroider and bake, even if my bread almost broke the beaks of the ducks we once fed in the park. But I was still the enemy.

"Rainer will be here soon," she said shortly before dawn.

I froze.

She was trying to cut through one of her rye loaves to make Rainer a sandwich, but I clutched her arm.

"Beate, don't let him take me. Either hide me or let me go. Please."

"God in Heaven," she said, sighing and arching her formidable eyebrows. "Look, do you really imagine he catches fish every afternoon? He's found a way to hide you, Birgit. He's already helped many others." She paused and looked up. "I only hope God will help him."

As soon as he arrived, Beate wrapped her meaty arms around him. When I saw the tender way he extricated himself from her, my instincts told me I should trust this man.

"I have arranged a new home for you, Birgit," he said. "My friend works in an armaments factory with a storeroom at the back."

"A storeroom will do," I said.

"No. It's less than that." He took a long gasp of his cigarette. "There's this cupboard in it..."

"So, Birgit has a cupboard. Perfect," Beate said, hurling things into my case.

"Er...no," Rainer said. He avoided my eyes by blowing a long plume of smoke above his head.

"What do I have?" I asked him. "Please tell me."

"Well, this cupboard, which is full of oiled screws and welders' goggles, has a false back. And behind that, there is a small gap."

"A gap?"

"Just big enough for you, Birgit. It's a good thing you're not built like...well, it's good that you are so slim."

Rainer and my uncle set to work. They carried the sofa and armchairs from the drawing-room outside to a van Rainer had borrowed. 'Upholsterer', stated the freshly painted lettering. On one of the trips to the van they struggled with a particularly heavy armchair. Inside it, deep within the hollowed and hastily re-stitched seat, I lay curled into a tight ball.

Just before I was hidden, I thanked my uncle for allowing me hope, and he whispered, "Remember, Eleora, God is your light."

"*Auf Wiedersehen*," Rainer called to my family as he started the engine. And I knew he was saying goodbye for me.

Once again I was taken away, this time wedged in too tightly to tremble, but as the van clattered through the early morning streets, my heart rattled along with it all the way to the back entrance of the factory.

"There's someone following us," Rainer said, as I unfolded myself. "I have lost him for now, but we must hurry inside."

A long time later, I learned my thwarted pursuer was the gravel-voiced driver who had brought me to my aunt and uncle's house, the driver who had told me all this was for my own good.

Before I grasped Rainer's hand and hurried through the narrow tin door, I took my last breath of fresh air for a long time. It tasted sweet and damp, the flavour of childhood, of old freedom. I licked a drop of rain from the metal door before I disappeared inside.

In the gap behind the cupboard I listened to machinery rumbling all day. The factory boss hauled me out after the workers had left in the evening to use the toilet. He gave me bread, which I ate standing in the storeroom before he pushed me back into black silence at night.

"God is my light," I murmured for hours. "God is my light."

But I saw nothing ahead, only more darkness. The urge to scream was almost overpowering. My legs ached as if the bones were being crushed through a mangle, although sometimes I felt detached and weightless, my mind drifting back to a time unknown, to the peace, perhaps, of my mother's womb.

Eventually, the Allied bombs threatened us all, both the shameless and degraded alike, but I could never risk being seen in an air-raid shelter. I stayed coiled in my space, half-demented with loneliness and pain, but no longer afraid. I began praying the fighter planes would destroy the city that had forced me into hiding. If the bombs succeeded in crushing Berlin and ending the war, I might be safe at last.

***

I have no idea how it feels to find out your parents have been spirited away to a death camp. I can't imagine being hidden in a hole after growing up like a little princess, your chandeliers, your doll with glass eyes and the grand piano all smashed to smithereens, and to end up queuing at Stan's for liver and trundling the sweeper over Grandma's carpets. I have no idea how I'd cope if I was sent away to a hostile place, even if a chauffeur drove me there with a beribboned sausage-dog on my lap.

This stranger's nightmare is my nightmare too. Without this Rainer, I would never have existed. I'm hardly here. I was never supposed to have happened. Berlin was being cleansed of crossbreeds like me.

If ordinary people can swallow stories about poisonous mushrooms, another war could happen at any time, and that means more questions without answers. Would I be stuffed into a gap behind a wall? Would Mum escape again, and would she take me and Victor with her? I'm not going to be stuck in a hole with him. And since I don't believe God is my light, I wouldn't keep clinging to hope, nervously plaiting my rosary-beads or whatever saintly prisoners do in films.

I try to write, but I'm too confused, so I draw an obese sausage-dog with a huge spider's swastika-shaped legs hanging over it.

This project seems impossible now. Mum has given me yet another picture of herself along with the wife who bickers with her husband, the daughter-in-law whose clawed fingers hover at the back of Grandma's neck and the middle-aged woman who slinks into her past the way other mothers creep up to the spare room to polish off the Jaffa Cakes. Now I see she is a liar. Even if I stack all these different transparencies over each other, I still can't find my mum.

Who is she? Quite pretty, for a mother. Awful cook. Fast walker. Can cut out felt shapes even with blunt scissors. She copes with Dad's dark side, although she did try leaving him once. Ever practical, she cut herself a sandwich first and was still slicing her cucumber when Grandma locked the doors and hid the keys under Deborah's millet. Mum tried to storm off, but when she saw Grandma watching her like a warder with her arms folded, she burst out laughing and crying at the same time.

But now she is as difficult to fathom as Bwa-Bwa. She's a stranger, cast out from two families, her identity changed twice. German by birth, English by circumstance.

Dad is quietly lighting one cigarette from the last. I smell the Bad-Moon girls gathering.

"We are soon at Beate's house," Mum says, crumpling her tissue and gripping Dad's hand on the gear-stick.

I imagine she won't risk speaking about the past again, but I hope she still says, "Tidy yourselves up a little", or "Take that disgusting gum out of your mouth, Jacqueline." I don't want her to be any more different.

The mood in the silent car stiffens. If someone clears their throat or searches for a glacier mint, it seems normal, but the tension winds back up again. It's a relief when Dad starts humming. He's wildly out of tune, but I think I can pick out "Puppet on a String". I wish I could close my eyes and open them to see the car turning into Audette Gardens.

It should have been called Odette Gardens after Odette Sansom, the French resistance worker tortured by the Nazis, but because the road signage official came from Yorkshire and pronounced her name "Ordette", the sign-printer spelt it as he heard it.

We drive into the modern Schillerpark estate, a maze of identical red-brick blocks with white-framed windows facing the sun. Dad points out how the neat, flat roads are named in an oddly un-German way. Cork, Edinburgh, Bristol, Windsor and Oxford.

"Britain and Ireland paved the way in social housing, you see," he says, breaking the tension.

Mum and I clear our throats and say "Oh," to urge him on.

"With all the shifts in government over the years, some Berlin streets keep changing names," he says, encouraged.

"Oh yes," Mum chips in. "A place named simply Chancellor of the Empire became the Adolf Hitler square. But now it is named after the liberal politician, Theodor Heuss, the first president after the war."

"Good old Theodor," I say to an explosion of laughter triggered by relief that we are speaking, rather than by actual hilarity.

"And once Stalin fell out of favour, Khrushchev had his statue chopped up overnight and renamed his street after Karl Marx," Dad says.

Crisis over. We are now reclassified back to Holiday Trip, instead of Descent into Hades.

The Schillerpark balconies are planted with flowers and the doors have square panels in bright, primary colours. A mass of glass, from the tall windows on the lower floors to the tiny rectangular panes that shine like a row of squinting eyes beneath the flat roof, are designed to let light from the courtyard gardens flood inside, although from down here, the mirrored glare of the sun flashes blinding reflections of the Berlin sky.

Grandma and Victor wake up as we park in Dublinerstrasse, where Beate's block is as trim as the rest. People probably have to enter and exit at regular intervals like weather-house people; a red lady in a dirndl for sun and a blue man in leather shorts for rain. I can't imagine a rag-and-bone man disturbing the litter-free streets.

There is no grand entrance, no stone lion greeting us here. In the narrow doorway stands an apple-shaped lady with darting monkey-eyes, a smile full of bad teeth and a face like a school suet-dumpling, a rather cold one. At her feet sit an extremely clean child in pressed trousers and an elegant Dalmatian with its head thrown back, howling in protest at these subdued visitors in their ridiculous wooden car.

"Beate, I presume," Dad says to Mum, switching off the engine.

"Is it?" says Mum.

"Well, you should know, Bridge."

"But it's been years, Roy."

"Was she short and fat before? With a moustache?"

"Oh Roy, you can't possibly see that from here. Can you?"

"Oh yes. And half her teeth are missing."

"The family once had a marvellous dentist. Beate wouldn't let anyone else look in her mouth. When he was forced to flee the country, her teeth dropped out one by one"

"Probably all that concrete cake," I say. Mum turns round and gives me a smile, but I don't smile back.

"I thought you said she was a shadow of herself?" Grandma chips in. "Looks like a bloody solid shadow to me, Bridge."

Mum's hands flutter on the door-handle, and her reflex bad-news-grin flickers on. She even grinned when she told us the fishmonger had dropped dead in his ice-crate. Nothing to do with Dad saying, "Are you squidding me? When's the funeral? Do let minnow."

"Roy, this is a mistake. Beate hates me. Why am I here?"

"Christ, Bridge, pull yourself together. We've just been on a death-defying drive in a car held together by a thread of nylon for this."

"Probably not even a thread, son. A gnat's prayer's all that's holding this jalopy together," Grandma adds, helpful as always. She hunts for a lost knitting-needle, unaware that T-K and Sitting Bull are jousting with it.

"Quiet, Ma. Look, Bridge, you're not running away anymore."

Mum looks stricken. We all sigh and the car heats up even more.

"Christ alive, Bridge, you've been brave before. You can do it again. Have a drag of my fag, look." Dad passes her his cigarette, takes off his car-coat and drapes it across her shoulders.

The peacock-spider unfurls a multi-coloured cape during his courtship dance. It's quite classy when he does it.

"Bloody ugh," Victor whispers, flicking bits of barley-sugar at the windscreen. "Not parent-love again."

But Mum can hardly hold the cigarette to her lips.

"I feel like an unwelcome guest again, Roy," she says, beginning to climb out of the car as if about to lay her head on the executioner's block. "The years tell a dreadful story on Beate's face."

"Come on," Grandma says. "The poor woman just needs a good English girdle and a decent denture. Let's not be judgemenial."

Beate's jowls concertina over one another and a large mole sprouts enough hairs for a backcombed beehive. Her hair is still wound around her head and she smells of sour milk, brandy and onions. She hugs each of us like a fierce bear, almost cracking Grandma's whalebone, but with Mum, the show of hugging is wooden-armed and the kiss stilted, with extended polite noises. If I had scissors, I could snip the air around them.

We troop into the sparkling kitchen, where Beate is preparing coffee und cake. The table is set with white plates and tiny forks on a black cloth. A theme of black and white has invaded everywhere. Not a single splash of colour. Snazzy, Gillian would call it. "Arty-bloody-farty," Grandma mumbles. In our mismatched, travel-creased clothes, we don't know where to put ourselves.

There are white and black vases with no flowers in them, a fireplace with painted flames and a shiny white telephone that has surely never been touched. We have just started renting one at home, primrose-yellow and already smudged with Victor's finger-marks. He keeps picking up the receiver and listening to the party-line.

Last week, he heard a woman say, "Quick, he's just this minute gone. And the bed's still warm, Mr Big-Love." I told him her husband must have suddenly died and she'd called the undertaker. Victor said, "But isn't he called Trevor Simpkin—Taking the Sorrow out of Tomorrow?" So I told him to stop listening to private conversations or he'd be next.

Because the telephone shudders when the party-line is in use, Grandma sometimes places her heaviest shoe on the receiver. When the vibration makes the shoe fall off, she moves like lightning, lifts the receiver without a sound and listens in, puffing her smoke away from the mouthpiece.

Nothing in Beate's flat looks fingered or dog-eared. Sebastian's toys are in a black box with the lid on. The television-set sits inside a white basket.

Beate's colourless scheme is a far cry from our room in the Clacton guest-house, with its ribbon of sea-view, the armchair with a golf ball for a missing castor, the serpent's-tongue crack in the pink wash-basin with its badly painted wreath of sweet-peas round the plughole and the tiny purple crayon-mark Victor once made on one of the cabbage-roses jostling for position on the wallpaper.

As for our semi in Audette Gardens, nothing is fitted and nothing matches. We have blood-orange curtains, a bright yellow lamp-shade with a pattern of blue circles and a swamp-green rug because Dad always says we can't afford to tire of last year's in-thing, or any-bloody-thing, if it isn't falling apart yet. This is why we still have Grandma's utility furniture in the front-room. But when other women stock up on clothes-pegs or dusters in Woolworth's January clearance sale, Mum buys their cheap paint. When Afghan Tan slipped out of fashion, our front-room became a giant sweating mushroom. Our bedroom gained a Hot Mustard ceiling and Groovy Gold walls. One side of the kitchen door gleams with Yo-Yo Yolk and the other with Public Toilet, as Grandma calls it. Mum has travelled a long way from those first years in Audette Gardens. Not literally. She hasn't been further than Clacton until now, and she still moves the cushions aside before she sits on the settee. But, despite Grandma announcing, "They like covering things up, the Germans," she isn't afraid to keep changing the surroundings with a pot of emulsion.

Mum coaxes us to sit on Beate's long black bench at the table. "The dog's on it," I hiss at her, but she makes us stroke Axel's big trembly head. Grandma finds out he coordinates with the surroundings too well when she takes the weight off her feet. "Oh Christ, I thought he was a spotted cushion."

All I can smell is my Gorgonzola-scented feet. This is the kind of house where you are obliged to remove your shoes on the door-step and slide about in your sweating socks, leaving hideous footprints on the gleaming floor.

Mum and Beate talk in German like two old women queuing at the bakery, courteous rather than sisterly. They could be saying, "Nice weather, duck", or "Will you be going for the crusty farmhouse, dearie, or are you having that last bloomer?"

Or maybe, "So you survived the war in one piece, dear?"

"Yes, thanks for shoving me in the dark for years."

"No, no, thank you, my dear, for nearly getting us arrested."

I take Victor and Grandma to the toilet, glad to escape. Axel follows, his claws clicking on the polished floors.

"Jacqueline," Victor calls out after a few minutes, "I don't know what to do. There's this little ledge inside the toilet."

"So what?"

"Well it's sat on there."

"What is?"

"Come and see."

"Oh God in Heaven, there's a stinky just perched there," Grandma says.

"The flushing water won't swoosh it down," Victor moans.

"Bloody hell, Victor, it won't shift."

"But I can't leave it. How does it ever go down?"

"Maybe German cackers behaves itself."

"Well, mine doesn't."

"Now why in the name of Engelbert Pumperstink would I want my doings to roost on a shelf? I suppose they have to inspect them before they flush."

We have to fetch Mum to deal with it and then go back for the coffee and cake. Victor has to hold T-K out of Axel's reach because there's already a puncture wound on his left pectoral. He and Sebastian are given milk in a triangular cardboard container. Victor folds his arms and says, "I'm not a bloody baby," but he's pleased with the straw. We only have them at birthday parties. He slurps away, teaching Sebastian to blow bubbles.

Sebastian sits in a high-chair painted white with big black polka-dots. Like a miniature man, he's wearing a spotless white shirt and black trousers. His unblinking navy-blue eyes, the only colour in the room apart from our crushed holiday clothes, stare at me as he drinks his milk, refusing to copy Victor's rude gurgling. I think he's drugged. When he speaks, I marvel at his fluent German until I remember he's not one of the foreigners here.

The cake is warm and buttery with stewed plum underneath and a crumbly topping strewn with almonds.

"Not that dratted Hun flan, is it, Bridge?"

"Plum flan, Nell. Same recipe as mine."

"Lord help us. Oh well, I can feed it to the dog."

Axel looks up at Grandma and grizzles with fear.

I add a dollop of sweetened whipped cream to my third slice. It's heavy-go-ing, similar to Mum's, but I'm starving, and at home we only have cream at Christmas. Victor slings his messed-about piece onto my plate when no one is looking. Beate piles on even more, beaming and saying I look half-starved. Mum frowns and Beate beams even more. She eats all the rest and clears the cream-pot. I feel like Twiggy beside her, but I imagine even Grandma does. Bessie Bunter would look like a wafer.

Grandma asks questions in steely, loud English that Beate understands. She offers Grandma a glass of Schnapps and Grandma produces her Three Barrels.

"Where do you light your bonfire, duck?" Grandma shouts. Presumably an important issue when you meet your daughter-in-law's long-lost sister.

"No fire," Beate says. "Not permitted."

"Strike-a-light, I'd love to live in this flat. You could stake your life on Mrs Pither lighting one the second Bridge puts the washing out. The smoke gets to my chest even with the window shut. Oh, it's terrible to be trapped in your own home." She lights a cigarette and sits a box of Liquorice Allsorts on the table. "Dig in, Beattie."

Beate smiles at Grandma and passes her a cup of tea.

"Is this real tea, love? You haven't put lemon in, have you? I only ask because you continentals have ideas. When Bridge was first in my house, she kept popping fruit in my cuppa. She didn't even know milk comes in glass bottles."

I feel a longing for home, even for the psychedelic carpet that Grandma says looks like someone was sick over it and for the chipped enamel let-down, which judders when Victor and I are eating our tea on it, especially if the one o'clock express is knifing through Oaking Valley Cutting at the time. When Grandma complains her teeth aren't up to Mum's stuffed hearts, I even miss Deborah squawking, "Suck it!" At least I think that's what she says.

The flat smells of fresh coffee instead of stewed tea, but reeks of cigarette smoke the same as everyone else's house. The tall ashtray with the plunger is similar to ours, except Beate's is black rather than tarnished brass with a dent where Mum once threw it at the tallboy. The same long bars of late sun paint diagonal stripes across the floor, just like at home.

Beate takes us for a walk in the courtyard garden, arm-in-arm with Grandma, although they've clinked glasses so many times they're probably propping each other up. A large hutch is tucked in a corner out of the sun. Victor gasps at the rabbits, one white, one black and one a patchwork of both. Beate hauls them out and fills his arms with them. Stroking the beautiful creatures, their lop ears silky in his fingers, he forgets the horror of stewed plums and strange toilets.

Beate and Grandma become such firm friends they freeze Mum out, the way Gillian and Gaye sometimes slot me into the ice-box. "Put three women together and one always gets a raw deal," Dad often says. "You end up with a trio of witches bent over a cauldron, two of them stirring with one spoon and whispering while the other has to sever the tongue of newt and dissect the liver of bat."

"Beattie says you remind her of Ilse, Jacqueline, and the joy of being young,"
Grandma tells me, cutting with ease through Beate's thick accent to the core of
what she wants to say. I would tell her it isn't all that joyful thanks very much,
but since their youth was all about fear and suffering, I just smile.

The trim curl of the moon emerges, and the rabbits are prised from Victor's
arms. We troop inside and Beate demonstrates every piece of her gleaming
kitchen equipment to Grandma, including an oven that roasts with steam—
"Don't your spuds go soggy, Beattie love?"—and an electrified bowl that spins
muddy potatoes clean—"Lawks, Beattie, that thing sounds like a Vesper with
exhaust trouble."

The evening meal is seedy: dark bread with seeds, dark ham with a seedy
rind and coloured bits in it and yet more cake, this time with the added surprise of caraway seeds.

"Do you know Sunblest? What about Battenberg? That sounds German
enough," Grandma says, giving up on the food and vibrating her Jew's harp
to twang out the seeds between her teeth. She opens her Elastoplast tin and
shares it with Beate, who is glad not to sully her elegant plunger.

By the time Victor and I are told to go to bed, I'm shattered and suffering
terminal indigestion. It's strange to have no stairs and just walk two yards into
another room for the night. Victor's hand slides into mine as we inspect the
twin white beds.

"Jacqueline," he says in his serious voice, "if you were stuck on the other side
of the Wall, I'd throw a piece of raw steak to the guard dogs, crawl under the
barbed-wire, dodge the mines and save you. Sometimes, with the small lamp
on, you're quite pretty."

Maybe he's had a nip of the Schnapps.

But until now, no one in this flat has mentioned the divided city. How does
Beate just carry on with her new black and white life while Ilse is stuck on the
dreary, grey-brown side? I suppose everyone is pretending this is an ordinary
holiday, if such a beast exists.

We are like a television-commercial family in our new brushed-nylon pyjamas. But we almost couldn't buy them because Dad said a man in the street
had swiped Mum's housekeeping money from his pocket when we all knew the
five-to-one favourite had fallen two furlongs into the three-thirty at Epsom,
and Grandma had ended up lending us a ten-shilling note from her funeral tin.

We keep saying, ooh, jolly nice plum-cake and ooh, apple-bloody-strudel
and how schön to have filter coffee with England full of tea-drinkers and
isn't life grand with no war looming over us like a great miserable buzzard.
But Ilse will never be here, and Mum's putrid lie has burst over me like pus
from a giant boil. What next? Maybe we'll discover Grandma's descended
from the Navajo.

Beate is staggering like a spider rescued from a glass of whisky. Grandma is
shouting for a leg-up into her bed. Dad is horribly quiet, practically smoking
two cigarettes at a time. And what the hell are these puffy things on the beds?

"Continental quilts," Mum says, breezing in and talking as if everything here is thrilling and we are a picture-book mother and daughter. Bloody ugh. "Feel it, Jacqueline. Filled with goose feathers. No need for sheets and blankets at all. Just this."

While she keeps patting it and fluffing up the feathers, as if she's trying to knead my surliness back into a manageable shape, I wander into Sebastian's little white room, where Beate is folding his clothes. Apparently they have to be perfectly square, not hurled inside-out into a festering corner. Dad looks in and spots a battered old copy of *Grimm's Fairy Tales* on the shelf.

"Ma read these to me when I was little," he says, brightening. "Mind you, she was far too good at cackling when the witch shoved Hansel in the oven."

While Dad shows Sebastian the picture of the gingerbread cottage, Mum stalks in and whips the book away.

"Not that book please, Roy," she says.

"It is a very good book, Birgit," Beate says, her moustache bristling.

"Do you not remember, Beate? The Nazis praised the young people in the stories for their awareness of purity."

Oh dear. If we were inside that gingerbread cottage right now, you could cut the atmosphere clean in half with a wooden spoon and the whole place would fall into slices.

"I thought the Allies stopped it being published in Germany," Mum goes on.

"But I have kept this for so long now. I have so little left from the past," Beate says, letting Sebastian turn the pages.

"You keep something the Nazis approved?" Mum asks, her voice so low that even Sebastian turns his head on his little white pillow and looks up at her in surprise.

She leaves the room, and Beate slurs a lullaby while the rest of us shuffle off to bed. Mum recovers enough to dart in and out of our room, checking we have all we need, showing off to Beate that we're her dear little kiddies. At home, she just shouts goodnight up the stairs before dashing away to fill Grandma's hot water bottle or hack the black crusts off her sponge cakes.

Beate lumbers in and out, puffing and sweating, to show us the lamp switch and the spare pillows in the wardrobe and how the fan operates. The room has white walls, white quilts and a white floor. My clothes look like a wrinkled rainbow on the chair. Beate tries to fold them, while I'm still struggling into my new nylon nightie, then gives Victor and me big damp kisses that smell of peaches pickled in alcohol.

I can't sleep under the goose-cloud. It feels like a flock of dead birds have landed on top of me.

"Jacqueline," Victor whispers, "why does Deborah have a mirror?"

"So she thinks she's not alone."

"Oh. She's not trying to kiss herself then, like you do?"

It's horribly true. I pout at my mirror at home to see what I'll look like when I kiss Peter.

"You look like a puffer-fish," Victor says, his voice quivering.

I beckon him and T-K to climb in with me and they don't waste a second. Although I would never admit it, the warmth that radiates from a cleanish seven-year-old boy is somehow utterly comforting.

"I don't like the noise of the feather quilt thing," Victor says. "Every time I move it sounds like a thousand army-boots marching through bracken. And why did she come in and kiss us? Will she do that again? Will she do that every night? How many more nights are we here for? Will she give us stewed plum every day?"

When Victor has a cold, he asks if he's going to be ill for three weeks, the longest span of time he comprehends.

"Jacqueline, I don't want to go see-sighting tomorrow. I'd rather stay with the rabbits."

"It's sight-seeing you clot. And you want to see the TV Tower they're building in the East, don't you?"

"But the Wall's in the way, twit-face. We can't walk through it like ghosts."

"No, but we can still see the tower, you pig-dog. Behind the Wall and behind the Reichstag. The East wants it seen from the West so they can show how good it is to be communist. It's their way of being noticed, like a person poking out their tongue in the background of someone else's photograph."

"Dad said they haven't finished it yet anyway."

"No, but it's quite tall and they're making a great big ball to stick on the top. When it's finished they'll be able to listen to Western radio and jam it so their people can't be polluted by us."

Victor considers this. "When the men in the crane at the top of the tower look down from all those millions of feet, can they see the Wall?"

"Don't know. Ask them."

"If they can't see it from up there, Berlin must look normal again."

"Nothing's normal here," I tell him, reaching for my notepad and writing that down.

Victor watches me draw another spider and takes off T-K's jacket. "I won't mind the sausages. They call them hot-dogs in America. The Germans just know how to make them."

"I think they come from Frankfurt actually, Victor, which is in Germany. They're called Frankfurters."

"No. Dad says they're hot-dogs. Because they look like those sausage-dogs. Oh sod it, T-K's foot's poking through his pyjamas. It's made a great big hole, Jacqueline."

I look at the nibbled plastic toes sticking out of the small paisley trouser-leg that is a scrap of my old skirt. When I remember Mum making the trousers as a surprise for him when he had measles, a great wave of homesickness slops about inside me. Either that, or the plums are seeking revenge. Or I recall how vile he looked with all those spots.

"T-K should cut his stupid toe-nails, Victor. Now turn out the light, will you?"

"But I can't sleep."

I throw off the quilt-thing and cover us with cardigans.

"How do we turn off the fan?"

"Go and ask Beate."

"No. I don't want her coming in here in that black shiny dressing-gown like a killer whale."

"She'll be nude by now."

"Oh bloody ugh."

As he falls asleep, his teeth grind like thirty cheese-graters scraping a blackboard. I resign myself to staying awake.

I want to forget Mum and the project, so I think about Grandma's fear of loneliness forcing her to come on this trip. It may be less the dread of being alone and more the dread of missing out. While your back is turned, other people invade your territory. Gillian's always terrified of losing my friendship if Lynette invites me for tea.

Now I can't help remembering the things Gillian said about me the other day, things I denied because I thought I knew exactly who I was. It was the day we sold the Sunny Smiles. Sunny? So-bloody-called.

***

SUNNY SMILES

Lynette, Gillian and I go out in a scorching shaft of evening sun to sell Sunny Smiles around Audette Gardens, but not with much actual smiling. It's more like pistols at dawn.

Because her mother is chairwoman of the charity, Gillian demands control of the Sunny Smiles booklets, which are filled with greyish photographs of children from a Home. All of them are beaming, some with teeth and some with gums; wide hopeful smiles designed to knot up people's throats.

"I hope they're all given a proper home soon," Lynette says.

"Oh for God's sake, Lynette," Gillian says. "They're probably all about forty-eight by now."

It's true. They're all wearing those ancient cross-over cardigans that feature on Grandma's prehistoric knitting patterns.

Lynette rattles her tin in the shape of a kilted soldier. She's already put in a washer and a Polo mint so the first person will suffer guilt if they don't give. The rattle is a trigger, not just for the first victim to find their purse, but for the Battle to Be in Charge—bloodier than The Little Big Horn and just as tribal.

"I should hold the tin, Lynette," Gillian says.

"But we've only just started."

"You had it the whole time last year."

"That's absolutely not true, Gillian. I didn't hold it at all. It was a Saturday, remember?"

Lynette has a deep, sultry voice like Lauren Bacall. Gillian says it's a Jewish voice. I practise it sometimes, sitting elegantly like Lauren does on top of a piano, except I'm just on my quilted stool with the foam-rubber bursting out. I have to do it when Victor's not in our room. He listened at the door once and thought I had Patrick MacGoohan in there.

"Oh Christ," Gillian says. "You and your bloody Sabbath. What with no pressing doorbells or carrying anything, I'm surprised you're allowed out at all."

"Please don't bloody it," Lynette says, clutching the soldier to her chest.

"And what else did you tell us you can't do on the Sabbath? Oh yes, no slaughtering, no fire-lighting, no winnowing. What's winnowing when it's at home anyway?"

"You wouldn't understand, Gillian," Lynette says in her huskiest tone. And although Gillian is my best friend, I silently support Lynette for defending what is hers. Plus, her mother makes fabulous bread. Gillian's always first in line for a bite of the challah.

"Well, let me carry the tin then," I suggest. Lynette hands it over and links arms with me. Gillian's face darkens. The battle-lines are drawn. Three's a crowd, they say. Mind you, if this were Victor and two other boys, they'd just punch each other, roll in the dust and forget it.

"Just because you're Jewish doesn't make you special, Lynette," Gillian says after we've rung the first bell and been told all the loose change in the house is already sealed in the football-pools envelope.

"I don't see it like that," Lynette says as we walk on.

"Well, I do. It makes you think you can get out of things, like the assembly last year about the Varto earthquake. I had to read out three Bible passages, stamp on Paul Postlethwaite's verruca to stop him singing "All Shook Up" and ended up with my eye blackened by a flying bouzouki."

"Bouzoukis are Greek..."

"And *you* didn't have to cut up your mother's velvet curtain to make a fez and stuff balloons down your trouser legs."

"But Gillian, you volunteered," I point out.

"No, Miss Whipp made me because Mother always has spare curtains. We have new ones every year. It'll be the fibre-glass sort next. Dirt can't cling. Falling-leaves pattern. Green and orange with yellow shadows. Drip-dry. Forty-three and six."

When I tell her it's clear she lives at the posher end of Audette Gardens, she smiles her dimpled cat smile and grasps my other arm, forcing me to give up the soldier tin. She grips it so hard her thumb dents his sporran.

A man, dripping and shiny from his bath, opens the door of the next house, a towel tied round his huge hairy stomach. His little girl comes running up behind him, slips on the bathwater puddle, clutches the towel and pulls it clean off. The man slams the door in our faces, saying he can't donate without his trousers.

We call back later, desperate after a run of door-bells echoing in apparently empty houses, but like most of the others, he pretends to be out.

"Let's look through the window at the top of his door," Gillian says.

No one can reach it, so she stands on his ornamental bullfrog.

"I can see a shadow behind his cocktail cabinet," she hisses.

We all hear the toddler laughing and saying, "My turn to hide, Daddy!" And then the trouser-less man, presumably trousered now, whispering, "Sh, Verity. You haven't found me yet."

We cover the Gardens from the crummy semis at our end to the new horse-shoe of buffed red-brick villas at the other, each with a long central channel of shingle beach set into the driveway.

"My mother says we have to be persistiannt," Gillian announces.

"Let's see how much we've made so far," Lynette says, wrenching off the soldier's busby.

"You're abscessed with money, aren't you?" Gillian says.

"I'm not obsessed. I just thought we'd see how it's going."

"Well, we've only sold two and at least three of the pennies are Scottish, which won't even buy the orphans a Jamboree bag. I think I should have the tin now. Mother's watching out the window and she'll be tired of seeing you in charge of it."

"All right."

I can hear the rusty cogs of Gillian's brain creaking, working out how to continue the sparring. It takes a while, but the gears crank up again.

"Why don't you come into assembly, Lynette?"

"I come in for the notices, just not the hymns and prayers."

"Why?"

"You know why, Gillian."

"Well I'm glad I'm not Jewish. Aren't you, Jacqueline?"

I don't want to speak. I know Lynette isn't actually my friend in the way Gillian is, but she already has a bad enough time being teased by the prefects who supervise the pupils sitting out assembly. There's a Jehovah's Witness, a girl with her neck in a surgical collar and a boy with low blood pressure who can't stand up for longer than it takes to sing a hymn with three verses, and even they snigger about hooked noses. I don't know how they get away with it because the Jehovah's Witness has a conk like a Conference pear.

I think Gillian is scared of Lynette being different and is trying to tease her out of our Sunny Smiles evening as if she's a spider cutting a stray leaf from her lair.

"Jacqueline?"

Under the baking sun and with Gillian staring, I can't think straight. But Lynette's deep, rich voice speaks for me.

"I'm sure Jacqueline's glad. She's glad because everyone just wants to be whoever they are, don't they?"

I breathe out, but I'm still doomed. Gillian will start on me now.

"So how come you're going to Germany then, Jacqueline?"

"Because my mum's family are there."

I swear she thinks I'm about to march through her front-door and annexe the settee or set fire to her father's newspaper.

"We've prepared for World War Three under the stairs," Gillian says. "We've got twelve cans of luncheon meat, three of my dad's army-blankets and a bottle of tonic-wine."

We wouldn't have such a good time. Our under-the-stairs cupboard is stuffed with depressed-looking plimsolls and a thermos flask that smells of evil.

"Did your mum have brothers or a father in the war, Jacqueline? Because one of them could have killed my Uncle Dirk."

"She just had Beate and Ilse."

"Were they actually in the war?"

"They had a bad time in it, yes."

"But they were still in it. They were against us, weren't they? It was Germans against English."

"You make it sound like the World Cup final," Lynette chips in.

"We beat them at that as well."

"It's really not the same thing," I insist. "Beate and Ilse had a terrible time. They're still having a terrible time now Berlin's got the Wall."

"Wouldn't fancy a holiday there then," Gillian says.

"It's not a holiday. It's just being with family."

"Even when they were on the other side?"

"There weren't sides for ordinary people."

"How come she came over here if her sisters stayed behind?" Gillian asks, turning her face to me in a bid to block Lynette.

"My dad found her. He sort of rescued her when it was all over."

"A bit like Geoff Hurst striking the final goal just as the crowd charged onto the pitch," Lynette chips in.

"Shut up about football for God's sake," Gillian says.

"Well it was only a minute before the end of play. The West Germans were frantic. They sent all their defence forward to try for an equaliser, but Bobby Moore got the ball and passed it to Hurst. People were already sprinting onto the field while he was busy scoring."

Gillian, not usually much of a match for Lynette, uses the commentary time to think especially hard.

"If your dad had to rescue your mum, Jacqueline, she must have been in a concentration camp or something."

Miss Whipp taught us about the camps, but she had to take Gaye Kennedy to the sick-room in the middle of it. Lynette was offered the chance to leave the lesson, but she stayed. She claims it was because the alternative was an hour in Mr Finch's Language Lab and she didn't want him rolling his 'R's in her headphones. But I think it was because she's incredibly brave.

"My mum isn't Jewish," I tell Gillian. "I would know."

I flick through the booklet and dozens of Sunny Smiles grin at me.

"My cousin works in a library," Lynette pipes up before Gillian can start again. "He says people use Sunny Smiles as bookmarks. And he's also found a rude postcard from Colchester, a black banana skin and a dried-out slice of continental liver-sausage."

Gillian strides ahead.

"You can't go off on your own, Gillian," we shout. "We have to stick together, don't forget, in case we knock on the wrong door."

Keep at least one to run, Miss Whipp always says.

"I'm going home," she says. "I'll sell the rest to my mother."

We catch up in Gillian's driveway. A whistling delivery-boy has just dared to trample through the sandy channel Dad calls the death strip, so Gillian's mother is combing every grain back into place with a toasting-fork. It appears she'd rather impale him on it.

Lynette tries to take her tin back.

"I need to count the money. Let go, you spastic," Gillian says.

Gillian is not cruel. She just has an under-developed imagination. But her mum looms up, marches her inside and upstairs to the pink vanity unit in the bathroom.

Their soap is the expensive kind with a gold label. Gillian's mother prises the bar from the rubber suction-pad that looks like a cross-section from a pink squid. She froths it up with the loud squelch that only men make when they wash their hands. She is built like a man, I suppose. She pushes the bar into Gillian's mouth.

"Stick out your tongue, Miss," she says, lathering until Gillian makes gargling noises. The tears stream down her face while her mother runs a soapy finger over her gums. Lynette and I try to make ourselves part of the long raised grasses of the hall wallpaper. We are pampas. The tin soldier lies forgotten on the shingle driveway.

The soaping shrinks Gillian and turns her eyes into boiled gooseberries, hot and tight with tears. A horrible thrill of what Mum calls Schadenfreude squirms in my stomach.

It is an actual disorder, not just me being vile. I saw Gaye Kennedy smirking when her best friend told the history teacher Martin Luther King was a German monk.

Woven through my years of friendship with Gillian, throughout the endless games of Knock-Out Whist during wet half-terms and the bottling of fallen petals to make eau-de-cologne-de-Oaking, is Gillian's long grisly battle for supremacy.

She is primed to attack and snaffle as many honours as she can. Whether it's Hungarian dancing exams or a game of Canasta, she aims to trump me. If she loses, I relish a shocking sense of triumph. Gillian has the disorder too, but the other way round. She can't bear it when I do well.

I'm not a battler. I coast along, cheering other people's victories. I'm happy to be in the House that never wins at sport and don't mind being the hockey team's last choice along with the girl who needs binoculars to see the blackboard.

But Schadenfreude stitches its way like a black thread through the plaid of girl-friendship. Only half of me is a good friend. Half is bad. I'm composed of too many halves.

***

Thinking straight is impossible during the cacophony of Victor's teeth-grinding, Mum's loud, rhythmical breathing and the clashing soprano and contralto of the snore-sisters. But more disturbing is the lack of sound from Dad. Wakefulness foreshadows a night-terror.

I hear him get up, not gasping for breath this time, just sighing deeply. Poor Dad, with everyone concentrating on Mum coming home, we have forgotten that Berlin is where he had to kill a young man.

I slide out of bed and follow him into the kitchen. Axel sits bolt upright. He might need one of Sebastian's dummies when the terror launches. The kitchen door clicks shut. Not like ours at home, which needs a firm back-heel to slam it.

I whisper, "Sh, Dad" a few times, hoping we don't hear the thump of beached whale in the passage.

Dad slumps at the table, his head in his hands. I creep up and poke a hanky into his fingers, hoping it will cover his mouth and smother the imminent racket. He shrieks and leaps up, the chair scraping the floor. Axel presses his face into his spotted blanket.

"Dad, shush. Please don't be loud."

"Christ, Jacqueline, what the bloody hell are you doing?"

"It's all right, Dad. Everyone's asleep. I'm here."

"Oh, Jesus wept, I'm not having a terror, love."

"So what are you doing then?"

"I just couldn't sleep."

"Are you worried about the car?"

"Sort of."

"What else? About what Mum told me?"

"Yes, that as well."

There must be more. His eyes are hooded, his jaw clenched, and without his Brylcreem he looks like an ape-man. That's probably nothing to do with being scared. It's just a bit scary for me.

"Is it about me and Mum going to see Ilse?"

"Oh Jacqueline, hold the bus with the twenty questions, dear. Pass my fags, would you?"

I watch him smoke, staring him out. I might not be as close to Mum anymore, but I know my dad.

"Tell me," I repeat until I make him laugh.

He tries to light another cigarette from the first one, but I steal the matches. "Not until you tell me."

He sighs. "I'll tell you once I've got a smoke."

I have to hold the match steady. He takes a deep gasp before he speaks.

"I never passed the driving test, love."

"What?"

"I couldn't disappoint your mum again, Jacqueline." He pauses to relight his cigarette. "Look, if she doesn't cross the border on this trip, she might never get the chance. Those East Germans make it up as they go along. They might seal themselves off completely and Mum'll never see Ilse again."

"But the bits of torn-up L-plate are in the glove-box."

"Well, I had to go through the motions, didn't I?"

"Dad, you shouldn't be on the roads."

"No. But don't tell your mother."

"Dad, it's not Mum I'm worried about. It's the other Germans. The ones with Alsatians."

"Stop it, Jacqueline."

"And ways of making you talk."

"Look, put a bloody sock in it, girl. And not a word to anyone. My British passport should be enough for anyone."

"But it might not. Not if the police stop you. They'll want to see your licence."

"Why should they?"

"Oh Dad, because you're driving a half-timbered car with conked-out brakes that's falling to pieces."

"I'll keep it strung together."

Strung is the right word. Highly blooming strung is how I feel.

"All it means is keeping your mouth shut. It's not telling a lie, Jacqueline. It's...supporting a secret. That's all it is."

I supported Gillian when she wanted the class to believe she had a mute albino sister called Lily. But the consequences of her lie...er, secret, would not have led to being tied up in a fetid cell and fed L-plate fragments.

I weigh it up while Dad watches me, his eyes twitching. Either I keep quiet and be as scared as he is the whole time. Or I tell Mum.

"I'll keep quiet," I tell him.

Breakfast is the same as last night's supper, a spread of ham, cheese, rolls, jam and a big iced seedy cake, like a birthday tea without cocktail-sticks. Grandma's plate is piled high. Victor is allowed to curl thin slices of bendy, holey cheese and dark-red ham into tubes and eat them with his fingers. It cheers him up after the long night with the fan wafting cold air up our cardigans.

Beate has appalling table manners, talking with her mouth full, plunging her great fingers into the meat pile and jammy knives into the butter. Coffee-rings and flakes of bread scatter the table-cloth.

But she clears at speed, her arms wobbling as she wipes, transforming every-thing back to monochrome and mess-free. She drinks tumblers of buttermilk, her breath as sour as a cheese dairy, but I detect a stench of alcohol too, like sozzled cherries. Gillian's great-uncle in Gloucester keeps a miniature bottle of gin in his Sugar Puffs box. She found it when she was rummaging for the free plastic frogman.

Beate's lodger, Konnie, a toothless train-driver with terminal BO, sunken red eyes and a drooping moustache, arrives at the table, doffing his leather cap. He digs in his trouser pockets and produces two guinea-pigs, an elderly ginger one wearing a veil and a white one with a black waistcoat and bow-tie.

"Christ alive," Grandma says, dropping her tea-cup. Beate takes her into the garden with the rest of the seedy-cake.

Konnie makes the guinea-pigs shake hands with us, even T-K. "I am exquisite to practise my English," he says. His eyes are painful to look at. I've seen bloodhounds look perkier.

He cuts his ham into small pieces and passes them to Axel while he talks, referring to himself by name all the time. The guinea-pigs nibble bits of peach from his hand, reminding me of Bwa-Bwa, who seems part of a far more normal time.

"Venn a young man, Konnie eat nineteen *Frikadellen* at one time," he says.

"What are they?" Victor asks me.

"Meatballs. Mum made them once and Grandma said they looked like ackack shrapnel."

"I think they sound like frogs' legs," Victor says. "But nineteen's an odd number, so one frog must have been a peg-leg."

"And ago six years," Konnie continues, "do you know summsing? Konnie see a man paint a line on the ground."

"Oh," Victor says, stuffing in the ham.

"You are how many years, young man?" Konnie asks Victor.

"Seven and a quarter, plus three days."

"Ah. Konnie's son was six. Johannes."

"Is Johannes here?"

"No. Johannes, he luff water. Oh, he luff it."

"Has he gone swimming then?" Victor makes breaststroke gestures and blows out his cheeks.

Konnie looks down and strokes one of the guinea-pigs. "Swimming? No. Johannes not swim."

"Not even with a rubber ring?"

"No, no, young man. Johannes dead."

"Oh. Oh dear."

"In River Spree. Oh, that water. He luff it."

"Oh. Did he drown?"

"Ah, drown. Yes. But also not." Konnie strokes the guinea-pig's sparse fur the wrong way. "They say drown. They say it. But it is zat line on the ground—the wire, the fence, the wall, it matters not how you call it—it is zee line. It kills him."

Victor tickles the guinea-pig under its chin. "Er, hold the bus a minute. Line?"

"Yes, zey painted it on zee ground to show where to build zee Wall."

"But there's no line in the river, is there?"

"It is everywhere, young man. Johannes play by water here in vest. Last summer. But River Spree, it belong uzzer side. It is border. He fell from vest side of the city, where we live, to east side. There, the Spree belonged to the Soviet sector. Guards wiz guns, zey stand on bridge. Some drive boats too. Zey watch everything. Zey watch my Johannes fall."

Victor twists T-K's arms into a butterfly-stroke position. "So Johannes fell into enemy water? And they opened fire?"

"No. Not fire. Nussing."

"They left him?"

"Yes, they leaf him."

Konnie's hands trap the guinea-pig against his chest until it squeaks for mercy.

Victor and T-K tilt their heads to one side. "So, the guards left him because he was the enemy? On the wrong side?"

"Yes."

"A little boy?"

"Yes, little Johannes was the enemy. And Konnie's wife, she is gone now. It is too hard for her to live wizzout him. You know, Konnie see the Wall go up and up, until it grows inside Konnie's head. The first day it come, I know the war is never over for us." He shakes his head until his chin wobbles. "And it is better," he says, "if lines connect, no?"

He puts his leather cap on Victor then he puts it on himself backwards. No one knows what to say, in either language.

"Can your train go through the Wall?" Victor asks him.

"Konnie drive it into East, but Konnie must not stop at the stations. Only pass through. No stopping. For the underground trains, Vest Berlin pays zee East in vestern Deutschmarks to drive in their tunnels. And there is a check-point at Friedrichstrasse, the only station under East Berlin where vestern trains may stop."

That's where Mum and I will have to go when we visit Ilse. It sounds like the point of no return.

Konnie gives Victor a guide-book in all languages and leaves the house with a polite salute to us all. From that point, we have a seven-year-old in charge of history while I'm given the job of bed-making. I can't master Hitler's hospital corners or make the wretched quilt-thing lie smooth. In the end, I think of Mum and give it a good wrestle, followed by a hearty pummelling to flatten it for good.

When we leave for our day out, Victor and I help Beate with Sebastian, slotting him into his push-chair with his plush white rabbit. The car stays put, looking as peculiar as ever and with a huge new dent in its backside where Dad whacked it with the hammer.

Dad seems less sure of his role without his gloves and car-coat, like Biggles without the helmet and goggles. He and Mum keep bickering. A dark glint in his eyes shows the Girls are slumped in the wings in their ragged fishnets, waiting to swan onstage later.

We leave Axel caged in his steel contraption with a black water-bowl and a white rubber bone and catch a bus into the lively city, deep into its broken heart, which teems with sunlit crowds of jolly men and women with fat tanned arms, children skipping along with German sweets and woolly-haired hippies roasting in Afghans. Huge shops are filled with beautiful things. Ice-creams and sausages are sold from smoky stalls, and cafés serve tall glasses of beer and Coca-Cola in ice-cold bottles. It's how I imagine London, just without rain and red buses and Wimpy bars looming out of the fog, and nothing like a city under threat.

I didn't know all of life would be here without a care in the world. I imagined dismal people standing in bombsites and staring at an even grimmer place over the Wall, which I haven't even spotted yet.

"You know, Jacqueline, we are enclosed here by a communist country," Beate says. "No one knows how long we can survive. East Berlin is guarded so tight not even a mouse can escape. And one day it might open its jaws and swallow us too."

I truly don't know how to sympathise with this, so I just say, "Gosh," which I realise is playing a bit fast and loose with the etiquette of commiseration.

"It all looks quite normal here," I add, hopelessly equipped to judge anyone's city, let alone this one.

"We are told to value this *normal* life while it is still here," Beate says. "But not me. How can I, while my sister is on the other side?"

And I can see how, inside her stylish, snazzy black and white shell, she is barely living at all.

As we walk further into the centre, the colossal, older buildings remind us of the war that is over and the war that still goes on.

"This is where Berlin fell," Beate says.

This is the elegant Reichstag, a sandstone palace with carvings, turrets and magnificent pillars. It reminds me of the tier of wedding cake in Gillian's grandmother's attic, the brittle icing jaundiced and the little plaster columns crumbling to powder. The blemished stone is flaking and patchy, as if it has a skin condition. Once crowned with a massive dome that wasted away in the war and was eventually demolished, it seems flat and bald. A crane stands in front of it now, like a huge protective arm.

"It's held itself together though. Almost dignified, isn't it?" Dad says, lighting a cigarette. "I mean, the Nazis torched it, the Soviets mutilated it with graffiti once they'd vandalised the place for souvenirs and it's been stripped of some of its statues as well, but here it is, still standing. What do you reckon, Bridge?"

Mum just stares at the huge edifice the way visitors look at a horribly disfigured hospital patient.

"The graffiti is covered with boards and plaster now," Beate tells us.

"Did it say 'Vladimir woz here'?" Victor asks.

"Worse than that," Beate says, frowning at the rows of blank arched windows.

"Did they write them with felt-tipped pens?"

"No, they used charcoal from the burnt timber lying everywhere," Beate explains. "They made an ugly mess. Nothing in Berlin was safe. But you know, those messages should not be covered. They tell a dreadful story. People should know it."

She turns away and rummages in the pushchair. I hear the chink of glass, the glug and gush of fiery liquid. Dad, wary of Mum's silence, reaches for her hand. "When I first met you, this pile looked like bloody Stonehenge. It's not so bad now they've tidied things up, don't you think, Bridge?"

Mum is still staring ahead, but she takes his hand, interlocking their fingers. "When the war ended," she says, "I saw the view of the Reichstag from across the River Spree. The dome was just bare bones. The building was shattered, rubble all around. I thought it would collapse. Then I noticed its reflection in the water. It seemed untouched there."

Dad squeezes her hand and wraps his other one round it.

"Parliament used to meet here, many years ago. But now we are governed from Bonn," Beate says, her shiny pink face bobbing up from the pushchair. "With the city cut in two, the poor Reichstag has no use now. War has changed its face so often, but each time it keeps something of the past. See the words carved into the stone above the pillars? They say, 'To the German People'. Even through the last war, they have stayed. When the Soviets stormed in, they saw only a Nazi building. The fighting inside lasted two days. And a new, even more terrible time began for Ilse and me."

She sinks onto a bench, wheezing with Emotion, not just from heaving her colossal bulk around in the heat. Dad has to leave Mum and put his arm around Beate's shoulders, like a Chihuahua embracing a Great Dane.

Beate pats the bench beside her and even though there is only an inch of space, I perch on it, my stomach growling from the tang of hot-dogs and onions wafting from a stall. Grandma takes Victor to buy some for everybody and I hear her ask him, "Won't be actual Alsatian in 'em, will there?"

With the colourful stalls and gift-shops enticing them, we won't catch a whiff of our sausage. Grandma could easily swallow three before the Black Forest weather-house gift-shop swallows her.

Beate has heard about my project from Grandma and wants to add her memories. I have left the notepad behind, along with my plans of writing in it, but shooting me a look that says, 'You can't duck out of your mission, you know,' Mum passes me a stack of old shopping-lists and a rickety biro.

I try to make Beate's harrowing words sound like a story about two sisters. But this is no fairy tale.

***

CONTRASTS PROJECT

Beate and Ilse, Berlin, 1945
Part Four - Aggression

During the final air raid, the house opens up like a tin. Beate and Ilse lie in the street beside their neighbour's body, a bleeding dog and their mahogany coat-stand with three jackets still attached to the hooks. Their front door, peppered with holes, leans like a shield against an empty doorway opposite.

People search the rubble, picking up oddments of this and that. Anything found is a fragment of hope, maybe a weapon or just something to hold. Ilse carries a pastry-fork, Beate a book. One man clutches a broken bird-cage and a couple cradle a piece of their child.

Beate discovers their grandfather-clock lying on the pavement. She tries dragging it upright, but Ilse begs her to leave it. The elegant hands that once circled its painted moon-face are broken. They honoured a golden time that has gone now. It will have to be burnt later. People without homes need to keep warm somehow.

They try to sleep on the cold floor of a damaged church. Nothing lights the darkness or protects them from the bitter air. The remaining walls shed cascades of dust, the stone turning to powder. During the night, people die from their injuries. When daylight creeps in at last, Beate and Ilse are among the few still breathing.

"We face another day of this?" Beate asks, her blank eyes staring at the shattered windows.

Ilse, only just seventeen, makes the decision to look after them both. "We may have nothing left, Beate, but here we are. We have woken up again."

They walk through the demolished streets, passing ruins with black, staring holes for windows, breathing air choked with sulphur from artillery fire. They stumble over corpses smothered in blankets of dirt.

Hope eventually arrives—an eight-day ration to celebrate Hitler's birthday. It includes a small tin of vegetables, a little sugar and half an ounce of genuine coffee, although Ilse has no idea how to find hot water or unbroken cups.

To collect the special allowance, they must join a queue that stretches along the street and winds around the corner. While they wait, so weak they must lean on each other, they watch boys of thirteen being forced to join the depleted army and ordered to take pride in dying for their country.

"So, the Third Reich is on its knees, and our little ones must defend Berlin against the advance of Soviet tanks," a man shouts.

"Hitler says they volunteered for the honour," says another.

The first man lowers his voice to reply. "Hitler also says that if they are discovered hiding, these children will be hanged."

Ilse and Beate shuffle forward another inch.

One of the boys, hungry and hopeful, wanders towards the line. Ilse smiles and asks if he has anyone left. This question opens most conversations with strangers. No more, "Good morning", or "How are you?"

"We were living in a tunnel under the canal. My parents drowned in the flood when it was blown up," the boy says.

"Soviets? Or was it the SS who set off the explosion?"

The boy shrugs.

"Then who knows which soldiers to fear?" Ilse asks.

No one answers.

"I have a grenade," the boy tells them.

Ilse gasps. "You have what?"

"I have to put it in the road when the Soviet tanks come through and detonate it when they are seconds away."

"Run for your life, won't you, dear?"

"Can't. I have to stand with it, make sure it goes off."

As he walks away, a single tear slides down his face.

Ilse steps out of line to follow him.

"Oh for God's sake, Ilse, nothing about war is a surprise now," Beate says, pulling her back.

"Well it should be. I shall give some of our ration to those children," Ilse says, pointing at a white-faced huddle of boys in their over-sized army uniforms. "Look at them. They're starving. How can they fight in that state?"

"But what about us?"

"We'll survive," Ilse says. "Trust me. We've come this far."

Hitler's birthday tea over, the linden leaves become too still, too quiet, and the late sun lights the underside of the clouds a sickly gold. The Soviets have already surrounded the gutted city and decide to add to the celebrations with an artillery bombardment into its core. The Allies add an extra present in the form of a colossal air raid.

When the shelling begins, the sisters find a damp cellar beneath a ruined hotel, already littered with shattered glass, plaster and brick. Ilse looks up at the sky for a moment before they hurry down the steps into the pitch-black room, watching the young moon with its ghostly halo, a bright crescent waiting to swell into its next phase.

"Fine accommodation for now," she says inside, spreading a grimy blanket over them both and trying to ignore the rustle and patter of rodent feet. "Who needs fine clocks and silver cutlery when they can have this?"

"Our soldiers will defend Berlin, won't they?" Beate says, resting her head on her sister's shoulder.

"They can try," Ilse tells her. "But they say the Soviets are destroying anything still standing to force their way in ahead of the Allies."

"Our soldiers will protect us." Beate repeats, pursing her lips and trying to plait her hair in the dark.

Ilse sighs. She has listened to the reports. Endless Soviet convoys are poised to thunder into the city.

They stay in their cellar for countless days, listening to the shrieks of the brutal Red Army perched high on their tanks, guns primed. One night, exhausted from lack of food and water, Ilse creeps up the steps to talk to the others hiding in the building.

Returning with a piece of bread, she has news for Beate. "It seems our soldiers fought a bloody battle, literally from room to room, inside the Reichstag itself. But it is the Soviet flag that flies on its roof."

"See. I said we'd fight back," Beate says, smiling and unravelling her hair to plait it all over again.

"No, Beate dear, I'm telling you Berlin has fallen."

"Can I have some bread? They'll bring us coffee soon. Thank God. I'm so tired of living in this cellar and being so hungry. I can taste that coffee, can't you?"

Ilse gives her sister the bread. "I'm afraid hunger isn't our worst danger now, my dear," she whispers.

Ilse blocks the cellar door with anything to hand. She smothers them both with debris until they become a pile of useless rubbish. Bits of wood, scraps of clothes and pieces of broken china are all that shield them from death.

"Not a sound, Beate," Ilse whispers.

Beate whimpers, clinging to her sister and begging God for help.

"Hush," Ilse says. "I'm here."

The pile of rubbish trembles. A half-saucer and a wooden buckle slide off Ilse's hastily-constructed shelter. The small crash on the hard floor echoes throughout the cellar.

"Sh," Ilse says.

"Our soldiers will come," Beate whispers, struggling to keep still.

"Beate, think about the cake you'll bake me when this is over," Ilse mutters. "Check the recipe in your mind. Remember the ingredients, the different weights. How many eggs? How much butter? Think of that, dear."

Nothing else slithers from the pile, although Ilse sweats, convinced the cogwheels of Beate's brain, whirring through pounds of flour and handfuls of almonds, might be audible.

The commotion outside intensifies. Women scream in the house next door. Boots trample through the rubble outside. The butt of a rifle thuds on the cellar door.

6

WAXING MOON

Grandma and Victor come back with greasy serviettes and onion breath, but my mind is too full of questions to ask for a spare frankfurter. Why didn't Beate and Ilse go searching for Mum? As far as they knew, she was still suffocating in her cupboard. She just isn't mentioned at all.

When Mum begged God to raze Berlin to the ground, her prayer was answered. Not by Him, but by the Allied bombers in the air and the storming Soviets who finished the task. She was one of the secret people in a city declared "cleansed of Jews", a victor instead of a victim. So why not reclaim her two "sisters"?

I don't know the answers, but I do know that this city, holding out against all the odds, never stops surprising me. My mission is all systems go again.

Beyond the Reichstag's perfect symmetry, the TV tower soars like a thin rocket in the East. An even harsher landmark, restraining a tide of people, keeping them in as much as keeping us out, is the Wall. People no longer queue for water in Berlin. The normal flow of ordinary life has dried up instead.

A wall is a wall. But this one is different, a prison wall in the middle of a city for ordinary people to be kept apart.

Grey and solid, it is rounded on top, so no one can attach grappling-hooks. People have painted words and pictures on this side. Some of the graffiti is ugly, some is graceful. Most of it seems angry. *Berlin*, someone has painted in huge bubbly writing. Not *West* or *East*, just *Berlin*, to remember the past, or maybe it's just a wish.

"Of course, lots of walls were built to stop invaders," Dad says, trying to soften its impact. "There's your Great Wall of China. And your Hadrian's."

"Yes, lad. But this is the only one built to keep people in," Grandma says. "I shudder to think what it looks like over there," she adds.

I imagine the death strip, raked and smooth, all set to show footprints in the sand.

"Can anyone paint on this?" Victor asks Dad, looking round as if someone might hand him a brush and palette.

"No one's supposed to. They have to be careful, son. The actual border itself is about a yard inside the West."

"So if you're graffiti-ing it this side, you're technically in the other half and they could shoot you?" I ask him.

"Bloody well right, Jacqueline. And you can bet your life there's no graffiti on their side."

Beate is weaving the pushchair on an erratic path through the crowds to the Victory Column. Mum tries to help her, but Beate thrusts out her elbows and ploughs on. Grandma makes us pile into a gift-shop to buy a cuckoo-clock for Elsie. We come out with three fluted ash-trays, a mournful wooden donkey that dispenses cigarettes out of his bum and a wind-up parakeet.

Beate lets her stow the packages in the push-chair, amid much clinking, and they push it together. Grandma lurches over Sebastian every few seconds, cackling like a witch with heartburn. Old people seem hell-bent on alarming babies, but he seems entertained by her, clapping and shouting for more. I'll never understand small people.

"Here it is. Our Victory Column. All sixty-seven metres of her in one piece. Not too damaged, no?" Beate says, puffing and fanning herself as we crane our necks to see the golden statue on top of a monumental, glossy red column.

Everything we see is defined by its damage. According to Victor's guidebook, mutilation creates a "noble survivor", while anything intact is an "unshakable guardian of the city".

"Is she a symbol of peace?" I ask Victor, looking up at the golden figure.

"No, this is about winning wars," he says, consulting the book. "It was going to be just a column, but when they finished building it, they'd won even more battles than when they started. So they bunged her on top as well. She weighs tons and tons. Probably more than Grandma and Beate if they were welded together. The Germans call her Goldelse."

Believe it or not, this triggers one of Mum and Dad's Rows. At least a Very Public Row forces them to keep their voices down, unlike some of their 'private' ones, when they shout at each other at the tops of their voices. Goldelse may have been created to commemorate wars already won, but now she's overseeing a skirmish in full swing.

"So what's Goldelse mean?" Dad asks Mum.

"Well, it translates as Golden Lizzie."

"Why?"

I hear the danger note in Dad's voice. I imagine he uses it when the inmates in D-Wing get out of hand. He becomes the ogre-faced net-casting spider. Meek and mild while he spins his web, dangling it casually between his front legs, but when his prey approaches, he stretches the net to three times its size and casts it, trapping the poor victim inside.

Dad is trapping Mum now, unable to help his ogre-faced tendencies. As Grandma always says, every family keeps a chained beast in the scullery. Visitors never know it's there until the day it slips its leash.

"Because Lizzie is a girl's name, Roy."

"Why not Elsie? Else sounds just like Elsie."

"Because it's Lizzie, Roy."

"I know it's bloody Lizzie. I heard you."

Victor and I step inside the column, leaving Mum and Dad to light cigarettes with their backs to each other.

The pedestal is meant to be decorated with bronze friezes, but Victor's book claims the French took most of them away.

"I bet it was to stop the Germans blowing their trumpets about all the wars they'd won," I say to Victor when he shows me the list of wars that inspired the column. "Especially the Franco-Prussian one," I add, pleased with myself. Victor nods, smiling, and it becomes one of those brotherly-sisterly moments of intellectual understanding. We don't have many.

Beate and Grandma want to look at the friezes, but most of them are just plain granite where the missing ones should be and Grandma says, "Bloody French," several times until it gets a bit embarrassing and eventually they wander off to buy a tub of potato-salad.

"I'm not fond of green though, Bat-Ear."

"Green? Ah, no, Nell. It is quite, quite white."

"No, salad's green, love. Cows and sheep eat salad."

"It has the mayonnaise."

"Oh salad-cream, do you mean? Heinz, is it? Sounds German enough, does Heinz."

Victor and I begin our ascent, leaving the fire-breathing dragons circling each other below us. Thank John Lennon I had enough Deutschmarks stuffed in my sock for the entrance fee. It's the only place to keep money when your mother makes you wear twin-sets—they never have pockets—and you prefer not to draw attention to Tufty's slogan *Set off for school with time to spare* emblazoned on the only bag you have owned from the age of seven. It is also helpful to keep cash in your sock when your father is fond of the gee-gees and knows the combination of your replica bank-safe money-box.

Two hundred and eighty-five steep spiral stairs take us to just below Lizzie or Elsie or whatever the hell she's called. From the viewing platform, even with the wind whipping my hair across my face, the beautiful city is spread out like a pictorial map. People are thunderbugs. Cars are polished ladybirds and beetles. Feeling majestic, I survey the tops of trees, the roofs of buildings and, way down below, the green fringed ribbon that is actually the long, straight sweep of the avenue. The trouble is, I've never climbed higher than Oaking Lido's junior diving-board.

"I can't do this," I tell Victor.

He tries to help me turn around, but I keep gripping the metal grille that stops us stepping into the Berlin sky. I imagine tipping out, gripping Lizzie's golden toes above, but missing them.

"Let go, Jacqueline," he says, sounding as calm as if we are on the ground. I hold tight.

He carries on talking. "They moved it, you know. This whole monument." Has he turned into Grandma?

"The Nazis had it put here and made it taller. It only had three blocks before. They added another one. I'll tell you what, if you take one hand off the bars, I'll tell you why."

I uncoil the fingers of one hand. "Just keep talking," I tell him.

"Hitler wanted to make Berlin into a super colossal city, but he couldn't do much about it because they lost the war. And because he was dead by then."

"Go on. Keep talking."

"Take your other hand off then. I'm freezing up here."

Trembling, I take it off.

"It's made of sandstone."

"Sandstone? Sounds like it could crumble at any moment."

"And it almost got blown up."

Lord alive, it's probably teetering.

He tells me to turn round and I do, but it takes an age.

"The book says moving the column might have saved it because, where it was before, it would have got bombed in the air-raids. Mind you, the French wanted to blow it up after the war. With dynamite. Tons and tons of dynamite. Ker-blam! Ker-runch!"

This human bomb reveals a seven-year-old boy instead of a saviour. Families are such a ruddy disappointment. Old Golden-Toes-Lizzie would be more help.

I am a small fly caught in a huge web. Mum should be here, but if I shout, would she hear? She seems even more distant since she told me her story, but somehow, up here, while she is a pinprick among millions of people, I feel close enough to almost understand.

When I'm with her, the resentment smoulders, but away from her, it cools down, and I can see the scared young woman, not much older than me, who hid in a wall to save her life.

I could ask the other people on the viewing-platform to help me, but apart from beaming occasionally at Victor as if he is actually human, they are absorbed by the spectacle. They probably wouldn't understand me anyway. Are they foreign or am I? That's probably a question for students of the Great Identity Crisis.

At the moment, Victor is my only ally. I would hold his hand if he wasn't so busy detonating.

Once every sandstone segment has been obliterated, he asks, "Are we going now?"

"No, thick-head, I still can't move."

At last, piercing through the German babble and Japanese camera-clicking, I hear a familiar, heaven-sent voice.

"Hold the bus, you lot behind me, I can't go any faster. Don't have much clue how to queue, do you? Now, let the dog see the rabbit. Ooh, wait a sec. I must get my breath first. Ah, there they are. Ooh-hoo, Jacqueline! Victor! Thank the Lord for my buffalo Shebas and my all-day padded corn-plasters. My feet don't hurt at all. Mind you, they only just fitted on those twirly-whirly steps. They should have a proper staircase fitted with decent bannisters. Come on Jacqueline, take my arm, love. I'm a touch dizzy. Oh, strike-a-light, the sky's far too close. Take me back down, duck. We'll go and find your mum."

Grandma knows I'm afraid from the moment she sees my face, which actually feels green. But she must have suspected something was wrong, otherwise she would never have braved all those steps, not in those tight stays. Perhaps the people who love you can work out how you feel, even from a distance.

I recover as soon as we reach the final step. Victor is bursting to tell Mum and Dad I nearly vomited over Victory, and I want to tell Mum I've seen Berlin from the sky. But we just stand about, looking down at the ground and waiting for normality, the way children do when parents are busy hating each other.

"They are not cannons, Roy," Mum is saying.

"They bloody are. Look at them. Cannon barrels that this lot captured from the enemy. I know a cannon barrel when I see one."

"Why do you say 'this lot'?"

"It's just an expression. Same as I'd use for D-Wing."

"Oh, so we are all criminals here. I see."

"Don't be bloody daft. I didn't mean you personally. I didn't even say you. I said 'this lot'."

Ah. The nit-picking has begun. It follows this pattern. They tear at the flesh before stripping it down and sucking the bones. Not a shred of Dignity or Decorum. Yes, Mum, I can read the dictionary too.

"Well I am looking at the one part without cannons," Mum says, screwing up her eyes against the sun. "The part with the golden garlands. You are not seeing the whole column, Roy."

Victor's book settles the matter. "Three of the sandstone chunks are encrusted with gilded cannon-barrels and the fourth, added when they moved the column, is adorned with golden garlands."

"You see," Grandma says. "They do move things."

No one smiles. The Row has cast a shadow over us. I wish the moon could control it, rolling it back like the tides.

"Typical," Dad says. "They had to keep something that glorifies war, didn't they? It's the cannons people notice."

"I didn't," Mum snaps. "I saw the garlands first."

"Well you're a woman."

This Row was probably brewing in England and has rested ever since in the shade like a lion, one eye never fully closed, until Lizzie nudged it awake.

"Women don't start wars."

"Women wouldn't have a bloody country left to live in if men didn't go to war."

"If men never went to war, there would be nothing to worry about."

"But someone always invades."

"I think I know all of this, Roy. Do not tell me."

Beate, rattling and clinking as if she has a pack-horse instead of a pushchair, takes Sebastian to buy an orange juice while we shelter from the sun under a huge tree, one of the long line of lindens I saw from the top of the Victory Column. The Row is contained beneath its beautiful heart-shaped leaves that sound as if they are breathing. Under other lindens, other families might be in the thick of similar rows, although the world I can see through the branches appears to be smiling and licking strawberry ice-creams.

Victor's hand creeps into mine, as Dad reloads his ammunition.

"You like the Wall, don't you, Bridge? You think it's better than war?"

"Roy, how can you? Of course I do not like it."

"But it's brought peace, hasn't it? It's holding back a future no one wants to happen."

"It is a monster, Roy. I do believe that it prevents a worse war, but this isn't the way..."

"So how would a woman do it then, Bridge?"

"I have not the soggiest idea. And I do not wish to discuss it anymore. Except to say that the Wall does not end the suffering. So please do not think it makes me happy. Do not tell me that."

"The past is like a boil never lanced," Grandma says, her Shebas stepping between them with surprising elegance. "The Wall is a plaster. A temporary measure. Not up to the job long-term. It'll sort nothing out."

At least Mum hasn't hurled anything. I always worry they might end up separating once the throwing starts. I did see her pick up the tartan bag at one point, but she held back. Just as well. It contains a full thermos, half a fruit-cake and a ceramic flugelhorn.

If Dad didn't live with us, we'd have even less money. Every Monday at school, the dinner-lady with cauliflower ears and a crew-cut would slap into my hand the special grey dinner-ticket for Pupils Who Can't Pay, grip my shoulders and steer me to the segregated queue clutching their wretched dockets of poverty, waiting miserably for the scraps at the end of second-sitting. But if Mum left us, I'd have to come home and peel potatoes instead of conjugating Latin verbs or lying across the pouffe watching *Blue Peter*. And whoever went, I would miss them.

Mum is tearful, but mothers are not supposed to cry. I try to glare at Dad for hounding her, but I spot The Girls peering over his shoulder, draping their grubby boas over him and smirking at me. Fishnet stockings full of extra holes from cigarette burns stretch over the lardy great thighs of Loretta, Cherie (the one with the cheroot) and seedy Sumatra. (Geography lessons were getting on top of me when I named her.) I wish Dad had suggested tigers, or even kittens. Anything more glamorous or fluffy than shady ladies. But I guess they're the proof of how degraded and grotty the moods make him feel.

"If I had my way," Grandma whispers in my ear, "I'd boot them in the arse, send them flying over Lizzie's-ruddy-Pillar and headfirst into the River Spree."

I don't know if she means the Girls or Mum and Dad, but she adds, "The whole bloody lot of 'em."

I try to give her a nod of agreement, but she knows I'm close to tears, so she shoves a spearmint-chew in my mouth and it's a known fact that you can't cry with your teeth stoppered together.

"Not here of all places, Roy," Mum is pleading. "This is where you rescued me."

"Oh Christ."

"You were leaning against the wreckage of a shop, lighting a cigarette. Remember?"

Terrified of enraging her even more, Dad concentrates on recalling the exact moment. The effort shakes off Loretta and discourages Cherie.

"Of course, Bridge. Your dress was...yellow?"

"Green."

"Yellowy-green, that's it! And I watched you walking along by that..."

"No. I came from behind. I saw you before you saw me."

They both strain at the starting-gates, ready for the off, the odds roughly even. There is silence.

"She hoped he'd remember. But men don't," Grandma whispers. "Sometimes your grandfather couldn't even recall his door key wasn't designed to fit the lock of the Slug and Lettuce."

"Where did you actually get married?" Victor asks them.

This innocent steward's enquiry halts the race in its tracks. Mum looks at Dad. Dad looks at Mum. Neither of them speak, but they both back out of the starting-gate, take off their blinkers and whinny with laughter. With utter relief, we all join in without knowing why.

"Do you mean you can't even remember?" I ask them.

They just keep braying, refusing to answer and somehow end up holding hands. Blood and sand, have we stumbled on another secret? How many more do they expect us to take on?

Grandma looks as if she's swallowed a slice of stale wedding cake, the kind that could, for all the unsuspecting guest knows, consist of dry sand baked with dead flies. For once, she opts for discretion.

"Daft pair," she says. "Let's shut up about it and get going."

The tension of the Row has eased. The Bad-Moon girls have retreated to the wings. The flugelhorn is still intact. We emerge from the trees, find Beate and plunge back into the bright, bustling life of the city until a policeman scolds Dad for trying to hurry us all across a road before the green man flashes.

"Bloody hell, the Nazis never left," he mumbles, clamping a cigarette between his lips while we turn back and cluster at the kerb to wait for red to turn green. Beate could have warned us, but she is glassy-eyed, whether from thoughts of the past or the miniature bottle labelled *Kirschwasser* clanking about in her bag, I'm not sure.

I sit next to her in the train taking us to the main square, Breitscheidplatz, ready to hear the next part of her story. Sebastian clambers onto my lap, reminding me of Victor at three, when he used to be almost sweet.

***

CONTRASTS PROJECT

Beate and Ilse, Berlin, 1945, Part Two
Part Five - Resignation

The cellar door shatters. Ilse and Beate try not to breathe. They listen to the crunch of boots in the rubble, the soldier panting close to their hiding-place and the thunderous echo when he clears his throat. Now they can smell him.

The rifle smashes into their pile, again and again, until it finds the soft, trembling centre of Beate's body. The soldier shouts in triumph.

But Ilse smashes her way out. "Leave her. Whatever you want, I'll take her place."

The young soldier's bewildered eyes are bloodshot and his breath reeks of Schnapps. Ilse keeps talking. She steers him away from Beate, encouraging him into the darkest corner. The talking ends. Beate stays rigid in the rubbish pile, listening to her sister submit to the enemy and praying they will both survive the night.

The next morning, both sisters crave daylight. Beate helps Ilse to crawl outside, covering her with a tattered tablecloth. Other women are rubbing soot on their skin, desperate to look unappealing, but for now, the Soviet soldiers are busy ransacking the shops. Among those standing guard over the spoils littering the road is the young man from last night. Ilse ducks out of sight, shaking.

"I'm all right," she says to Beate. "I am still alive."

"Look, food," Beate says, tugging at what is left of Ilse's sleeve.

"Not for us," Ilse whispers, her raw, swollen lips thickening her words. "They'll shoot."

"Ilse, what you did for me last night..."

"Stop. We have another day to face. Just don't cry. We have no strength left for that."

"Our soldiers will come, Ilse. They won't let us down."

The Soviets set up soup kitchens and water hydrants. The survivors watch and wait, weighing up the danger of starvation against the acts of savagery that happen in broad daylight and without warning.

"Keep your head down, Beate," Ilse whispers, crouching low. "We'll crawl to the hydrant later. Let's wait until dark."

But Beate stands up. "Water," she says, as if she sees champagne.

Ilse, wincing with pain, struggles to pull her sister down beside her. The water, only fifty yards away, might as well be on another planet.

"Be quiet, Beate," she hisses, watching the soldiers. "They appear from nowhere, from everywhere. Look how they move, like angry ogres. No grace and no mercy."

Beate has found a rusty bucket, shot through with holes. The handle creaks in the wind.

"Try to keep that thing quiet," Ilse whispers. "But thank God we have it."

"It isn't ours though, Ilse. Ours was a fine steel. It matched the watering-can I used for watering the vegetable patch."

"Well there's a new kind of ownership now, Beate. Take what you can and guard it with your life."

"Oh God in heaven, look!" Beate says. "Gherkins, Ilse!"

"We aren't risking any more of my virtue for gherkins, dear."

"But I can already taste them."

"Good. Keep it that way. Imaginary pickles are safer. That brute we had the misfortune to encounter last night has opened the jar to tempt us out. But we haven't stooped that low yet."

Beate scratches her head, her dishevelled plait so infested with lice, it moves of its own accord. "You know," she says, "the Hitler Youth would have driven this rabble out. No woman would have been torn to pieces."

"For God's sake, don't forget the horror," Ilse whispers. "We had to turn Birgit out. She's probably dead. And what about cowering in the shelter and finding nothing left of our parents, nothing we could recognise? Being alive is a miracle. The Third Reich is over. So, no more talk of the past. Let's turn our backs on it now."

"I can't forget Rainer."

"I know, but don't make him some sort of golden symbol rising out of the blood and mess. He was another casualty of a regime that treated none of us like humans."

"Remember the wonderful cakes I made for him?"

"Oh dear God, I could never forget, dear."

"I had found the man I loved. And then *she* came."

"Birgit is yet another victim of the times. We all are. But you and I are lucky. We're still here to see if the future can improve on the past."

"I still say the Hitler Youth group was the ideal community, Ilse. Learning to bake, to look after children, swimming in the cold lakes on Saturday mornings. Everything that would equip us for the perfect existence. I had such faith in it."

Ilse tips back her head and laughs quietly. "You were always stubborn, Beate."

"But you loved it too."

"No, I just endured it as I'm enduring this life now."

Beate shakes her head. "I thought it would go on forever."

"It was fatally flawed, my dear, being based on exterminating everyone who didn't fit."

"The future isn't worth having now," Beate says, gazing into the distance as if Rainer will materialise, bearing coffee and strudel.

"We aren't dead, Beate," Ilse says, touching her sister's shoulder. "We just don't know how to look ahead yet."

After dark, the sisters are able to smile at the sound of water as they scoop it from the bucket at last. They settle with relief in their new cellar, which is so damp, filthy and infested with vermin that no one else has tried the door yet. Hope returns in the form of these small miracles.

As the long days pass, despite the yells of the cold-hearted Red Army and the tormented screams of women, the faintest wind of peace approaches the city.

The sisters wake in the morning and watch the sun climb up the sky. They huddle on the remains of a bench in an unrecognisable park and later find a mattress in an old air-raid shelter. Wretched though it is, it has to be enough. Ilse talks about old luxuries; soap and milk, cushions and music. "Don't torture me with your goose-feathers and rose-scented lather," Beate complains, still trawling her memory for recipes she will make again one day. Ilse tips her head back to laugh quietly about it all, because there can be nothing worse to come.

Small battles over food break out, but the survivors have little appetite for more fighting. Poverty and disease have made neighbours hard to recognise, but they hope to become old friends again.

Everyone takes what they can. A scrap of looted blanket is a blessing. Half a book is bliss. Sometimes the day brings nothing but crouching in a bombed-out doorway, famished and frozen. Sometimes it brings joy.

"Hey, Beate," Ilse might say. "That Red beast with the breath of Satan, he has not made me pregnant. I must have died and gone to Heaven."

Ilse tries in vain to keep Beate out of sight of the soldiers. All she can do is warn her that struggling against brute force is pointless.

"If you resist them again, biting and kicking, they will kill you. The only way to survive is to be tolerant."

Beate learns to be docile.

When you have nothing, the ordinary takes on a new status. A morsel of meat and a cup of water become a bowl of soup.

One day, they cut up a cow. They are drenched in its blood, desperate to bite into the raw flesh. Its stench turns into the sweetest perfume. No one knows where it came from or who killed it. An old lady keeps begging for a piece of its tongue or a slice of its liver. Ilse and Beate become butchers, unaware they possessed such a skill, just as Ilse didn't know she could pacify a soldier threatening to run her through with a wooden broomstick. They never view themselves as exceptional. Desperation has become resignation, turning ordinary people into unflinching survivors.

Beate treasures her book and Ilse guards her silver pastry-fork. She wipes it every day on the hem of her dress, only taking it out of her pocket after dark.

"The way it feels in my hand, the texture of its engravings, remind me of home," she tells Beate "No one's cutlery is the same as your own."

When other people take their own lives and Beate asks if she and her sister should do the same, Ilse insists they must have no intention of missing the future.

"I once asked Birgit if we would die and the answer was no. Let's hold her to it."

The water is still pumping. Food can be found. The Allied forces will soon arrive to reconnect the pieces of the city.

***

In the centre of Breitscheidplatz, the jagged silhouette of the rugged Kaiser Wilhelm Memorial Church takes pride of place in the middle of the road. Immensely tall and elegant, its dark, distorted steeple was damaged by bombs during the war and looks like a giant's broken, hollowed-out tooth.

"Almost elegant, the breakage," Dad says. "Defiant really."

"Yes, isn't it?" Mum agrees.

"Gallant and unflinching," he goes on, looking over Victor's shoulder at the guide-book.

Grandma pitches in. "Looks like it needs a good patching up to me, son."

"No, Ma. It's best to leave well alone."

"Berliners asked that it should please stay like this," Beate says. "It has survived in this broken state and we catch our breath every time we see it. I remember when we thought it would fall."

"A memorial," Mum says, no doubt remembering its former, intact elegance. My throat swells a bit when I hear her sigh.

"A hopeful sight, yes?" Beate says, looking at me. "This city is used to hoping, especially since the Wall."

"It's always best to turn your back on a bad place and keep it behind you," Grandma says. "Down Widgery Lane there's a tramp who might read your palm for a bag of salted peanuts and a squirt of eau de Cologne, but then he…"

I give Grandma a toffee and concentrate on the squat modern chapel and soaring hexagonal tower that have been built beside Kaiser Wilhelm.

"Like grandchildren grown almost taller than their grandmother," Dad reads from the book. "Berliners have christened these two additions the powder box and lipstick, as if the old church just needs sprucing up. A dusting of rouge for the old woman, a waft of powder to coat the cracks."

"Enough of the old woman, son," Grandma says, pursing her lips around her Senior Service. "And those new bits look like pre-fabs to me."

It is true. The powder and lipstick buildings are actually made of prefabricated concrete, like great slabs of honeycomb with thousands of tiny inlaid blue-glass windows. But even though they seem like structures from the space-age, our eyes are drawn back to Kaiser Wilhelm with his, or should it be her, lost pinnacles and teetering arches.

"Losing a bit of height won't stop her," Dad says, his arm across Mum's shoulders. "You can see her blemishes, but this old girl lives on and on."

Grandma, cheesed off with old lady comparisons, blows her smoke in his face.

Breitscheidplatz has a strange beauty. The old and new merge together, the wrecked and the renewed side by side. New offices, high-rise blocks and a massive shopping complex loom over the decayed and damaged buildings. And despite being surrounded by the new season's bikinis, this one stricken church is the most striking of them all, its chipped-tooth spire showing the terrible price of war.

We walk to the Europa-Center, a huge, boxy shopping mall beside a glassy tower topped by the Mercedes trademark, a colossal metal star within a circle, visible across Berlin.

"The Mercedes star spins," Beate says. "And it glows at night. In a storm, it turns into the wind for protection. It can never break. Never be moved."

It must outshine any ordinary star at night, a symbol of prosperous, brand-new West Berlin stamped in the sky.

Inside the silky newness of the monstrous shopping complex, the elderly ruins of the city disappear, as if the doors open into a futuristic world. Mum looks startled, Grandma guarded and Dad terribly small and grey in his dog-tooth Home Stores sports jacket. Victor and I have never set foot in a shop larger than Spotwood and Mole on Oaking Parade, where Grandma once lost us in Ladies' Separates and was almost arrested for helping herself to fig-rolls in the staff restroom.

When I overcome my fear of heights, I will transform into Tuesday. *Dienstag* in German. Doesn't have quite the same ring to it. Tuesday will flourish her shorthand pencil in one of the top-floor offices of the Mercedes tower, with a view of every corner of the city, answering a purring telephone at a glass desk by one of the long windows and so far from ground level that no one could possibly look up her mini skirt.

The intimidating boutiques with wall-to-wall psychedelic patterns throb with music and are jam-packed with women like Amazons in their stilettos and bee-hives. Not one twin-set. Dad asks if I want to have a look, but I feel as if I'm ten years old, three feet tall, and my socks have plummeted to my ankles. I prefer fashion between the covers of a magazine. If I could be transported to Spotwood and Mole and given a ten shilling note for a fair-isle pullover, I would be in clover.

"No thanks," I tell Dad and he gives me a brief grin of relief.

But the exhausting, endless maze of a hundred shops, teeming with a million people and two million damp armpits, attract Grandma like iron filings to a magnet. We have to restrain her. There are only so many ash-trays a family needs.

"It'd be handy to put one on the corner of the bath, Roy. How about that statue of the widdling boy. Look, you stub your cigarette out in his little puddle."

Dad ignores her, probably desperate to leave the shop so he can light up.

"Can we get something to eat now?" Victor pleads, dragging his feet.

"It is not time for Sebastian to eat. Not for ten minutes," Beate says.

"Ooh you're a slave to your schedules, Beattie," Grandma tells her. "Come on. At least take the weight off your bunions and get a banger butty inside you. Will this café have proper sausages, d'you think, love?"

"What an enormous place," Mum says, glancing at Dad while Grandma locates a café.

Silence.

"There's even an ice-rink, Roy."

No response. Not that Dad's ever strapped on a skate in his life.

In the café, Sebastian whines for his white rabbit then throws it at a nun drinking from a water-fountain. After delving in the pushchair, Beate tips the contents of a tiny bottle of Schnapps into her coffee. Victor is fiddling with the disgusting bits and pieces that breed in his duffle-bag. One day, it will walk off on its own. Last time I dared look, I found a pre-historic apple-core, a picture of Franz Beckenbauer with his front teeth blacked out and a flattened shrew.

"I'm going for a wander first, Bridge," Grandma says while we wait for our food. "It does my knees no good to sit about on these plastic chairs. Do the Germans not know about foam rubber?"

"Not on your own, Nell, surely? You will get lost."

"Oh, I'll not go far."

"But your corns?"

"Jacqueline can give my feet a rub later."

Bloody ugh.

And off Grandma goes, a seasoned tourist, her white cardigan draped over one arm. Mum looks as if she's been deserted and left for sacrifice.

The atmosphere is stifling. No one can breathe. The café clanks and clatters around us. A ceiling-fan stirs the air, thank Ringo, but the breeze barely reaches us. Mum prattles on, fanning herself with the guide book, watching Dad all the time.

"This building used to be a beautiful Romanesque patisserie. Do you remember, Beate?" she says. "It had two pretty towers and rows of arched windows."

Beate gives her a stiff nod, but doesn't chime in with a memory, so Mum keeps trying.

"It was such a charming meeting-place for artists and poets and actors before everything changed."

"It looks much more charming now," Beate says, slurring her words and wiping her moustache.

"It was 1943 when the Nazis stormed the café," Mum drones on. "Friends of my parents were here." Her voice trails away. She looks around, as if a group of pensive bearded men in smocks, paintbrushes tucked behind their ears, might replace the sun-tanned family in shorts at the next table. I would kill to be wearing a sun-dress instead of this twin-set. It's like living inside a kiln.

Mum reaches for Dad's hand, but he doesn't notice her hold it between hers. I try not to look at him. I don't want to see Loretta, Cherie and seedy Sumatra vying to light his Woodbine.

Instead I imagine canvases and fountain-pens and paints scattered across this floor, trampled by a hundred jack-boots, a flurry of artists trying to escape through the massive glassy entrance, the echo of the doors slamming shut.

"You know, Birgit, it was the Allied air-raids, not the German troops that destroyed the building," Beate says.

"But an era had been lost, no matter which side caused the damage."

"A circus used to perform in the ruins," Beate continues, ignoring Mum. "Then two days after the Wall went up, this magnificent place was built to remind the world that Berlin had come alive again. It shows the East how good life is here. Better than just survival. But it is not a symbol for the whole city."

"I do not look at it that way, Beate. This is still my Berlin. I see the signs left by the war, but I do not see the division at all."

Beate pushes her cup away, slopping coffee into the saucer. "I wish I could watch my Ilse's face if you say that to her tomorrow. You will never understand, Birgit, how hard it is to live here. We have to be so strong. Survival is exhausting."

"I know all about that, Beate."

"No. Not like this. You missed the worst of it."

No one knows what to say. I'm sweating from the tension as well as the heat. The awkward silence around the table is smothered by the air-conditioning system finally bursting into life, but the blast of cool air causes a startled guinea-pig in a pink tutu to leap out of Victor's duffle-bag.

Mum and I squeal. People at nearby tables nudge one another as if we're hired entertainment. The wretched creature scuttles about, knocking over cups and depositing disgusting pellets like greenish liquorice torpedoes all over our serviettes. Good job the sausages aren't here yet.

Victor grasps the animal at last and thrusts it at Mum in a pathetic attempt to endear her to it. She backs away, resisting the temptation to throttle him.

"Konnie said it likes going out," Victor says, stroking the horrible animal. It smirks at us with its yellow teeth, baring them like a row of sweetcorn kernels.

Mum marches Victor outside. "I shall take this little beast back to the house," she says. I assume she's referring to the guinea-pig, but who knows?

She strides outside, her old city beckoning. "I am Berlin," she might be saying, a tad more accurately than President Kennedy did. Victor has given her the perfect escape. Who says a geriatric guinea-pig doesn't have a silver lining? This one even has sequins.

I imagine Mum peering round old corners, slipping into side-streets, revisiting the old life without Beate directing her. I hope she doesn't go to Bernauer Strasse with Victor instead of me.

On schedule, Sebastian eats his jar of small-boy food and falls asleep in his clammy pushchair. I'm enlisted to rock it backwards and forwards while Beate wanders to the Ladies, sailing back in a cloud of peachy vapour. She even pours something clear into a hollow in Sebastian's dummy. As he falls sleep, he sucks the strong-smelling liquid through the rubber teat. Gripe water? Ten-to-one it's gin.

We spend the afternoon waiting for Mum and Grandma. Only Beate eats, nodding and pursing her lips with approval when the food arrives at one o'clock sharp. Crumbs fly from her bread over Sebastian's head and she sweeps them out of his hair with a soft brush she keeps in her bag.

"I found it in a hairdresser's shop after the bombings," she tells me. "It was for sweeping the cut hairs that fell on the customers' shoulders. It was the only thing still in one piece. A broken scissor also I took, for protection and for cutting up dead animals. I can never forget the smell of the animals frying on a fire in the ruins."

I begin writing on my scrap of paper, but it might not be big enough to list the many pieces of Beate that will never be fixed.

"My Sebastian, he has lovely hair, no? Just like Ilse's. You know, Jacqueline, somehow we survived the worst, Ilse and I. Never apart. And here, at last, we have something to celebrate. We have my son. But she cannot hold him, not even touch this soft, soft hair that is so like hers."

To distract her from plucking at the poor child's curls, I ask her what she and Ilse used to do together before the Wall.

"Ah, Jacqueline, it was heaven back in the fifties. We shopped on the Stalin Boulevard. Anything we could not buy there could not be bought anywhere. A huge sign showed the sun shining on the jolly folk of East Berlin, with West Berlin under cloud. Music played from loudspeakers and loud messages were announced. 'Workers, raise your standards!' We drank good coffee and strong Romanian beer. Jolly folk, we certainly were."

I look up, but the memory of the Romanian beer has sent her scrabbling for her hip-flask and soon she is weeping over Sebastian's head, remembering the day he was born.

"My labour lasted two days. My body had never mended from the damage a Soviet soldier did on our last night in the cellar, almost twenty years before. Because I was shaking so badly during the birth, the hospital bed rocked across the floor and the nurses had to tie my hands and feet to the bed-frame. It felt like being in the cellar again and I screamed for Ilse until the baby was born. He was blue. It took the doctors hours to save me and days to give hope for Sebastian.

"Two weeks later I could wait no longer. I dressed over my gown and went with the baby to the Wall. I could not telephone Ilse because the lines in the East were cut. I asked a policeman to stand with me and borrowed a stepladder from a builder. For the first time, as I shouted my sister's name into the silence, I saw how bare and desolate it was on the other side. I called out the address that was once mine too and that she drove a tram. I even shouted the name of the café where I hoped she still drank her coffee. At last a woman went to look for her.

"After two hours, Ilse was standing on two crates to see Sebastian through a pair of binoculars. After one minute, a guard told her to climb down. She blew her nephew a kiss. There could be no more.

"The only people released from East Germany are the very old, those no longer useful to the state. There is no hope of freedom for someone as strong and hard-working as Ilse until she becomes a burden to them. Then she will come to me and Sebastian, if we survive that long."

Beate falls silent for a moment and we just sit there in the hot crush of bodies.

"My husband was a broken man long before Sebastian was born," she says, her voice cracking. "You know, the first time I met him, his quiet voice and the way he smoked a cigarette reminded me of Rainer. He was not my Rainer of course, but he was a man I could care for. I had hope at last, Jacqueline, because I could see he had none left. This was my chance to look after someone more damaged than me."

It was too late for Beate's brood of eight and in any case, there were no medals for that anymore. But her dream of looking after a family of her own had never wavered.

She can hardly go on. I just about grasp that, unlike all other husbands the world over, hers wasn't chain-smoking in the corridor during the labour. He passed out. By the time the baby let out its first, weak cry, he was in the Emergency department three floors below with a swelling on his temple. The nurses tried to make a joke of it, but Beate knew he was beginning to fade.

I pass her a hanky and while she talks, she bunches it between our hands.

"The night after his father died, I went outside with our baby to show him the full moon. It lit up the whole street. A piano was playing in one of the flats and it reminded me of the times when Rainer visited every day and I watched him dance with Ilse and Birgit. The music kept taking me back further, to the safer time before Birgit came. I knew I must stop thinking about the past, but what was left? The Wall had taken me from Ilse, and the war had destroyed my husband and parents. My life was in pieces, but I had this beautiful child, who deserved a future. I told him this great, bright moon was shining on both sides of the Wall, but as I said the words, it was impossible for me to believe it."

Although Miss Whipp will love the part about the miracle of birth (grimmer aspects removed), Beate's story is one of the saddest contrasts so far; the pain of separation scoring through the joy of a new baby.

I think about her calling for Ilse over the Wall, across the death-strip, her voice echoing down those miserable streets, and how she drinks syrupy wine for breakfast now, barely a survivor at all.

"Do you think you'll ever be allowed to visit Ilse one day?" I ask, a bit choked.

She keeps hold of my hands while she answers. "Passes for West Berliners are hardly ever given, Jacqueline. Two years after the Wall came, they did open the checkpoints at Christmas, but not all of us were allowed a pass. There was no good reason. And this summer, no passes were given to West Berliners."

She sighs and takes out a cigarette. Dad actually reaches across the table to light it for her, cupping his warm hands around hers. I could hug Beate for helping him stay connected, if only by a thread.

Since the East Germans make things up as they go along, Gillian should be a member of their secret police. Once, to duck out of playing rounders, she pretended she had an iron lung, not realising it was a breathing machine you climbed inside. She thought it was a metal body part that could be implanted. Miss Monger shook her head, muttered, "No wonder you struggle to hit the ball, dear," and sent her out to bat first.

Children are useful for wiping your fingers on. They don't seem to mind. I used to mop jam off my hands on Victor's rompers. Beate picks Sebastian up, settles him on her lap and leans over him, possibly for sausage-grease absorption, but mostly for drying her eyes.

She is also singing softly to him. And although she is way off-key, and he must be sozzled by the fumes, not to mention the gin-dummy, it seems to soothe him. And despite this being an unscheduled moment, she looks perfectly at home.

When Mum appears, with Victor grinning beneath a green feathered hat and clutching a miniature cone of sweets, I sense her becoming herself again. Her appendix isn't even growling. She links arms with Dad, trying to blast him with her fizzing joy, but he doesn't look up. The thread is beginning to fray. She had better not break it.

"Thank you for taking me home," she says. But he says nothing.

The atmosphere is edgier than during a row, especially without Grandma here to distract anyone. While we wait for her, Beate and Victor stuff sweets and push Sebastian around our table, the glory of West Berlin forgotten. We could be anywhere at all.

A shaft of artificial air wafts a cobweb on a pillar. The spider panics. His legs buckle, his silk tightrope all that exists between safety and the unknown. A breeze can sometimes help a spider by catching up the first thread of the spin and fastening it wherever it happens to land, but it depends which way the wind is blowing.

The air-conditioning breaks down again, allowing the web to settle and the spider's legs to slacken. While he surveys the damage, Grandma arrives at last, thank the Fab Four. I notice she's wearing her best lipstick, the way she always does for special occasions, like a small red bow-tie in the centre of her mouth.

I wish I could say, "I missed you." But we never talk like that, especially not to Grandma. She sits on the hard chair she wouldn't sit down on before and lights a Senior Service. No one asks if she's all right. Mum and Dad are too bound up inside their own bubbles. When Sebastian starts fidgeting in his push-chair as if he's fighting his way out of a strait-jacket, Beate marches us all back for dinner.

I sit next to Grandma on the bus.

"Lawks, don't these German drivers put their foot down? Oh, I've gone and sat on my little Fräulein, and her head's only made of mashed paper, bless her." Out of her cardigan she pulls a hideous crimson-lipped doll in wooden shoes.

"Grandma, she's terrifying, like the posters of Bette Davis in *Whatever Happened to Baby Jane.*"

"Ooh, I might call her Jane. Thanks, love."

"But her lips are all smudged and her eyes are wonky."

"Well you can't expect much from a market stall full of rejects. And there's a two-vinegar coin in her apron pocket."

"It's two pfennige, Grandma."

"That's what I said, duck. Now, where were we with this project of yours? I know, Stan and me were having tea and I made him eat a bit of my boiled fruit-bun because he looked so pale. He tried to tell me how those Jewish kiddies on the train must have felt to lose their home and be sent so far away. But he couldn't. Clammed right up, he did. But, you know, folk say a lot without talking."

And folk with a mouthful of Grandma's boiled fruit-bun have a non-functioning jaw anyway.

Grandma takes off her glasses, rubs them on her cardigan and goes on.

"Anyroad, Stan stopped for a bit of dinner. Lincoln-pea soup, rabbit pie and mash, it was. And as it was December, my box of Christmas decorations was on the table. I can see him now, touching a worn bit of old tinsel..."

Grandma pauses with the memory, swallowing hard before she carries on.

"Stan said, 'Never had a Christmas of course, those children.' And he looked as if he wanted to take that tinsel back to the station, pile it into their arms and give them ten Christmases all at once.

"'Did Santa not come to the orphanage then?' I asked him.

"'Well, it was a Jewish orphanage, Nellie,' he said.

"'Santa a Nazi? Dear oh dear,' I said. 'What's the world coming to when kiddies can't have Christmas?'

"Anyroad, Stan was trying to get a grip on hisself, and I knew the best thing was to give him something useful to do, things your grandfather never did for me. So he got my Ascot working and let out all his upsetment trying to bash my mop-cupboard properly shut with the meat-mallet."

"Grandma, that door's still all crooked now."

"I know, Jacqueline. Your grandfather fetched it off its hinges, three sheets to the wind, and after that it was never quite right. Mind you, neither was he. Not after I whacked him one with my decorative ladle from Clacton."

"The Nazis should have come to England, Grandma. You'd have fought them off single-handed."

"Well I did my bit, duck, during the Blitz. Tch, those Doodlebugs were buggers. No mess like it. I was having none of it, so I joined the ambulance service with Elsie. Can you imagine her ladyship in overalls checking tyres? Oh, did she ever stop bleating? But I took to it from the first day. Drove this bad-tempered Ford V8 with its arse-end sawn off and a tarpaulin over. *Ersatz* emergency vehicle, it was called. That's me speaking me English all posh-like of course."

"Did you have to operate on injured people?" I ask, handing her a biscuit from a packet we bought in the Center.

"Good Lord no, dear. We just ferried them to the makeshift hospital. It was too much for Elsie in the end. She caved in when the depot gave us a rollicking for reporting back without our full kit. Well, we knew fine well we couldn't afford to lose two blankets. Trouble was, most of the poor young mother we'd been tending was stuck to them, you see. Rendered down to the bone, she was. Looked like the end of the day on Stan's meat counter."

"Oh, Grandma, don't."

"Well, that's how it was. No good getting all droopy-drawered. Elsie was sent home with her blubbering. She'd thought she'd be tucked away in the depot cellar until the raids were over, not driving out to the injured as soon as the bombs dropped. But that's when people needed saving, you see, love. We had to be at the sharp end. Of course it was all a big upsetment. But it weren't Elsie's baby still lying in that poor young mother's arms, was it? And it weren't her toddler that was blown clean into the fireplace. She took that bad. We all did. But it was a case of either cave in or cope. My job was to find the hearts still beating and keep 'em that way. Elsie was no more use than a lace umbrella."

"Horrible," I say, sounding pathetic because I can't imagine the horror.

"More hopeless than horrible, she was," Grandma says.

"I mean the Blitz, Grandma."

"Oh, the Blitz. Yes," she says. "Christ alive, call these biscuits? More like week-old cat-litter. But it wasn't all sad, you know, love. Put that in your project for Miss Whippet. One night we found an old man crying. He couldn't find his wife because their street had just been blown to bits. People were staggering around, all confused. He just stood there in his dressing-gown and slippers, waiting. I held his arms, trying to coax him into the ambulance, and blow me down, he said, 'There she is. There's my Joan.' Sure enough, a woman covered in muck was being pulled from the rubble further down the street. Even from that distance we could see a part of her face had gone. 'Are you sure?' we said. 'Course,' he said. 'She can never stop her stockings crumpling. I'd know them wrinkly ankles anywhere.'

"They were reunified for a full five minutes before she seemed to pass on, and by way of a thank you for making her tidy-like, the poor man fried me his week's quota of best streaky on a coke brazier. But just as I took the first bite, I saw Joan's eyelids flicker and gave her the kiss of life. I didn't get to finish my rasher while it was still hot, but I'm glad to say I saved her bacon."

While Grandma searches for her Trebor Mints, I realise she was doing all that life-saving while Dad was away fighting. She never knew if she'd come home to the dreaded telegram and was never sure if 31 Audette Gardens wouldn't be the next house blown to bits.

"So where have you been today, Grandma?"

"I tried to find the burnt-down orphanage, love, on the off chance they'd have rebuilt it."

"Why on earth did you do that? And you don't even know any German."

"I just wanted to give them something. Stan had told me the street name from the labels the orphans wore round their necks. But I went round in circles, duck. I would have asked a policeman, but they aren't terribly approachable here. Not in those long boots and jodhpurs."

"So what did you do?"

"I gave up, duck," Grandma says, sighing. "There I was with three white matinee jackets, ten pairs of assorted bootees and an apricot layette. But not an orphan in sight."

"You knitted things for German orphans?"

"Well they weren't for Khrushchev, duck."

As the bus glides towards Schillerpark, Grandma crunches her mint and I wonder where exactly she deposited the baby clothes.

"I was about to leave them on the steps of some great building where the steps were swarming with young city gents," she says, reading my thoughts.

"Since my rib-stitch is second to none, I thought they could take them home to their deserving wives."

"Do they have city gents in Berlin, Grandma?"

"Not our kind with a bowler hat and a well-rolled brolly, they don't." She takes another mint and ponders for a moment. "In the end, I happened to see a pram parked outside a shop and I'll tell you this for sixpence-five farthings, the baby inside it was wearing a very ill-fitting jacket and a bonnet that put me in mind of a worn-out tea-cosy. So I did the poor mite a favour and piled all my woollies on his pram hood."

I let her pat my hand because I can tell how chuffed she feels to have made this gesture for Stan.

"Batty's going to boil me a duck egg in the morning, you know," she says. And when I smile at her, she looks so happy, I slide out my hand to give hers a pat too.

Back in the flat, Beate makes the rabbits a newspaper parcel of cabbage leaves as if she's wrapping a present. She lumbers to the hutch with Axel, his toe-nails tapping on the concrete, but when she wanders back in with the dog grinning beside her, she's still clutching the damp parcel of newspaper. Her speech is so garbled from all the Schnapps glugging out of the bottle while she hacks at the meat for dinner, no one, not even Mum, can understand her.

I don't blame Beate. Mum has invaded her family again. Tomorrow, she can even nip across the border to hug the sister who isn't really hers.

"Ever used sheets and blankets, Bat?" Grandma shouts from the table where Sebastian is sitting on her vast lap and bashing her necklace against her mountain-range of a bosom. "They're what you need to make up a proper bed, love. Bridge said you all learnt it in Hitler's Youth Club. Where these quilts came from, I don't know. It's like lying under a ruddy cloud. You make a good scone though, Bat."

They are more like puffy rounds of fried bread sprinkled with sugar, but whatever Beate does, Grandma seems to like it better than anything Mum cooks at home. I think it's because Mum tries to cook English food while Beate has been practising her beloved old recipes and made some of them quite edible. That and the fact that Beate uses masses of butter. No better way to soften up Grandma.

Konnie hurries in from his shift with maps for Mum and me.

"Konnie show you zee ghosts of Berlin," he says, spreading them out on the table and earning a grimace from Beate because our places are already set. Pie-eyed or not, the schedule continues, more regimented than Victor's tin cavalry.

"Trains on tracks between Vest and East must stop at zee border and turn back. But some vestern lines in the city centre pass through a short piece of East Berlin. No trains can stop there."

On our map of the West, a footnote refers to "stations at which the trains do not stop." These 'ghost-stations' are even crossed out, as if they no longer exist. On the East Berlin subway maps, no western lines or ghost-stations are shown, as if they have never existed at all.

"Sometimes people hide in zee ghost-stations," Konnie explains. "Zee doors in our German trains can open when the train is still moving, even wiz top speeds. But zee train, he go so slow through ghost-stations that someone hiding in the shadows can jump on, if zey ask a friend on the train to open door quick. It is one way out of the East to the Vest. But always there stands a guard on the platform with gun, waiting and watching."

I imagine the roof dripping, the echo of the splashes, the glow of the guard's cigarette. Mum is studying the street-plan, her finger hovering over the thick pinkish shading that encircles West Berlin, and Konnie doesn't need to explain that. She steps back from the table, and he folds the maps as if he's collapsing the bricks of the Wall, managing to make them small and square again. Dad should learn how to do that, but at the moment he is wandering in the courtyard alone.

In one of those rare useful moments, just as the steam from the stewing meat makes me feel queasy, Mum asks me to go for a walk with her.

I hesitate on purpose, keeping her waiting even though I know where she wants to take me. I want to go there too, but I still can't forgive her. Even if I swallow the bile now, it will come back, more bitter than a grudge.

A grudge is what Gillian bore after Pamela and Derek took Gaye and me to see *The Sound of Music*. For three weeks afterwards, she clapped her hands over her ears whenever she saw us. Mind you, we did keep singing "High on a Hill Stood a Lonely Goatherd", especially the yodelling bits.

But I feel something else as well. An Emotion. A warm feeling. Not the kind I feel about Peter. Sympathy, I suppose it is, the kind I felt when Gillian had her mouth washed out, until the Schadenfreude arrived.

I don't have the heart to say no. Beate is being monopolised by Grandma and Dad by his loony lunar Girls. Victor and Sebastian are kneeling on the couch, apparently flying a Messerschmitt. The guinea-pigs would be better company.

"All right," I say, and Mum and I walk to Bernauer Strasse together.

It is unmissable with its hacked tenements and rubble spilling out onto the pavement, forcing us into the gutter. Railings protect what is left of the once-tall houses, all of them chopped to ground-floor level. But despite the disturbing bleakness, the majestic line of trees makes me walk in a dead-straight line. The wind has taken their seed to grow saplings in the empty space behind the façades. If you look straight ahead, not glancing at the beheaded buildings, you could believe this is an ordinary stroll with your mum on a summer's day.

But the street is too quiet and still, these ordinary homes like ours, and the workplaces that were once busy all day, now part of a solid barricade. The rough brick squares were once windows. The boarded doors used to open and close a hundred times a day. I imagine the lives of the past still inside the rooms that are left, caught in time beneath decaying layers of wallpaper or under buckled lino. The sky here once turned brown with coal-fire smoke in winter.

In summer, housewives out shopping in their short sleeved frocks paused to talk, resting their baskets on this pavement.

"It feels as if the war never ended here," Mum says.

I agree, noting the guards on the watchtower on the other side and their huge flood-lamps that must make the nights strangely strip-lit.

We hear voices behind us and turn round to see a group of men in suits. Some are English, visiting for a conference. A German man is leaning a wreath against a railing, honouring the anniversary of a lady who died trying to escape. Mum and I try not to impose on the quiet ceremony, but after a minute of silence they invite us to join their tour. Mum looks like an actress being escorted to meet her public. Her Terylene tunic and short skirt give her the look of a blonde Jackie Kennedy, just a bit more British Home Stores than Chanel.

They usher us away, pointing out the East Berlin police taking photographs through a gap in one of the blocked windows. They take us to another street where we can climb onto the flat roof of a police post for a mind-blowing view of the city. People are dashing along, trams are running and a thousand car-windows glint in the evening sun. But the division soon becomes obvious.

"It's terribly grey and subdued over there," one Englishman says.

"Yes. Impossible to believe it's the same city," another agrees.

"See how the Wall dissects the tram lines," a German says, concentrating on the visible facts.

I imagine having to leave the tram at the last stop before the Wall, when once I might have travelled on and on across the city.

"I was at the Brandenburg Gate the day the Wall began," the German says. "It was a wire border at first. The bricks came later. We were all so angry that the authorities feared we would break the wire and storm through to the Soviet tanks all around Berlin. We did walk towards the soldiers, but we did not cross over."

"Were you not awfully tempted?" one of the men asks.

"No. Not when we saw such very young soldiers, their guns shaking in their hands, scared like us. No one crossed. The Allies did not touch the wire. We all just watched. Nothing was done because no one wanted war again. Not for this city. Not for these young men. Not again."

A softly-spoken German man points to a window on the third floor of a tall building and says, "My grandfather is sitting in that room."

Planting his feet wide apart, the man begins to wave, his arm sweeping through the air in a huge arc. We all step back to give him enough room. If I let my vision swim out of focus, this seems like an ordinary day with an ordinary man greeting someone he loves across the street.

"I'm not expecting to see him again," he says. But he waves on and on, hoping his grandfather has spotted him.

The Englishmen look away.

Mum and I thank the businessmen and walk back to Bernauer Strasse. I forget the eyes and cameras and guns on the other side, feeling somehow protected by what is left, and by the patient ghosts of interrupted lives.

We walk the entire length of the street, our sleeves touching, and pause at the felt-shoe factory. But it looks so blind and broken, I don't want to stay any longer.

"It has a purpose now that the shoe-maker could not ever have imagined," Mum says.

I hear her swallow. It sounds painful. When we turn away, she takes my arm and I don't pull it away.

When we reach the end, the sun rolls out of a cloud and a breeze raps the millions of leaves, sending out a metallic rustle like thousands of coins tipping out of a treasure-chest. In the last tree on the street, a bird sings his heart out, and I can still hear it after we have turned the corner.

On the walk home, darkness sets in. Lights are blinking on. People are strolling to restaurants, meeting friends, wafting perfume. And over on the other side of the Wall, the drabness of the day has transformed. Security-lights are blazing, flooding the area of watch-towers, anti-tank obstacles, trip-wire, the dog-corridor, alarms, anti-car trenches and electrical fencing. It is blinding, and utterly silent.

***

Back in Schillerpark, we sit round the table for dinner, Victor frowning because he's already in pyjamas the same as Seb. Beate has given them both a rounded fork and spoon even though Victor's been using proper cutlery for five years. Dad's daily quota of Brylcreem has sweated away and Mum tries to sweep his hair back. He actually grunts, "Geroff it, Bridge." So the Girls haven't quite captured him yet, in spite of seedy Sumatra's attempts to lasso him with her boa.

Blotto or not, Beate has cooked us a feast. The meat is juicy and delicious. There are two kinds of roast potatoes, some salty and some sweetened. I don't know if the sweet ones are meant to be sugar-coated, but they're strangely edible. Even Grandma is piling them onto her plate. Flashing a hideous grin of triumph at Mum, she proclaims them "delicious for foreign muck."

The wine is turning Mum hideously red-faced and giggly. She tries to make Dad take a sip from her glass, but, apart from his Christmas sherry, he never drinks alcohol on account of the many occasions he had to scoop my grandfather out of the rhododendron border. With Mum trying so hard and Dad not trying much at all, a sickly surge of homesickness swills inside me, because at home I can try to hide from all this. Not that it helps much. Bad Moons and bad mothers cast their nauseating light throughout the entire house, fingering into every corner.

I'm allowed to drink the revolting wine, taking a glass so Dad is not the only one to suffer the humiliation of being coaxed. Even a few polite drops make me dizzy. I keep thinking about Peter, but he seems to be floating. I become the exquisite Tuesday who kisses him. A hot blush starts at the roots of my hair and seeps into my face. I'm not listening to the conversation. When I say conversation, I mean Grandma gabbling on about meat, Elsie and her beloved Big Stan.

"Elsie said I flirted with Stan when all I did was tell him I preferenced his sweetbreads. And it seems I pant—*pant*, she says—when I start waxing hysterical about his chump-chops. And I plant—*plant*, mind you—my bosom on the counter. I said, never. Not on a counter piled to kingdom-come with blood and gristle. Of course the gristle got her going. 'My Stan has only the very best end,' she says. And I say, 'I know that fine well, Else.' Tch. She's got all the charm of a ladleful of cold tapioca."

My mind tunes in and out, but I sober up in the middle of all this when I realise Victor is sobbing.

"What's happening?"

"Well, Victor asked me what kind of meat it is," Mum explains. "But he has not taken it well."

"It is from the largest," Beate says. "The white one with the black patch."

It takes half a minute for light to dawn. Bloody, bloody ugh. Rabbits for eating. A skinned rabbit in bloody newspaper, no longer matching the décor.

And Mum knew we had a pet on our plates. She should have lied to Victor. If we were at home with no wine on the table, she would never have let this happen. And if I had known, I would have kept it a secret. If only she knew how well I do that.

Victor rushes away from the table in tears, and I hurry after him to our room.

"Did you stroke its ears, Jacqueline?" he says with great gulping sobs. "They were really soft. Where are they now?"

Oh, help me, Mr Lennon.

"Look, animals don't mean the same to Beate as they do to you," I explain to the back of his head, his face being buried in the feather quilt thing. "She had to kill a cow in the middle of the street once."

But that makes him howl even louder.

"Look Victor, if this is how other people want things, it isn't up to me to change the way they live."

"I want to go home."

"This is home. For now."

"Isn't."

"It is, because we're all here together."

"It's a horrible home."

"Well, home means different things to different people."

"Mrs Pither thinks hers is a castle with a moat and a drawbridge."

"Yes. And Oaking Borstal is still a home. And the Children's Home."

"Even though it looks like a prison?"

"Yes. And even though the children probably hope their sunny-bloody-smiles will take them far away from it one day."

"Will you tell me that story about the moon-rabbit?"

"Aren't you too old for that now?"

"I'll give you something if you tell me."

He scrambles out of bed and fusses about.

"I don't want a chewed bit of rubber or a rewrapped Spangle you've already sucked."

He comes back to bed empty-handed, but I tell him the story anyway.

"Once upon a time, some animals wanted to do a good deed, hoping for a reward. When they saw an old man begging, the wolf brought him a lizard, the otter a fish and the monkey gathered fruit. The rabbit panicked. With nothing to offer, he crept into the old man's fire, prepared to give himself. But the old man was really a god so the rabbit wasn't hurt. And to honour him, the man drew the rabbit on the moon. He's still there. At full moon, you can see the smoke around him."

Victor falls asleep, the tears drying on his face. I flick through my notepad and let it drop on the floor. I hold Victor's hand while Mum's wine-tinged laughter echoes down the hall.

7

ACCLAMATION

The next morning, the breakfast table is piled high with cold meat. Slipping back into the bedroom again, Victor and I make a pact not to be forced to eat any, resurrecting an old rhyme we made up to fortify us for Mum's dinners.

Touch your forehead,
Slap your knees,
Stuff your pillow with mouldy cheese.
Eat something horrid
And catch a disease.
Bagsy I'm not the first to heave.

When we come back after several repetitions, suitably bewitched to withstand any adult who tries to make us eat, the table is groaning with eggs, peppery black bread, pale cheese, warm, gritty cake and rashers of bacon fried especially for us English folk.

"Is that really bacon, do you think?" I hiss in Victor's ear.

"Could be rats' tongues," he says.

We settle for cheese.

Beate and Grandma are both tittering away. In Beate's case it's because she's already breakfasted. The fumes accost us the minute we enter the room. The clear drink in her cup looks as innocent as water, but smells like liquid fire.

In Grandma's case, the tittering is because her boiled duck-egg gives her an excuse to play Decapitating Khrushchev.

"Oh, there we are, Beat. Off it goes. Good-looking without it, isn't he? Lovely yellow belly."

Konnie, coming in from his night shift, turns his hat back-to-front to have a look. "Oh dear, zee brain has melted all over Nell's egg-holder. Nussing left inside, see? Wiz his scull off, Khrushchev is...how you say...hallo?"

"Hollow, duck," Grandma says, inching away from his guinea-pigs.

I don't understand what I'm crossing into today, but it might be a better deal than staying with this lot. After playing Khrushchev's Head with a second egg, a procedure that includes a horrendous disembowelment by buttered soldier, Beate says, "Birgit, you have your pain today, no?"

"She is so white. Like her English sheets," Konnie adds, cutting up ham stubbled with black peppercorns.

"But I will still go," Mum says in a bring-on-the-wild-horses way.

"There is nothing of our old home left," Beate says, draining her glass.

"I know. It's Ilse I want to see. And I'll be able to tell you how she is, Beate."

"Ach, I know well how she is. I am allowed no contact with my own sister, but I know how she lives. I went back and forth with her every day, Birgit. No people in Berlin cared about borders before the Wall. We were free enough until this other war drizzled in like rain through a crack."

"Is true," Konnie says, wiping his moustache. "Konnie saw how it was. Before they draw the line, one city."

"Is correct, Konnie. One Berlin, Birgit," Beate says, her currant eyes glittering. "Thousands of us from the East came here every day to work in the shops and offices, wearing our shapeless Russian-peasant clothes and scarves. We could never buy leather in the East. My Ilse must still carry a cheap, horrible handbag. That is life there. Every bag the same."

Konnie pats Beate's shoulder and I imagine he has comforted her like this countless times.

"West Berlin became small and quiet. Like zat bacon there," he says, pointing at a forgotten rasher seizing up in the pan. "It was all over, zee freedom. My old friend, he used to come here every day from the East to work in his bookshop. We had long talks, making zee world right again until one day, he did not come. He never opened his shop again. I am told he is 'having new training' in an East Berlin factory. His daughter was student here in the university. A serious young Fräulein with her broken old spectacles stuck togezzer wiz chewing-gum and her little case of books falling into pieces. She disappeared too, one of hundreds of young people who came in the underground trains from East to West for learning, but I never see her again. After the Wall, it was over."

Mum looks at me and says, "It is not over for us."

I know she's excited, but she just sounds plain hard. Beate gets up to wash the pots and pans, her glass beside her on the draining-board and her shoulders slumped, while Mum lowers the rifle T-K is aiming at Beate's back.

Grandma has been staring at our East German city map. "Well this is a fine tarradiddle," she says. "Look, Jacqueline. Roads and rivers and churches on their side, but if you ignore that egg stain, they've left the West plain white. See? Fancy printing a map with a mistake like that. Did they run out of ink?"

"Nell," Konnie says, "the vest does not exist."

"Well, I'm here, aren't I?"

"Zey do not agree. Zey pretend it is not here."

I have to gather up the map, sensing Mum's desperation to leave them to it. She is wearing her linen dress with matching jacket and her lurid Gay Geranium lipstick, but has bundled her hair into an old paisley scarf.

"Going for the gypsy style today, Bridge?" Grandma says.

"I wish to look smart, but not too smart, in front of Ilse, Nell."

"You run with both the hare and the hounds, you do," Grandma says, lighting a cigarette.

"What does that mean?"

"It means you don't know who you want to be, duck," Grandma says, not unkindly.

Mum ignores her and holds out my cardigan and Tufty bag, unaware T-K is now training his machete on her backside. Time to go.

Clinging to her leg, a strange sight in his striped pyjamas and Tyrolean hat, Victor begs Mum to stay. Blimey, she's already forgiven for complicity in last night's bunny butchery. "Don't go, Mummy," he says. He never says Mummy these days. It changed to Mum when he learnt words like soccer, offside and camouflage. Sebastian, clean and pink from his seven o'clock bath, is staring at him with the great wisdom of a three-year-old.

Beate's wiping surfaces as if she's bursting with energetic good health, but I know better. Miss Lobb once showed us a revolting liver soaked in alcohol.

It's not just Beate's liver that's in a rotten mess. There's her heart. Not its ventricles and atrium. I mean the contents, the Emotions. Hers must be a pouch of pain. She is reaching for a carton of buttermilk from the row of chilled milks, chocolate, banana and vanilla, standing to attention in the fridge. Her eyes are cloudy, as if they are full of buttermilk too. Bottles of wine are hidden all over the house. I saw one behind the toilet when I was looking for a brush to swipe over the damned ledge this morning.

While Mum's busy being forgiven, I slip into the garden to find Dad walking on the damp grass, flattening it with his dark footprints.

"Beate's drinking buttermilk this morning, Dad. What is it?"

"Settles her stomach, lines it ready for the Schnapps."

I don't know why we're wandering about in the chilly dawn. We don't usually do anything as stirring as that. But this morning my stomach is tied in more knots than Beate's liver and I need Dad. At least he's walking and talking today. That's good enough for me.

"I feel stuck here, love," he says. "I miss the driving. It was good for me, that."

I don't know what to say. I wasn't expecting him to speak about how he feels.

"You'll be driving all the way back to England soon. You've still got that to look forward to."

Strike a light, I've just said a sentence that belongs in the Parental Guide to Annoying Phrases—or How to make your offspring practise their range of death-glares that question if you were ever young.

"I wish we could just drive home now, Jacqueline."

He means it. He's not even smoking. He's standing in the dew and just looking at me, so close to sliding into sadness. It's like a hole in the road that widens as you come closer until there's no way around it.

He's so much happier in the car; reaching across Mum to check the glove-box is closed properly, pushing the ash-tray in and out, jogging back to us after a wee-stop in a glorious hurry for the road, and rasping his leathery hands together before turning on the engine. The Bad-Moon girls could slink in here today, their filthy red feathers at odds with the black and white flat, and smother him one by one. Beate will be no help at all. She might even try to get Dad sozzled. When he went to the Kennedys' Hogmanay party last year, they hid so much whisky in his ginger ale, he ended up putting on their eight-year-old's kilt and dancing the hornpipe.

But Grandma is here, cackling away in the kitchen, playing Patience with Victor, her backside not pulled in yet and her teeth still in a beaker. But she is here, and she loves my dad.

I stay outside with him, still not knowing what to say, savouring the cool air before the sun bakes it again. Mum is calling me. But through the window I can see Beate slicing cold meat, and I can't bear to witness any more evidence of pet slaughter. It might be Axel this time.

We pace about. "I don't know what to say, Dad," is the best I can come up with. He emerges a little, poking his head out, tortoise-like.

"Jacqueline, don't upset yourself about the rabbit. Beate's lived in Hell and beyond. And no one survives that without pulling on a thick skin. Fluffy bunnies don't make her feel all soppy. She can't afford to be sensitive. Her heart got left behind, over there." He jerks his half-thumb eastwards. Well, I guess it's east. He has no sense of direction. "Plus," he adds, "booze deadens the senses."

I pull a pointed leaf off a miniature tree, its growth stunted to fit in a pot. A dewdrop hovers in the central vein. "I understand about the rabbit," I tell him. "And I've explained it to Victor. But Mum's senses are sometimes deadened as well. She never listens. She never tries to feel what I feel. And even Grandma tries."

The words tip out like coal into the bunker. Horrible words with an accusing edge. Black words that sit in a pile between us. But when he speaks, his voice is soft with understanding.

"Fear of loss, Jacqueline, that's what drives people. Mum lost herself years ago. And she's terrified of losing you. While she's watching you grow up, she's remembering what happened to her when she wasn't much older. It makes her withdraw because she had to learn not to show fear. She couldn't afford to, not with the enemy's rotten breath blowing down her ear-hole."

I watch the dewdrop wobble on the leaf. "You don't smell with your ears, Dad."

"You probably can when some sod's trying to kill you. And when it can happen while you're walking to the shops or even just sitting in your own home. Mum lived with it so long she doesn't dare let herself go. So think what it cost her to tell you the truth."

I tilt the leaf and the dewdrop quivers on its tip.

"I get afraid too, Jacqueline," Dad goes on, an awful tremble in his voice. "Afraid of the past. Afraid of seeing you grow up and losing my girl. It all comes straight out though, my misery. Like I've had a dose of Eno's. I just can't help these terrible days. And I'm so sorry."

I look down at the leaf as if my life depends on it. He's never said sorry for the bad times before. He's looked sorry. But this morning I hear the word for the first time, out there in the garden while the first spear of sun pierces the blank sky.

"It's like being two people," he says, clearing his throat. "Or like a worm cut in half. I'm scared of myself. I wish things weren't like this, Jacqueline. I really wish that. I don't know what I've become. It doesn't even feel like being human sometimes. And when I feel better, I know it's only until the next time. I'm so scared of losing you all. And I'm so, so sorry."

I poke the dew with my finger, but it sits back up. Dad lights a cigarette at last, inhaling and holding his breath for what seems like forever.

"Parents aren't supposed to be scared," I mumble, the proud bubble of dew staring back at me.

I sense Dad nodding while he takes another long gasp. "I know, love. But even Grandma's scared. We all carry fear about with us. Mum can seem a bit distant because she's trying to keep it from you. And when Grandma's mouth starts motoring before her brain is in gear, it's just to settle her nerves. I made up the Bad-Moon girls to help you and Victor. Don't know if it works. I just hoped it might show you how I'm feeling, if that doesn't sound bloody nuts." He flicks his ash. It perches on a blade of grass. Beate will probably come out here later and sweep it into the black bin.

"The moon you see is round and chummy," he says. "Mine's hard and hollow. And not lit."

"I know."

"I don't need locking up. I'm not mad. But I get scared. Scared of losing my mind. And I can see you're scared too. But I only see that after the Bad Moon's gone. I can't see anything while it's here."

"Dad, are you scared someone might lock you up?" My stomach squirms at the question that has waited long enough.

"Yes," he whispered. "Yes, my love."

I lay the leaf on the ground. The dewdrop trickles away in a miniature river. He's never said "my love" before.

Mum's calling me for the final time.

"Be careful today, Jacqueline," Dad says as we start to walk inside. "Watch out for your mum."

"I'll try."

"And remember, no eels or asparagus."

It's true. Konnie showed us a list of food items that East Berlin believes would have an upsetting Western influence on their people.

"Perhaps some vegetables are known to *leek* secrets," I say, hoping to make Dad smile. Pretty pathetic.

"Or some fish might be considered carp-italist," Dad says. Hopelessly pathetic.

We grin at each other, not because of the hilarity of the so-called jokes, but because they make us feel oddly better.

"The problem is, I feel strange with Mum now," I tell him. "She lied all that time."

"I know. But people who've suffered can't always talk about it. And she wanted to spare you the misery."

"The misery of being different?"

"No. That's not it. Not the being different. She wanted to spare you the misery of being treated different."

"Different*ly*."

"All right, all right. I'm not bloody foreign, you know."

"You are here."

"Sometimes I am anywhere."

He's running his hands through his hair. It's really floppy today. A bad sign. He's usually fanatical about his Brylcreem. Victor once got hold of it and plastered it on, slicking it all to one side. He looked like a boy Hitler, if such a creature ever existed.

Dad is waiting for reassurance I'll take care of Mum. He wants me to be adult about this. And someone blooming well has to.

"All right," I tell him. "I'll watch out for her. But hold the bus a minute, Dad. Isn't she supposed to look out for me? I'm the minor here. I still get into the Lido half-price."

He almost smiles. When he speaks, his words are gargled, as if they can't quite leave his throat. He clutches my arm. "Come back safe, girl."

When we step inside again, we find Mum talking non-stop, blind to everything but the day ahead, while Beate keeps hacking away at another carcass. I wouldn't have thought it possible to look so completely defeated with a cleaver in your hand.

"Come on, Jacqueline," Mum says. "Hurry now. Make yourself recent. There is a grass stain on your skirt. Do make an effort. You are driving me round the corner."

"It's *decent*, Mum. And I drive you round the *bend* actually. Anyway, just hold the bus, will you?"

Ignoring her exasperated sigh and trying not to think about the nature of this particular batch of flesh, I walk over to Beate and sink my hands into the meat, lumping it into the basin with the onions she's been slicing.

"Goulash," she says, drawing me inside her yeasty alcohol cloud. After the freshness outside, it feels like stepping into a distillery.

"Mm, very nice," I tell her.

My help might be feeble, but she smiles and strokes my hair. I can't bear her fingers on it, but I don't pull away. I plunge my hands back into the meat and carry on helping.

"Mix it with this, please, Jacqueline," Beate says, handing me a jug of red meat juices.

I don't know how I'm kneading a dead thing chopped up with a pint of what looks like fresh blood, but I have thrown myself in and am even thinking hard too.

"Dad wants to drive you, Grandma, Sebastian and Victor out somewhere today," I tell Beate over the squelch of the meat. I had no idea I was going to suggest this. It just emerges, a sort of desperate solution similar to the time

Dad and I trowelled the remains of Mum's Christmas pudding into the dark soil beside the coal bunker. It was exactly the same colour. We pretended to have eaten it. Irresistible, we said it was.

"A drive?" Beate says, round-eyed at the prospect of a change in routine.

I put Victor in charge of Dad's fag-lighting (dreadful, but seven-year-olds in all the best families have to take their turn) and general humbug-passing. He throws his feathered hat in the air in triumph. I tell Beate to sit in the back with Grandma and to take no notice of the strange noises coming from underneath. It will either be the dodgy floor or Grandma. Turbulence or flatulence.

As I throw Dad his driving-gloves, Sebastian catches the excitement and bounces about. I didn't know he could move. I thought he was stuffed.

The project is prodding me again. It is still my mission and I don't want Gillian beating me. I wasn't planning to carry on, but I woke early this morning and looked at my picture of the felt-shoe factory with gruesome fascination. Yesterday it gave Mum and me a connection that had nothing to do with feeling lost or growing up. It was about something beyond us and something between us.

Our taxi to Wollankstrasse station is rumbling. Time to leave.

Konnie starts preparing for a lie-down after his late shift. This consists of turning his cap sideways, then curling up on top of his bed with the guinea-pigs, a picture of Johannes watching him from the chest of drawers.

He yawns loudly, too tired to speak in English now, but Mum translates his last words as he shuffles off. "Konnie has no time for cars. He says the train lines weave through and below the city, tracking its mood, part of its nervous system, linking people together. Cities are held in one piece, able to survive, only because of their railway."

Climbing into the taxi feels like stepping into a pit of quicksand. Bugger the central nervous system. My nerves are utterly jangling.

As the taxi glides away, Mum starts to gabble, the maps on her lap twitching away. "The Reichsbahn, the railway is called, Jacqueline. East Germany runs the whole system, you know."

"What?" I snap. "I'm so confused. I thought I had it worked out. West one side. East the other. So how come Konnie works for the other lot? It's the same as British Rail suddenly becoming a Chinese company or something, is it?"

"Well no, Jacqueline, East Germany has been in charge of it for a long time. At the end of the war, the Allies kept the railway under one control. The drivers are trained over there and employed under their laws. Part of Konnie's pay is in their currency and he has to spend it over there because no other country accepts the eastern marks. But it is nice for him. He can buy things over there and bring them back home. We will not be allowed to bring much back with us, but we must still buy some of these eastern marks. It is the law. They need our money."

"Why?"

"Because their own is not worth much."

"But they don't have anything to buy. So how come it's nice for Konnie?"

The sun blushes like a ripe peach in a blue bowl and the taxi might as well be an oven. I can smell the ginger-coloured bread and the perspiring mottled meat slices Beate insisted we bring with us. Why does food smell so horrible in a car? I try to write some more of my project, but the pen nib splits even further apart and makes irritable-looking ghost-words.

"They have all kinds of food, dear. We must buy Beate some *Knusper Flocken*," Mum says. "East German chocolates. Konnie says they're very good."

"Really? They have chocolates?"

"Of course they do, Jacqueline."

"Did you know Beate's finished up our Five-Boys? She doesn't deserve any *Knocken Fluster* or whatever you call them."

So far, Beate has acquired Mum's peppermints, Dad's lighter and Victor's multi-colour Biro.

"What sort of chocolates are they?" I ask her, suddenly longing for a Mars Bar to settle my edginess.

"Ah, very different from English. Not much cocoa, I understand."

"What's inside them?"

"Flakes of crispbread."

"What, the slimming stuff Dad says is actually hardboard?"

"Yes."

"Well, that says it all."

I slump in the taxi, confused, hungry and scared of the day ahead. It was hard leaving Dad. I gave him a kiss on the cheek before we went, and his stubbled skin smelt like home. I told him we'd just be a stone's throw away, but it is so much further than that.

"Konnie said a rotisserie chicken restaurant has just opened over there," Mum says.

"I like Wimpy better than chicken."

"Well, don't expect that, Jacqueline."

"I wasn't expecting bloody anything."

"Pardon? Did you just bloody?"

"No."

Mum rustles the maps, trying to fold them and giving up, crushing them into her bag.

"How long are we staying?"

"We must leave the East before midnight."

"Will we stay that long?"

"Oh, Jacqueline, I have no bloody idea."

I just want to meet Ilse and leave. Will we even have a conversation over there without guns jabbing at our backs or black cars pulling up outside to spirit people away before they've finished their crispbread?

"So what would happen if Konnie has a grumbling appendix when he's driving his train on the other side?" I ask, determined to find a question Mum can't answer, trying to poke holes in this tangled old web of a city. I'd like to take a stick and swipe it out of existence. "How would he get to hospital? Would they just fling him on the next train back to the West?"

"Oh, in an emergency, the railway authority would let him use the hospital over there. It is absolutely free, their healthcare."

"It's free everywhere, isn't it?"

"No. Not at all."

"Oh."

After ten minutes we reach the station, a pretty building with a tower and arched windows. Under a tree, a group of young people huddle in their coats despite the heat, their eyes glassy.

"Are they drug addicts?" I whisper.

"Perhaps," she says.

"Are they homeless, even on this side?"

"People are homeless everywhere, Jacqueline."

I make her walk in an arc to avoid them, and there it is, the Wall, looming out of nowhere, its greyness at odds with the friendly brick of the station, like a huge uninvited guest, a hulking intruder on the doorstep. It is taller, so much more menacing here than in the city centre.

"*Mein Gott*," Mum whispers, stepping back. "It follows us."

I don't usually touch her, but I have to clutch the sleeve of her cardigan. She doesn't generally smoke in the streets, but she lights up now.

"That...that thing was just part of the city yesterday. But here it has its own life. It comes towards us," she says, sucking on the cigarette so hard her cheeks cave in. "Konnie said this station used to be in the East. So we stand on the absolute edge. On the border."

I see what she means. The Wall has twisted around its east side, leaving the actual station within West Berlin's railway system. Entrances to the East are closed with bricks. Only people on this side can use it.

Mum turns a bit green and I pass her an Opal Mint. I can't think of anything else to do. I chew a mint as well and it tastes of my bedroom, the car and somehow the dregs of Grandma's ash-tray, of everything that isn't here.

"I want Dad," I say at last.

"Me too," she says.

I don't know if she means her dead father or mine. I don't mean Dad is dead, although when his days are really dark, I think he might wish it.

"When our train comes in, could our driver be an East German?"

"Yes. A state railway driver. He is one of the few permitted to exit for the purpose of his job. But that is all. He cannot have a life here."

"If the station we're going to..."

"Friedrichstrasse."

"Yes, that one. If it's inside East Berlin, why don't they just get on the train there, come over here and get out? Then they'd be free. Mixed up with all the crowds on the platform, people could easily slip on without being noticed. Why doesn't Ilse do that?"

I have discovered a way, surely? We could just wait for Ilse to bob across. She could live with Beate and rediscover her portly pastry-chef. I'm only guessing he is portly because I can't imagine a puny pastry-chef.

Mum grinds out her cigarette, shaking her head. "Friedrichstrasse was once the starting point of escape for the millions behind the Iron Curtain. Only West Berlin gave hope of freedom, until the Wall cut all connections. Access to the train service travelling west from Friedrichstrasse was closed to East Berliners."

Ah. They have everything covered.

"No way through," she says, in case I did not fully understand.

A guard appears, strolling in the sunshine while he waits for the train to arrive. It takes him a moment to register our hesitation. He walks across and helps us onto the platform, his rapid-fire German rattling over my head. Mum is like a seaside donkey at first, the worn little heels of her sling-backs digging into the sun-softened tarmac.

I glance up as we follow him into the station, my arm linking with Mum's of its own accord. At the top of the Wall, a thin white butterfly pauses, the sunlight streaming through its white-tissue wings before it flutters across to the other side.

The train is old, jam-packed and stuffy; the ride drab and bleak. Scrubby pine trees and endless grain fields flash through the morning haze. Every so often, the train crawls through a dimly-lit station, and we all stare at our own faces reflected in the windows.

I write down what I see, almost sad for Miss Whipp that there are no gambolling lambs or clucking chickens to mention. I consider adding one or two, but they don't fit into this bleak landscape. It's probably the wrong season anyway. I'm not sure because it's been a few years since I did my pig-and-poultry project.

Villages have been sliced apart like a Battenberg cake, only they look less pretty. Long stretches of barbed wire dissect the farmland. Watch-towers grow out of the soil. Fields that might have grown from the same batch of grass-seed are now divided. An extra couple of paces and a farmer's boots can walk into no-man's land. One more step means sudden death. His own land becomes out of bounds, his own feet turn into enemy feet. Every blade of grass is drenched by the same rain and parched by the same sun. But if that farmer takes one step too far, he's dead. The only harmony is underground, where the roots remain undisturbed by the rift above, free to travel, spread and tangle at will.

"Border villages are being left to crumble," Mum says as we pass them. "The people who live there are ordered not to repair or rebuild."

"Why?"

"Because the government here is unhappy about its people living so close to the enemy."

"What harm would the West do?"

"None at all. But with it so close, there would be too much temptation to escape."

The border between the two countries consists of a ploughed strip, an anti-tank ditch, miles of fencing and concrete watch-towers, but in front of it there is some neglected land that Konnie told us belongs to the East Germans. Special patrol-guards look out for anyone careless enough to stray into it from the West. They bundle you through hidden gates and no one sees you again.

The Wall escorts us all the way to Friedrichstrasse. I watch Mum biting her nails to shreds, keyed-up about seeing Ilse again, or perhaps contemplating the madness of bringing me, her only daughter, over here.

I think of the desperate people who dig tunnels under the Wall only to be double-crossed by their friends and caught halfway through in the beam of a Stasi torch. Some swim the canal in the dead of night, but drown in barbed-wire traps underwater.

I don't want to feel scared, because I've promised Dad I'll watch out for Mum. And I've promised myself I'll complete this project. I force my nerves to knit themselves together and take the map that looks like a dog's dinner off Mum's lap and fold it along all the right creases into a square, the first of the family to achieve it.

"We know where we're going," I tell her, stowing the map away in my bag.

It's a good thing one of us is being mature. When Mum looks up at the signs that tell her she can smoke, I have to take the thing out of the packet for her. I light it after an age of waiting for it to stay steady between her lips, ramming it in place with one hand and striking the match with the other while she tries to hold the box still.

She looks quite nice in her peasant clothes. If President Kennedy's wife wore a headscarf and a camel cardigan, and had a small cold-sore distorting her upper lip, then that's a fair picture of Mum. At least she doesn't have butcher's arms and flashing cod's eyes like Gillian's mother. Mum's eyes are a black-treacle colour, but too bright with pain and worry.

We listen to the rhythm of the train while she smokes, watching the progress of the Wall.

"Are you nervous, Mum?"

"Yes. I have no idea exactly why. Maybe that's why I am nervous."

"Yes, it probably is."

We look out of the window in silence when the train takes us into a subdued world of smoky slate-grey tenements. Many of them are derelict, roofless since the war. One or two coloured blocks flash by and on some of the shabby high-rises I notice surprising painted patches: muted red or sea-green or a hopeful sort of turquoise. But hundreds of unpainted concrete apartment blocks are still pitted with war damage, their grim curtains often closed. A tattered poster shows Uncle Sam with devilish fangs and deadly weapons, and insists that *Americans Go Home*.

Soon we are standing beneath the vaulted glass of the frantic Friedrichstrasse station, feeling the thunder of trains in the underground maze of tunnels under our feet, tunnels that turned into emergency hospitals, and the trains into wards, during the last days of the war. And we begin the quest to cross the border.

In between the two main platforms at Friedrichstrasse station a barrier under armed guard, watched by cameras, sniffer-dogs and the State Security Police, cuts two distinct halves. One half is for people in East Berlin, separated from the world they cannot enter, and the other for travellers like us. Whenever a train stops, the guards and dogs swarm over it, inside, underneath and on top.

Our queue inches forward.

"We are standing where thousands of children waited for a train to take them away after Kristallnacht," Mum says.

I look up at the glassy dome way above the rumbling platform, the sun striking my face. How would I feel if I were an orphan in a long queue, leaving myself behind, holding hands with a little boy like Victor who is leaving his mother forever?

I might envy him for having a mother or pity him for being torn away from her. If the Nazis barked at him to stop crying, I would tell him to stare straight ahead without blinking to hold the tears back and grip his hand tighter. A stranger's hand is sometimes all there is.

And what about the little boy's mother? Until the moment he was out of sight, she would smile and flap a farewell handkerchief. After walking out of the station into the sun, she would listen for the last vibration on the track to settle before her smile disappears and she dares to cry. She would hesitate before turning away, scared to go home and see his clockwork train at a stand-still, his ranks of cowboys and Indians waiting. Her own torture and death lie ahead, and the one bittersweet comfort is that he will soon be hundreds of miles away, somewhere safe enough for him to call home.

I feel Mum's hand in mine and I should squeeze it tight, but I am not ready.

We trudge through three passport checks and customs control, cooking to death in a waiting room for two hours. It reeks of Alsatian, perspiration and fear. I feel more ill than I did in the car.

A woman with a blue suitcase sits bolt upright, staring into space. Her baby cries without a pause for an hour while her travelling companions try to soothe it. The woman speaks in broken sounds. Even I can tell it's not German. It isn't any language. Without a hint of emotion she takes the sweating, sleeping baby, plonks her in a basket and strokes the blue suitcase on her lap as if it's a cat.

Her companions understand. They glare at anyone staring. This is their Bwa-Bwa. She lives in East Berlin too, in this yellow-tiled halfway house that leads to everywhere from anywhere.

At the counter for compulsory currency exchange we swap our western marks for our dutiful five eastern marks at the shocking rate of one for one. Like Cinderella's gown and coach, the money will be useless after midnight.

"I'll look out for the Ryvita coated in cack," I whisper to Mum as she puts the money away, hoping she's less resistant to rude words today.

"Indeed, right so," she says. "Shite pretendin' to be chocolate."

This is a perfect take-off of Gaye Kennedy's Irish grandfather who is always saying, "Jaysus Mary Mother of Christ, now isn't this world just full of shite?"

"He had Friedrichstrasse in mind, to be sure," I tell Mum. She gives me the flicker of a smile.

The wait stretches into the third hour and our nerves stretch with it, the final guard peering at the visa and squinting at us far too long. He asks to see Mum's bag and flicks through all its contents, peering at her Trebor Mints and used tissues and twiddling her lipstick up and down. He's suspicious of her Oaking Library membership card, turning it over and over, the plastic cover shining under the strip-lights. He slips it out of the cover. Back in, back out. He asks a lot of questions about the library and about Oaking, that infamous hotbed of anti-communism. It probably is, actually.

I groan when he pulls out the picture of Dad with the Oaking Eleven. Mum always keeps it in her bag because it falls out of Dad's pocket with his cigarettes and matches. The guard is fascinated in his wary, oily way. He wants to know all about Dad, how old he is and how he met Mum. I can't understand much of the conversation, but the long wait is making me sweat. I can smell the dogs. I can hear them straining against their leashes, braced to spring out of corners. The room is bristling with guns.

Nothing, not even Cybermen starting World War Three in the school showers (which is the most dreaded place on earth when your mum provides a towel the size of a postage-stamp) could make me feel this anxious. I told Dad I would take care of Mum, but how can anyone look after someone here? If you took off all your clothes and did the Twist on top of the vending-machine in an English railway-station, your polite fellow-passengers would turn away. But here, everyone is raw meat on a butcher's counter. I can hear blades sharpening. Or is it the release of a safety-catch, the click of a trigger? I really must stop peeking at Victor's *Commando*.

Mum is still knee-deep in conversation, trying to explain the rules of cricket. A man with an ironing-board under his arm is whistling. A woman in the next queue has a shopping-basket on wheels with a tyre missing. It squeaks when she shuffles forward and she keeps apologising. A giggling child bounces a balloon on a string. A puffy-cheeked family play pass-the-parcel with a purple-faced baby in a papoose. An old man sighs as he slots another cigarette into the gap between his front teeth. And all the time, the blank-faced guards in their polished boots show no hint of our Emotions. It's hard to believe they are ordinary people.

They watch me watching them, making me feel sick with nerves. The orange juice I drank at breakfast rises in my throat as throat-scorching bile. I hope they don't demand a fine from people who spew in Friedrichstrasse station because my sock is clean out of Deutschmarks. I feel the colour draining from my face.

A voice asks do I want a seat. I think it's the man with the ironing-board. But when I sit on a chair and take a deep breath, my eyes focus again and there's a young guard crouched down beside me, his Kalashnikov three inches from my leg.

"OK?" he says.

I nod, not trusting myself to speak. He is terribly good-looking.

"Sit. One minute, yes?"

I nod a great deal more and start breathing again. I hope I don't land him in trouble for stepping out of line. And I hope I'm sitting with poise like Tuesday, not some hopeless square. Before he returns to his spot, he wishes me a nice stay in his country as if I have just arrived in the Garden of Eden.

"Jacqueline, stay with me," Mum calls, before turning back to her guard's questions about our two years' worth of bus tickets and her dog-eared invitation to Dad's work's dance. There are twenty minutes of interrogation about Dad's job. The guard approves of him being a prison-warder. We should have brought an autographed picture of him with D-Wing. Gillian's mother has a signed photograph of Roger Moore with one eyebrow arched. She met him when she was lumbering after an escaped budgie, but lost sight of him when he soared over the liver-paste plant. The budgie, that is. I doubt Roger Moore has ever taken flight over Oaking Potted Meats.

The conversation makes less sense than the squeaky wheel or the clanking ironing-board. The queue sighs and shuffles. The guard turns back to our passes. He sighs, flicking through the pages, prolonging the agony just because he can. I imagine him ironing his uniform in a tiny room painted the colour of oxtail soup. I strain to see his sinister, long boots behind the desk.

The officials here are the same as any; prison warders, policemen, Salvation Army officers, traffic wardens, Girl Guides. When Gaye Kennedy was made Sixer of Kingfisher patrol, she turfed a trespassing Scout out of her jamboree, but not before he scorched his elbow on her camp-fire. He was only dropping off a batch of his auntie's drop-scones. The uniform changes people, especially if there are badges attached to it. The man staring at us and our papers has become a human barrier. Keeping people in. Keeping people out.

He stifles a yawn as he works through our pile again, maybe masking a greater fear than ours. Everyone, uniformed or not, is being watched here.

His routine is precise and unhurried. Papers, one at a time; glasses on, glasses off; passports, one at a time; gather documents into piles; glasses on; straighten the ranks of rubber stamps already lined up; glasses off. There is no smiling. He's not much older than me, but he already has a trio of sharp vertical creases between his eyebrows. A feathery wisp of ginger hair has strayed out of his cap. His skin is raw from shaving at dawn with cold water and a cold blade.

He sneezes, an odd bark of a sneeze, which interrupts the official proceedings. He sneezes nine more times in a Germanic rhythm I recognise from dance classes. Mum passes him a tissue, which he drops. Muttering and red-faced, he picks it up and trumpets into it. He looks at the tissue with such disbelief I can feel a vibration from Mum, the smallest muffled snort that has nothing to do with fear. Flustered by the unscheduled sneeze, he sends us on our way. The barrier rises. Mum and I are free to leave, whatever that means here.

We have time to explore before Ilse finishes her shift, but Mum looks lost. Mothers are supposed to know where to go when they bring their children into their home city, but I suppose if I returned to Oaking twenty years from now and the enemy had blown Audette Gardens sky-high, I might be lighting a fag and saying, "*Gott im Himmel.*"

"Mum? Come on."

She drops the cigarette and crushes it for ages under the sole of one sling-back.

"Mum, it's all right. It's just different this time."

She stops crushing and looks up.

"Absolutely correct, Jacqueline. This time, I'm with my daughter."

We link arms. Thank you, Mum.

If West Berlin is a buzzing hive of activity, East Berlin is a single bee asleep on a flower. Not just subdued, but utterly silent, apart from the occasional lawnmower-rattle of a Trabant chugging by, trailing its fog of bluish smoke.

But East Berlin is somehow spectacular. They didn't just take a meat-cleaver and cut though the centre of the city like Stan splitting a lamb carcass. The Wall wriggles, skirting around huge stubborn monuments, lassoing some of the best into this side; museums, theatres, cathedrals, some of them crumbly and casting crazy shadows, most of them blemished. Their mouldings have shed chunks of stone and corners have been shaved from walls. Carvings are chipped and facades are flaking, but the deep-red town hall and the ornate cathedral are more beautiful than the buildings in the West. East Berlin is more than plain cake. It is an iced fancy, if rather a squashed one.

Mum points out the remainder of the once grand Hotel Adlon, alone on the grassed-over square that was once brimming with beautiful embassies. Although the air-raids scarcely touched the hotel, it perished when the Red Army arrived, drank the contents of the wine cellar and set it on fire. At least East Berlin has preserved its one remaining wing and given it a new, if less dazzling, frontage.

It used to have the swish address of Number One, Unter den Linden, but East Berlin has renumbered the street, beginning at their end, making Hotel Adlon the less impressive Seventy-Seven.

"I was taken inside as a small child," Mum says. "A pianist played part of the Mendelssohn concerto I grew to love, the slow section. I tried so hard to learn that piece. I never tired of it."

"Isn't a slow part easier to play?"

"No, but it is soothing. If I hear it on the transistor, I think of being a child. For a few moments, I have a sense of time being held back especially for me, a luxury that was lost a long time ago."

When I try to imagine Mum playing the piano, she looks like a different person, one that only she might recognise.

"I will never forget the beautiful palm court and the oriental fountain surrounded by its carved black elephants," she says. "But I remember most the... how do you say it...the gentleness of that time."

"Do you mean genteel?"

"No, I think I mean gentle."

Despite the sun, the atmosphere is frosty, as if the fancy cake is in cold storage. In the hushed, ghost-town stillness, our Western heels, however flat and worn, sound thunderous. On this side of the city, we don't weave around pillars smothered in advertisements or bustling crowds or girls in mini-skirts. Instead, we are dwarfed by the imposing French and German cathedrals, the striking concert hall and the elderly palace Peter Fechter was helping to repair before he tried to escape. All the grand buildings are still wading in war wreckage. Mum remembers gracious domes and pillars, a sculpture of a chariot drawn by griffins and a winged Pegasus. I try to imagine them, realising she wants to draw my eye away from the outcrop of socialist housing, great dark slabs of it in the background, shadowing the heart of the city.

Mum whisks us onto a tram that trundles past the crusty carcasses of bomb-blasted buildings, but without warning, we emerge from desolation onto the wide swoop of Karl-Marx-Allee, a sparkling six-lane boulevard with grass along the middle and two massive skyscrapers at the end. The pavements are lively with people scurrying ant-like at the feet of monumental yellowy blocks that look like square beehives sponging up the smoke and grime. These are the showcase workers' palaces, their frontages decorated with lavish ceramic tiles carved with toiling workers. In a veil of mist, the unfinished TV Tower looms, watching the whole show.

"This street is the East's great exhibit," Mum says as we climb out of the tram. "Made-in-Moscow. Designed to make the people feel fortunate and protected, but also tiny. It keeps them in their place."

"I do feel sort of insignificant," I tell her, looking down at my clothes, which, despite their unintentional communist appearance, seem smug and Western now, utterly out of place.

"You are," she says. "We are all insignificant here."

This is the spectacular street where Beate shopped with Ilse when East and West could merge. These people on spindly chairs outside the milk-bar, sitting beneath loudspeakers tied to street-lamps, are the 'jolly folk' of the miracle mile.

Beate would slice her overfed chins off to be here with Seb and Ilse. Even if she had to pour her cherry brandy down the split-level toilet to reverse time ten years, she would. But there is more chance of unearthing their old grandfather clock than recreating their wonderful past.

We travel back towards Unter den Linden and wander into a clothes store in a side-street. The subdued shop offers no choices, just one sort of each basic essential and many empty shelves. No colour. No fashion. No surprises. Not many patterns. A choice of two scratchy-looking jerseys. No background music. Just our shoes tapping on the hard floor.

We buy nothing, even though the money must be spent at some point, and continue along Unter den Linden. Once designed to be the grandest avenue in the city, the Cold War has changed it into a no-through road.

"I had not expected so much to survive the damage," Mum says, gasping at each flawed, familiar sight.

"Will they ever patch things up?"

"Maybe not without the...what does Dad say... teddies?"

"Reddies actually, Mum. And by the way, English slang doesn't sound right when a German says it."

"Well, whatever it may be called, they have none of it."

"No wonder they snatched our money at the exchange."

"Yes. But I think they might leave some of this damage on porpoise."

"Purpose."

"Yes. To remind us of the horror. "

"Do you need reminding?"

"Everyone needs reminding, Jacqueline."

Unter den Linden is lined with a thousand lime trees that Hitler tried to replant with Nazi flags. Little boys who were caught hiding in fear when Hitler insisted they join the depleted army were strung up from some of these branches and hanged.

Beate and Ilse trudged through the ruins here in 1945, faint with hunger, pushing a handcart without tyres, hoping the Americans, who had bombed Berlin by day while the British attacked it at night, would arrive before the Soviets. But, building by building, the Red Army soon completed the destruction the Allies had begun, leaving Berlin and many of its people butchered.

In the silence of this patched-up city, with Mum pausing every minute to look at the distorted relics of her past, I imagine the road scattered with smashed military vehicles, fires raging, tanks storming through, buildings with walls sheared off and most of the furniture splintered into firewood by falling beams. Perhaps, here and there, a heavy table or ornate sideboard stayed upright, the polished surfaces crusted with dust and debris.

Beate and Ilse picked up odd shoes, blood-splattered rags, a broken pair of spectacles, anything, no matter how pitiful, that could be exchanged for food. They searched the wreckage for cigarette butts, the best currency of all, feeling for them in the pockets of the dead. They ate the corpses of animals lying in gutters. And here are Mum and I, her purse fat and jangling with money that we are too snooty to spend.

We stroll in the sunshine to the New Guard House, where we will meet Ilse at last. It looks like a Greek temple with tall fluted columns and carvings of goddesses that represent battle, victory, flight and defeat. It used to commemorate the fallen German soldiers from World War One, but now the same building, bristling with guards, is a memorial for Victims of Fascism.

Mum keeps reaching for my arm. I allow her my sleeve, which she pleats between her fingers over and over again. Since the sleeve-pleating is a worse torture than waiting in border-control, all I can do to occupy her hands is light her a cigarette, which tastes of rotting leaves stewed with ear-wax. I have never lit up before, but then I've never stood anywhere like this.

Ilse appears in the crowd, small and slender in a dreadful frock, her copper hair lit up by the sun. I would know her anywhere because of the way she's looking at Mum. And she looks nothing like a victim of anything.

I whip the cigarette from Mum's mouth and step on it. She and Ilse hold onto each other with something I can only call grace, with an Emotion no biology teacher could explain. It feels like a beginning and an end.

They kiss each other's tears and reach out for me. No one stares. This is a city of tears.

We all speak at once, but Ilse holds up her hand. "One moment. The guard is changing."

The young soldiers perform back-to-back in pairs then nimbly spin to face one another again, as if ready to begin a romantic dance. When they march, it is not a jolly brass-band sort of marching, but a silent goose-step, black boots rising high and pointed, stiff right arms whipping mechanically across the body.

"They're just boys," I hiss.

"They probably have just met their very first girl-friends," Ilse whispers back.

"And just shaved their first bit of bum-fluff," I add. Judging by her puzzled expression, this is not a phrase she knows.

"And have mothers who still want to hold their hand to cross the road," Mum joins in.

"But only when the green man says they can," I remind her.

Mum's smile soon disappears. "Even after all the lessons learned from the past and with their mothers still wiping their noses, still they dance the dance of war."

Ilse slips between us, holding our hands like a school-friend. "Let's treat ourselves to coffee," she says, as if we are about to sashay into a Lyon's tea shop.

As we walk along, warm air rumbles up from ventilation shafts in the pavements.

"That is the West Berlin subway," Ilse explains. "We feel it and hear it, this forbidden world under our feet." She tips back her head and laughs about this while Mum watches the breeze scoop up a few leaves and toss them down the subway stairs, where they join the pile at the blocked entrance.

The café is the front-room of a house with bullet-holes in the window. Ilse doesn't flinch or make apologies, having known far worse places than this.

None of the leatherette-jacketed coffee-drinkers inside the bleak little room look up, but all of them know we are here.

Ilse orders me a Club Cola.

"Our very own," she says with pride. "Bottled here in Berlin. We got it earlier this year."

"It looks just like ours," I tell her, examining the bottle and wondering whether I should lower my voice. I pull in my chair and the legs shriek on the concrete floor.

"Well, of course," Ilse says, grinning. "Anything you can do, we can match it here, you know."

It tastes like ancient dried herbs in melted tar.

"Lovely," I say with a bright smile.

"It feels like war time," Mum whispers. "Nothing much has changed, Ilse."

"And yet everything has," Ilse says, rolling a cigarette.

"No one looks happy," Mum says. "Everyone is standing on the blade of the knife."

"It's called living on a knife's edge, Mum."

In an even more toe-curling moment than my chair-scraping, Mum smiles round at the other tables. It has no effect. We are unable to improve or blend into this dreary atmosphere, because at the end of the day, everyone knows we can leave.

The young man on the next table is staring out of the window at the shop opposite. It has a display of rubber hot-water bottles, their faded red the only colour among these worn-out houses and bare shops. He opens a tin, scrapes out his last dusty shreds of tobacco and rolls a cigarette that he puts in his pocket. His eyes are empty too, blanked out like the boarded windows in Bernauer Strasse.

It feels like a sodden autumn day inside the café, the misery clinging like damp leaves to the soles of shoes. I can't finish my Club Cola.

Ilse notices us looking round and says, "Enough of here, I think. Come. It's quite a walk to my home."

Mum pauses at the young man's table and gives him some of our marks.

"Mum, what the hell are you doing?"

"We cannot spend this money in a day, Jacqueline."

"Let's give it to Ilse then."

"She is too proud."

Ilse smiles at Mum, and they hold hands as if they're about to run hell-for-leather to the trout pond again to escape the tension in the house.

Other relatives like us with one-day passes must feel this kind of love, but without the Wall, it might be the short-lived kind, like a match struck in the wind. One quick flare and it's gone. In the ordinary world, they might be the kind of people who spot their relatives turning up at the front door and dash out the back to hide in the coal-bunker.

But Mum and Ilse share something that has stayed alight all these years. It would scorch you if you touched it.

We walk past a tiny old man carrying wood scraps in a shopping bag. I have to stop Mum giving him money too. We need to keep enough for our *Knusper Flocken*.

Two women in starched white uniforms are pulling a strange cart stuffed with two rows of four fat-cheeked toddlers sitting opposite each other on red metal seats and clutching a central hand-rail.

"Their job is to care for children while their mothers work," Ilse explains when she sees me looking at the women.

I wouldn't mind having children if I could offload them onto a trolley, hop on Ilse's tram and model for Biba by a fountain all day until I scooped my babies off their red seats and breezed home to put on an apron and cook Peter's schnitzel.

Ilse's flat is in a grand bullet-scarred corner house with a carved arched door and a stately staircase. It smells of school floor-wax. Painted slogans have bled into the walls of the stairwells and landings, but the atmosphere is calm and peaceful.

The flat itself, despite the high, carved ceilings, is like a tall cardboard box with a few pieces of thin square furniture, the functional kind, mostly fitted against the walls in units, and a few hard, low-level chairs. Everything is terribly brown, similar to Grandma's utility stuff, but without its chunkiness.

This is not a house where people dash about or keep being interrupted by doorbells and telephones or milkmen. I can't imagine anyone shouting or throwing a toad-in-the-hole at the walls. It is tidy, although there is little to keep tidy. Ilse clearly values everything, from the neatly arranged food-packets on the flimsy-looking kitchen shelves to the solid-looking cake under a glass bowl on the sideboard.

The beige and brown wallpaper is brick-effect. The wall-unit is made of pretend wood, the grain in orderly stripes. Two yellow apples sit in a bowl with a bunch of keys and a worn pencil. The bowl sits on an extravagant lace mat that has been saved from some long ago time. Otherwise, only a few books, an orange candle stub and an empty vase sit on the shelves. No flowers.

Ilse's television-set has the central spot in the unit. No plant with heart-shaped leaves, no glass ash-tray full of toffee wrappers and tooth-picks, no photograph of children with pudding-bowl hair-cuts on top of it. Just a proud coat of polish.

"We have West German programmes here, you know," Ilse tells us with a grin.

"I am surprised," Mum says, looking around as if she's expecting to find a *Radio Times*.

"Well, as our leaders cannot block television signals so easily, they tell us how wicked the West is with *Der schwarze Kanal.*"

"That means the black channel," Mum tells me.

"It is very clever," Ilse goes on. "In the German language a second meaning of *Kanal* is perhaps 'gutter' or 'drain', I think."

"'Sewer'?" Mum suggests.

"Ah yes. Sewer. The black channel, you see, is a recording of the programmes they do not like us to see, but with a communist voice that comes through and tells us how things really are."

It must be like watching *Crossroads* with someone shouting out that Amy Turtle is a covert train-robber. I would resent the interruptions, although living with Grandma I am probably immune to them.

I sip the coffee and try not to shudder. Just sitting here with Mum, who seems younger with Ilse, I breathe in the hushed air, listening to the plain clock's gentle tick and the polite creaking of the floors above. Feet tread with respect. Other people's doors close with a soft click. The genteel past is still here, out of tune with the crude graffiti in the stairwells and the porridgy stuff they have plastered over the damaged walls.

"Mostly chicory," Ilse tells us, nodding at her coffee-cup. "I'm used to it now. It tastes a little better than the pig-mud we drank in the forties."

Her long-suffering smile reminds me of wives who shake their heads and tut about their husbands always disappearing into the shed or leaving the toilet-lid up when you know they don't expect things to be any other way.

"Later you shall meet my friends from the other flats," Ilse tells us. "They want to teach us the Lipsi, our new approved dance. We learned the steps from the television." She smiles and rolls a cigarette. "Oh yes, the government allows art forms to enter our culture, as long as they have a strong socialist heartbeat. The Twist, for example, is far too shocking."

I know what she means. Last year, I saw Otis Redding singing "Shake" on *Ready, Steady, Go!* There were gyrating dancers, flailing limbs and at least one bare midriff. Tch-tch. How would that go down here? Dad said, "Blood and sand, I'll have to cover my eyes," proceeding to glue himself to the screen, and Grandma said, "Ooh, haven't the black and white minstrels got a lot to answer for?"

"Our dance is...how you say it...demure. Suitable for young and old," Ilse says, winking at me again. "You see, we need protection from evil. We are children always. Not to be corrupted."

Everything seems less sinister the longer I sit in the brown chair and stir the melamine cup of brown sediment that passes for coffee. This is a proper home and for the first time since we arrived, I am not damp with nerves. If I had the latest *Mandy* on my lap and could forget the world outside, it would all be fine. *Petticoat* feels like a step too far now. Tuesday has stepped onto a catwalk that runs for more than a million miles, and she's just not ready.

Soldiers are pacing the streets below. Fractured families pray, or plot an escape that could end in a hail of bullets. The Wall is closing us in. But I feel so safe with Ilse that the fact that I have only ever danced with a partner once before—a terrifying gallop around the junior gym with Gary Bust, whose Way-Finder shoes kicked my shins so hard his secret compass flew out of the heel—I don't even feel anxious about learning the Lipsi.

Life must have followed this homely pattern after the war was declared. From what Grandma tells me about those times, one minute it was pass the ginger-nuts and let's all have a sing-song by the fire with *Peg's Paper*, and the next minute was...exactly the same. Just less sugar in the tea, less coal for the fire. Shortages meant solidarity. Home mattered more than ever. With less to have, they stretched what was there. Nothing smug or stiff-upper-lipped about it; it was just how things were. Ilse's life has taken a chilling twist, but that same spirit is here in this flat.

She passes me a slice of the cold-dog cake she made for us this morning. It's one of those cocoa, crushed biscuit and melted margarine mixtures that set hard in the fridge. It reminds me of the unique taste of school cookery-lesson food when it isn't cheese-pie or semolina. We're meant to take it home, but can never resist it in the bus queue, except when Gillian and I made the Christmas pudding that put us in mind of Pedigree Chum. Ilse's cake isn't exactly choc-olaty, but it is *lecker*, which means 'bloody luscious'. Especially if your mum's cakes have the consistency of a cliff face, the chalk kind. I lick my fingers while Ilse and Mum light up cigarettes.

"I can't believe they let women drive trams," Mum says, looking for an ash-tray.

"Why not, Birgit?" Ilse says. She passes Mum a small ash-tray piled high with dog-ends.

"But when we were young," Mum says, "we were taught that the heart of a German woman's life should be the three Ks: *Kinder, Kirche, Küche.*"

Children, church and kitchen, apparently, a principle dating back to Kaiser blooming Bill. "For Beate," Mum goes on, "that is still her belief."

For Beate, there should be a fourth K, for *Kirschwasser.*

"Yes, my dear Birgit," Ilse agrees. "But since the war, it has become a ridic-ulous saying. Beate and I became rubble-women. We helped to rebuild the ruined city. We cared for the wounded, buried the dead and rescued any-thing and anyone we could. We had no children, no kitchen. And as far as I was concerned, since it was roofless, if the rain was pouring we also had no church. But as Germany recovered, the West returned to the old ways. Women were back in the home again, cooking and having babies. In the East, we became workers as well as housewives. Women can do it all here you know."

Mum, who concentrates with varying degrees of success on two of the three Ks, the church not being a feature of our life in England, struggles to take this in.

"And the state help you with this?" she asks.

"Birgit, we are encouraged so much, you would not believe."

"It sounds fabulous," I tell her.

"Fabulous? Ah, perhaps it is, Jacqueline."

"Well, you must have more choice of things to do. It's exciting. I mean, women here don't have to polish their sideboards all day."

Ilse winks at Mum. "But Jacqueline," she says, "choice is the one thing we do not have. So many men have died in the war or escaped this country that women *must* drive trams and dig ditches! The country would not function without us. We are expected, not asked, to do it."

I swallow the dusty dregs of the disgusting chicory-coffee, which tastes of old leaves, to show her I don't mind it at all. She watches me and her laugh bubbles up.

"So polite," she says, shaking her head in wonder and seizing Mum's hand. "I hear the English have beautiful manners and now I know it's true."

She shows me two presents she has bought for Victor. One is a comic about a yellow teddy-bear called Bummi, which he'll love just for the name. The other is a kit similar to Lego bricks for building a modern East German block of flats, pre-made in white plastic panels with red window sills and quickly assembled to the height of twenty storeys. He will love it. T-K can lie on the flat roof to snipe at people or whatever he does when he's on top of a building. It reminds me of the pre-fabs in Oaking, except they have only one level and are meant to be temporary homes.

Every pre-fab has properly fitted cupboards and a gas fridge that tucks into the corner. Our cupboards at home have gaps between them where the steam and grease stick disgusting balls of dirty fluff to the sides. Elsie's pre-fab can be cleaned throughout in fifty minutes flat and is so compact she can keep an eye on Big Stan at all times. When Grandma used to stay there, before Elsie put a stop to that, she slept in the tiny second bedroom, which was home to Elsie's parrot, Neville, and all Stan's spare knife-sets and old boxing-gloves. But his great boxing and butchering hands also tenderly glued a bedside shelf onto the headboard for Grandma and placed Elsie's spare pink-frilled lamp and a chipped porcelain lady in crinolines on it. Grandma said, "Sheer blooming luxury to have your own special shelf right beside you, even when you sit up and bash your bonce on it."

"I have friends who live in these brand-new boxes that are made in factories," Ilse says, pointing at the toy pre-fab. "But I am glad we found this beautiful old house. Beate and I moved in here with many other homeless people and refugees after the Allies came. The owners had fled the country long ago before the Nazis could catch up with them. It somehow survived the air-raids, although the roof is still so badly damaged we must catch the drips. Beate used to love taking charge of the buckets! The rooms were still grand before they were turned into apartments."

"It is like my old home," Mum says, lighting another cigarette. "Imagine the parties here, the chandeliers and a grand piano, a ballroom that took up more space than two or three of these flats."

"Yes, there was still a piano here when we arrived. Sadly, the Soviet soldiers had not treated it well. As for the ballroom, even if the owners had still lived here, the state authorities would have cut the house up into these flats. The pretty carvings along the walls are still here, at least parts of them, but the war has wiped away most of its history. And the need to make lots of these sensible workers' deposit boxes has removed nearly all the rest." She gives me her usual smile and wink, stubbing out her cigarette with a hint of controlled fury.

***

We visit Ilse's friends, trailing up and down the beautiful staircases because the lifts haven't worked for a while. In the other little brown flats, all with identical furniture, we meet Silke, Uwe, Barbara, Karin and Dieter, all close comrades, they tell us, their work binding them together. They are machinists in a textile factory and make jokes about their hearing being poor from the racket in what sounds like a vast windowless shed stuffed with needle-pounding contraptions.

Barbara has calloused fingers from the unforgiving work. Silke, older and with an even more delicate frame, has misshapen hands and a useless right ear.

"Our factory has clubs after work. We must attend them for the friendship it provides," Uwe tells us.

"You can't have much time at home," Mum says. "Especially the women with children to collect and meals to cook."

"Women are allowed time off to have babies," Barbara says. "They can raise young children without being afraid their jobs will not wait for them. It is so easy to return to work because we have the State kindergartens. It is very modern here. Oh yes."

She doesn't have Ilse's mocking tone and looks shocked when I tell her hardly any mums work in Oaking. Gaye Kennedy's aunt is a go-go dancer by night. Every New Year's Eve, when she insists on singing "Hey Big Spender" in their front-room, they have to hide the budgie in the attic. The central nervous system of a bird is not designed for that sort of shock.

"In East Germany," Ilse explains, "women have the same rights as men. The difference is that mothers are allowed one day at home with their children every month. And they are also paid for having babies. *Mein Gott*, what stops us having a whole army of them, you may ask? Easy money, no?"

"So, the more you give birth, the more you are paid?" Mum says, her mouth gaping.

"It's like collecting milk bottle tops for guide dogs," I point out to her. "Fifty's probably enough for a paw, but you have to drink gallons to get half a puppy."

Giving Ilse a glance to reprimand her scornful tone and me a dark look, Barbara says, "It costs us very little money to bring up a family."

"That is because there is nothing to buy," Ilse chips in.

"Rent never rises," Uwe says, ignoring Ilse to support Barbara's party line. "Prices are low."

Uwe and Barbara seem grateful for their plain homes and grisly clothes and harsh jobs, for their daily guarantee that this is all there is and everyone has the same, ruling out jealousy or poisonous grudges.

"East Germany is all about hard-working families," Uwe tells us in his smooth English, his words marbled with pride.

"Oh sure, they want us girls in the kitchen as well as in the bedroom as well as on the machines having our ear-drums blown to pieces," Karin says, rolling a tight cigarette on her lap.

"What else?" Uwe booms, imposing and beefy in his square donkey jacket and work-boots, despite the sweltering day.

He speaks as if work is their right and their duty, for men and women, mothers too. It's so hard for me to understand. I know nothing other than fathers setting off to work while mothers make up the fire and stir the porridge. And in the afternoons, fathers come home to warm their hands and sit their children on their lap while mothers stir the stew. That's how I imagine it will be for me and Peter.

"And one day when I'm married," Karin says, hands on her hips, "my children will stare at the posters on the kindergarten walls all day long and learn their messages by heart. 'For Peace and Socialism, Are You Prepared?' When I carry them home after ten hours at the factory, stopping to queue for meat and butter on the way, I will listen to them sleepily singing 'When I Grow Up I'll Join the People's Army'."

I'm fascinated by her green nylon trousers. They are the most awful shape, the fabric washed so many times it's bitty and thin. She sounds angry and plucky, her spirit more alive than her fashion-sense. As she licks her cigarette-paper, her small eyes dart like tadpoles in my direction, as if I come from Mars. Tuesday would have given her such a glare, but I smile because however bad my clothes are, compared with those nylon monstrosities they look like something from Biba.

***

In her own flat again, Ilse shows Mum and me her copy of *Sybille* magazine, smoothing its thin cover before she opens it.

"The clothes in this country are so, so bad," she says with one of her winks, her eyes rolling upwards to Karin's flat, where the green trouser-legs flap and the plastic flatties pace. "But *Sybille* is a way to fight back."

She glances up again before opening the magazine, spreading out the dress patterns printed on cheap paper inside it.

The pictures show beautiful girls in truly elegant dresses, but they are only connected by a thread to the latest fashions. One page reveals girls posing in a tumble-down street, their romantic ballerina dresses billowing in the wind, their expressions fierce. They look as if they have danced their way out of the rubble to light up the grim background.

"These styles are all created by unknown designers," Ilse says, turning another page. "None of the dresses are for sale. Our stores never stock fashion. We have one size for all on the racks. We must make do with any material we can find to sew the *Sybille* patterns."

Mum and I watch the pages turn. *Sybille* is hollering a message to all East German women, telling them they could look a little less prudish and dull. For once, there is no State propaganda. Women are beckoned beyond their dismal world and shown how to make something of their own.

"The patterns are our promise of escape, even if the escape is only in our imaginations," Ilse says. "Uwe knows a model who works for *Sybille* and she says the Central Committee is watching the magazine. All the staff and models are under surveillance. The articles in here often have to be changed. If they don't conform to the way the State wants us to think, some are refused permission and cannot be published at all. The model's last cover picture was forbidden because she was posing behind a barrier."

"What?"

"The State wishes us all to look free, Jacqueline. East German women do not stand behind walls. They stand in front of them."

I imagine an Englishman in a bowler hat scrutinising *Woman's Realm* and shaking his head at the cable-knit cardigans.

"The models are not professionals," she explains. "They would not appear in your...what do you have in England?"

"*Petticoat*," I tell her in a respectful tone.

"Well, they would not appear in there. But not being professional makes them very natural," Ilse points out.

It's true. They have Tuesday's awkwardness, but with style. And they look as free as it's possible to be.

"*Sybille* sells out fast. I'm lucky to have this copy," Ilse says. "I so wanted the dress pattern. I can now unite fashion and politics. When I sew, every stitch is a small protest."

"But can you buy the material?" Mum asks.

"No, Birgit. Not in the shops. We have to make it up as we go along. The young mother on the ground floor made a white pleated skirt with nappy cloth. And Karin's family has an allotment so they gave me some plastic sheets for protecting strawberry plants. I can make a raincoat from those."

"A plastic raincoat?" I yell. "They're in fashion in England. I've been wanting one for ages. Not the fold-up type for men on bicycles. A snazzy sort."

"Well, there we are," Ilse says. "This is the proof that I am a secret fashion expert. Just don't tell the Stasi I'm snazzy."

"I'll keep it under my hat," I promise.

Being in East Germany is like swimming in an underwater world. Everything is distorted by its own atmosphere. For Ilse, this is just the way she lives. She is not disturbed by it, just amused.

Even Karin's trousers have their own obstinate style, a sense of belonging here, and she wears them with her own hard-chinned flair, not quite willing to view this life as entirely normal.

I swear I can hear her match striking every half an hour upstairs while she irons all her friends' factory overalls.

"She takes on the ironing to stop her going mad," Ilse tells us. "Karin is being watched, you see, followed by cars that creep behind her when she walks to work. And the manager at her factory has moved her to a boring job in a different section. Just to keep her in line."

Ilse suspects the hearty Uwe of being a possible informer, although she doesn't think there's much to tell. Karin toes the line, even though she is outspoken.

"But Uwe is Karin's friend."

"Eyes are everywhere, Jacqueline. On the streets. At work. Even in your own block of flats," Mum reminds me.

"It is so. Exterior eyes. Interior eyes," Ilse whispers, her eyes serious for once. "None of us are truly alone. I watch myself all the time. My own eyes see more of me than anyone else's can."

While the goulash simmers we have time to visit the supermarket.

"Meat here takes a long time to cook," Ilse says, taking a string-bag from a hook by the door as we leave. "No tender cuts, I'm afraid. Mystery meat, I call it."

Mum smiles. "The meat we ate as girls fell from the bone," she tells me, linking arms with Ilse. "The veal moulted in our mouths."

"Melted, Mum."

"I remember the strong smell of the butcher even now. And the cooked meats in the next shop, smoky and peppery."

Ilse breathes in hard. "Oh Birgit, I can smell it now, even here." And for once she doesn't break into peals of laughter.

Victor and I go shopping with Mum during the school holidays. At two o'clock we walk to the parade and weave in and out of the shops, filling our basket with loaves and chops and iced buns and shampoo. If Dad hasn't pilfered Victor's piggy-bank, he uses his pocket-money to buy yet another kit for making stuffed felt creatures. He isn't all war comics and Messerschmitts. His collection is almost complete, with only a stern-faced kitten and a demented-looking zebra to go.

In summer, Mum buys us ice-creams if she has a spare shilling. I think she goes without the Brillo or the soft toilet-paper to make sure of it. In winter we huddle in the warm bakery before braving the rain or the ice again. Victor moans about wearing a balaclava, but if Mum lets him take it off, he whines about his freezing ears. He is such a square.

But East Berlin is nothing like Oaking Parade. In Ilse's district, queues grow out of the shops and take root along the pavements. Older women stare and shift their weight from one leg to another. Mothers try to ignore the tedium and heat, their children tugging at their hands. If the shelves cannot be restocked, everyone has to come back in the morning.

"Sold out for now," Ilse explains as we pass a long line of people breaking up and heading home.

At least we are going to the supermarket, rather than waiting for loaves or fish. I imagine it will be like Mace's, but with peculiar brands. At least it will be cool inside. Mace's is cold even in summer, especially the refrigerated section.

But this shop is no Mace's. It's thick with horrible heat and sweat from all the people waiting to pay. The shelves are scattered, rather than filled, with goods. Ilse picks up a packet of dried lentils and the last jar of gherkins. We wait to pay, Mum and I exhausted by the long walk and the longer wait. It's normal for Ilse. She sets off to work at six every morning. At night she drags out her zinc bath and waits ages for the water to heat. There is always a queue to use the one toilet in her block.

After her shifts, she dashes up and down the stairs from one flat to another with a piece of paper, taking lists and collecting cash from her elderly neighbours and rushing out again to the shops.

"They hand their money to me with great hope," she says. "But often the shop is empty and I must let them down."

"I know you drive a tram, but are women allowed to drive cars too?" I ask her. "Because it would save you all this walking."

"Oh of course, Jacqueline. Women are treated exactly the same. They drive. They earn the same pay. We all work a fifty hour week. But, you know, that has made it harder. As well as having a job and raising families, women must cope with having nothing to buy for the table. The Nazi belief in the perfect family, with the smiling mother roasting meat for everyone and polishing their home, lives on here in East Germany. But we are also expected to be the same as men in a country that has no money and no imported goods. The old tradition has become impossible. And as for my car, I am waiting for one, the same as everyone else."

"Roy saved for three years. How long will you have to wait?" Mum asks.

"The waiting list is long. It's not just about saving the money. Trabants are only made here in this country and we do not always have the materials. I expect to wait fifteen years. But I am happy to walk, you know. I like to breathe the air after driving the tram all day."

I admire her thin legs, the calf muscle standing proud beneath the hand-sewn frock with its red ric-rac edging. Her ballerina feet never move while the queue is static. Mine fidget and Mum's shuffle about. Ilse has the poise and patience of a statue.

But fifteen years is endless, longer than I have lived. And after all that waiting, not even a choice. Practically every car we see is a Trabant. Clattering and smelly, they churn out clouds of black exhaust.

"The petrol goes into a tank above the engine," Ilse explains. "There is no pump. Only gravity sends the fuel to the right place. So if the front end crashes into something there's a terrible danger of fire. Trabant drivers are like doctors with sick babies. They must do some kind of surgery on them every day to help them last a lifetime. But I am still looking forward to mine. My name is on the list."

"How can you look forward fifteen years?"

"Because that is what we do."

"Can't you have cars from other countries sent over? We saw all different kinds in West Berlin."

"Other countries aren't interested in our worthless currency, so nothing is imported." Ilse lowers her voice. "You know, this country does not exist. The West does not recognise it. Nothing and no one comes in. And no one can leave."

There is no ice-cream cabinet in the supermarket. No Corona in tall bottles. No imperial mints. Nothing much at all. Tiny trolleys that look as if they're made for dolls rather than people. I suppose they don't need to be very deep or strong since there's nothing to put in them.

"My God, the prices," Mum says. "Are they real? They seem to have frozen in 1936."

"Yes," Ilse says. "That is correct."

Mum shakes her head and stares at the miserable shelves. Not much good having cheap things if there's nothing to buy.

Ilse spots a man carrying a tray of minced-beef portions at the far end of the shop and asks us to keep her place while she dashes over to him. I wish he was offering iced ginger beer.

Before the assistant can pile his meat onto the little counter, the crowd has taken it all. He can barely hang onto the empty tray as the discs of meat are snatched up. He's left to gather up the fluttering circles of bloody waxed paper that sandwiched them together.

Ilse is one of the lucky few. She turns away from a bent old man in a sagging checked shirt still holding out his hand on the off-chance someone will take pity and let him have their miserable piece. No one can afford to be generous to him. Hopeful people are waiting for Ilse back at the flats, including a pregnant widow and a woman of eighty in a wheelchair.

As she carries the meat back to us like an athlete with a trophy, she throws it to me and veers to another part of the store like a rugby-player on course for a try, returning with rumpled hair and an armful of toothbrushes.

"Such a crowd," she says, panting. "No one has been able to get these for so long. The factory caught fire, you see."

"One toothbrush factory for the whole country?" Mum asks.

"Yes, just one."

She has six toothbrushes. One is for Silke. She squeals at the prospect of giving her the good news. She will stockpile the rest with her boxes of dried peas and jars of strawberry jam, all the same type, which form a tower in a corner of her bedroom. She has to take what she can whenever it appears, an art she has been perfecting for over twenty years.

War is supposed to end, one way or another. Here, where it has set in cold stone, this is how she will always live.

While we drag our feet forward another inch, Mum says, "I could have brought you a toothbrush."

"No. You must never worry about me," Ilse says, squeezing Mum's arm. "East Germany is the most wealthy and well-equipped of all the socialist states in Eastern Europe. I am very lucky."

Her clear voice carries, just in case that tired-eyed lady serving at the counter is an informer, or that bent old man clutching his haul of toothbrushes, sweating in his ancient suit and tie, or the harassed assistant with the meat-tray who has just slapped down a pound of shredded liver. Ilse ducks out of the queue, dives towards him. But a throng of old ladies in head-scarves tackle him first. She shrugs and grins as she comes back to her spot.

"Ah, little Ilse," Mum says, hugging her. "You could almost be English, you know. They accept hardship with good grace. Roy even eats celery if we visit someone's house for a meal. What is it, Jacqueline, that the English always say?"

"Put up and shut up, Mum."

Ilse bursts out laughing, winking at me. "Oh, Birgit, in that case, I have much in common with you English. If ever I can come to see for myself, I will fit in so well that no one will guess my past."

It's such a small wish.

We walk back to the flat with the toothbrushes and the few other items of shopping. The course of the Wall has made the route longer than it used to be.

"I still expect to walk along a favourite street I've known all my life, but as I turn the corner I remember it is not possible now. I must change direction at the last minute."

"My dear Ilse, I cannot imagine how you manage here."

"Oh Birgit, never worry about me. Too much sadness would rot me like a fallen apple. And I do not wish for wrinkles. I am happy, you know. I have my good companion, Silke. She understands me better than anyone. We have a special friendship, one that may not be so easy in the West. I have my place in this society. My job is secure. I'm needed. I'm paid. I have more food than in those bad years. If I become ill, the hospital is free. I have friends who all understand how my life feels, because theirs is the same."

Ilse's eyes are fixed like two dark fish in a frozen sea. Mum and I pretend not to notice her long silence that follows. We just keep walking, our feet in rhythm until we reach Ilse's building with its long history and stubborn beauty. The pre-fab blocks we have passed on the way may take a few years to acquire the same soul.

Ilse pauses on the top step, her key in the lock.

"Look, I have accepted this life. I have survived. I helped Beate to survive. Now she is over there and I'm here. Both surviving still."

"Is that enough?" Mum asks.

"If you had stayed in Berlin after the war and lived here in those times, you would not say that now. The people of Berlin keep this city open, Birgit. And our survival made me realise something. To find happiness after suffering, you must concentrate on the facts, on all that is real and true, even if life is not perfect. Even if a wall appears in the middle of the night. Never concentrate on hope. You will be disappointed. Manage with what is here now. And be glad it's not that same terrible war."

She rattles her string-bag of toothbrushes and laughs to show her sadness is parcelled up now. We will never see it again.

***

Ilse's friends squash into the living-room and flick through *Sybille*. Some of them even admire my clothes. Not with envy, just curiosity. We squat on the floor to eat the thin goulash and a powdery chocolate blancmange. Ilse hands the food through the serving-hatch that is actually a very modern feature and I pretend Peter is standing the other side of it, passing me the braised cucumbers.

It is an age before Ilse switches on her skinny little lamp. She has to be careful about the electric bill. I bet if you wait for the red-print one, like Dad does, you get arrested. The lamplight shines on her prized red telephone and I wonder how often it rings, and who else listens.

Telephoning the West is impossible and mail is checked by the secret police. If the pastry-chef ever writes, his letters wouldn't reach her, or possibly just one censored page. Saying "I love you" might be code for "Let's bundle you over the border in the boot of my bread-van."

Ilse and I slice gherkins in the plain little kitchen.

"I love your skirt," she says. "Such fine fabric."

Blimey, no one's ever said that before. I shall see Spotwood and Mole's Young Fashion department in a whole new light now.

"I'd like it shorter though. And more A-line. More Biba."

She gives me a look of total incomprehension.

"I'm not supposed to know about fashion yet," I tell her. "But I look through *Petticoat* magazine when I get the chance. That's where I find out about clothes. But I haven't an earthly chance of being allowed them."

"Nor me," she says.

Aunt Ilse and me, both banned from reading *Petticoat*. I catch her eye and we both snort with laughter. Then she actually guffaws, really meaning it, not just being a good sport, the same as Gillian and me when we have hysterics at school.

"My darling Jacqueline, I hope you are permitted to read it before your youth is over. Otherwise you may be too ancient to enjoy your, what do you say, Beeber dresses, and will have to wear this stuff instead." She screws up a handful of her cheap frock and laughs like a drain.

She is pigheadedly feminine, even though she has to work like a man in a man's job. She must even wear trousers on the trams. She also knows how to unblock a drain. Life here is wedged in the past, but a planet from the future has crashed into it, a combination of the Dark Ages and *Lost in Space*.

After the food, Mum and I are taught the Lipsi.

Dance should be about moving in a way that suggests something more. Belly-dancers on television make me blush. And as for the Tango, what with those long strides up and down and the man flinging the woman backwards, then leaning over her, practically horizontal, you can't slide a wafer between them. And, not as high-scoring on sex-appeal, I suppose, there's the Mashed Potato.

"Do you peel the potato first?" Karin asks in her deadpan way. I never know if she's joking or not.

The Lipsi is in a league of its own. The East German authorities insist their dances are performed without a whiff of sauciness. They have supposedly tried to make it exciting, but have stripped the thrill out of dancing like whipping the Flake out of a Ninety-Nine. It's just a series of plain steps, a dance without dancers.

In pairs, we step right and left, tapping our feet politely, and flinging out an arm here and there, like children acting out "I'm A Little Teapot". No touching, of course. A few of the steps remind me of tap class when I was four, but most of them are a dead ringer for the march of the stiff young guards we saw earlier.

Finally, we swirl round and the man holds the woman around the waist. No pelvis involved.

"This is faster than other dances we've known, you know," Karin says, poker-faced as she and Uwe pick their way through the steps with painstaking accuracy. "So modern, the Lipsi."

Ilse dances only with Silke, neither of them mastering the steps, but giggling like I would at school with Gillian. When the dance is over, they sit on the floor. Ilse turns her back and Silke's legs wrap around her. Silke tidies Ilse's rumpled hair with long strokes of her comb until it's a smooth, copper curtain again.

Mum and I dance together until she asks to sit down and watch. Her eyes lose focus as the hours tick by, and she prepares to miss Ilse all over again.

I dance the Lipsi with everyone in turn. Dad would have loved it. Despite all the restriction and shortage and bleakness, life here is a party.

"Who needs Elvis?" shouts Dieter.

Who indeed?

8

FULL MOON

Before we leave, Mum visits the dismal loo on the floor below—no dreaded ridge, but no seat either, and dozens of fat carved cherubs still blowing their trumpets from the high ceiling.

While the primitive plumbing is belching away and echoing in the stairwell, Ilse hands me a creased photograph and some papers.

"Jacqueline, I used to keep this safe inside a book of fairy tales that Beate found in the ruins. It never left her side. She even took it into the hospital. I hope she has it still. This picture was taken just before my last ballet lesson. Birgit was planning to come with me to play the piano, but the British air-raids started that night and there was no more dancing."

In the picture, Mum's smile is hesitant, her dark eyes huge, her hair bleached platinum. Beate's hair is so severely drawn back her features are stretched into a grim mask. Ilse is wearing her satin ballet-shoes and her wide smile. Mum, guarded and uncomfortable in her own skin, stands in the middle, trying to stretch her arms around the others. Ilse leans in towards her, but the shadow of Mum's thin fingers barely reaches Beate's shoulder.

Even without the badly-dyed hair and contrasting black eyebrows, it would be clear that Mum did not belong with these girls. There is a serial in *Mandy* about a Polish ballerina on the run from the Nazis, who says things like, "The polka is now the dance of death." I showed it to Mum just before we came to Berlin, and she sat down with the tea-towel bunched in her lap while the washing-up water turned stone cold. I would never have shown her the comic if I had known her own story.

The papers Ilse gives me are covered in musical manuscript, a composition Mum's father wrote for Ilse and Beate's mother.

"Our mother kept it in the attic, beneath a floorboard," Ilse says. "It was one of the few things saved. Perhaps Birgit will play it one day."

"We don't have a piano though."

"Perhaps a friend has one?"

Gillian's mother has a baby-grand that none of the family can play. She just likes having something to French-polish. I would like to see Mum sit on the quilted stool and play the piece, providing Gillian allows her to march across the threshold.

"Jacqueline, does your mother sometimes seem to disappear?"

"All the time."

"I sense that she hides herself. But, know this, she is tied to you with the strongest knot in the world."

I tuck the photograph into my bag, my hands shaking a little.

When the sun rinses the sky with brownish-orange light, Ilse walks with us to the station, eking out every last minute.

"Is there any time to see Bernauer Strasse from this side?" I ask her.

"Bernauer?" she says. "No, Jacqueline. Too many guards and dogs patrolling. And nothing to see."

"Do you think it will ever be rebuilt?"

"I think not. The people who lived there will have new lives now. Why not change your project to something happier?"

She gives me a bright smile and I push my notepad back in my bag. Ilse is too clear-cut for contrasts, not clouded by any of the shadows I had imagined.

We have to keep walking in case we miss the train. Mum and Ilse are holding onto each other, knowing this is all they will ever have.

"Oh Ilse, I wish you could climb into your tram one morning, turn to the West and keep driving," Mum whispers.

"Hush, Birgit. In any case, the West would not allow me in."

"The West would not allow?"

"Crazy, yes? In the fifties, the West allowed only men to drive trams. And so the wise people in charge of public transport here in East Berlin insisted that all our trams crossing into the West were driven by women only. Of course the West refused to let them in, so East Berlin were able to complain that this time, it was the West stopping the flow of border-traffic, when really it was yet another way of keeping us here."

Ilse tips back her head to laugh. I would join in, but the craziness is beginning to feel like a nightmare.

In Pariser Platz, we stand at the Brandenburg gate, a massive archway built hundreds of years ago as part of an ordinary city wall, the triumphant entrance to the city. A bronze sculpture of a chariot pulled by four horses graces the top.

"The driver of the chariot was the goddess of peace," Ilse says. "But Napoleon took her. Berlin got her back after Waterloo and she became Victoria, symbol of victory. But in 1945..."

"In 1945," Mum continues for her, "this gate was one of the few structures still standing in this square. The copper horses were badly damaged. The one on the right was your favourite when you were young, Ilse."

Ilse looks up at her charger. "But after the war," she says, "he lay on his side. After drinking half a bottle of brandy Beate found in a broken pram, I remember yelling, 'Someone call the horse vet!' And the horses did get their treatment—they were melted and reborn in bronze. A quick recovery, yes?"

She smiles as if this is all a huge joke, then becomes deadly serious.

"This beautiful avenue, even in ruins, still swept through the Brandenburg gateway. But now we must all stop here, at Khrushchev's solution."

Mum and I look at the Wall. The blue uniforms of the West Berlin police line up on one side, the green uniforms of the East German people's police form ranks on the other, and the red flag flies above.

"We have inherited two cathedrals, some magnificent museums and our glorious Unter den Linden," Ilse whispers. "But Socialism prefers everything dark and ugly. And so, in the middle of all the splendour lies this monster! But I have found the answer. The best way to bear it is to let the...what do you call it in your project? Ah yes, contrast. Let this shameful contrast expose the great building's charm. Concentrate beyond the painful sight, let it fade, and you will see only the old glory."

Mum looks up at the horses silhouetted by the sinking sun. "If our great gate must now separate the city," she says, "is that victory?"

"Birgit, we have to accept how we live now."

"Yesterday I thought I recognised Berlin. But not now, Ilse. The soul is missing."

Ilse shakes her head, smiling. "No. Your head makes too much of it. You do not see the plain facts, Birgit. Half of the city is all of the city to me."

Mum will never see that. Mothers resist adjusting to change. Years ago, all Ilse wanted Mum to tell her was whether they would all die. To still be alive against all the odds is enough for her.

"And look," she continues, "the Brandenburg gate is still here, Birgit. East Berlin rebuilt it, West Berlin mended the chariot and horses and it is still seen from both sides."

But for Mum, Pariser Platz is desolate, the famous arch a barrier like the Wall itself; the glorious and the grim thrown together. Mum refuses to see the dignity Ilse tries to unearth. She walks away and, without hesitating, I take her arm.

"Remember, everyone thought Oaking Borstal was a hideous eyesore," I remind her, prattling horribly, adopting the style of mothers everywhere. "But when the *Gazette* said it had historical significance and the skyline would look bare without it, they all changed their tune. It was all oh, look at the pretty weathered stone and that magnificent oak door with its fifty-odd bolts. I bet the wayward boys inside didn't say that when it clanged shut behind them."

She smiles in her far-off, watery way and clutches my arm tighter. It's a bit painful with my Tufty bag all squashed up in there too, but it feels fine, I suppose.

When I look round, the TV Tower is watching, stalking us. Majestic from the other side, it seems menacing over here. I turn back to the view of the West. If Dad and Victor were standing over there now, they would be thirty seconds away. But tripwire, guns, dogs, mines and guards make them our deadly enemy. The walk through the gate of peace would be the walk of death.

"I stand here often," Ilse says.

I wonder if she's watching the ghost of her pastry-chef and an outline of the sister and nephew she will never touch. But she says no more, just laughs at herself again.

While we wait to cross the intersection of Unter den Linden and Fried-richstrasse, I notice the illuminated traffic-light men.

The plump, arm-swinging, hat-wearing characters are the only bright colours in East Berlin. The red one holds his chubby arms out to make a warning barrier and the marching green one's nose and hands are softly rounded.

Wait here. Be careful, one says. See my hat. I'm in charge.

My turn now, interrupts the other. Cross now. Your wait is over.

I look back once we reach the other side of the road. The red man reappears, bright in the evening sky, his arms outstretched once more.

No going back.

Ilse and Mum pause on the corner of the road to the station. This is their last chance to speak.

"Birgit, I cannot let you go without saying sorry," Ilse says, taking hold of Mum's hands.

People skirt around us. Wafts of cheap cooked chicken float past from the new rotisserie. Its strip-light flickers.

"Why sorry?" Mum says, gripping the small hands that clasp hers.

"We kept you safe all that time, then behaved as if you had never existed. We sent you out like a cat into the night. Forgive us."

Mum looks as if she has carried a sack of sponges on her back through heavy rain and someone has just squeezed all the water out.

"Ilse, I put you all in danger. You sent me away so I could live. And look at me. Look at all I have now."

Mum kisses her sister's hands. As they hold each other for the last time, two border guards walk by, boots clicking, leather holsters squeaking. They smell of communist chicken dinner, pungent cigarettes and cheap washing powder. I hear them mutter something about time and the next train. They know what we should be doing and where we should be.

Ilse's hands drop to her sides.

"Birgit," she whispers as the guards stride away. "I know now how it felt for you to bury yourself."

Mum has received genuine Sympathy now, a heartfelt, finer feeling from someone she loves. I hope this is the moment she finally climbs out from her brittle hiding-place.

We break into a run for the train. Hurtling along the street nearly finishes Mum off. She is clutching her side and sweating. My heart thrashes about in my head. I can hear nothing except my own gasping. Ilse, programmed never to be late, has a more efficient running style than ours.

We won't be on time. Our pass will expire. I have a stitch. My legs are not working. Mum and Ilse are leaving me behind.

Oh, thank you, thank you, blessed Beatles. They're slowing down, almost at the entrance now. I can catch up. There's still a hope of getting out.

Another guard appears from the dusk, under a yellow street-lamp. Oh God, he's talking to Mum and taking things from her tartan bag. He's brandishing a folded magazine, looking at the cover, asking questions.

I walk closer. The guard is leafing through the pages, holding the magazine at arm's length like a madman with a fizzing bomb. I can see it now—an old *Woman's Realm* that has been lining the tartan bag since its inner nylon melted. Grandma bundled dozens of little sugar sachets into the bag when we were in the restaurant on the boat. The trouble was, she forgot she was holding a lit Senior Service at the time.

How could we have been idiotic enough to bring in the degenerate *Woman's Realm*? It must have stuck to the bag when they turned it out at border control. Standing between us and freedom are new-fangled diets without starch, knitting patterns to delight the cardigan-hungry man in your life and tips on cheering up his mid-week fricassee.

This man might take my mum away. I dash towards them, but have to stop. The street is spinning. The echo of the guard's boots pounds in my head, like brisk hand-clapping.

As my head-rush clears, the echo fades. He is walking away alone, the magazine under his arm, as if he just wants to borrow it. And thank you, dear Lord George Harrison, you have somehow held back the hands of the huge station clock. We have a minute to spare.

"Hurry!" Ilse calls.

Not long ago, Ilse and Mum were dancing the Lipsi, spinning time around one another, but not with the strength of spider-silk. Inside the station, Ilse reaches her boundary. We are now in the Palace of Tears.

This is the room where the visit ends. Mum and I must pass through a door that leads us deeper into the station. East Berliners are forbidden from taking another step.

The party is over. Hundreds of people are saying goodbye. This is the worst division of them all, where tears flow in rivers.

The trains are rumbling in, the clock clicking without mercy. The guards' clipped voices cut through the crying. We must proceed. Everyone in the desolate room is wrenched apart without saying a word that makes sense. No point in whispering, "See you soon," or "Bye for now." And those left behind can never say, "I'll come to you next time."

"Goodbye, Ilse."

"Goodbye, my dear Birgit."

Mum cries for Ilse's lost freedom, but Ilse no longer mourns it. Her tears are all for Mum. I have to prise their fingers apart. Before she turns away, Ilse winks at me, but not with a smile this time.

Echoes of tears rebound from the walls and ceilings, following Mum and me through the tedious checks and braced guns. One man is howling like a beaten dog. A woman carrying a cockatiel in a cage weeps while the bird watches her, its tiny yellow head tilted to one side.

I never cry much, but my eyes sting as if they are bleeding. I can't see very well and Mum can probably see nothing at all. We are the blind leading the blind.

Mothers are not supposed to cry. Daughters are not meant to be the ones with clean hankies. An old man carrying a black loaf gives me a paper tissue as he hobbles by.

I separate its two layers and blow my nose with one.

"Come on, Mum." I pass her the other flimsy half, which disintegrates and sticks to her face the moment she drenches it. Clearly a communist tissue.

I lead Mum towards the next queue, linking arms to encourage her forwards. I still can't quite forgive her, but I want to remind her that she still has me.

Mothers are supposed to know where they belong, but I suppose daughters sometimes have to take them there. At least, after peeling away the wet tissue, Mum's awful Gay Geranium lipstick is shed with it.

We are herded through the checking procedures again; the queuing, paperwork and passports, the harsh lights, secured exits and underground platforms. We watch the guards search a train inside and out, climbing onto the roof and crawling underneath it with mirrors. Armed guards clutching hungry-looking dogs keep vigil from the bridge across the line.

As the long process is about to finish, a guard appears from nowhere and asks to check through our papers once more. Mum has to empty out her bag. Please, no more contraband. Don't let there be a *Commando* in there.

The guard whisks us into another room where even more are waiting and watching. One of them separates us and tells me to sit down in a bare waiting area. He takes Mum into another room. I catch a glimpse of a thin table with an old-fashioned typewriter on it and a chair each side. Nothing else, apart from a portrait of Walter Ulbricht on the wall. Mum has to sit facing him. The door closes.

Louder than the grating and squeaking from the guards' boots, guns and stiff uniforms is the thump of my heart.

I have no idea where to look or if I'm allowed to ask a question. They might shoot me on the spot. The inside of my mouth is sandpaper, but when I finally manage to swallow, it's so deafening they all look at me. I dare not move, but I have no control over my quivering legs.

I must look as green as asparagus. The heat of welling tears gives me a focus. If I work at not blinking and think of something perfect, these men won't see me cry.

I think of Peter Fechter, wild with joy at the prospect of escape. I am surrounded by his killers, but they must never see inside my head. I imagine him soaring into the air and clearing the Wall. In this drab, creaking room with the squeak of leather and the smell of sweat, Peter is alive again, and free.

Not a single tear falls.

The door of the little room opens. The guard with Mum leads her out, speaking in stern German. Not that German sounds anything but stern to me. He leads us both to another office and a long procedure of more paperwork with Mum scrabbling in her purse for money.

"Are you being arrested?" I hiss while the forms are rubber-stamped.

"No."

"Then what the hell's happening?"

"I'm so sorry, Jacqueline, but I kept some of the eastern marks. I was going to leave them for Ilse's friends, but in the rush I forgot. I have to pay a fine, the same amount again in western marks."

"Is that all? No prison?"

"Yes, that's all."

Mum turns out her pockets and scrabbles inside her jacket where a pfennig has dropped into the lining. "Um, do you have some reddies, dear?"

"You're as bad as Dad."

"Two peas in a pod, yes?"

"Don't mention specific vegetables or they'll lock you up."

I have no money in my sock and make a mad search through my bag, but I know there is nothing in it. Too easy for Dad to find. But, miracle of miracles, screwed up inside Victor's none-too-clean hanky are a few Deutschmarks—my payment for the moon-rabbit story. Thank you, blessed Victor. And I have never said that before.

Time rushes past the train, suspending us inside the stuffy carriage and giving me a chance to ask Mum about her time in hiding.

"Mum, when Beate and Ilse were living like tramps, where were you?"

She takes off her headscarf and folds it, then fiddles with her matches, testing out her memories like the tip of a tongue seeking a sore tooth.

"I fell ill in my hiding place. I felt my insides were coming out."

Bloody ugh, Mum.

"One night, the owner of the factory checked on me. He saw I was near death. He did not want a body hidden behind his wall. The city was swarming with Nazis and Jew-catchers. They would soon discover me anyway, dead or alive. So in the middle of the night I was carried to the Jewish hospital."

"A hospital full of poorly Jewish people? Surrounded by Nazis in the middle of Berlin? Are you sure, Mum?"

She pulls out a cigarette that trembles between her fingers. "It saved my life, that wonderful place. It became my home."

I shake my head. "But how come a place like that was allowed to exist?"

"Astonishing, yes? But it was so. A place out of time."

This is like solving a difficult crossword. Thank Lennon Gillian isn't helping. I have known her to cram three letters into one square to force a word to fit.

"So you were scooped out from the gap in the wall and carried to this hospital?"

"Yes, close to death with a gastric blockage. I stayed there until the war was over. Once again, I survived by the skin of my feet."

"Teeth, Mum."

"Ah yes. Teeth. I never understand that saying. Teeth have no skin, do they?"

"That's the point really. Just go on, Mum."

"Well, by the autumn of 1944, the Nazis were desperate. They were losing the war. There was a great push to get rid of all the remaining Jews. They gave the order to kill us all. If the Soviets had stormed Berlin just three days later than they did, I would not be here. When we heard the cry of a new baby, born alive to a dying woman on the day the war ended, it was the first sound of hope."

I can't speak. My mum saw death coming round the corner so many times and kept dodging it. I look down at a goulash stain on my dress and watch it blur.

Mum reaches for my hand and I let her hold it in her lap as if I was six again. "I was lucky, Jacqueline. Remember that. I am still here. Please, never torture yourself with all this. If we do that, my freedom will count for nothing."

I still can't speak. I can only think of my mum listening to that new baby.

"I left the hospital after the end of the war, still weak, but improving," she says. "A nurse gave me a room in her house in Wilmersdorf, a British-occupied sector of Berlin."

"And you met Dad?"

We listen to the chug of the train for a moment. Mum blows her nose and wipes her eyes, but tears are still streaming when she speaks.

"Yes. He made me the luckiest woman in history, my Roy. And that is why I have this terrible guilt. There was always an exit. Every time danger came, someone stepped in and cleared a path for me. Ilse and Beate suffered more than I shall ever know. And still suffer. Yet they have not deserted their country."

"But you married a man from somewhere else," I remind her. "That's not the same as running away."

Mum's lips whiten around her cigarette before she says, "Beate is a broken woman."

"Yes, but not Ilse. She said if she was living in the West, Beate would interfere with her life, with her friendships. And poison her with bitterness. She's relieved they aren't together."

"I know. I am too greedy, trying to let go of all my regret."

That's greed? Eating a whole pack of stale Blue Riband in one break-time is greed. And Gaye Kennedy won't be allowed to forget it because the pack belonged to Gillian, and she'd brought it in for Harvest Festival.

Since surviving a war seems harder than being in the middle of one, I ask Mum about life in the hospital to take her mind off the life that followed.

"Oh, we created our fun. We even made chess pieces. My knight was a screwed-up cigarette packet and some old bandage. Once we ate a roast goose that some kind soul had left on the hospital steps. There was enough for one sliver each and nothing had ever tasted so good. By that time, hundreds of Jews were being rounded up every week in the city and never seen again. And there I was, sitting in bed with hot food, playing chess on the blankets."

I stop asking questions and look out of the window. Deserted, half-lit stations pass by, the train sounding thoughtful as it slows. Konnie says the train-tracks were laid to take Berliners to anywhere, to set the city free. Sealing the stations has broken their crucial links.

Our train brakes almost to a standstill beside the abandoned platform of Oranienburgerstrasse, a tongue-twisting name for a cheerless station. A guard haunts its shadows, his Kalashnikov glinting in the gloom, watching us watching him.

The ghost-station is rotting. Tiles have slid off the walls. Rubble is strewn in heaps. Pillars have crumbled. Colourless posters are flaking. A weak light seeps in through the gaps caused by decay, or perhaps because light can always finger its way in. Not many places are pitch-black, even if they seem thick with darkness at first. Dad says you should let your eyes become accustomed to it. If you wait long enough, outlines always appear.

We all sway and lurch as the train stutters alongside the platform. Mum stares at the rocking ghost of herself in the window, the hollows beneath her eyes smudged with dark shadows.

There is no roar from the wheels, no clattering expectation. In the ghost-stations, you feel the rhythm falter.

As we gather speed, the ghostly guard slips away. No doors slam. No whistles blow. The platform without people slides out of sight and we leave the station behind as if it no longer exists or was just a mirage. My reflection disappears in the flood-lights from the death-strip, but returns as the dimming city rattles past, as if I am in two places at once.

I fall into a half-sleep as the train picks up its normal, faster-than-fairies beat.

Someone is cutting my hair. I have a Sassoon five-point bob. Thirty-six shillings in a London salon. A dream come true. But I'll miss my long hair. It keeps my neck warm in winter.

Here is Victor with a comic under his arm, wearing fifty pairs of shorts and with a Sassoon bob too. He has grown as huge as Grandma, waddling one side of the line. And there are Ilse and Beate, blowing kisses that turn into flying spiders. And Bwa-Bwa, her voice clear, telling me she is home.

T-K, towering over me, wraps an arm around my shoulder.

"I promise I won't build a wall in Oaking," he says, lying down and vanishing into a black pool, one hand waving a handkerchief with an embroidered "B" and the other a tarnished pastry-fork with the prongs of a devil's trident.

Naomi Sims emerges from the pool wearing Grandma's glass beads and strides along saying, "There ain't no one nowhere who's foreign."

Dad is wrapping his arms around one of the fat West German pillars with advertising posters pasted all over it. Victor throws himself against it, hugging it too. They stretch their arms round until their fingers touch. They melt into molten marble, setting rock hard, ghostly in the half-light.

Konnie, with a blindfolded guinea-pig sitting in his pocket, drives a train that becomes a sewing-machine punching out back-stitches to and fro. He has invented a miracle. It looks like a camera to the Stasi, but has a secret lens that can see through walls. Millions of seeds rattle inside the camera. It turns into Deborah's cage. Her bead-eyes stare hard, willing me to notice the moon trapped inside her nesting box.

The moon-lens transforms lives, Konnie says. For a split-second, it can switch the vision into solid life. You can touch someone you love one more time.

Gillian and Lynette want me to skip on the tracks. They swing the rope and chant, "Salt, mustard, vinegar, pepper."

They want me to join in. "Come on," they say. "Come on, Tuesday, or whatever you call yourself now."

They pass me a note speared to a fishing-pole, but there are no words on it, just hundreds of musical notes.

I am blind again, apart from hundreds of red and green flashing stars. I want to stay and watch them. Stop, go, stop, go.

"Come on, come on," my friends shout.

"Where's the door?" I ask them.

"Where it always is, you twerp," they say. "Where you left it, of course."

And looming in front of me, the black lettering clearly painted, is the Jewish hospital. I can even hear Mum's voice, telling me a story the way she did when I was a child.

And while she speaks, in the breath of a sigh, more ghostly stations pass us by.

***

CONTRASTS PROJECT

Berlin, 1944
My Mum, Eleora

"She's almost dead, Rainer. I don't want a body in my wall. The smell will give her away. The Gestapo is breathing down my neck. Enough now."

"I will move her. Don't worry. Thank you for turning a blind eye all this time."

"The Jews are disappearing, Rainer. And people like you who love someone they shouldn't, they are disappearing too."

Rainer nods. He has given up talking these days. The anxious, clammy, kind-eyed manager in his oily overalls has allowed Birgit to hide in his factory for so long and given her bread and water. Now he is frightened and can no longer be trusted. Not even doctors can be counted on to stay silent about the whereabouts of a Jew.

Birgit's skin feels like moist paper. Rainer has brought her medicine, stroked her damp hair and massaged her cramped legs, but he cannot keep her to himself any longer.

"How about the Jewish hospital?" the factory owner asks. "I don't know if it's safe. It could be the worst place of all to take her. But it could also be your last hope. I guess someone is watching your apartment."

Now that the Allied air attacks are expected, the Berlin night-sky is blacker than molten tar. Even so, Rainer still takes care to choose a moonless night to carry Birgit through the city. It feels like carrying no more than a thin coat.

He side-steps under the lindens and holds his breath whenever a torch beam flickers across his path. At last he reaches the Jewish hospital, a softly-lit enclave, a place out of time. But he and Birgit could be flies about to land on a spider's web.

A nurse opens the door to his gentle knock. She appears hesitant, even hostile at first, then gasps at the wretched state of the young woman he is carrying.

"How do you know about our hospital?" she asks Rainer.

"I have heard talk," he says, "but I didn't believe it could exist. I see you even have electricity."

"Yes. And running water."

"Please, my Eleora is so weak. Will you help her?"

The nurse can see now that he is not the enemy, just an ordinary, anxious man.

Rainer helps her to lay Eleora on a trolley. Her face is whiter than the sheet and her hair, no longer blonde, lies in lank strands of indeterminate colour that snake over the pillow. The nurse motions for Rainer to stop smoothing the blankets and sit down. He obeys, his heartbeat steadying in her cool, starched presence.

"How many patients here?" he asks, taking out a handkerchief to wipe his face.

"Eight hundred."

"And you have enough doctors for them all?"

"Oh yes," she says. "The Nazis may have stripped Jewish doctors of their qualifications, but they still allow them to treat Jewish patients. Nazis are scared of sick Jews."

"So it pays to fall ill?"

"And to remain ill, Sir. This is not just a hiding-place. It is a ghetto. They are gathering us here in preparation for the camps. But they only want those who are well and thriving."

"You're saying it's dangerous to recover?"

She nods, consulting her clipboard.

Rainer can no longer sit still. He paces, his shoes screeching on the polished floor. He takes a deep breath of the sweet, disinfected air, wishing he could stay too.

"We will do our best for her," the nurse tells him. "This is a community. The patients in recovery look after the garden and grow vegetables for us all."

She smiles for the first time, a brisk smile that tells Rainer it is time for him to leave this extraordinary refuge. Dawn is about to break. He can ask for no more. Eleora is finally at home.

***

"Nurse, the man who brought me here, can he visit?"

"If he came, we would let him in, Eleora. But he would be taking a risk. We are always being watched. He could be arrested for helping you."

"But he brought me here."

"It was dark. Now please rest."

"How long did he stay?"

"He waited until he knew you would live."

"How long?"

"All night."

Eleora sinks back into the pillow, closes her eyes and prays for his safety.

***

I open my eyes as the train's rhythm falters again, preparing to pass through another ghost-station. A man in our carriage gets up and stands at the door. Mum warns him the train won't stop, but he stays there.

The ghost-station is almost pitch-dark. The train lumbers through, like a polite gent doffing his cap at a tramp.

The man pushes the window down.

"Er…" Mum says. "*Nein*…!"

The man wrenches the handle. The door swings open. A young woman leaps inside, into the man's arms. He holds onto her with one arm, wrapping her in his coat, and slams the door shut with his free hand. They huddle together on a seat at the end of the carriage, while the train gathers speed.

It happened in seconds, but it takes me another moment to realise what we have just seen. Even above the racket of the train, I can hear the woman catching her breath in a series of gasps.

"What happened there?" Mum whispers.

"Oh my God, they only had a split-second."

"What?"

"They must have had it all planned, Mum. He must have got word to her somehow. Told her which carriage he'd be in, so she could watch out for the door to open."

The woman is free now. To the guard on the platform, she was a shape, a slight movement in the dim light. He had no time to raise his gun. In the murky shadows, she made the smallest shift. One turn of the kaleidoscope.

"I wonder, is she going home or leaving it?" Mum says.

"Going there, surely?"

"But before the Wall came, she might have always lived in the East, Jacqueline. Escaping to the West may mean she is leaving everything behind. Her job, her flat, her friends and relatives."

"Mum, can't you see the way the man's looking at her? And the way she looks at him?"

Mum thinks about this before answering. Why does she always have to do that?

"They do look so very relieved," she says.

"Exactly. And I bet she didn't bother bringing him any bloody *Knusper Flocken*."

"But she still has her life there. Some things she will miss."

"Mum, they're crazily in love. Head over heels. Can't you tell? No, don't look at them."

"Yes, I suppose so."

"Suppose? It's written all over them. I'd say she's definitely coming home, no matter how many packets of cacky crispbread she's left behind."

I hope they have a bottle of champagne waiting at home.

While we sit in silence, thinking about the couple and all they can look forward to now, Mum keeps pressing her hand to her side. "Oh, Jacqueline, it hurts so badly."

She has never gripped it this much, as if she is trying to push the pain deep inside. I remember Victor calling it a grenade and pray it is not about to detonate in this carriage.

9

REALISATION

A baby babbles. The family fuss over it, making those incoherent noises people offer babies. Mum's hands are cold and clammy. Her face is gleaming like pearl. Even her hair looks paler against the dark roots I have never noticed before.

She groans and I stand up in a panic. Mothers are not supposed to make grunting noises. The family with the baby scowl as if we're lunatics.

"We should ask them to stop the train, Mum."

"Jacqueline, no. For God's sake, don't tell anyone."

"But I don't know what else to do, Mum. You look as if you're about to faint."

"Just keep talking. Singing. Anything. Take my mind off it, Jacqueline. I can cope. Just help me get back home first. I can't be taken off here."

"But you said they have National Health Service in the East, so we won't have to pay."

"I'd rather bloody pay."

"All right. I suppose Beate will know what to do," I tell her, although I imagine Axel would be more use. "It won't be much longer, Mum, until we're back in Schillerpark."

"No, Jacqueline, I mean let's change the ferry crossing and leave in the morning. I want to go home."

"To Audette Gardens?"

"Of course, dear."

I swallow the lump in my throat, remembering how she ran all the way to collect me from my first day of school with her slippers on, because she couldn't wait to see me. I never believed Grandma when she said Mum needed to be first at the gates because German blood starts pumping nineteen-to-the-dozen at the slightest whiff of a contest.

"I won't stop the train, Mum," I promise her. "We'll go on to the end."

Dad will jump behind the wheel and Victor will grab T-K faster than he's ever moved since the day he recreated the battle of the Little Big Horn on an ant hill. Only Grandma, as always, will object to the sudden uprooting.

"At least if we can't stop at the ghost stations," Mum gasps, "we can't be trapped in the East. So if I die in this carriage, we can't be taken prisoner."

"Mum, shut up."

"But I would be another casualty of the Wall."

"Yes, you would."

I sing "Jerusalem" and "There is a Green Hill Far Away" until I sound like a frog with laryngitis, but Mum doesn't mind. When I run out of hymns, I resort to the Elf song I used to sing at Brownies, with a finale of "These Boots are Made for Walking" and "Last Train to Clarksville". The wheels on the track strike up a faster rhythm, and we reach Wollankstrasse with Mum croaking along to the chorus.

"Thank you, Jacqueline," she says, staggering out of the station. "You have matured here in Berlin."

Singing the Elf song is mature, but I'm too young for a Berlei Gay Slant? Strike a light, I'll never understand mothers.

As we step around the people living rough, my brand-new maturity makes me realise that being homeless is actually more likely this side of the Wall. Ilse said evictions are never necessary on her side because rents are low and state welfare is given to the sick and the drug addicts. Everyone is accounted for. No net to slip through.

Dad and Victor step out of the gloom, the Traveller parked behind them like an almost trusted friend. It feels like three lifetimes ago since we last saw them. I'm relieved to smell Brylcreem, tobacco and the essence of grumpy seven-year-old boy. I don't even care if the Bad-Moon girls are hanging around. I might even light Cherie's cheroot for her. I am an adult now. I might even stop checking behind my bedroom door for Ronald Biggs. I know people can be monsters, but it's less exhausting to just accept that they exist.

And thank Ringo, Dad is smiling and hugging Mum so hard she is almost off her feet, although that might be down to her quietly passing out.

He piles us all into the car, exhaling smoke in dragon-like triumph. "God, I'm glad you're back. I kept thinking of you being interrogated at the border. Victor and I went to stand as close as we could to that Brando Burger Gate thing, hoping we'd see you."

"What time were you there?" I ask him.

"All day. I couldn't drive anywhere. I just kept going round in circles."

"Oh, Roy, it was so kind of you to worry."

"Well, no, I got lost actually, Bridge. Reading the map made Victor spew up, Ma never stopped prattling and Beate was caterwauling to Sebastian. Christ, German lullabies are fierce. It sounded like chucking-out time at the Slug and Lettuce. When the petrol was running low and my ear-drums were fit to burst, I dropped Mum, Beattie and Seb off in Schillerpark, then Victor and I went to the Brando. I just wanted to see you. We waited there until your train was due."

"All bloody day," Victor whispers in my ear.

"Well if you'd been with me," I tell him, handing over the hideous crispbread and watching his expressions change, contrary to the Five-Boys child, from delight to despair, "you'd have been dancing and eating chocolate that tastes of shite."

How easy it is to make a great day sound utterly hideous.

Victor constructs the pre-fab on the drive back to Schillerpark, where Grandma is reading stories to a wakeful Sebastian and Beate is stirring a vat of goulash. Lord alive, twice in one day would be too much even for a Hungarian.

"How was my Ilse?" Beate asks, swaying in the doorway. Her white dressing-gown is loosely knotted and her hair is working its way out of its bun, as if she is falling apart.

"She is well," Mum says, easing herself into a chair. "Thin and tired, but happy, do you not think, Jacqueline?"

We tell Beate about the bones of the day, but not its essence. She is incapable of taking it in.

"Sit and eat," she slurs, sawing haphazard slices from a dark-brown loaf. Dad pours Mum a glass of water and I rescue the goulash from burning. Mum's dilemma is carved into her face. How will she tell Beate we're leaving?

Beate stumbles and the knife slices into her finger. Mum has to stagger across and hold it under the cold tap while Dad and I sit down, white-faced.

"Ach, *mein Gott*, Beate. You are not fit to hold a knife. Why have you drunk so much?"

Beate tries to pull her finger away. She nearly falls over a whimpering Axel, who is trying to blend in with the tiled floor. "Leave me alone, Birgit. I am in enough pain. You make it worse."

"How so?" Mum turns the tap off.

"Ilse is my sister, not yours," Beate says, the words welling up as if they have festered in a stagnant pool all day. "Now I have lost her to you."

Mum clamps her hands onto Beate's shoulders. "Now hold the bloody bus." Victor gasps.

"Ilse and me sleeped hand in hand," Beate says, shrugging Mum off. "We are tied together. You are the outsider. But you see her, you touch her. You should be behind the Wall. Not her. You invite yourself into our lives. You used us. And you are still using us now to have all you want."

"It's slept, not sleeped," Victor whispers. "And she shouldn't shout at Mum." But Mum, grenade and all, shouts back.

"*Mein Gott*, Beate. How deep does your hatred go? I paid a price too. I lost my home, my parents, and then my home with all of you. My life became worthless. I hoped I would not be found. But, you know, even more than that, I wished I had never lived. I was hated just for existing and I was too dangerous for the people helping me. I have lived my life believing I must hide."

Beate, dripping blood from her finger, shouts back. "And what about us, Birgit? You put us in danger for years. In our own home. You even kept that photograph back from the fire."

"You saw?"

"Yes, I saw how you thought only of yourself. You almost had us all slaughtered." Her voice is harsh, the bad years hunting her down. She pants and sweats, spitting out the bitterness she has been tasting for years.

She bangs her great fists on Mum's chest, a sickening series of thumps that go on and on before Dad can pull her off. Even his most hardened prisoners are not built like Beate. She crumples in his arms, her hair unravelling all over him.

"Bloody hell," he says. "I can't breathe in here."

"After the war," she whispers to him between sobs, "I stopped Ilse searching for Birgit. I told her she was dead. I even believed it myself. I wished her a million miles away."

The war years are hunting her down and she is trying to drag Mum back there for punishment. I know I'd be bitter if Victor evicted me to save himself. But although he caused my banishment from the front-room one Boxing Day, snitching to Mum and Dad about me snipping Pong-Ping out of his *Rupert* annual with my new pinking-shears, he would never turn me out. At least, I hope not.

"Listen, Beattie," Dad says, pushing her further away from Mum. "I was Bridge's enemy too, you know. Think of that. I was right here, with a gun. My country was raining down bombs on Berlin. On my future wife's home."

"But that is war," Beate says.

"Exactly. War's a bloody party-game. Follow-the-leader. Blind Man's Bluff. Playing parts. Taking sides. Dressing up in silly uniforms. What makes it a rotten bloody game is that the fucking dice get thrown for you. I had to be a soldier. You had to keep your home fires burning. And poor bloody Bridge had two parts to play; your sister and your enemy."

"Dad said..."

"Shut up, Victor. No one noticed."

"I blooming well did."

Beate crashes onto a chair while we all listen to the black minute-hand clicking around the blank white face of the kitchen clock. I think of Beate's moon-faced grandfather-clock lying in the bombed-out wreckage, now a fallen pillar of ash, buried in another time.

"You must understand, Roy," Beate says, twisting her handkerchief into a knot. "Germans will never know peace, not in our heads. Twenty thousand Berliners helped the Jews. Not many out of four million. I tried to help Birgit, but not with a good will. And then I turned her away and never tried to find her. I do not count as one of the few who chose not to join your game. And Germans like me are now too ashamed to speak of the bravery of those twenty thousand people. If we do, it means admitting we had the same choice and ignored it. And that is our guilt, to be carried for the rest of our lives."

Mum tries to take her hands, but Beate snatches them away and holds them up to hide her face.

"The Cold War keeps us on the edge of danger," she whispers. "West Berlin is an occupied city. Every morning, we wake up and think, is this it—the last day?"

After the ordinary August Sunday when Berlin woke up to discover home was no longer where it was supposed to be, Beate moved into this orderly, joyless home with her kidney repaired, but no longer a survivor. I cannot imagine her ever recovering now.

"Beattie," Dad says, pointing his cigarette at her. "Look love, I had to kill a youngster my own age. He was looking straight at me. Pleading. And I shot him. I had a duty. I didn't want to kill. When I loaded my gun I thought of Ma and pulled the trigger. My enemy hadn't even lived long enough to unwrap his first razor-blade. He just froze. My eyes looking into his were the last thing he saw. And Beattie...he had a mother too."

I look up to see Grandma in the doorway.

"Bear-Tear, it's no wonder life doesn't always make sense to my Roy. On bad nights, he talks to the young man he used to be. Well, he can't just leave him behind, can he?"

So the gentle, faraway sound I hear after a night-terror is Grandma's voice. She wakes up and goes to sit with Dad, singing in the low voice I never knew she had, to help him through the rest of the night.

"Beate, you are even more trapped than your sister," Mum says, clutching her side. "Your life here in West Berlin may run like clockwork, but you have not found your way home yet."

Beate lifts her head and looks around at the black and white room that mocks the greyness of her life.

A barn-spider normally repairs the same web throughout his whole lifetime. But sometimes he wakes up, goes berserk and tears the whole structure down. In the cool of the evening, he spins again. But whether he restores or rebuilds, his home is the same; the same strength, the same silk, the same amazing blend of delicate toughness.

The white squares on the kitchen floor are Beate's beloved traditions trying to line up with the black squares of war, a long way from the haphazard mosaic tiles from her golden time. The rabbit-hutch is a barbaric miniature of the grand kitchen with its beef-bashing boards and pantry full of strudels. I am glad that despite the occasional batch of sour cabbage, Mum has not tried to recreate Berlin in Audette Gardens.

"Beate," Mum continues, "all I did was try to survive, the same as anyone else. One photograph of who I was, that was all I asked. I never wanted to make you unhappy. Please be happy now. No one could fight harder than we did. Don't let it be all for nothing."

Mum breaks down, crying for her lost sisters, her broken childhood and her load of rotten guilt shedding like coal on the shining floor.

"Beattie love," Dad says, holding onto Mum. "Bridge was stuffed into a hole in a wall for bloody years. Years of shining a torch on her one photograph. So put a sock in it, love, and give up the grudge. All this rage over one picture? Strike-a-bloody-light."

No one else speaks. This is Dad taking charge. He hasn't finished yet.

"Your own blood, Beattie—that drop with a touch of Hebrew—could have bubbled to the surface any time. It wasn't just my Bridge who knew her way round a bowl of chicken soup and a bagel, was it? She's come to make peace with you, love, not start World War Bloody Three. So leave my wife alone."

Not even a wink from seedy Sumatra could stop my dad now. He's hooked them up by the scruffs of their sequinned necks, for now.

"I'm so ashamed," Beate keeps saying in a tiny, hoarse voice. "So ashamed." Axel patters across to her and lays his soft black and white head on her lap. Tears drop on to it and I keep expecting the black spots to bleed into the white fur.

But Mum is crying too. The pin is falling out of the grenade.

"There, there, duck," Grandma says, shuffling across and patting her arm. "Tch-tch. We'll soon have you put right."

Grandma holds out a hand to Beate. "Now you sort yourself out as well, Beattie. A blind man lives with his white stick, but he doesn't beat himself with it. For the love of God, let it rest, duck."

I have no idea if Beate understands all this, what with all her chins wobbling and her brain pickled. She starts crying into her hands. "There's no peace in Berlin," she says in an awful, strangled voice.

Dad sighs and lights a cigarette. "You can't change the past, love. But you can change this." He shakes her empty bottle.

"One drink leads to two, duck. And two leads to ruination," Grandma adds for good measure. "And if you really let it get a grip, it can lead you straight underneath the rag-and-bone man's cart."

Bloody hell, it was grisly how my grandfather died.

Beate begs us to eat the goulash, slopping it out all over the place, but those bits of meat could be anything. Dad points at my plate and whispers in my ear, "Where the hell *is* that spotty dog?"

Unable to face the food, I keep staring at the dotty scarlet pattern of Beate's finger-blood splattered over the black and white floor. In any case, Ilse's goulash left me utterly satisfied.

"One of my prisoners was a drinker," Dad says, waving his fork. "Fell in with a bad crowd in Borstal. Brushed his teeth every morning still full of drink. Probably brushed his teeth *with* drink. Couldn't walk as far as the bend in the road without it. Prison's his salvation. Had the shakes for a few days at first. Sweating something evil, he was. Now he doesn't want to be released. Too easy to sink a few celebrating. And then that's it. The beginning of the slide. He's telling us to throw away the key."

Dad gives up on the goulash and lights a cigarette. "This lad wasn't persecuted by Nazis, Beate. He didn't see his home bombed or have to hide from the Red Army. But he's got a demon inside. We all have."

"Dad's got three awful girls who sit on the moon," Victor says.

Beate looks even more bewildered.

"Shut up," I hiss, giving him a quick dead-leg. T-K gets me back with a machete to the rib-cage.

"When things get rough, I told this lad, frame it into a picture," Dad tells Beate. "His is a swamp full of alligators. Whisky isn't much help against them. Not even a bottle of good malt."

I shall keep it to myself that, to save her life, Ilse once had to stab a Soviet soldier in the eye with her pastry fork, but she suffers no demons and sleeps soundly at night.

I think Beate has listened to Dad. And he has managed to avoid the dip in the road, leaving his girls to hitch a lift from some other unfortunate soul. I love him for who he is, demons and all. I love him in the sun and under the moon. I love him to the ends of the world and back again. And it feels like that's how far we've gone.

Konnie comes in from the late shift, swivelling his cap as if he's not sure whether he's coming or going, and listens. He picks up a bottle hidden behind her electric potato-peeler, swinging it in his fingers. "You have zee most important and *wunderbar* thing. Your son, safe in his bed. Never forget. "

He hurls the bottle through the open door and we all stiffen as it smashes. While Axel whimpers and slinks into the corner, Konnie says to Mum and me, "Good you come back." But he doesn't wait to hear about our day over there. He has the guinea-pigs to put to bed.

Beate stares into the buttermilk Grandma has poured for her, staring at her own swamp of alligators while the rest of the world spins somewhere else, way beyond her walls.

Grandma wraps Beate's white apron around herself and washes up. She leaves masses of drips and splashes on the surfaces, but for once Beate doesn't start wiping. Grandma lights up a Senior Service and leans against the breakfast-bar, flicking ash tidily into the apron pocket.

"So, how was Ilse really?" Beate asks at last, turning to me, her voice cracking.

"Very well," I say with absolute truth. I almost want to say, "As well as can be expected," like they do in hospital bulletins. But Ilse is far better than that. Over there, she is well. The Wall casts a darker shadow on this side.

When it's time to go to bed, we discover Victor humming Sebastian to sleep. It's no lullaby. More like "Ging Gang Goolie". But it's working. I notice how carefully he extracts his fingers from Sebastian's fat little fist, covering the little boy up to his chin with his white blanket and tucking in his black cloth rabbit.

Deep in the night, I am jolted awake. Dad is having a terror. I try to struggle out of the mountain of feathers, but something is different this time.

A gentle voice is saying "Sh, sh, Roy love."

I pull the quilt back over me. Dad is in safe hands.

"Sh, duck. It's all right, son. I'm here."

And when Dad is calmer, the voice says, "Bridge, I'll heat you both some warm milk. Lawks though, I can't fathom this fancy stove. Shall we try it together?"

10

CONNECTION

Mum has fallen asleep with her mouth open and her head lolling.

"Bloody ugh," Victor mumbles. Yes, it is a ghastly sight when a mother sinks into oblivion, but at least her pain has eased, for now.

"Her appendix probably looks like a bit of school liver," Victor observes.

I agree with him for once. "Probably a bit the caretaker's bull-mastiff's been chewing."

"Christ, we've only got a teaspoon of fuel, Ma," Dad says.

"Better hurry to the petrol-station before it runs out then," Grandma tells him before she starts snoring to the tune of "Nancy with the Laughing Face".

The car windows stream with morning damp. Victor's finger gets straight to work on the glass. Without even turning to look, Dad says, "Victor, if you must write rude words on the window for other road-users to read, at least have the sense to write backwards."

He seems anxious to keep driving before the car falls apart, or maybe Sumatra is trying to catch hold of his car-coat. I don't know. What I do know is that when a little brother leans on you and falls asleep with a block of flats assembled on his lap and both hands clasped over it, everything feels all right. I shall never tell him that though.

Although it isn't easy with Victor pressed against my arm, I write the final paragraph of my project, based on something Beate told me just before we left. It reads like a scene in a sad, old film. When I close the notepad, I begin to have second thoughts about letting Mum see this part. It might crush her.

While I brood over it, rain begins to fall, and I close my eyes, listening to its metallic drumming on the roof. I hear Mum wake up and after a long sigh, she says, "Roy, do you think I should forget my sisters?"

"No. It took us long enough to find them. You didn't come all this way to let go. You've started building a bridge, Bridge."

A match strikes, a flame flares. Mum's seat creaks. I guess she is twisting round to look at me and assumes I am asleep.

"Roy, I know why Ilse's so happy. She has a special friend, Silke. They are in love, I think."

"Poncy name for a bloke, Bridge."

Smoke curls up my nose. The car rattles on. I must be dreaming. Gillian says women sometimes love each other, but they always wear bowler hats and grow a slight beard.

"Silke's a woman, Roy."

"What, a bloke who dresses up, you mean? One of those drag artists?"

"No, she and Ilse are just two women in love. They are discreet about it, but the laws are a little more tolerant in the East, I believe. Besides, Beate would have difficulty accepting it, so it suits Ilse to live on the other side."

I can hear Dad pulling hard on his cigarette, wanting to understand. I don't know if I do. What about the portly pastry-chef?

"So how about that fat cook then, Bridge?"

"He might have been a woman too. Beate never met him. Her."

"Maybe Ilse just liked his Danish pastries, Bridge. Or perhaps it was a half-baked relationship."

I want to laugh, but stifle it.

"Oh, Roy, my poor sisters. They are not as lucky as me."

I hear a horrible sound of Mum kissing Dad's cheek multiple times.

"Hold the bus, Bridge. I'm driving, you know."

Another match strikes, then Dad pats her knee. I can hear his driving-gloves catch on her dress. The car fills with smoke.

"I had no right to be saved, Roy," Mum says. "Rainer took such a risk, bringing me food and water and carrying me to the hospital when I was ill. But my life had no value after I went into my gap. I wasn't worth it."

"Bridge, this Rainer helped you as a favour to Beate. He was doing it all for her. So you shouldn't feel bad. He made his choice."

After a long silence, Mum strikes another match, taking five attempts to light it. Her voice is so quiet I need to strain my ears.

"Roy, it was not exactly like that. You see, Rainer loved me. I begged him to love Beate instead. But he said that however easily people can be forced to feel hatred, they cannot be made to love."

The rain pauses. I hold my breath for Dad's next words, which makes me a bit light-headed because he smokes an entire Woodbine first.

"So...did you...love him back then, Bridge?"

"Roy, I did not love a man until the moment I met you."

I can hear Dad's relief in his long, quivery sigh, followed by a painful-sounding swallow. Fathers are not supposed to cry.

"Beate never knew, but I believe she guessed. Oh Roy, imagine if someone you loved with all your heart was in terrible danger because they loved someone else."

"Leave the guilt here, Bridge. The sins of the Third Reich aren't your property. All you did was try to live."

"Rainer sent me a note while I was in hiding. I managed to keep it."

"What does it say?"

"It says, 'They may uproot you and replant you in a foreign field, but your dream of returning home flies with you, like a seed in the wind. Nurture your dream, Eleora, in exile, and you will instantly, and constantly, keep coming home.'"

"And now you have come home, Bridge. Back to Berlin."

"I did not belong here, Roy, or anywhere, not until I met you."

Rain patters on the car again. The windscreen wipers click and thump as they sweep it to and fro.

"What happened to this Rainer bloke, Bridge?"

"I was looking for him when I met you, but I never found him."

"If you had..."

"I would have thanked him for my life, Roy, and wished him well."

The rain pours in torrents, the wipers struggling under its weight. When it quietens again, Mum says, "Sometimes I dream that I am still in my gap. Even when I wake up, I do not believe I have enough air to breathe, and I am about to die."

"I'd die if you did, Bridge."

They don't say any more.

No one should be different. No one should be marked. Everyone deserves to be wanted. My eyes burn for my mum, and for everyone without a place to go.

***

CONTRASTS PROJECT

Beate, 1944
Ashes

Beate senses something is wrong. Someone else is driving Rainer's train.

"Think of yourself, for God's sake," she has told him so many times. "She has led you in too deeply."

"I am already in," he has told her. "Up to my neck."

Beate leaves the train and walks to Rainer's house. As soon as she turns the corner of his street, she can see his front-door is hanging off its hinges. The air-raids have shattered Berlin, but she knows that if a survivor's front door stays intact, they keep it closed.

She steps inside, but there is no point in calling his name. Sheet-music, a Mendelssohn sonata, is scattered over the floor. Furniture is overturned, a coffee jug smashed. In the ash-tray on top of his piano, Rainer's cigarette has burnt down to a column of cold ash.

***

I pretend to wake up after a few more minutes, open my notepad and make the decision to cross that last part out.

I doodle a special spider underneath the obliterated words. *Argyroneta aquatica*, the diving-bell spider, lives a lifetime in slow-moving streams within a spun-silk bubble. It surfaces sometimes for air, which it traps under the hairs on its legs and carries back down. It darts out of the bell to catch prey that happen to touch it as they swim by.

The bell is like beautiful silver velvet. It glimmers when the moon is reflected on the water. But even concealed within the underwater chamber she rarely leaves, the diving-bell spider can still make connections, not to mention laying dozens of eggs as a result.

All she has to do is wait, with infinite patience, until the male builds a bell next-door. He spins a romantic tunnel with silk strong enough to tether a lion, connects the two bells with that silk, and breaks through her wall to find her.

***

Still in Berlin, we're driving at about fifteen miles an hour. The morning sun is leaking through the sky like a mixture of blood and honey, striking peculiar patterns on my thighs. It reflects the face of Victor's toy wristwatch on the car's ceiling like a tiny manic moon.

Everyone yawns. Our disgusting dawn breath fills the car. Dad is in such good spirits he picks up Helmut, an Austrian rambler in feathered hat and green shorts with bib and braces, although rambling is probably quicker than being driven at this speed.

"I voz supposed to be on a mountain by now, but I vent off course."

"A mountain in a city?" I ask him.

"He must mean fountain," Grandma says, the snoring having come to an abrupt halt when Helmut broke open his tablet of Swiss chocolate.

"No, I am coming to Berlin to climb the Teufelsberg, mountain of the devil," he says.

"Teufelsberg is made of war rubble," Mum explains. "The Allies piled it on top of a Nazi training-school for soldiers. The school would not collapse, even when they tried gunpowder, so they made it into a little mountain instead."

If we all jumped about in the tin-huts they call classrooms, our school would fold like a pack of cards. Miss Lobb and her beloved skeleton would be the only fixtures left standing.

"Not real mountain?" Helmut asks.

Mum shakes her head. Helmut has walked all this way to discover the Teufelsberg is just the dust of hundreds of thousands of homes.

"I do not vish to see such a mountain," he says. He looks so glum that Grandma thrusts a handful of green Newberry Fruits under his nose. T-K had better not crank up his Messerschmitt or the poor chap will burst into tears.

The squash in the car is agonising, but Helmut teaches Victor the beautiful Austrian word for apricot, which is *Marille*, while T-K demonstrates how to perform the splits in full combat gear while shouting, "*Achtung.*" Once Grandma is banned from relentlessly repeating that Hitler was an Austrian, time continues to pass in this fruitful way.

But just as the hopefulness of morning streams through the windows, the car judders to a halt.

Dad tries everything.

"It won't start, Bridge. Oh Christ, I reckon we've had it, love."

For a moment, the car feels like one of East Berlin's red trolleys and we become mute, helpless babies stuffed inside it.

"Do you need a stocking to make a fan-belt?" Victor pipes up.

While I imagine a Sunflower stocking holding the engine together, gradually cooking to a crisp, Dad climbs out and heaves up the bonnet, cursing when it falls back down on his fingers.

"Bloody ouch. Christ, I can't believe this. Traveller, my arse. Not much travelling going on now, is there? Bridge, bring us a tissue, would you?"

We all climb out, Mum pale and shaky, her hand clutching her side. Swearing and smoking, Dad strides around the car. Victor copies the manly pacing.

I sit on the rain-soaked grass beside the road. Mum asks Victor to haul some bags out, which feels like being back at the checkpoint again. We pass round a packet of soft, gingery German biscuits and wait for Dad to work a miracle. But we do have the advantage of an eager Austrian on board.

"I help," Helmut cries, haring off down the road like a loony leprechaun.

Grandma is shaking her head. "Half-shaft's gone, I reckon."

I think she means the car, not the Austrian. I don't know whether it's a shaft, half or otherwise, but the thing has definitely given up. We are going nowhere. I pray the Bad-Moon girls don't sashay onto the verge.

A small sheet-weaver scuttles across my arm and onto the tartan bag, beavering up its canvas bulges and into its faded valleys, contemplating a place to spin its sheet-shaped web. Other completed webs, decorated with quivery dewdrops, are already sparkling, masterpieces of weaving, suspended above ground and supported only by the grass. If a cat prowls through and swipes them away, the spiders would just wait until it seems safe to start again.

People can become stronger by being brave with spiders, but Mum still screams if she sees one and, according to seven-year-old boys, real bravery is about parachuting off the Empire State Building with a gun in your sock.

"When the car's fixed, Dad, you can be Jackie Stewart," Victor says. "I'll be the man asking questions after the race. I'll ask you how it feels to drive at two hundred miles an hour. And you can do your Scotch voice."

Dad says nothing. The sun may be out, but the remains of the moon are still glinting. I help Grandma to sit down next to me. She takes out her Elastoplast tin.

"Men, eh?" she says.

I nod as if I understand them too.

"Mind you, duck, he's a good lad, my Roy, for all his ups and downs. Turned out better than his father, that's for sure. Before the drink sent him off the rails, my Bill had a good job at MacFisheries. He was such a ladies' man in his youth, you know. Stole me from Stan's arms at a tea dance. Whisked me off into a terribly unsuitable rumba. Stan tried to put a stop to it. He called Bill a pigeon-chested streak-of-piddle. But I was a young woman with a mind and a heart of my own and Bill's fresh scallops were second to none. But he was far too free with his salmon-tail, so Stan was always telling me. Young housewives would find a bit extra in their fish parcel, like a calling-card, shall we say? A wink or two later and they'd be waiting for him after dark at the back of the gutting-station. I knew I should have stopped trusting him when his prime cod turned out to be a load of cheap pollock. Oh, I wish I'd left it at that one dance. But dreams and wishes are slippery fishes."

She's right. Dad's king of the road dream is slithering through his hands faster than a shoal of sardines.

Victor starts kicking the tyres.

"Stop it," I shout. I have to be parental because Mum is in agony and Dad is about to give up on the car. Victor folds his arms in protest. Even at seven, every male knows for a fact that tyre-kicking is an essential part of the diagnosis.

"Action, that's what's needed," Grandma says. "Help me up, duck."

She prowls around the car, pursing her lips in concentration and rolling up her white cardigan sleeves.

Helmut comes back at a fast jog, calling, "I haff spanner!"

While the pale moon makes way for the white sun to beat down, he does surgical things to the engine, letting Victor hold the spanner from time to time. Grandma watches the entire operation, arms crossed, as protective as a mother with a poorly child.

Eventually Helmut cries, "Is done!"

His hair flopping out of its Brylcreem, Dad climbs in and switches on the engine. Reluctant at first, it finally starts to purr. "My angel!" he shouts.

"Not last long," Helmut says, pointing at the car and shaking his head.

But the engine is chugging and that's good enough for Dad. He leaps out, shakes both Helmut's hands for ages, then plies him with spare cigarettes and Grandma's emergency marshmallows.

"Ready for the off then?" he says, rasping his hands.

"Not yet. Now police come," Helmut says. "I haff call them, in case we not fix."

"No, not the police," Dad keeps repeating. "Not the police."

"They will just make sure the car is safe to drive, Roy," Mum says.

"And if it conks out again, we'll get a ride in a police-car," Victor adds, as if this clinches it.

Pale as a ghost, Dad struggles to light a cigarette. "I don't want to get involved with German paperwork and all that bloody jazz. And that's final. Everyone just get in. We'll make a bolt for it."

"No," Mum says. "We do not need to run away, Roy."

"Get in! Now!"

"You are *Dummkopf*, Roy," Mum shouts at him. "Why can you not be a normal man?"

"Hold the bus right there, Bridge," Grandma says, drawing herself up to her full height and standing beside Dad.

"He is bloody normal," I tell Mum, glaring.

Dad climbs back into the driver's seat. He doesn't shut the door. He just holds onto his precious steering-wheel, the edge of his car-coat flapping in the breeze. All the anger has drained out and he is part of the car, broken and running short of hope.

"I am sorry," Mum says. "But I do not understand."

"You never bloody do, Bridge," Grandma says.

I don't want to let Dad down, but I ought to tell Mum the truth. She looks so confused I feel sorry for her. But Grandma beats me to it.

"Christ alive, Bridge, open your eyes. There's not just a wall in Berlin, is there? There's one in your daft head. Look at Roy. Look at him. What do you see? I'll tell you, shall I? His eyes won't look at us. See that? And when did that last happen, Bridge? Well, I'll tell you when. It happened the day he came in and said he'd passed his driving test."

"Nell, what...?"

"Lord preserve us, can't you see? He didn't pass. He's been pretending. And all for you, for your Berlin."

As Mum gasps, a siren blares and Dad's face turns whiter than milk.

"How did you know, Ma?"

"I'm a mother, that's why."

"But you tore up the red L," Mum squeaks. "The pieces are still in the gloves-box."

"Anyone can tear up a bloody L-plate, Bridge," Grandma says. "It doesn't always mean victory."

"Here zey come!" trills Helmut.

"Jesus wept, it really is the *Polizei*."

"The secret ones, Dad?"

"No, that's the other side."

"We wouldn't be able to see them if they were secret, would we, duck?" Grandma says.

"Don't worry, Dad. You're King of the Road," Victor reminds him.

"Thanks, *Herr Kommandant*."

"Roy, please."

"Sorry, Bridge."

But his hands are so tense on the wheel that his blue-white knuckles poke through the holey pattern of his gloves.

"Get out, son. Hurry," Grandma says.

"Look, the bloody Gestapo's coming, Ma. I don't need orders from you as well."

But Grandma insists. "Shift it, son. Quick. Let me get in. Ooh lummy, does this seat go back a bit?"

"What the...?"

"Don't forget I drove an ambulance in the war, son. My licence is in my bag."

Helmut takes one look at Grandma in the driving seat and refuses to get in. When the police eventually allow us on our way, we leave him standing in a blackish cloud of exhaust.

***

"Wow," Victor keeps saying.

"If you say that once more, I'll throttle you," I tell him.

"That was T-K speaking. Don't you know anything?"

Mind you, wow is the only word. Blue lights are flashing in the distance. Grandma can't keep up with them, but she keeps yelling, "Come on, girl. You can do it."

I don't know if she's talking to herself, to Mum in the ambulance storming ahead or to the Traveller she's now nursing along, but I do know that Dad is holding Mum's hand in the ambulance and we have left the Bad-Moon girls way behind us, for now.

Mum has hung onto her appendix for much too long. When she doubled over and screamed, the policeman pursing his lips at the car called an ambulance and the ambulance-man said the grenade was about to explode.

I feel grown up and fabulous sitting in the front seat. I am an office junior earning six pounds a week, chauffeur-driven every day. I buy myself real flowers and have Bwa-Bwa's perfect fingernails. The chauffeur says, "What's that wonderful perfume? I wish every woman smelt like you." And when he turns round to give me a diamond-ring in a velvet box, guess who he is—wait for it—only Paul-bloody-McCartney.

A fur-trimmed telephone glides out of a mahogany box and I ring Gillian, who has broken out in terminal acne, and tell her, plus the entire party-line, that I am engaged to a pop-star and about to fly to Cannes for my tea.

"Got any Poppets left?" Victor says. I ignore him. Office juniors shouldn't be pestered by small boys.

I know T-K is flashing a Nazi salute behind me before hiding out in his prefab, but I don't care. I'm allowed to light Grandma's cigarettes and she keeps saying, "Thanks, duck. Don't let on to your mum."

As the car splutters on its way, I try to think about Peter, but he is asleep after laying our new carpet. In any case, I can't help worrying about Mum and wondering how painful it was for her to reveal her great secret. This is the first time I have thought of it as a secret, rather than a lie. Perhaps if you are meant to know something, people will tell you when the time is right for you to hear it. Maybe she thought Berlin was the perfect place to let me in on her special news, as if it had been waiting there, hidden spy-fashion behind a loose brick in a wall, for us to open together. I guess she hoped I would be mature enough to understand, but I threw a fit instead. In spite of all the biology lessons, I didn't think once about her Finer Feelings. So in the future, before I start tramping over other people's Emotions with my own spiky-heeled opinions, maybe I should change into my felt shoes first.

A person's blood-history shouldn't be important. It's what follows that counts. And what follows is the Traveller's doors falling off.

"Blood and sand, Jacqueline, what's Victor up to back there?" Grandma shouts, the force of her massive weight on the brake slowing the car down.

"It's not me," he shouts. "It's the bloody doors! And the tartan bag. And the suitcase. They're all on the ground!"

We become an island surrounded by hooting cars. A sea of confused faces presses at the remaining windows and surges into the open back.

"Oh, do come in, everyone. Have a cup of tea and a French Fancy," Grandma titters, flicking ash into the thermos.

The spectators look bewildered, as if they want to know why an English family would be so daft as to drive all this way in this flea-bitten half-timbered wreck. Well, the wreck is our temporary home, thanks, I wish I could tell them. And the dreams? Well, that's holidays for you.

Before we know it, we are sitting in a very clean lorry towing the Traveller. When it deposits us at a repair shop, Grandma gives the driver a wodge of money from her spare denture pochette.

"Is that from the accumulator the day before the holiday?" Victor asks. He knows far too much about turf accountancy.

"No, lad, from Helmut. Best your dad didn't get his mitts on it," Grandma says. Saved by the Tyrolean bell.

The head-shaking, lip-pursing mechanic, the same you find the world over, tells us that under the floor, the main body of the car is just cardboard and old newspaper.

"Ooh, you don't half look like Claude Rains when he's not smiling. Only handsomer," Grandma tells him, applying her standard flirtation technique for making sure a repair-man does a good job. But this is a German repair-man.

"Grandma, I think he's saying the car isn't going anywhere."

"Strike a light, Jacqueline. We have to get to Bridge in the hospital. Have you got any more of those dratted tosh-marks?"

"It's Deutschmarks, Gran. And Victor's the only one with any money."

But this time even Victor can't come up with the reddies.

"Jacqueline," Grandma hisses in my ear, "get your project out of the car, and let's hop it before Claude Rains makes us pay him."

"We can't just leave it, Grandma," Victor says.

"I'll tell him we'll be back in a minute," Grandma says. She points at her watch and shouts, "Other fish to fry, Claude!"

Lord Ringo knows what he'll make of that, but we manage to scarper. The walk is long. Grandma is wheezing, Victor whining and I develop three blisters and a black toe-nail. We trudge on, deflated to leave the car behind, Dad's dream in tatters.

At the hospital, I become utterly adult and pretend to Dad, just for now, that the car is still in one piece. Grandma's orders.

"White lies are all right," she says.

"What about Victor? He can't keep secrets."

"T-K can ruddy well gag him."

Grandma starts thrusting threepenny bits in the chocolate-machine. Dad, grey-faced, comes back from Mum's room for a smoke and I am allowed to see her for a few minutes.

She is woolly-headed from the pain-killing medication, but I have to show her the project. I can't wait. I spread the notepad out on the bed and turn the pages for her.

I read out Mum's memories of her life before and during the war and the new memories she will have of her crushed city, rebuilt and cut like a cake into slices, and of the time we spent together, crossing the border on the train.

She listens like a child, so intent she almost forgets to breathe.

She even manages to smile at me. I can see my mum is not a hard person. When she ate the rabbit and laughed at Victor, she was trying to see eye to eye with Beate. All her different selves are either ill or scared in this city. She is never here at the right time.

She asks me to show her every page again, not wanting it to end.

"Have I started seeing double?" she asks, frowning at the words with their feathery shadows.

"No, Mum, my pen nib's split."

"And I have lived the life of two people, I suppose."

She laughs at this, although I can tell it hurts, and keeps looking, asking me to turn the pages time and time again, reliving her incredible life.

When she sees the picture Ilse gave me, taken so soon after she became Birgit, she weeps to see this glimpse of herself. And when she unfolds the music her father composed, it is too much for her. Her hands tremble so much I take the papers back with a promise to arrange her a session on Gillian's piano. I hope I can sit in their lounge, if Gillian's mother allows me to dent her new white sofa cushions, and listen to Mum play it.

"When must you give this to the teacher, dear?" she asks, reluctant to let the project go. I tell her I have no idea because I am wavering about handing it in. This is Mum's story, plus a little of mine, and something about the two of us together.

"I think it might be a bit too much for Miss Whipp actually, Mum."

She smiles, but her eyes are closing. I notice Dad has taken her sewing out of her bag, the dress with the endless running-stitches, and left it on the bedside locker, hopeful she will soon be well enough to carry on where she left off. And for the first time, I realise this is a task she will never finish. She always unpicks the thread and then starts again, never able to decide whether or not she wants those stitches running round the hem and the arm-holes.

"Jacqueline, dear," she mutters. "I have seen Berlin."

"I know, Mum."

"But I do not recognise it, dear. They have cut out its heart. I came here because of the past, but I did not find it."

"I know, Mum."

"It has cut me in half too, into the person I was and the person I am."

"A bit of you will stay here, Mum. Perhaps the bit they are going to cut out, the useless bit hurting you."

A tear rolls down her cheek and we are silent for a while until it seems like the right time for me to say, "You could get a job at the mop-and-brush, Mum, if you want, for when me and Victor are at school."

It sounds mad; Mum with a card to punch, a time to clock in and a time to clock out. Her own position.

"I would like to be handed my own envelope of money every Friday," she says, her cloudy eyes brightening. "So *wunderbar* to buy your new shoes without having to wait for the racing results."

And she needs somewhere to go. Not the place that belongs to Grandma, where she is a wife, a daughter-in-law and a mother. Not a hiding-place. Not exile. Just a place she has chosen herself.

"I miss my mother, Jacqueline," she mumbles. "Her name was Idit, you know. A gentle lady, she wore silk and the sweetest scent. She taught me to waltz. She always kept a pure-white handkerchief in her sleeve, the lace edge poking out. Her beautiful life was cut short, but because of how much she loved me, I still have mine."

I imagine trailing dresses that ripple on a marble floor a long way from the front-room of Audette Gardens, a voice never raised, the perfume of mauve roses wafting from long, dark hair; a perfect mother, even though her name is sadly awful. Mum says it means 'choicest'. Sounds like one of Stan's expensive steaks or a brand of tinned dog food to me. I can't imagine Lennon and McCartney writing a song about an Idit. Even so, I'm glad to have it. And I wish the original Idit, my other—utterly different—grandma, could have known about me.

I hold onto Mum's fingers and, because of her delicate state, squeeze them as much as I dare, but enough to show how glad I am she survived.

"I am so happy I saw Ilse and Beate," she says. "But I will never come back here again."

The nurse comes to get her ready for the operation, but just before I go, Mum whispers, "Jaqueline, do you think we should give your project to Beate? It is her story too."

I have to think about this. The project is a bridge spanning me and Mum, or at least the beginning of one, and, in spite of the coffee spills and doodles and crossings-out, I am proud of it. But Beate probably needs it more than we do. And afterwards, she can close the notepad and tidy it away in one of her white baskets, knowing we have all listened to her and tried to understand.

"Yes. Maybe Berlin is the right place to leave it, Mum."

"Mind you, Jacqueline, it is a shame we will not have the chocolates."

"True. Not to mention having to put together another project. It might have to be blooming Sandie Shaw after all."

Mum is woozy now, so I give her a quick kiss, trying not to trespass on the grenade.

"By the way, just a final thought, how about I call you Eleora now?"

"Mum is best," she whispers. Or *Mutti*?"

"I'll stick with Mum, thanks. And by the way, your roots need doing."

"No they don't," she says, her voice woozy. "I shall damn well grow out the blonde now."

When I am back with the others, Dad hands me a dog-eared copy of *Petticoat* with a coffee stain on the cover. The pages are falling apart and the fashions are out of date, but I am actually holding the sacred magazine in my hands.

"Mum spotted it in the waiting-room," Dad says, coming back into the ward. "And even before she was drugged up to the eyeballs, she insisted I steal it for you."

During the long wait while they operate on Mum, I clutch the sacred *Petticoat* and think about the instalment of *The Girl in the Iron Collar* that will be in this week's *Mandy*, as well as the Blitz Sisters, about to stumble upon an unexploded bomb, not to mention the repressed Red Indian outcast from Granite Gulch and the two Australians who inherit a dilapidated steamboat.

I lay the *Petticoat* aside. It is designed for "the new young woman", but she is Tuesday, Peter's utterly grown-up model wife, a woman of the future. Lawks, is he still drilling the holes for that serving-hatch?

"Ma, did we bring those insurance papers? The ones that pay for hospitals and that?" Dad asks Grandma.

"Haven't the foggiest, son. I remember lining the cage with a load of papers. Blood and sand, I do hope Elsie hasn't put her Neville in with my Deborah. It's the sort of thing her ladyship would do, you know. Stan will soon put her right though. He knows my Deborah's heart's too weak for all that shenanigans."

"Jesus H. Christ," Dad says. "I'll go and look in the car right now."

"No!" Victor and I shout.

"Over my dead body," Grandma whispers in my ear.

"Dad, hold the bus a minute. Will you tell us all about your motorbike and side-car?" Victor asks. "I need to take my mind off Mum's operation."

Strike-a-light, seven-year-old boys can save the day too.

Dad turns a bit misty-eyed. Once he starts, it's like trying to turn off the fuzzy noise on a faulty transistor. He remembers Mum banging on the prison doors with her waters breaking when she went into labour with me after flagging down the ninety-three bus to get there.

"The Governor said it was the first time anyone had ever begged to be let into the place," Dad says. "Roared to the hospital in no time, we did. Wasn't too easy stuffing her in the side-car though. Christ how I miss that bike."

Whether he is misty with the memory of my birth or his bike, I am not sure, but it keeps his mind off the car and the rest of us breathe again. Grandma passes round the last of her Poppets and gets out her knitting. Hopefully not another twin-set for me.

"I've run out of fags. Jaqueline, got any cash left, love?" Dad asks, biting his nails.

Victor manages to unearth a few spare coins from T-K's duffle-bag, just enough to tide Dad over for now. And then? The Fab-Four only knows. The car is dead, but thankfully Mum is not. In a minute, Dad will go outside and have a look at his dream that is not there. We will all have to walk back to Claude Rains, and he'll be smiling even less than before. Then we will have to telephone Beate's flat and ask if we can stay until Mum is well again. Help.

I tell Victor to distract Dad for a bit longer by bringing up the World Cup and, if necessary, steering the conversation round to the Grand Prix.

"You're not a bad lass, are you?" Grandma says.

"Not too bad, I suppose."

"Well, you come from good stock, duck. Damn good stock. On your father's side of course."

Grandma may love me, even though I am half-foreign, but I suppose she can never completely love Mum, because foreign or not, Mum stole her son. That was where she went wrong.

Holidays never turn out how you think they will. For example, T-K has changed his name to Johannes Freedom-Fighter. He can clear a pit of rattle-snakes in one leap. Good for him. Perhaps he knows how to get us home. But however we manage to get there and however long it takes, we all know it will be waiting. In the meantime, we must make a temporary home out of the wrecked car or the hospital waiting-room, or even back in the monochrome flat in Schillerpark. Anywhere will do.

If a spider's web is broken, the spider starts spinning again straightaway. The silk thread keeps unravelling. The work never ends until the spider dies. He rebuilds anywhere he can, throwing out the dragline to get the work underway for the millionth time. Once he sets to work on the new web, he has already forgotten the one that's gone.

I pick up my notepad for the last time. There is one final paragraph to add.

***

CONTRASTS PROJECT
Ida Siekmann, 48, Bernauer Strasse
Home

Early one August morning in 1961, when men arrived to brick up her ground-floor windows and front-door, Ida Siekmann had to make a decision.

She used to cross the border daily just by opening her front door and setting foot on the pavement. But earlier that month, when a man painted a line on the ground, fifty families fled Bernauer Strasse before it became a wall.

Ida made her choice.

She threw her most treasured possessions and her bedding from the third-floor window, and leapt out.

Ida died on the way to the hospital, the first victim of the Wall.

If people are caught up in madness that they cannot fight, it can crush them. But if they puzzle out how to crawl away from the ruins, after hundreds of twists and turns they might find their way home. If the sign-posts are confusing, they turn back and start again, or they try a different way.

If they survive, they might need the strength that ties down lions or the patience to wait for the moon to turn the tide, but they keep on looking. Home can be anywhere. All they have to do is find it.

ABOUT THE AUTHOR

Joanna was born in 1960 and grew up in Hayes, Middlesex. She was too shy to speak to anyone outside the family, but she invented stories about them all the time.

When a perceptive nursery school teacher let her spend playtimes with a stack of books in the classroom, Joanna taught herself to read and has hidden in corners that turn into many other worlds ever since.

Today she lives near Stroud, Gloucestershire. While pretending to be her husband's secretary and learning all about life from her three daughters, Joanna's love of the written word has led her to become a writer. All kinds of literary and commercial magazines and anthologies have included her prizewinning short stories.

As part of her degree course, which included the study of East Germany, Joanna lived in West Germany for a year, where she taught English. All the people she met showered her with kindness and were keen to share their experiences of both the Second World War and the Cold War in which they were immersed. Most of all, they were enchanted that an English girl could, despite past and present hostilities, choose to live in their country, learn their language and try to understand how the ordinary person felt.

Tying Down The Lion was inspired by "A Temporary Uprooting", a short story about the Bishop family. After Joanna had written it, they kept insisting on their own novel. The only way to silence Nell was to write it.